P9-BYG-024

There was so much more to consider here than a mere kiss.

If she gave in to this attraction, it would only complicate things. Not only their friendship within these walls but how they acted when out in society. That was a massive risk for Cal. And what about her job? If their friendship changed to romance, she couldn't imagine a man would be thrilled with the idea of his lover sprinting down dark lanes, digging out secrets in alleyways, and shepherding her flock of pint-sized informants.

But she ached for him. After two years of denying her feelings, the opportunity to let them out now felt freeing—allowing them to fly like the bird she'd carved today.

A heavy heat settled low in her belly, enticing her to give in and taste what he offered.

Even if it was only once.

"It's still a risk," she said, but the protest sounded thin as her body swayed closer.

"What if I dared you to kiss me?" he teased.

She'd wanted him forever, and here he was daring her—practically begging her—to take a risk on them. How was anyone supposed to resist that?

"You're right. I want you, and it scares the devil out of me." She took one step forward.

"I dare you to do it anyway."

PRAISE FOR BETHANY BENNETT
AND THE MISFITS OF MAYFAIR SERIES

"Everything I adore in a Regency—wit, steam, and heart!"
—Grace Burrowes, *New York Times* bestselling author, on
Any Rogue Will Do

"Filled with gripping drama, strong characters, and steamy seduction, this tantalizing story is sure to win the hearts of Regency fans."
—*Publishers Weekly*, starred review,
on *Any Rogue Will Do*

"This is a fast-paced and spicy debut, with likable characters and a feel-good finale that boasts a just-right blend of tenderness and groveling."
—*BookPage*, starred review, on *Any Rogue Will Do*

"This debut novel has everything regency fans love—wit, drama, loveable characters, steam, and romance all in an entertaining story."
—All About Romance on *Any Rogue Will Do*

ALSO BY BETHANY BENNETT

Any Rogue Will Do

West End Earl

BETHANY BENNETT

FOREVER

New York Boston

This book is a work of fiction. Names, characters, places, and incidents are the product of the author's imagination or are used fictitiously. Any resemblance to actual events, locales, or persons, living or dead, is coincidental.

Copyright © 2021 by Bethany Bennett

Cover design by Daniela Medina
Cover illustration by Judy York
Cover copyright © 2021 by Hachette Book Group, Inc.

Hachette Book Group supports the right to free expression and the value of copyright. The purpose of copyright is to encourage writers and artists to produce the creative works that enrich our culture.

The scanning, uploading, and distribution of this book without permission is a theft of the author's intellectual property. If you would like permission to use material from the book (other than for review purposes), please contact permissions@hbgusa.com. Thank you for your support of the author's rights.

Forever
Hachette Book Group
1290 Avenue of the Americas, New York, NY 10104
read-forever.com
twitter.com/readforeverpub

First Edition: June 2021

Forever is an imprint of Grand Central Publishing. The Forever name and logo are trademarks of Hachette Book Group, Inc.

The publisher is not responsible for websites (or their content) that are not owned by the publisher.

The Hachette Speakers Bureau provides a wide range of authors for speaking events. To find out more, go to www.hachettespeakersbureau.com or call (866) 376-6591.

ISBN: 978-1-5387-3570-1 (mass market), 978-1-5387-3569-5 (ebook)

Printed in the United States of America

CW

10 9 8 7 6 5 4 3 2 1

ATTENTION CORPORATIONS AND ORGANIZATIONS:
Most Hachette Book Group books are available at quantity discounts with bulk purchase for educational, business, or sales promotional use. For information, please call or write:
Special Markets Department, Hachette Book Group
1290 Avenue of the Americas, New York, NY 10104
Telephone: 1-800-222-6747 Fax: 1-800-477-5925

For Gram, who never got to see her name in print.

And for Gram's namesake, my Ladybug. You've given me endless laughter, the ability to love someone more than myself, that weird white hair in my eyebrow, and enough material for a library of books starring brilliant smart-ass girls in pants.

In light of all that, you scored only half my sarcasm DNA, and this book dedication. Sorry, kid.

I love you. Thank you for still being here, making the world better with your light.

Acknowledgments

Little did I know that second books have a reputation for being a roller coaster. This one didn't disappoint. I couldn't have done this without a crew of people behind me.

Alexa Croyle, for loving my characters so well, she knew what Phee smelled like before I did.

The Let's Get Critical group for emergency Zoom interventions and endless Marco Polo conversations while I whined about Cal and Phee trying to break me.

Hotness, for his amazing ability to love me unconditionally, buy my happiness with kittens, and handle our life when I'm on deadline. I still thank God for you every day.

My agent, Rebecca Strauss. I'm so damned lucky to have you in my corner. Don't think I don't know it.

Madeleine Colavita, the phenomenal editor responsible for tackling my words, who was somehow undeterred by that "some assembly required" tag.

A special thank-you to Sam Brody, for her generous gift of time and attention to this story.

The team at Forever, for their tireless efforts that bring

my Misfits of Mayfair to the hands of readers, reviewers, and retailers. You're making my dreams come true and looking awesome while doing it.

And finally, to you. The reader. I know we're just getting to know one another, but I treasure you.

West End Earl

Chapter One

London, May 1820

*F*ew things were more terrifying than Almack's on a Wednesday night.

When an unmarried man in possession of a fortune entered the room, young women straightened their shoulders to put their bosoms on display, donned smiles, and went on the hunt, with their mamas acting as guides. Likewise, if a gentleman wanted a wife with a dowry and a good family, he merely had to show up and survey the options. Anyone who attended knew what they were getting themselves into.

Tonight, he wasn't the one hunted. Emma was. And the chit seemed to be having the time of her life.

As the evening progressed, the room filled with wedding-hungry mamas and white-muslin-clad dewy-eyed girls who should be in a schoolroom—not in the arms of these decrepit lechers, most of whom were old enough to be their fathers.

His sister swept by in the arms of a man who, if his hand crept lower than Emma's waist, would be dead by morning. Bow Street might never find the body. Not all of it, anyway.

The stark color palette for gentlemen attending the assembly rooms was another annoyance on his growing list of grievances against this evening. Cal sighed, running a hand over his black embroidered waistcoat. It would be a shame to spoil this perfect cravat with blood—Kingston would have a fit, and exceptional valets were hard to find—but if young Lord Cleavage-Ogler didn't rein in those wandering hands, the linen would be collateral damage. Cal narrowed his eyes and tried to send a silent threat to the man holding his sister.

He'd thought he would have weeks before Emma waltzed in these hallowed halls. Permission to waltz was precious and not something you could plan for if you were a debutante brand-new to the Season. He'd watched in silent dismay as one of the Almack's patronesses had given her blessing. The woman had sent a beaming smile at the top of Emma's gold curls as his sister made a perfect curtsy.

"A fellow Saint Albans girl? And so lovely too! Waltz, enjoy, and please pass along my regards to Headmistress Lunetta. It's been an age, and I owe her a letter."

Damn.

Cal turned to one of his closest friends, Adam. "Puppy, I'll give you one hundred pounds to marry my sister—on the condition that you never touch a hair on her head." It was said in jest and desperation, but once the words left his mouth, the idea gained appeal. Someone stable, reliable, and honest like Adam would be ideal for headstrong Emma. Adam worked for him now but would gain a tidy fortune upon his next birthday. He didn't have land or a title, but he was a gentleman's son and had character.

"No thank you. Emma's a beauty, I'll grant you that. But my pockets aren't so dusty that I need to sell myself just to relieve you of your brotherly duty." The Puppy, known to everyone else as Adam Hardwick, nursed a glass of lemonade, grimacing with every swallow.

The famous Almack's refreshments claimed another victim. "I object to your strong moral fiber. But I hate to see a friend suffer. Here. Brandy helps the lemonade go down easier." Cal slipped a small flask from his waistcoat pocket.

"Don't they need lemons to make lemonade? Whatever this is, it has never met a lemon. I'd bet my final shilling." Adam dumped a generous serving of liquor into the small punch cup.

"Are you down to your final shilling? Because again, I offer one hundred pounds."

"Watching you suffer is better than a king's ransom." The Puppy took a tentative sip and made a grunting noise Cal assumed denoted relief.

On the dance floor, Emma's partner said something to make her laugh. The charming sound rose over the notes of the orchestra, complementing the music. All around the room, heads swiveled toward her like sharks scenting blood in the water.

"Two hundred pounds. What if I dare you?" Even to his ears he sounded desperate.

"I hate saying no to a dare. But I'm not that gullible." Adam didn't even have the grace to sound apologetic or look away from watching the action on the dance floor.

"Why? Only an hour ago you said she was beautiful."

"She looks too much like you."

There could be no doubt he and Emma were siblings. But thanks to his father dipping his quill in every available inkwell, the same applied to several others in the room. The fair hair and dark eyes were distinctive. At least the number of his father's by-blows present tonight ensured three—no, Lady Wallace just arrived. So there were four eager mamas who wouldn't be pushing their daughters toward Calvin as potential matches. As silver linings went, it left much to be desired.

"Did you know your left eye twitches? It hasn't stopped since Emma's partner splayed his fingers towards her bum." Adam said it to tease, but he wasn't wrong.

The betraying eye twitch made itself known again, and Cal couldn't do anything about it. "For that, I'm taking my flask back. Get your own liquor, Puppy." He tucked it inside his coat.

"It's almost empty anyway." Adam took a healthy swig of the considerably doctored lemonade.

Cal glared at the couple on the dance floor. "Don't you think they're too close? Where's a patroness when you need one? I should have kept her in school for another year."

"Eighteen is a perfectly respectable age to come out."

"Sisters are the bane of a man's existence. There is nothing worse than launching them into society."

His friend raised a brow at him. "I realize you're being dramatic, but try not to be an arse. I can easily think of a dozen worse things—several of which I witnessed firsthand on the way here tonight, and one in particular I wouldn't wish on my worst enemy. And considering I know exactly who my worst enemy is, that's saying something."

Just like that, heat flooded Cal's face. Damn. He'd officially earned the title of Worst Friend Ever. "Apologies. That was insensitive."

Adam offered a jerky nod, then returned to studying the room.

"I'm a lousy friend tonight and an ungrateful wretch to complain to you of all people. You would have been happy to launch—devil take it, now I'm forgetting your sister's name." Did the title of Worst Friend Ever come with a crown? Perhaps a spit of land somewhere, like a deserted isle on which to maroon oneself?

"Ophelia," Adam murmured. "Phee. She would have been out for a couple years by now. Maybe she'd have married already. Or she might be firmly on the shelf at the ripe old age of four and twenty. Twins, you know."

Cal hid a wince behind a sip of his lukewarm quasi lemonade. Adam wasn't a terribly handsome man, so it seemed implausible that his twin would have grown to be the toast of the Season. He might never fill out beyond his slender frame, but Adam was young yet. To call the Puppy's hair merely "red" was rather graciously understating the situation. In reality, his hair was the color of bright-orange carrots and curled wildly in fluffy, feather-like tufts if allowed to grow longer than an inch. To be fair, Adam had full lips and a fine nose. If Ophelia had shared those features, she may have been pretty in her own unique way—although she likely would have lingered on the fringes of society with a minimal dowry and genteel but not high-born connections. Painfully thin, flat-broke, ginger-haired girls were not a sought-after commodity.

"I am sorry," Cal said again.

Adam accepted the apology by toasting him with an almost empty glass, then downing the contents in one last swallow. "I'm tired. You stand here and stare daggers at every man with the audacity to flirt with your gorgeous sister. I'll get a hack home." Adam gave Calvin's chest a firm pat in farewell and made his way out of the room, his bright hair acting as a beacon in a sea of black coats.

Well, that went poorly. Rubbing a palm over his chest, Cal turned to the dance floor. If he could convince Adam to return for next week's Almack's assembly, it would be a miracle. As it was, he'd bribed, begged, and cajoled several weeks' worth of vouchers for his friend in hopes of not having to face this ordeal alone. But after essentially telling the Puppy he was lucky to have a dead sister, Cal might deserve to suffer Almack's without support. The haunted look on Adam's face whenever he spoke of Ophelia created a guilty roll of unease in Cal's stomach that had nothing to do with angst over watching Emma and her partner—both of whom looked to be having a wonderful time.

Tomorrow people would declare her the belle of the ball, as they had with many events before this one. In the short weeks since she'd moved from school into his townhome, Emma had found her footing within the *ton*. Cal couldn't help feeling a surge of pride as she conquered society one smile at a time.

The waltz ended, and her dance partner led her, with

obvious reluctance, toward where Cal waited. Emma's cheeks dimpled prettily at her partner, the picture of demure beauty.

What an act. She might be a handful, but he loved her unreservedly. No doubt after tonight, she would have an even larger league of suitors following her about like ducklings in a line after their mama. The drawing room would look like a hothouse by this time tomorrow.

Across the chalky floor, a patroness led several young men, and some not-so-young men, toward them, with a determined expression that signaled more introductions. Almack's wasn't the place to play loosey-goosey with niceties. Within these walls, etiquette ruled as king. Even Prinny needed to behave if he expected to stay. Although, since Prinny *was* nearly king, he may hold more sway with the powers that be.

Eagle-eyed patronesses and their social constrictions had felt claustrophobic on those rare Wednesday evenings when Cal had attended Almack's as nothing more than an eligible bachelor. But as Emma gathered attention, those myriad rules were a comfort. Within these assembly-room walls, he did not have to worry about his sister's safety.

Emma welcomed the introductions with a cheerful curtsy. God, to have that much enthusiasm. She was probably reining in the need to bounce on her toes while pretending to be the perfectly polished gem of femininity their parents had paid that school to create. At least the gentlemen were circumspect enough to not let drool dribble off their chins when facing Emma's dimples, rumored dowry—and, er, assets.

The damned flask was empty, and too many hours remained to smile through. Hell and blast. If given the option of escaping in a hack and leaving early like his friend, Cal would jump at the chance.

Three torturous hours later, a footman finally closed the carriage door behind them, and Cal breathed a sigh of relief.

"Didn't you think it was the loveliest evening?" Emma launched into a retelling of the night, hardly stopping to breathe between sentences, while Cal rested his head against the wall of the carriage and closed his eyes.

Her excited summary lasted through the entire ride home and continued as she trailed behind him into the library, where Cal poured himself a drink.

"Seeing you enjoy yourself made me happy for you. I couldn't be prouder." That stretched his diplomacy as far as it would go tonight. After an evening of watching men he personally knew consider his sister in a carnally appreciative way, he'd wanted to start throwing gentlemen—using the term loosely—out of the room by their lapels. This was his baby sister. Didn't they know that only a few short years before she'd been in pigtails and catching frogs to put in the governess's bed? Now she possessed bouncy, soft bits that scrambled men's brains and that Cal would prefer to pretend didn't exist. He missed the pigtails and pinafores.

"Perhaps you will find the future Lady Carlyle at one of these events. Wouldn't that be grand? If we both had weddings this summer? Or maybe next spring—we wouldn't want people watching my waistline after a rushed engagement."

No, they wouldn't want that. Calvin let her talk, giving an occasional grunt that she'd interpret however she wished. A lifetime of experience had taught him that those words rattling around within Emma would come out no matter what. She even talked in her sleep, as if the day's leftover syllables needed an escape.

Such a drastic difference between the siblings. The first time he'd visited the Marriage Mart, his reaction had been nothing like this. It had been a disquieting experience to see the speculative gleam in women's eyes and wonder if they were weighing his fortune and looks against the chance that he'd grow into the kind of man his father was. It made one feel like produce on a fruit seller's cart, examined for soft spots and signs of rot before anyone committed to a purchase.

In the end, his talent with growing his personal fortune, and those of his friends, went a long way toward encouraging society to ignore his father's indiscreet mating habits. The man used less self-control than most animals, so the term was apt.

"Didn't you think Lord Roxbury's shoulders were divine?" Emma sighed dreamily.

"Am I really the person you should talk to about this?" He settled into his chair and hoped she would run out of air soon so he could go to bed. The chatter intruded on his favorite place in the entire house. This chair had been a peaceful oasis until now. Last year, when his best friend Amesbury stayed with him while wooing his now wife, the evenings had usually ended with the two of them sitting in these chairs, winding down from the day. Conversations had been far more limited, and Amesbury hadn't drunk his brandy— unlike Cal's sister, who obviously believed she was pulling one over on him by sneaking a nip now and then. This used to be a bachelor home. Those were the days.

"Who else should I talk to about these things? You're

basically the only person I know in London besides my Saint Albans friends. I can't talk to Henrietta until tomorrow, and Clementine glared at me tonight, so she might be jealous."

She had a point. Emma's success in London meant the gentlemen and hostesses welcomed her, but the implied hierarchy of diamond of the first water set her apart from many other debutantes. Lord willing, Emma would make more friends soon, so she could save these talks for a gaggle of giggling ladies. And yes, Miss Clementine Waters's jealousy of Emma's success this evening had been obvious to everyone there.

"Roxbury has an unsavory reputation with the ladies that would make our father proud. As to shoulders—" Calvin shook his head, not quite believing he'd given in to this conversation. "I can see why you'd find them impressive. But you must remember I spend a lot of time with Amesbury. Everyone else is tiny by comparison. My metric is significantly skewed." He sighed and closed his eyes.

"True. That man is as big as a barn. Trust me, Lord Roxbury's shoulders were delicious in that evening coat. I thought he'd pop a seam." The rustle of skirts, followed by the light thud of her slippers hitting the floor, meant she'd taken her place beside him, sprawling with her stocking feet slung over the arms of the chair like the hoyden she truly was. Cal knew her so well, he could paint a picture in his mind based entirely on the sounds she made.

He opened his eyes to level a look at her. "Roxbury runs with a fast crowd. I have heard nothing about him being on the lookout for a wife, so don't set your heart in that direction.

Enjoy the flirtation—a *light* flirtation—and the dances, but keep your eyes open. Be on your guard."

She pouted her bottom lip. "You sound like an overprotective papa."

"No, I sound like an overprotective brother, which is far worse. A papa would not know these men as peers. I've seen Roxbury drunk. I've heard how he speaks of women. Why not look towards someone kind and safe? Someone honest."

"Someone boring, you mean?"

"What about Hardwick? He's not boring, but he is a stand-up fellow. He's honest. And he'll come into his fortune soon. Earlier if he marries." Cal tried to sound casual, but subterfuge had never been his strength.

"The scrawny redhead you cart around with you like an accessory?" The horrified scrunched-up face was not a pleasant look on her. "I hardly think I need to set my sights as low as that. You must be desperate for me to not encourage Roxbury if you're pushing me towards Mr. Hardwick." She studied Cal until he grew uncomfortable. That searching look could pull secrets from a dead man. "Have you already said something to Hardwick? Are you playing matchmaker, brother mine?"

Cal refused to meet her eyes. The joking offer he'd made to Puppy earlier in the evening lingered in his mind.

"You have, haven't you? Oh, you beast! What did he say?" She would relish the failure of Cal's attempt at pairing her off with someone who wouldn't hurt her the way their parents had repeatedly hurt each other.

"Refused the whole plan, then emptied my flask and left me alone to deal with you."

"Maybe I could like him after all," she wheezed through a belly laugh.

A knock on the library's door proved a welcome interruption. "Come in!"

Higgins entered with a note on the silver salver. "A message from Mr. Hardwick, my lord. One of his urchins delivered it but did not wait for a reply."

Odd. The street kids knew if they waited for an answer, they'd collect payment for the reply. The Puppy hoarded his salary like a dragon clinging to gold, but he loved sharing coin with the children in the neighborhood of that hovel he rented. They came in handy when Cal sent Puppy digging around London in search of information. Children witnessed far more than people realized. That this one hadn't darted around to the kitchen to wait while they begged treats from Cook meant no reply was expected.

Emma's brows knit. "Is everything all right?"

The note was brief and to the point. Very Adam.

"He's going home to Northumberland. The vicar in his village—essentially the only decent father figure he has—is not doing well. Adam leaves on the early mail coach."

"Northumberland? He might as well ride to the moon. Why take the mail when he can borrow one of our carriages? I'm sure you would have offered," she said.

"Because he's a stubborn mule. Refuses to accept help most of the time and gets huffy when I offer. He won't even take a room here as part of his employment. Claims he has everything he needs in that drafty single room he rents."

"Then I wish him safe travels. It will be a while before you can continue your misguided matchmaking. That's something, at least."

Cal folded the note, with its neat, loopy penmanship, then tucked it into a pocket. "I'm going to bed, brat. I suggest you do the same. And stay out of my brandy."

Chapter Two

〜

They say time marches on, but when it marched through Northumberland, it must have bypassed the village of Warford to sow seeds of change elsewhere. The dirt road that ran through town with the pub at one end and the church marking the far boundary was as rutted as it had always been. No new buildings pushed those boundaries farther, and on the streets the same signs hung—nothing called attention to a fresh business venture.

She adjusted the satchel she'd packed for the journey, and stepped back to avoid the carriage wheels as the coach pulled away. It was odd to move, assume an entirely new life, and return to find that the only thing changed was her.

About three miles beyond the village stood the cold, solid stone house where the Hardwick twins had lived in misery for five years after their parents died. The small manor squatted on the land, as unyielding and lacking in whimsy as their uncle.

Memories of their time with their parents were warm, centered on their small family's contented life in the country. After the reading of their parents' will, the children had arrived on Milton's doorstep, and the memories of their time there were decidedly darker.

For children reeling from the loss of their parents and their comfortable life, there'd been one haven in the town. The vicar and his son had become a small pocket of normalcy, affection, and acceptance when everything else was topsyturvy. Milton had refused to pay for a governess, so the twins had attended lessons with the other village children at the vicarage until Adam was old enough to be sent away to school.

Vicar Arcott had helmed the church's pulpit, confronting sinners and comforting parishioners, for as long as anyone could remember. But during those hours of lessons, it had been his steady demeanor, calming voice, and gentle affection for all the children that had made her feel safe when everything else seemed tumultuous.

John, the vicar's son, had become a dear friend and readily accepted that the twins were a team. Where one went, the other followed.

The small vicarage stood behind the stone church that dated from the Norman times, content to exist in the shadow of the Lord's house as the centuries slowly passed. The blue paint on the door faded in a diagonal line where the sun hit it each day before continuing on to shine through the stainedglass window of the church.

Beyond the vicarage lay the village graveyard. In the third row, fourth from the end, a simple headstone read

"Ophelia Hardwick 1795–1808." John had written that he'd planted and groomed a small patch of flowers on the grave. Spring came later in these parts, but tiny petals would just be unfurling. A splash of cheerful color in a place of loss.

The wind whipped, flinging mist like needles and threatening to dislodge the hat Cal had passed along last week. A carriage rumbled by, and she tilted her face down toward the ground so no one could identify the lone figure standing before the church.

John opened the door to the vicarage, his familiar face creased with lines of stress and the grief one feels when they know loss is imminent. He sagged against the wood frame. "Oh, thank God, Phee. He's been asking for you for days."

Although the relief soaking John's voice was a welcome balm of familiarity, the name felt like a slap. "Don't call me that." A furtive look over her shoulder showed the surrounding area free of lurkers.

After eleven years, Ophelia knew the first rule in assuming someone else's identity was to be them in every possible way. The endeavor required complete commitment—all or nothing. Think like them, dress like them, talk like them. If she tried to keep the real her alive in any way, this would fail. She must *be* Adam. Most days she felt more like her brother than herself.

Ophelia, the adolescent girl she used to be and the woman she would become, lived in a tiny iron box in the recesses of her mind, under piles of chains and locks. Phee allowed herself to think of the future only under very specific circumstances. And standing on the doorstep of the vicarage with her gravestone only a few yards away was neither the time nor the place.

"I am Adam. Do not forget it when we are in public."

"Public? You're practically in the door already." John rolled his eyes but stepped aside for her to enter.

When she shouldered past him, Phee threw a brotherly elbow to his gut. "Practically in the door is not actually in the door. Let's get inside before someone hears you."

"Is that her?" came a warbled question from the next room.

"Yes, Father," John called. "We will be there in a moment." He turned to Phee, all traces of teasing gone. "You need to prepare yourself. He isn't well. Every morning I expect him to simply not wake. He's weak and only a fraction of the man he used to be. Physically, at least. Mentally, he's still sharp, thank God."

Emaciation and illness were not much of a shock after years of living in London's poorer neighborhoods. Here in the villages of Northumberland, neighbors relied on one another to help when needed. While people were people, no matter where she roamed, Phee noticed in the city that after a certain point the poor—and often the sick or those who would never recover from the war—became invisible to the stronger masses, who frequently weren't even willing to make eye contact. Like ghosts, the stick figures of the poor drifted among the living, waiting to cross over.

To think of Vicar Arcott in such a way felt wrong on every level, but she nodded and braced herself. John's father, while not the largest man in the room, always made up for his lack of physical stature with a booming voice and an all-encompassing smile. Once he opened his mouth or caught you in his intelligent gaze, he no longer seemed like an average man.

Wisdom was his first language, and kindness his second. Although he'd been present for only five years of her childhood, he'd been a father figure to her, reinforcing in her young mind that good people still existed. That not every adult male manipulated others with his position or used words as weapons.

In the vicar's room, open curtains welcomed what meager light the day's sun offered, while an oil lamp next to the narrow bed filled in the remaining shadows. Vicar Arcott's pallor seemed gray, and the blue eyes that always held kindness and unconditional love for her now had a watery, blurred quality to them, as if on the edge of tears.

A sickroom often had a certain scent—the sweet syrup of medicine combined with a body fighting disease or the ravages of time. Being a kind man, the best she'd ever known, he should smell like butterscotch candies and sandalwood shaving soap. Not like this.

She sat on the chair beside the bed, and John perched on a stool at his father's feet. Her hand found Vicar Arcott's on the faded quilt, and with a movement that looked to take more effort than it should, he rested his other hand on top, like they'd done a thousand times before. The last time she'd seen him, his fingers hadn't been this bony. But then, it had been a year. No, nearly two.

"You're too thin, sweetheart. Don't they have food in London?" Arcott's reedy voice would never carry from the pulpit to the vestibule these days.

"I don't need much." Encroaching tears strangled the forced cheer.

The effort of speaking made Arcott close his eyes, although he kept his face turned toward her. "That uncle of yours is still providing for you? There's a rumor around the village that Milton had several large investments fail. He's fired most of his staff in the name of economizing."

As usual, the mention of her uncle made a ball of unease bunch in her gut. "We all know he has never been generous." Or loving, or warm, or kind to small animals— let alone young children left under his care. That he'd become the guardian of her and her brother spoke more to their lack of living relatives than to a preference on her parents' part. At least, she hoped so, since no one in their right mind would give Uncle Milton children on purpose. Economizing might mean Milton lived without dipping into her modest fortune—or it could mean he'd run through not only his money but her parents' as well. And until her birthday, there wasn't a damn thing she could do about it.

The vicar's chuckle and John's snort told their own story. There was no love lost between Milton and anyone who'd made his acquaintance outside the realm of his business holdings.

"I get by. I've taken a position as a land steward. The job isn't like anything I expected. I handle a lot of personal errands and a few bits of correspondence." The hardest part of the job revolved around making sure no one caught her staring at her employer. It was impossible not to stare. If he'd been merely gorgeous, admiring him would have been an unemotional, detached experience. Like appreciating a beautiful painting or a finely built horse.

But given his humor and sharp mind, her objectivity disappeared. Some days the furtive glances at her employer and the response Cal triggered in her body were what kept her from forgetting she wasn't actually her brother.

"A steward? Where is the land?" John asked, pulling her from her thoughts.

"A hundred acres of forest a few hours from here, actually. Cal claims I got the job because I am familiar with the area and know the mentality of the people." In reality, her time was usually spent canvassing the areas beyond the safety of Mayfair, using her network of street urchins to gather information on investors for Cal's extensive financial holdings. The man was thorough with his research and determined to keep his businesses honest. If an investor's name came with a bad report, Cal cut all ties and didn't look back.

"Cal, is it?" John's question held an edge. Phee straightened in her seat but kept her hand with the vicar's, avoiding putting pressure on his gnarled knuckle joints.

"Yes, Calvin, Earl of Carlyle. He's become a friend. A godsend in many ways."

"How did you manage to get tangled up with an earl?" John scoffed.

"I was working at a secondhand clothing stall, and a dissatisfied customer was making a fuss. It drew a crowd, so the owner of the stall felt like he had to make an example of me. Sacked me on the spot, even though it wasn't my fault. Cal and his friend Lord Amesbury witnessed it all." Phee smiled at the memory of the two handsome aristocrats insisting the stall owner pay her wages before they took her to a coffeehouse.

"They took me out for a cup of coffee, and Cal sort of adopted me like some stray kitten they'd rescued from a sack by the river. Lord Amesbury says Cal did much the same with him." Only, Amesbury had been floundering in society and well on his way to ruining himself when Cal swooped in.

"Oh, so fancy, with your aristocrat friends," John teased, but his tone made her feel defensive.

"They're good men. Because of Cal, I can eat. And he passes along clothing so I don't have to worry about a tailor. I alter everything myself."

"Good to see one of your wifely skills is coming in handy," John said. There could be no mistaking the utter lack of teasing.

Phee shot him a look at the same time Arcott barked with surprising strength, "That was uncalled for. Apologize."

"Sorry, Phee," John mumbled to his clasped hands.

"If your apology isn't sincere, then I have no use for it. Do we need to discuss something, John? Vicar, I hate to bring tension to your bedside. We can take this outside."

Vicar Arcott tightened his grip. "Stay. You two have always bickered. It's a comfort to hear you together again, as it should be. John, ask her."

"Ask me what?" She wasn't feeling particularly generous toward John at the moment. Verbal jabs were not the way into her good graces, no matter how long-standing their friendship.

Sighing, John stood reluctantly from his stool. Gripping

only the tips of her fingers, he said, "Ophelia Hardwick, would you do me the honor—"

Phee jerked away, sending her chair clattering behind her. "Hell no! What do you think you're doing?"

"Oh, thank God." John sank onto his seat. People usually reserved that amount of relief for escaping a death sentence.

An urge to kick the stool out from under him nearly overwhelmed her. Instead, Phee righted her own chair and glowered at the supine man in the bed. "Did you encourage this?"

"I have to make this right, Ophelia. God is calling me home soon. How can I rest in peace if you aren't safe? You're like a daughter to me." A single tear trailed over Arcott's papery cheek, and the fight drained out of her.

"You've already made things right by me, Vicar. Don't you see? I wouldn't be here, alive and well, if it weren't for you."

"We erected a lie on consecrated ground. Every time I pass Adam's headstone with your name, I apologize to him and the Lord. But I can't apologize enough, can I?"

Guilt pounded at her with cruel fists, but that was her burden to bear, not the vicar's. The man may have salvaged some good from the situation, but she'd caused it to begin with. Phee wiped a second tear from the old man's cheek. "No boy of thirteen should die. It's not fair. He drowned, and there's nothing we can do about that. Your quick thinking saved me from a living hell. Not only the one I lived with Uncle Milton but also the one he'd arranged for me. Everything you did—lending the weight of your influence to hurry the burial, guarding Adam so the doctor didn't examine him naked, and then keeping my secret—all that worked for the greater good. If not for your tutelage, I never could have returned to boarding school as my brother and kept up. And at the end of the year, when I turn twenty-five and Uncle has to hand over my inheritance, I will have the means to start over somewhere else as a woman. America, or the Continent. Somewhere. You say you can't apologize enough, but I can't thank you enough." A new year, with a new life and a new name in a new country.

Phee glanced over at John. "I owe both of you a debt I can never repay. Thank you, John, for attempting to protect me, however misguided. I know it was your father's idea, but I appreciate that you were willing to saddle yourself with me. You're a loyal friend. But you're also an arse."

John laughed, shaking his head. "You'd be lucky to land a gent like me."

Her earlier irritation at him slipped away. No wonder he'd been grumpy and making comments about her lack of wifely skills—he'd been envisioning a loveless future with her.

"No woman wants a man who's in love with someone else. I'll never be Daisy." He'd had eyes only for the delicate blonde for as long as she could remember. Still did, judging by the vibrant blush visible at the mention of her name. "Marry her, if she'll have you. If she's as sweet as I remember, you have a greater chance of survival with her, anyway. Lord knows I'd smother you in your sleep within a week."

With a grinning nod, John accepted her verbal peace offering. "I'm sorry I made that crack about you sewing your clothes. 'Tis a fine coat."

She smiled. "Cal is a bit of a dandy. I always replace the

buttons with more sensible ones. But the gold and silver ones bring a fair price. When the time comes, I'll have a tidy nest egg in addition to my inheritance."

"Will you stay here, or shall you take a room in the village?" John asked.

"I have a few days before I need to return. I'll make a pallet and stay here if you don't mind. Uncle might hear of it if I stay at the inn." She'd slept worse places than a floor, more than once.

"Take John's bed. He's been sleeping in here all week anyway," Arcott said.

"He's right. I'll sleep in here. Father, are you hungry? Mrs. Courtland stopped by earlier with a cottage pie."

"Feed Phee. Girl needs some meat on her." The fading reply from the bed left her and John exchanging a look.

In the kitchen, John served two generous helpings of the cold meal onto plates, then another portion so small it would barely feed a child.

"Does he only eat that much? He's so slim, I worry," Phee said. At John's amused glance, she rolled her eyes. "I know. Pot calling the kettle black. But I'm skin and bones by nature—your father isn't."

"He eats a few bites once or twice a day. Not much else for weeks now. That's one reason I think he's not long for this world."

Tucking a cloth over the cottage pie, Phee set it in the larder and poured three glasses of milk. The utensils were exactly where they'd always been; the kitchen hadn't changed in the sixteen years since she'd first set foot in it. The butcher-block counter still smelled of the same oil the vicar, and now—she assumed—John, used every month to seal the wood. There was a bottle back in her room she kept for whittling, and the scent reminded her of home each time she opened it.

A deep gouge in the countertop made her pause as she organized their meal on a tray. When she'd made this cut, she'd cried, fearful the vicar would be mad at her for not paying attention when she sliced her sandwich. Phee ran a finger over the wood and smiled at the memory now. That day years ago, Vicar Arcott had wiped her tears, made sure she hadn't nicked herself when the knife slipped, then told her she'd simply made her mark on the house. That every time he saw the scarred wood, he would think of her.

After this trip, she might never come home again. Home. The idea made her throat tight. Knowing the story behind scuffed counters and the location of the forks might be an odd definition of home, but if she were asked for a reference, this tidy vicarage would be it.

"What will you do when he goes?" It was a struggle to get the question past the looming grief.

"I've accepted a teaching position here in the village. Since I'm not stuck with you forever," he teased, "I'll court Daisy properly."

That made her smile. As long as John would be happy in this corner of England with the baker's daughter, then something in the world was as it should be.

A few hours later, as the sun dipped below the horizon, the days of travel packed into the mail coach caught up with her.

"If you yawn any bigger, your head will fall off. Go to bed," John said. The vicar had been dozing for a half hour, and they'd dimmed the lamps so as not to disturb his sleep.

Nodding, Phee shuffled outside to the privy to take care of business, then returned inside to John's room. As she crawled between the sheets, the moon peeked in through the small paned window. It hung like a lantern in the sky, giving plenty of light to see the familiar bedroom where she, John, and Adam had passed countless winter days.

As a child, she'd daydreamed of a different life, one in which her parents survived to see her grown. Now an adult, she'd accepted the loss of them. Memories faded over time, lost their crisp edges. She couldn't even remember what her mother smelled like, or her father's laugh.

Adam was the ghost she clung to.

But there was no denying life would have been better if her parents had lived. It wouldn't matter that Milton was a despicable human being. At thirteen, she wouldn't have learned she could be sold and traded like livestock—a commodity and not a child. All it had taken was a business associate of Milton's wanting to take her off his hands.

Life would be so different. *She* would be so different. Adam might still be alive.

With only the moon for company, it was easy to become maudlin. Phee closed her eyes and rolled over, breathing in the traces of the fresh herb sachet Arcott used in his linen cupboard.

The vicar had stopped including lavender in the sachets when, at the age of ten, she'd launched a persuasive argument on the properties of other herbs and declared her unshakable opinion that lavender smelled of cat piss. He'd used only thyme and rosemary after that.

Some things didn't change. Yet nothing remained the same.

Chapter Three

〜

Y ou look like hell, Puppy. Are you sure about this?" Cal yelled over his shoulder as he removed his coat and unwound his cravat, because he already knew the answer. Just like he had a propensity for taking a dare, Adam didn't back down from a fencing challenge. Of course, that assumed Cal offered a challenge, which was debatable these days. Adam had been a quick study. Given those dark circles under Adam's eyes, Cal might actually stand a chance today. The lad had been traveling for days and looked like he might need a day or two to recover from bouncing about on a mail coach.

"I could beat you if I were half-dead and blind drunk," Adam said, grabbing his favorite fencing foil and inspecting the blade in the light by the window.

"An appropriate boast, since you appear half-dead." Removing a foil from its storage cupboard in the corner, Cal zigzagged the tip of the sword through the air. It might be unsportsmanlike to challenge the lad when he clearly needed a few more hours of sleep, but sportsmanlike conduct rarely came into play with close friendships.

"I'm fine. I can sleep and be back in top form. You can't sleep and get any younger. Now take your position," Adam said.

Cal grinned. "Oh, it's like that, is it? Big words for someone whose bollocks probably only dropped last year. Prepare to be trounced, whippersnapper."

They took their places, face-to-face in the long gallery. Adam rolled his eyes as he shook his sleeve off his cuff, then adjusted his stance. "My bollocks are perfectly adequate, thank you."

Cal dropped his sword arm and stared in horror. "Puppy, under no circumstances does a gentleman ever refer to his bits as merely adequate. Perhaps you should work on other skills. Not every man can be blessed below the belt, so learn to make up for it in alternate ways or you'll end up a lonely, sexless old man."

"Like you?" Adam quipped.

Cal glared and tried not to laugh. "I don't even have a decade on you."

"A lot can happen in a decade."

"*En garde*, smart-arse."

It had been a while since he'd had a lover, but that was perfectly normal. These things ebbed and flowed. He'd been too busy to spend his energies in that direction, and he was tremendously picky.

Metal clanged against metal as they fell into the familiar parry and thrust movements, traveling up and down the long gallery. Whenever Cal thought to slip his blade through a gap in Adam's guard, his friend caught the motion at the last moment and corrected.

Hell and blast. He might not be able to win, even with Puppy half-asleep on his feet. Just as he thought it, Adam scored a point. The tip of his blade tapped Cal's shoulder as he tried to dance away. When skill couldn't cut it, a distraction might work in his favor.

"Do you plan to stay all day? If so, I have a situation that could use your talents." The words came out heavier than he'd like in between breaths. Small consolation that Adam appeared to be working harder for each point today too. He usually bounced through the day with barely restrained enthusiasm. Good to see he didn't actually have springs for feet and unending energy reserves.

The Puppy took a swipe at Cal's chest and nearly scored before Cal jerked back and blocked with his blade. "Are you trying to distract me with work?"

Cal flashed him a grin and wiggled his brows. "Is it working?" Teasing opened him to attack. It took only a split second of distraction, but Adam took advantage and scored a final point.

Resting the tip of the foil on the toe of his boot, Adam breathed heavily. "What's the situation?"

"I need some ears at the docks. The *Wilhelmina* was due in port last month with a valuable cargo hold. When I ask around, I get the placating 'don't worry, milord' speeches. See if I need to break bad news to worried investors."

"Wasn't your father one of those investors?"

"One of the largest, yes. So you see my concern."

"Sending your errand boy all over Town when he's only just returned home?" Emma said. Cal turned and spied his sister. Light flooded the narrow space and made her curls shine where she leaned against the wall and bit into an apple. "Good match, though. You're quick, Mr. Hardwick."

Adam saluted with his blade and sent her a cheeky wink. "Thank you, Lady Emma, but Cal nearly took that last point. I'm lagging a bit today."

Cal wrapped his blade in oilcloth and set it in the cupboard with the rest of the fencing gear. Without a word, he held out a hand to Adam for the other foil, then wrapped and stored that sword as well.

A glance at the pair showed Emma eyeing the Puppy's waistcoat appreciatively. "That fabric is beautiful. I wouldn't have pegged you as a dandy."

The clothing in question had been Cal's a month ago, although Adam probably wouldn't say so, and neither would Cal.

Adam brushed a hand over the brightly colored brocade waistcoat, his cheeks a vivid pink to match the fabric. "It's my one extravagance. Everything else I wear is black, white, or brown. I think it's far enough away from my head that I can wear whatever I want, without worrying it clashes with my hair."

Emma cocked her head, then nodded. "I imagine that would be a problem. You're lucky you don't have to worry about wearing color beyond a waistcoat. Fifty years ago, it would have been a different story."

The Puppy's giggle sounded young and so different from the usual tone he used with the other men that Cal glanced over. "Can you imagine the horror of me in a rose silk jacket?" The pair laughed like longtime companions.

If Emma would fall for Adam, maybe Cal could sleep at night, content knowing his sister was safe from her unfortunate propensity to flirt with men as dissolute as their father.

"Calvin?" Her sweet tone jarred him from wishful thinking.

"What do you want, brat?"

"Lord Roxbury is taking me for a drive in a half hour. When would you like me home?"

Roxbury. The man's attention seemed fixed on Emma. Cal gave her a hard stare. "I notice you aren't asking my permission to go for a drive with Roxbury. You know how I feel about him."

"Oh, please, Cal," she said in a wheedling tone. "He's ever so handsome and he really likes me."

"They all like you, Emma. You have a pretty face and a healthy dowry." Cal looked to the ceiling as if the patron saint of annoying siblings would sprinkle more patience from heaven on him. Lord knew he needed it.

"But he might make me an offer. He's hinted as much, and I would like to know him better before then. Catching a husband is the whole reason I'm in London, is it not?"

"You make it sound like it's a pheasant hunt and you're beating him out of the reeds," Cal said. Emma would do what she wanted no matter what. The more he kicked and screamed about damned Roxbury, the more appealing she'd find the reprobate. The way through this situation was to come at her from the side, not head-on, otherwise she would raise hell. He'd need to have a chat with Roxbury himself. "Be home in an hour. Stick to the public parks. If he arrives in a closed carriage, I'll box his ears, and everything I've agreed to will be null and void. Am I clear?" Thank God she'd have her maid with her.

Emma bounced on her toes, clapping her hands like she used to when she was younger and not a complete pain in the backside. "You're the best brother ever!" After a kiss on his cheek, she skipped out of the room.

The enthusiasm would be endearing if it wasn't for someone like Roxbury. Cal intercepted a glance from Adam. "Don't look at me like that. Give her time. She'll annoy the spine out of you too."

"Think she'll be all right?" Adam asked.

"I hope so. If he lays a finger on her, I'll chop off his stones and shove them down his throat." Still, the worry niggled his brain. A conversation with the scoundrel needed to happen soon. "I could use some coffee, and you look like you're ready to drop from exhaustion. Let's go downstairs. You can tell me about your trip."

Their footsteps thundered on the stairs to the first floor. Without discussion, Cal headed to the library and Adam followed, their strides falling into synchronization. It was good to have him home. During the last couple of weeks, he'd turned around to talk to his friend countless times, only to find Adam gone. Having him back in the house, resuming their usual schedule of fencing and sharing a meal while discussing work and life, soothed the remaining tension from the conversation with Emma.

As was their habit, Adam rang for coffee before settling into the same leather chair Amesbury had preferred when he'd stayed here. "I missed this place," Adam sighed.

"London, my house, or this library in particular?"

"This chair specifically, but I was referring to the library."

"I'm sure the chair missed you too. It's been quiet around here. Not that I mind you taking the time off. I went to Almack's without you. Twice." And it had been boring but for the worry over Emma causing his eye to twitch.

"Oh, the horror," Adam deadpanned.

"It was, rather. Not that I deserved any less punishment after my appalling behavior. I know I apologized already, but I feel awful about the comments I made that night."

"I appreciate that, but think no more on the matter."

It didn't seem like enough, somehow. Perhaps because he'd had two weeks to stew in his guilt. "I'd love to have known Ophelia. Especially if she was anything like you. I'm sorry for your loss and my careless words."

Adam cleared his throat. "I think she'd have liked you too. Thank you."

"And how was the vicar? Do you think he'll recover?"

"Arcott insists he has no intention of going to be with God anytime soon, but I said my goodbyes just in case. John was right to send for me." He clapped, as if slamming the book shut on that conversation. "Now. Tell me why Almack's was a horror, and leave nothing out. I want to hear how miserable you were without my glowing presence."

Cal sank into his seat and leaned his head against the padded wing of the chair. "Roxbury danced with her twice this week—one of them a waltz. He might as well have fallen to his knees right there and declared himself. But then he danced the other waltz and a quadrille with that Dowling chit.

Emma ranted about it." He closed his eyes at the memory of the tirade he'd endured on the way home.

"Remind me again, why do we hate Roxbury? Beyond his general abhorrence of civil conversation, I mean. I remember looking into his name a while ago, but not the specifics."

"That thing last year with the opera dancer and my father? Roxbury took up with her next and shared every indelicate detail she spilled in private."

Understanding dawned in Adam's expression. "How could I forget the marquess's-mini-member jokes? You're right. We hate him."

Cal's father, the Marquess of Eastly, had a penchant for opera dancers. That one in particular hadn't appreciated receiving paste gems as a parting gift. Her revenge had been brutal and effective. Now not only had every man in Town discussed or heard discussions of the size of his father's allegedly uninspiring cock, but there'd been rampant speculation that Cal shared the condition. The whole situation struck him as juvenile, but really, he should be used to it by now. Father seemed incapable of staying out of trouble. A character trait Emma might share, if this budding relationship with Roxbury gave any indication.

"Roxbury's attention to Emma doesn't sit right. I can't believe his intentions are honorable." Worry nagged at him. Emma would be safe enough in an open carriage with a maid in tow, but the social restrictions didn't seem like enough when applied to his baby sister and a rotter like Roxbury.

"Honorable intentions seem in short supply with that one," Adam agreed.

A maid entered with a rolling cart piled high with coffee,

cream, and sugar. Cook had a soft spot for Adam and shared Cal's determination to fatten the lad, as shown by a stack of sandwiches that could feed five men.

The friends ate in silence for long moments while they drank coffee in front of the empty grate. The day was too warm for a fire and would only get warmer. Early summer in the city meant an odd mix of gorgeous blooming flowers, greenery, and the scent of filth baking on the streets and in the Thames.

Here in the dim cool of the library, thick velvet curtains muted the sun. Shelves of books and foil-pressed wallpaper created the illusion that those streets were a world away. The silence grew.

"Are you falling asleep over there, Puppy?"

"Almost. Those days of travel took it out of me. I can't seem to sleep enough," came the drowsy reply.

"Finally, a sign that you're getting old."

"The coffee should wake me up in a few minutes. I'll ask after the *Wilhelmina*. If she went down, there will be talk. But we both know the ship could have simply run into weather."

"Agreed. Let's hope for the best. I received three letters from investors this week and need to be prepared for every event, though." Another letter sat behind him on his desk, and Cal was fairly certain it pertained to the same topic. When ventures paid out, everyone was happy. But one constant in finance—whether playing on the Exchange or dabbling in trade—investments carried risk. Like any game of chance, the risk was part of the fun but could be the ruin of a man. And Eastly had invested more heavily than Cal had advised.

"Maybe take a nap when you return. There's a room upstairs at the ready for the day you quit that hovel you rent and decide to embrace creature comforts."

"I'm not having that conversation again. I'll go home after the docks, then see you bright and early tomorrow."

Cal sighed. When God had created this particular Adam, he'd crammed a lot of stubbornness into such a skinny package. "Fine. Be careful on the way home."

Chapter Four

❧

*J*t was official. Calvin wanted to throw Roxbury into the Thames just so he could enjoy his coffee and toast in peace.

Cal had called on the bounder four different times and each time had been told at the door that he wasn't home. He'd looked for him at the club but come up empty. Roxbury always seemed to show up and call on Emma when Cal was out of the house, so he'd managed to take Emma for a drive several times over the last few weeks. When Cal instructed the servants to turn the man away, Emma bumped into Roxbury while out shopping, or at the museum with her Saint Albans friends. There was no escaping it—Cal was being outmaneuvered.

With such focused attention from Roxbury, everyone suspected an offer would be imminent.

Like hell. If there were even the slightest chance the man's intentions toward Emma were honorable, Cal might wish them happy. But he'd bet the pot of Cook's delicious strawberry jam in his hand that Roxbury was only toying with Emma. Entirely unacceptable.

The talk had to happen today. Even if he needed to run the man to ground like a fox, Cal would finally have a one-on-one discussion with the reprobate. Then perhaps he wouldn't have to sit at breakfast enduring yet another monologue on Roxbury's charms.

Reaching the end of his patience, Cal threw his serviette onto the table and grabbed his cup. "Excuse me."

Coffee in hand, he marched down the hall, past the library, and through the front doors and kept walking across a narrow lane to the residence of his best friend Ethan and his wife, Lottie. Dawson, their butler, would be horrified if he simply went inside, so Cal knocked, then took a sip of his steaming coffee while he waited. The street wasn't too busy yet, but a man pushing a cart of wooden crates gave Cal a questioning look as he walked by.

Because of the exceptionally long term of Parliament, the newlyweds had spent more time in Town this year. Typically, Lord and Lady Amesbury preferred the country, doing whatever country dwellers did. Something to do with sheep and hops—that was what he'd say if Ethan asked him to explain the workings of their estate. Cal knew damn well Woodrest crafted delicious ale and would eventually sell to the finest houses in London.

Building a production and retail endeavor from the ground up with Ethan had been a unique challenge. Their efforts were looking to pay off nicely as long as this year's crop yielded the projected harvest. Not that Cal ever willingly or enthusiastically discussed such things. Ethan and Lottie could go on and on about crop rotation and not even notice that Cal was on the verge of dying of boredom. That was why he handled the business side of things—because playing in the dirt sounded awful.

Cal took another sip. Dawson's knees must hurt today. That would explain the wait.

Another moment passed before Dawson opened the door and stepped aside. The butler was as ancient as Methuselah, with jowls that hung from his face as if exhausted from years of clinging to the sharp edges of his facial structure. "My lord and lady are in the breakfast room," he said.

"Thank you, Dawson."

A floral arrangement on the slim table by the door caught his eye. Little touches like that told everyone that this home belonged to a lady who cared about the details. Without Lottie, Ethan would have been content to let the place exist as a vast echoing marble chamber with a random distribution of half-read books piled on every available surface.

The smell of breakfast led Cal to the sunny room where the pair preferred to start the day. Pushing through the wooden door, he immediately felt better. No one here would rhapsodize about damned Roxbury's shoulders.

"Good morning," he said.

Lady Amesbury gave him a wave, and Ethan jerked his head toward the sideboard, where platters of breakfast options lay, making a silent offer.

Moments like this reminded him that his family was pretty brilliant. They didn't share blood, but they would do anything for each other.

Cal loaded a plate with all his favorites and topped off his coffee. He might be a disgrace as an Englishman, preferring coffee over tea—and Ethan assured him regularly of this—but they always had coffee on hand for Cal during breakfast. Sometimes he smelled coffee on Dawson's breath, so he was fairly certain he wasn't the only one who appreciated the black nectar of life.

"Are the Lords not meeting today?" Cal asked.

Ethan took his role in the House of Lords seriously, although he wasn't as politically active as some. Calvin assumed his seat in the House only when he had nothing better to do. Which admittedly wasn't often.

"I'm not going tae sit through whatever Whitfield is goin' on about today. Besides, I was, er, detained longer than expected before breakfast." Ethan grinned and Lottie smirked, obviously proud of herself. "Did you have a particular reason for stoppin' by, or are you just here tae eat my sausage and kippers?"

"Your bacon, actually. I'll leave your sausage for your wife to enjoy." Grinning at the choked laughter from Lottie, Cal sat across from them and swallowed a hearty bite before continuing. "I need to talk about my sister, otherwise I may not survive her Season. Or she may not survive. Lord Roxbury might not make it out either. Regardless, one of us will have to go. I'm going to hunt him down this afternoon and finally talk to the man. He's raising expectations, and anyone with a brain knows Roxbury isn't the marrying kind." *Maybe Emma liked a challenge.*

Fine, he might be indulging in a bit of dramatics.

Thankfully, his companions didn't comment on that. Lottie bit her lip as she smeared strawberry preserves on a piece of toast. Ethan shook his head and grinned over at his wife, then leaned back in his chair. "The papers called her an Incomparable. A diamond, even. The lass has her pick of anyone. What could possibly be the matter?"

God, their bacon really was amazing. Amidst his general annoyance with life at the moment, the salty perfection stood out as a bright spot. "My cook needs to talk to your cook and discuss this bacon. It has to be something in the curing process they do differently. As to Emma—she could choose anyone. So why the bloody hell is she so focused on Roxbury?"

Lottie grimaced in sympathy. "Some women are drawn in by pretty charmers."

"Can't she see beyond the face? He's a handsome fellow, I'll grant you that. But there has to be more to a man than appealing shoulders."

Cal tried not to roll his eyes when Lottie stared at Ethan's impressively wide shoulders and her expression evolved into a heated look more appropriate for their bedroom.

The two of them were adorable in their own twisted way. As sentimental as it sounded, Cal supposed love made all the difference. His parents hadn't exhibited the concept of love—not with each other at any rate. If he could find what Ethan shared with Lottie, he might consider the institution of marriage.

Preening like a peacock, Ethan winked at his wife before returning to the topic at hand. "Will you think anyone is good enough for Emma?"

"I offered Puppy two hundred pounds to marry her and keep his hands to himself. But his morals are too firmly entrenched, I fear. He laughed at me, then drank my liquor and left."

The couple snickered. Lottie said, "I like Adam. He's young, but he has kind eyes."

Pushing the now-empty plate aside, Cal cradled the coffee cup between his hands and tried to relax his shoulders from where they'd crept up near his ears. "Young, but he's a solid fellow. We're taking Emma to Vauxhall tonight, if you'd like to come along."

The couple exchanged a look, then Lottie nodded. "Let's dine here first. Their portions are appallingly small."

Ethan sighed. "Aye. Elf food and fireworks, it is."

"Perfect." Cal refilled his cup from the silver carafe and rose. "With that to look forward to, I'm afraid I need to go. My schedule is full. I'm due at the tailor's in a bit, but first I have to deal with Roxbury. Which is sure to be a fun time. On top of that, Father requested I call. Let's all hope he hasn't spawned another illegitimate child."

A short drive later, the butler at the club informed him that Lord Roxbury had left for home after gaming all night.

Cal's carriage pulled up three doors down from Roxbury's tidy residence. He called up to his coachman, "Hobby, have someone check the mews behind the house. Make sure his lordship is home."

Ten minutes later the young tiger, Walter, returned, slightly out of breath. "He arrived about a quarter hour ago, your lordship."

"Very good. Circle the square. I won't be long."

Cal whistled a cheerful tune as he made his way down the pavement and climbed the steps to the town house. The butler answered his knock but didn't bother glancing at Cal's card this time before stating that Lord Roxbury wasn't at home.

Donning his most charming smile, Cal tipped his hat brim at a rakish angle with one finger. "Then you won't mind if I wait inside. Roxbury is expecting me," he lied.

"I'm afraid, milord, that won't be poss—"

Cal missed the rest as he brushed past the butler and strode up the staircase to where he assumed the family rooms were. Behind him, the retainer gawked, and Cal waved a hand over his shoulder. "I'll tell him I overpowered you. This will only take a moment."

A maid in the hallway on the second floor pointed the way to the master's rooms. Cal gave a cursory knock on the door, then walked in.

"Your butler is sputtering in the front hall, cursing my name, and will probably send a burly footman to drag me away posthaste, so let's make this quick, shall we?" Cal kicked the door closed behind him, then turned the key in the lock to buy him a few extra minutes in case his prediction wasn't far off.

"What the devil do you want, Carlyle?" Roxbury's jaw was rough with late-night bristles, his eyes were red-rimmed, and a pungent wave of alcohol and perfume—thankfully, not Emma's preferred scent—wafted across the room when he spoke.

Wincing, Cal said, "You look like hell, man."

Roxbury shrugged. "I'll be right as rain once I sleep. I repeat, what do you want?"

"I need to know your intentions regarding my sister."

The other man chuckled, which turned into a full-on guffaw while he shrugged out of his evening coat. "Did she put you up to this? Damn, dance with a chit a few times and they hear wedding bells."

A glassy calm settled over Cal, not unlike the smooth surface of a peaceful loch hiding a sea serpent in its depths. "My sister's emotions aren't a laughing matter. But I fear you're toying with them, and that is not something I will stand for."

"Emma doesn't have any such reservations. In fact, she's been most...eager to get to know me." Roxbury smirked as he unwound his limp cravat and dropped it on the floor, then started on his waistcoat buttons.

At the implication, Cal's hands clenched, but nothing would be solved if he blackened the man's eye. Although it would be bloody satisfying.

"You won't speak of Emma that way. Not now, not ever. Are we clear? You obviously don't have honorable intentions, so your involvement with her ends now. No more rides in the park. No more dances. If she approaches you, you'll greet her civilly, then walk away." Such treatment would break her heart in the short term but save her future pain. It would be agonizing to witness, but Cal couldn't stand idly by while she wasted her debut Season on a scoundrel like the sot before him.

"You want me gone?" Roxbury's waistcoat joined the pile of clothing on the floor, and for a moment, Cal pitied the man's valet. Cal's manservant, Kingston, would make his life hell if Cal dared disrespect his clothing like that. In his shirtsleeves, Roxbury sauntered toward him.

"She deserves better than you. If you're not planning to marry her, then you need to leave her alone."

Roxbury seemed to consider that, but his smirk didn't bode well for the conversation. "Two thousand pounds."

Cal cocked his head. "I beg your pardon. You expect me to pay you to do the right thing? We are talking about protecting a young lady from a good family. The daughter of a marquess."

Roxbury untucked his shirt from his trousers. "You want me to leave your precious sister alone? Two thousand pounds. For that, I'll abandon the field to a suitably pasty fellow of your choosing."

Crossing his arms to appear casual as he leaned against the door, Cal weighed his options. Roxbury had no honorable intentions toward Emma, and likely no honor in general. If paying him off was the quickest way to end the situation, then so be it. The whole business turned his stomach, but in the end, this was similar to paying a spurned and dissatisfied mistress, or a pregnant maid—and God knew he'd done that for Eastly enough times. "For two thousand pounds you'll agree to stop your pursuit of Emma?"

"Quibble about it, and the price goes up," Roxbury said. "Besides, it's not as if passing around that Carlyle fortune is new for you. How many women have you paid to keep quiet after your father's done with them? This is no different, really. But I didn't have to see the marquess's mini member to get my lump sum. Two thousand, delivered today. Or I'll take a check."

A knock at the door behind his shoulder made Cal glance at the lock. The cavalry had arrived.

"I'll write a check now and have it done with. Call off your dogs while I use your inkwell." A small desk against the wall held a messy pile of papers, four empty wine bottles, and an inkpot and pen. The quill nub could have used a good sharpening with a penknife, but it wasn't Cal's job to maintain this man's writing tools. Shaking his head at the clutter and disarray, Cal pulled his checks from his pocket and scratched out the information required to draft such a large sum.

At the door, a bare-chested Roxbury told whoever was in the hall, "He's here to pay a debt. You can escort him out in a moment."

Signing his name with sharp strokes, Cal curled his lip. "There. Don't smudge the ink, for I won't be writing you another." He handed the paper to Roxbury on his way out the door.

"Pleasure doing business with you," the bastard said, then closed the door.

The footman looked more like a boxer, with the kind of nose that had clearly been broken more than once and a brow so bisected by scars, the hair had given up any attempt to grow. With a jerk of his head, the servant motioned for Cal to walk ahead, escorting him from the home in threatening silence.

But it was done. Emma was safe from one of London's

many scoundrels. Thousands more to be on the lookout for, but that was a problem for another day.

There was only one way to salvage the morning—a visit to Bond Street.

A half hour later, Cal tugged the bottom of his new waistcoat down so it fell exactly where breeches met shirt, then turned in the mirror to inspect the seamlines. Perfectly straight without a pucker or unwanted wrinkle in sight.

"Well done, Carter. Beautiful fit as always."

"Thank you, milord. It's always a pleasure to dress someone of your refined tastes."

Cal shot him an amused look. "Laying it on a little thick, don't you think? You're just relieved it's not a pair of trousers so I can't make my usual dangling-cock jokes."

Carter, predictably, bit his lip against a smile in an effort to keep his professional demeanor. It had become a sort of game between them, with Cal free to be as outrageous as he pleased, and Carter trying his damnedest to keep a straight face.

On top of that, the man really was an exceptional tailor.

"Now the coat, milord?"

The dark-green wool settled over his shoulders like a hug. "That will do nicely. You were right about the onyx buttons. They highlight the fine weave of the fabric without distracting from the lines."

"I'm pleased you are satisfied with it, milord. If there won't be anything else today, shall I wrap these and give them to your footman?"

"Yes, thank you."

There was a pregnant pause as Carter helped him out of

the coat, then handed it off to an assistant. "As always, we are honored to receive the continued patronage of the Carlyle and Eastly houses."

Cal glanced over as he shrugged into his original waistcoat and fastened the buttons. "Has Eastly been in recently?"

"Last week, milord."

"All right, then I'll settle his account before I leave." Otherwise, his father would live on credit until doors shut in his face all along Bond Street.

Carter nodded. "Very good, milord." He cleared his throat gently. "I believe your father also visited the glovemaker two doors down as well."

Of course he did. Cal smiled ruefully. "Then I shall stop by there next. Thank you, Carter."

As predicted, the glovemaker was relieved to have Eastly's account settled. A pair of leather gloves for Puppy and a delicately beaded pair for Emma helped reaffirm goodwill with the shop.

Sometimes he wondered if it would be easier if the shops simply sent the bills directly to him. Giving Father pin money made more sense from a financial perspective, except for the tantrum Father would no doubt throw.

On the street, Cal climbed into his carriage and tossed the two slim glove boxes onto the empty seat across from him.

He sighed and relished the quiet of the few minutes it took to get to his father's town house. Just another day in the life of Lord Calvin Carlyle, caretaker of the Eastly family. Once he dealt with his father, he'd be free to anticipate Emma's first trip to Vauxhall. She'd love the fireworks, and he could hardly wait to see her excitement at the acrobats.

That was something to look forward to. The morning might have been a trial, but at least the day would end well.

Or so he thought, until he found out why his father had asked him to drop by.

"At any point in this horrifically misguided thought process, did it occur to you that human beings are not currency? This isn't a tailor bill or a new pair of boots. This is too far, even for you." Cal scrubbed his palms over his face and wished he had ignored Eastly's summons.

The marquess appeared discomfited for the first time in recent memory, avoiding Cal's gaze to fiddle with a crystal paperweight on the desk in his rarely used library. "Well, you see, it's like this, Son."

Cal sighed. When the marquess started calling him Son, it always spelled disaster.

"Everything will be fine once my investment in the *Wilhelmina* pays out. The debt is rather sizable," his father said.

"Rather sizable? Or crippling?"

"It'll ruin us, Son."

"No, it will ruin *you*."

"I don't know if the estates can recover from this," Eastly said.

Cal took a moment to process those words and still couldn't quite make his brain accept them as real. The estates were healthy. Sizable. Sure, he paid Eastly's Bond Street accounts—but because his father was irresponsible, not broke. Cal bit out words through gritted teeth. "What was it? Cards? Horses?"

"Lady Winslow," his father muttered.

"I'm sorry—Lady Winslow?"

The marquess took a deep breath as if preparing to tell a tale, and something told Cal that was exactly what this would be. A story for the record books of ridiculous wagers. Depending on how utterly preposterous it turned out to be, it might even be true. But he hoped this one time, his father would be honest and have the grace to feel ashamed of himself.

"Lady Winslow tends to be ... well, let's say, not so loose with her favors," his father began.

"You mean she's faithful to her husband."

"Yes. Odd duck, that. Baron Rosehurst and I bet about who could get under her skirts first."

"And you lost." Did that mean the baron overcame the lady's determination to stay faithful to her husband? Curiosity won out over the anger long enough for Cal to ask, "How did Rosehurst manage that?"

"We set a time limit. Neither of us won the lady, so we each owe a forfeit."

Ah, there was the utter lack of forethought or logic he'd come to expect from his father. At some point Father's scandals had turned from opera dancers and mistresses to blatant recklessness, and Cal had failed to notice. Or perhaps he'd become numb to it all, and the escalation of consequences had sneaked up on him. "So, you were so confident in your ability to woo a lady—who by all appearances actually loves her husband—that you put a time limit on this bet, with a default that will cripple our estate's ability to function."

"Unless you marry the chit, yes. But in all fairness, the baron defaulted too."

"Please tell me the baron's default is some kind of boon to this situation."

For the first time in the conversation his father's face took on the animated excitement of a little boy receiving a present. "Mason's Square. The prize stud from his stables. Gorgeous, leggy bay. His offspring will bring a tidy sum."

Cal's fists clenched so tightly his fingernails cut his palms. "A horse. A woman and a horse. You thought a *horse* equal to a default that threatens the financial security of our entire family? You literally traded your own son's future for a *horse*."

"He's a beautiful horse," his father said sheepishly.

"Forget the fact that we don't have a horse-breeding operation—let me get these details straight." Cal cleared his throat, hoping in vain to extinguish the fury threatening to close his airway. "Either I have to marry his daughter, or we pay a monetary default that will drain the coffers. In exchange for my freedom, you gain one single blasted horse."

"A prize-winning stallion," his father interjected.

Cal wouldn't honor that with an answer.

"Very generous of Rosehurst," his father said, bobbing his head as if he could somehow nod hard enough and with enough enthusiasm that he might sway Cal through sheer force of will. Classic Marquess of Eastly.

"And if I don't marry her, we're ruined," Cal growled.

"Unless the *Wilhelmina* shows up soon, yes."

"Why don't you marry her?" Cal shook his head with disgust. "A marquess is a better title than an earl. Or renege on the bet. You wouldn't be the first gentleman to do so."

"I can't go back on my word. A gentleman's word is

sacred." Eastly placed a hand over his heart as he made that entirely hypocritical declaration. "Rosehurst thought she'd fancy you more, since you're closer to her age. Just wants the best for his daughter, after all."

The first instinct battling for action demanded Cal punch his father in the nose, march out of the house, then have a stiff drink or five while repeating his determination to never speak of his sire again.

To the marquess, the title was God-given destiny, and since he hadn't done anything to earn it, he didn't see any reason why he should exert effort to safeguard it. But what Eastly never seemed to grasp was that this was about more than the title. Their homes and tenants were full of people who depended on them. If Cal simply refused, the estate and those families who relied on them would feel the impact.

Not only that, but Emma's marriage prospects, and eventually Cal's own, reflected Eastly's rank in society. Containing his father's scandals—and now paying off an inappropriate suitor of Emma's—had always been more about protecting their futures than Eastly's personal reputation.

What a mess.

"I'll have them announce the banns." His father rose from behind the desk and had the audacity to clap a hand on Cal's shoulder as if they were partners in this ridiculousness.

"Don't you dare," Cal said, plopping his hat on his head while his brain whirred, searching for a way out of this.

"Sorry, what did you say, Son?"

"Tell the baron you'll settle the debt when the *Wilhelmina* returns with your investment. That will buy me some time to find a way out of this coil. I'm not making a decision right now."

"There's no decision. You have to do this. You can't ruin me, Calvin."

"And yet you think nothing of ruining me." With that, Cal stormed out, slamming the library door behind him. He climbed into the carriage, his chest tight with an acrid mix of worry, frustration, and red-hot fury.

The city passed by. Buildings with dirty doors on packed streets, only blocks from gleaming townhomes with tidy gardens surrounded by ornate ironwork fences, like elaborate cages of their own making. Thousands of those people would think he lived a blessed life. Bet they didn't have family members who traded their sons like livestock. Hell, he'd been traded *for* livestock. Granted, matches in the *ton* happened all the time for reasons that had nothing to do with affection and everything to do with finances, connections, and politics. Yet the marquess hadn't even pretended there might be some higher noble purpose at work.

Just a horse. What a mess, indeed.

Chapter Five

❧

The evening was warm with a breeze that made her cravat flutter against her chin. Normally, she'd never venture into this part of Town in her evening wear, but Phee was due at Vauxhall in an hour. Behind her, a lantern hanging beside the door to the tavern offered enough light to see the hands on her watch. She snapped the case closed and tucked it away.

Laughter and shouted conversations made their way through the window to the street where Phee stood. She could make out Peggy's sharp cackle as the barmaid went about her rounds, refilling drinks and greeting customers by name. Not only did Peggy keep company with one of the sailors on the *Wilhelmina*, but she could read and write. A steadfast devotion to her sailor beau meant a letter waited for him in every port, and he sent a reply before returning to sea. During their interview, Peggy hadn't voiced concerns about whether her lover was alive or dead, which spoke well to the fate of the *Wilhelmina* and her crew.

Frankie, one of the street children Phee often worked with, would be back from the docks any minute. That grubby little girl saw and heard everything and could make herself invisible at the drop of a hat. As long as Frankie's report didn't conflict with Peggy's, Phee would consider the information she'd gathered tonight reliable.

"Coin first, as usual." Frankie appeared around the corner with palm outstretched.

"Of course." A flash of money from pocket to tiny hand, then Phee stepped with the child beyond the circle of the lantern light.

"Ship hit weather at the Cape and took on damages. They've gone to port in Africa to make repairs," Frankie said.

"Peggy told me something similar. Any word on the cargo?" On that topic, Peggy hadn't been helpful. Her focus had been understandably on her man, not the contents of the hold.

"No. I left messages asking around. It might take a bit to find someone who knows, but I'll send word when I hear anything."

Phee slipped the child another coin. "Well done, Frankie. Send word when you get it."

Without another sound, the urchin melted into the darkness, and Phee turned toward the nearest cross street. Keeping alert for unsavory characters, she ducked around the building and jogged between the traffic toward a hack parked across the road.

"Vauxhall, please," she called up to the driver, then settled on the seat. Opening her pocket watch, Phee checked the time again and smiled. She might not be late after all.

A short while later, the smells and sounds of the docks were another world away as Phee met Cal's carriage outside the gates, then paid her admission.

"I spoke with Frankie," she said in a low voice, for Cal's ears only, as they made their way toward the dining area.

"The *Wilhelmina*?" he asked.

"She hit weather and took on damages. Stopped for repairs after rounding the Cape. No word on the cargo, but Frankie is on it."

A groove appeared between Cal's brows. "Keep me apprised of the situation, as usual."

"I always do."

"Carlyle!" someone cried, and the worry disappeared from Cal's face before he returned the greeting with a cheerful one of his own.

"What would I do without you?" Cal clapped a hand on her back.

"Lose money and be taken in by cheats and liars."

He laughed. "You're not wrong, my friend. I made do before you came along, but you make my life easier."

The spot on her shoulder blade where his hand had rested tingled. Phee tilted her hat at a jaunty angle with one finger and shot him a smile.

Viscount and Lady Amesbury were already cozy at a table, sitting a few inches closer together than entirely proper. The viscountess was rosy-cheeked and laughing, resting her considerable bosom on her husband's arm, when Phee approached with Cal and Emma. Amesbury didn't appear to mind, as he not so subtly appreciated his wife's cleavage.

Phee had fought against a similar expression a few minutes

ago when Cal had exited his coach and wrecked her equilibrium. The forest-green evening jacket he wore highlighted the angle of his shoulders and the lean lines of his body.

He offered a seat to Emma, then took a place across from Ethan, gesturing with a nod to a spot for Phee.

Emma craned her head about, trying to see everything all at once, but kept glancing toward the darker paths, as if expecting someone to appear. She might think herself subtle, but the furtive looks put Phee on alert. Thank God Emma wasn't entirely her responsibility—although, in good conscience, she couldn't let the girl wander off alone.

At Vauxhall there were myriad spectacles to enjoy, and this was Emma's first visit. Fresh-faced, eyes sparkling with excitement, Emma looked lovely tonight, as if she floated through the crowd with an enchanted glow about her.

Phee couldn't remember ever being that wide-eyed toward the world. Not with innocence, anyway. Trepidation, sure. But by all appearances, Emma lacked that emotion altogether.

Cal was a watchdog of a big brother. Considering how happy-go-lucky he was in so many other areas of his life, these protective instincts and this desire for rules with Emma tickled Phee to no end. Judging by the grin on Lord Amesbury's face, Phee wasn't alone in her amusement. Calvin wearing his big-brother hat in the face of Emma's enthusiasm was comedy at its best but also incredibly sweet. It made her heart go soft, so she tried to avoid looking at him.

Across the table, Lady Amesbury laughed at something her husband whispered in her ear, then murmured a reply that made Lord Amesbury grin wickedly.

"Sorry we're late," Cal said, nodding to a footman who

offered a glass of wine. "I hope you two haven't been waiting long. How much champagne has Lottie imbibed?"

Lottie hiccuped. "Just enough to think you're pretty." She shot her husband an amused look. "Not as pretty as you, love. But nice all the same. All that shiny hair is like a halo. False advertising but quite attractive."

Everyone laughed until Cal's amusement cut off abruptly.

Two men approached their table. Rising with slow movements that spoke of his reluctance, Cal made a bow to the Marquess of Eastly. "Good evening, Father. I didn't expect to see you."

"Calvin! We were just talking about you. Well met, Son."

Phee and Amesbury stood as well when a younger woman trailing behind Eastly and his companion joined the group.

"I'd like to introduce Miss Violet Cuthbert and her father, Baron Rosehurst. Close friends of mine I mentioned earlier today. A fine young lady, as you can see."

The polite expression Cal wore seemed wooden to Phee, but others might be convinced. Years of training likely overrode his fairly obvious urge to flee, as he bowed over the lady's hand as expected.

Eastly had talked to Cal earlier today? Strange that their meeting hadn't come up in conversation before now. But then, she and Cal hadn't exactly been glued to each other's side today. In fact, they'd met only briefly before she left for home to dress.

Phee flexed her hands and enjoyed the supple slide of the beautiful new gloves he'd presented her with. She shrugged off the question. If the interview with Eastly had been important, she was sure Cal would have mentioned it.

Besides, this wasn't the first time she'd witnessed Eastly throw his son into an awkward situation with bull-in-a-china-shop exuberance. It pained her to see Emma's expression change from unrestrained enjoyment to a polite mask as she waited for her father to acknowledge his daughter's presence at the table.

Cal's "Pleased to meet you" and "It's an honor" sounded perfectly sincere, but anyone who knew him could tell his heart wasn't in it. His interest—as far as she knew—remained unstirred, despite Eastly's numerous matchmaking attempts. In two years of friendship, Phee hadn't seen him do more than look at a woman, and they'd never spent their evenings at brothels or chasing actresses at the theater. A lucky thing, since that could have turned very awkward very quickly.

Out of the corner of her eye she spied Emma rising from her seat and murmuring something about the ladies' retiring room. Lucky girl to escape so neatly. Their footmen standing at attention beyond their box would help her find the way safely, so Phee returned her attention to the three men who still stood.

The baron held Cal's hand captive between the two of his, seesawing his arm up and down like the handle of a water pump. In a graceful move, Cal managed to free his hand before clapping the baron on the arm. Smoothly done—he'd extricated himself from an overly enthusiastic greeting and still looked friendly.

"We have enough room at the table if you'd like to join us. Although some notice next time would be appreciated, Father," Cal said, and Phee heard the reproach, even if Eastly didn't outwardly acknowledge it.

No one seemed inclined to address the niceties, so Phee helped Miss Cuthbert to a seat and gestured to their footman to fill her glass of champagne. Miss Cuthbert murmured her thanks before Phee took her seat as the other men finally found places at the table.

A shout from the jugglers and acrobats in the crowd caught everyone's attention as a fire-eater blew a gust of flame toward a shrieking woman.

Depending on where they fell in their political leanings, the revelers were primed for either a fight or a celebration now that Queen Caroline had ended her exile in Italy. The performers played to the heightened emotions of everyone, mingling with the vibrant mix of low and high class. In another hour, the fireworks would begin, which was always Phee's favorite part of the night. But until then, their entertainment would be provided by watching men belch fire and Cal fend off the baron and his mortified daughter.

Pity stirred within Phee for the daughter, though. With her downcast gaze studying the hem of the serviette in her lap, Miss Cuthbert, at least, seemed to recognize her father and Eastly's boorish behavior.

Lord Amesbury brought his mouth to Lottie's ear, and whatever he said sparked a wicked gleam in her eye. Without further ado, Lord Amesbury rose, offered his hand to his wife, and led her out of the box.

The viscount and his lady wove through the throng of revelers toward the dark paths beyond the seating pavilion. Lady Amesbury pulled her husband's head down to say something, oblivious to the man walking a tightrope above them.

In another life, Phee might have been as determined to

escape toward the area of Vauxhall that made it so appealing to revelers with carnal intentions. If she had a lover, she would gravitate toward the darkness too, with no worries beyond stealing another kiss. Helpless to resist the fantasy, she let herself drink in the picture Cal made under the swaying lanterns, with his perfectly packaged good looks that her fingers itched to muss and unwrap like a present. The too-long hair he restrained in an orderly queue that would fall free if she tugged that black ribbon loose. She wanted to unwind the pristinely folded cravat to expose the bristles of beard that would peek out in a few hours. It was the fantasy of a moment—until the men's conversation interrupted her daydream and ruined everything.

The baron and Eastly were singing Miss Cuthbert's praises in the most general terms. Excellent stock, fine needlepoint skills, biddable—that word alone made Phee clench her jaw. Miss Cuthbert didn't preen under the attention—she remained mute, worrying the edge of her serviette in her lap. Surely, it would irritate anyone with a modicum of self-respect to hear herself discussed like a horse at the races.

Lordy, when would the baron and marquess stop talking? Although his face remained impassive, Cal's hands clenched tellingly around the fork beside his wineglass, which an obliging servant kept filled. Cal tried to draw Phee and Miss Cuthbert into the conversation several times, but the other men seemed determined to dominate the discourse.

As the minutes dragged on, the older men talked, and Miss Cuthbert inched away from the fathers until she'd nearly crept into Emma's vacant seat.

Wait. Emma. She had been gone for some time and hadn't

taken a chaperone. No doubt a footman accompanied her. Unless the girl had talked her way out of a watchful eye, which would certainly be in character.

How far away was the retiring room? Phee didn't know, having never been in one at Vauxhall. Most men stepped off a path and used a handy bush or tree. Thanks to the carved, hollowed-out piece of wood resembling a phallus she kept in a panel inside her breeches, she'd devised a way to pee standing up years ago. Most gentlemen considered it bad form to check another's wares—so to speak—while relieving oneself. The pocket pizzle might not be the cleanest option, but it had saved her more than once and had been vital to avoiding discovery at boarding school.

The orchestra began a piece that may have been lively and joyful but to Phee's ears only added to the noisy environment.

The footman Phee had expected Emma to take stepped into view, opening a fresh bottle of champagne for the table. So Emma didn't have a servant with her after all. That settled it. Phee murmured her excuses toward the others at the table, who ignored her, then she set off to look for Cal's sister.

After a few subtle inquiries Phee found the ladies' retiring room, which did her no good, because Adam Hardwick couldn't march in and look for her. After waiting outside the door for five minutes, Phee flagged down a passing matron.

"Pardon me. I realize this might be an odd request, but could you please ask in the ladies' room if there's a Lady Emma within?" A moment later, the matron came out shaking her head. Phee tipped her hat at the matron with a murmured thanks.

Surely, they would have crossed paths if Emma had returned directly to their dinner box. Perhaps she'd seen a friend and stopped to talk? Didn't she realize how risky this place could be to an unescorted miss? Anything might happen in these corridors.

Thousands of lanterns filtered light through the trees, creating pockets of well-lit space and acres of shadowy temptation. So many labyrinthine paths available to a headstrong lady like Emma. For a moment Phee considered sending an attendant to their table to raise the alarm. But with her luck, they'd find Emma quaffing champagne and chatting with friends. They'd all look like fools, with Phee as the king of them all.

Nearby a bell rang, spurring an uptick in the excited hum of conversation around her. The mass of humanity swarmed, then surged in one direction. Ah yes, the bell signaling the imminent start of the cascade show. The man-powered artificial waterfall ran for only about a quarter hour each night. Maybe Emma would be there. The spectacle was famous, and this was Emma's first visit, after all. The flowing-river illusion crafted from tin, with accompanying thunder and rain sound effects, was a highlight of Vauxhall. The first time Phee paid her handful of shillings to enter the gardens, she'd stood spellbound for the entire fifteen minutes.

Moving like a fish downstream with the others, Phee followed the crowd to the waterfall. A painted curtain pulled back, letting the lanterns shine on the bucolic scene. Hidden from view, men operated cranks and wheels, making the tin flats shudder. The storm sounds crashed all around as Phee stood on her tiptoes, searching for golden curls with pink and white plumes attached with a jeweled pin.

Wherever Emma was, it didn't appear to be here.

One path led to another, which led to another, which led to yet another. No Emma. Handfuls of moments passed, pulling bile higher in her throat. The risk of raising a false alarm sounded more appealing by the minute. Perhaps she should return to the table and demand Cal hunt for his own damn sister. It might be the perfect escape from Eastly and the baron.

Turning on one heel, Phee paused. A sound, and then a slightly louder noise, followed by a male chuckle and the admonishment to be quiet.

Oh dear. By the sounds of it, she'd stumbled upon a pair who were well beyond the kissing and shy hand-holding she'd seen other couples doing this evening. They must be on the other side of the hedge, ensconced in an alcove of assumed privacy.

Rolling her eyes at the ludicrous notion that anyone would consider privacy an option in a public place like this, Phee took another step toward the lights of the crowded dining area. One of the pair let loose a breathy moan, her voice catching at the end as if words escaped her entirely. Clearly, they were enjoying whatever was happening on the other side of this leafy barrier.

As she walked away, the woman's cries built in a crescendo that chased her through the dark.

"That's it, Emma. Just like that. You're always so eager, love."

Phee stopped in her tracks. *No. Please, God, no.*

Icy cold dread settled at the base of Phee's spine, replacing her earlier worries with an even worse reality. "Stupid girl. Stupid, stupid girl."

She ignored the poking branches as she shoved through the shrubbery and fell through to the other side with all the grace of an aggressive jack-in-the-box. The scene before her didn't fully register before her mouth moved. "That's quite enough. You're done."

Roxbury had the audacity to laugh, as if shagging a debutante in a hedgerow was just another average Tuesday for him. Emma shrieked, covering her face and leaving her bodice around her waist.

Phee rubbed at the dull ache behind her eyes. This was bad. Very bad. "Lady Emma, please cover a different body part. Your face is the least of your worries right now."

With frantic movements, Emma tugged her dress into place, refusing to meet Phee's gaze.

Roxbury casually buttoned the placket on the front of his trousers and smoothed his waistcoat. "We were done anyway, weren't we, Emma? Just saying our goodbyes."

The blighter.

"Don't tell my brother," Emma hissed when Phee led her away with a firm grip on her elbow.

Cal would absolutely lose his mind, and there wasn't a damn thing anyone could do about it. "Do you have any idea how serious this is? You can't ask me to lie. In fact, you should tell him yourself."

Emma dug in her heels, drawing them to a halt in the middle of the gravel path. "You needn't lie. Not really. Just don't tell him the truth."

"What am I supposed to say? That I found you watching the cascade?" Phee rolled her eyes. She'd never been so young and convinced of her ability to control the world.

Emma bounced onto her tiptoes with a happy noise. "That would be grand. Thank you so much, Mr. Hardwick!"

"I didn't—" Phee turned her head, right as Emma kissed her cheek in flirtatious thanks. In a slow-motion slide, Emma's lips brushed Phee's cheek, then landed directly on her lips. They both froze. Before stepping away, Phee noted softness, warmth, and a dozen other sensations—all of them foreign. None of them particularly welcome.

Without a word, they turned and headed toward the dinner boxes. It was an accidental kiss from a girl who'd thought she'd gotten her way. No more.

The orchestra grew louder when they left the treed paths. A few yards from their table, Emma grabbed Phee's hand. "If you tell my brother what you saw, I'll tell him you kissed me. Don't think I won't."

"What? That's not even close to what happened—" But Emma charged ahead, chattering in her bubbly way to their dining companions about the marvelous cascade. "Son of a bitch."

Chapter Six

❧

To hear Calvin and his set describe it, Shoreditch housed criminal masterminds, petty thieves, and the lowest dregs of society. While those kinds of people absolutely lived in her neighborhood, similar personalities lived in Mayfair. They just wore better coats in Grosvenor Square. Or in Emma's case, petticoats.

The nerve of the girl, trying to strong-arm Phee into lying for her.

In reality, the residents of Phee's neighborhood were like her—desperately trying to survive and play the hand dealt to them. Obviously, Phee's circumstances were more favorable than most. With connections to the *ton* and secondhand clothes to appear respectable, she had a more comfortable life than others.

But who knew when that tenuous connection to the aristocracy would disappear? Cal had hired her on a whim and could fire her as easily. Sure, they'd become friends.

And no, Calvin wasn't a fickle man. But eventually, something would happen—like Emma convincing him dear old Adam kissed his unwilling sister—and who knew what her income or circumstances would be then. That meager nest egg of squirreled-away pay and pawned silver buttons meant security. Independence.

So she did her best to live within the means allotted by Uncle Milton. Referring to those as *means* was a bit of an overstatement. In actuality, she suspected his severe restriction of funds under the guise of a living allowance was his way of trying to keep her—or rather, Adam—home and under his thumb. As ploys went, that one hadn't worked so well.

The hackney pulled to a stop. "King Street. Cart's blocking the road, so you'll get out here, lad."

The cramped buildings piled one on top of another, and the lack of streetlamps didn't make her neighborhood look inviting. As the temperatures increased in June, so did the danger in these tight streets. Only a fool would lounge about on street corners in the dead of winter. Now the underbelly came out to play.

A warning ripple of unease slithered along her spine. She shook it off. Such a ninny. The door to her lodgings stood only four buildings away. Besides, the landlady, Mrs. Carver, appreciated that Adam Hardwick paid his rent on time, so she ran interference when the local lads were on the prowl for new marks. Almost two years living on this street, and she'd had only minor encounters with the riffraff. Phee kept her nose out of everyone's business and avoided trouble.

The local crime syndicate, led by Joseph Merceron, didn't care for peons like her. Merceron craved bigger fish to fry—

like lords who rode around in fancy carriages. And Cal wondered why his friend Adam refused to accept rides home in a carriage with the shiny Carlyle crest on the door. No, sir, hacks were good enough for her. Yet another thing Cal didn't understand about the world outside Mayfair. He was at ease beyond Mayfair, but he lacked the street sense to truly blend in elsewhere.

Phee dug in her pocket for the fare before hopping from the hackney, then tipped her hat at the coachman's mumbled thanks. A breeze whistled along the street, blowing air redolent of hot refuse and cabbage soup. Sidestepping to avoid a puddle with unknown but likely foul contents turned out to be a wasted effort. The same hack she'd just left rumbled by, hitting the puddle and splashing the water—and God only knew what else—onto her trousers.

"Blast." She shook her foot, attempting to leave the water on the street rather than her evening shoes. Thankfully, the doorway to her building was only a few yards ahead. Changing clothes as soon as possible was vital in order to salvage these trousers prior to the nasty water setting in.

Before she could reach the door, a cudgel behind her knees brought Phee to the cobblestones, followed by a blow to her head that made the light in her sight flicker.

Shaking off the blow with a pained groan, Phee attempted to rise. It had been years since she'd taken a hit like that in school. Those scuffles had been more about establishing the hierarchy than true intent to harm. The two situations were truly incomparable.

Her attackers outnumbered her. Hands reached into pockets, tearing seams. Buttons gave way to greedy fingers, grabbing all the money she'd carried for the night out—which thankfully wasn't much.

Blood dripped, metallic and thick on her tongue. Someone rolled her over like a limp doll, removing her coat, while someone else slipped her free from her waistcoat. Rough tugs at her feet left her lying in the street wearing nothing but torn trousers, a filthy lawn shirt, and a single glove. Blinking to focus, she attempted to identify her attackers. With this big of a group, it might be some of Merceron's men after all.

"Takes a hit better than expected, eh? Who'd have thunk it from such a skinny rat," said a gravelly voice. Another knock to the head threatened to take her under. A nervous chuckle made her force one eyelid open and narrow her gaze through the murky shadows crowding her vision.

"Nelson?"

The butcher's son met her gaze for only a split second before shuffling back a few steps. "Sorry, Mr. Hardwick," Nelson mumbled.

The last thought before she lost consciousness was that the butcher would hear about this tomorrow.

When she came to, considerably gentler hands were picking her up under the arms, carrying her inside. Mrs. Carver fretted in high, sharp tones somewhere nearby.

Not everything translated through the haze of throbbing pain, but Phee caught "Lad works for a fancy man. Take a message to Hill Street, by Berkeley Square. Lord Carlyle."

Damn. She'd never hear the end of it from Cal. The man

worried like a mother hen already, feeding her and clothing her in carefully curated donations of perfectly fine castoffs.

"No," she tried to say. But her voice came out thready and feeble, too quiet to be heard over the din.

The shouted inquiries from her fellow building residents made her brain rattle in her skull, but their concern was sweet in a way. In some houses, everyone would have slammed their door shut, hoping to block the bad luck from rubbing off on them. Mrs. Carver ran a friendlier ship. People in this building tried to help one another with their resources or talents. Phee leaned heavily on one of the hands holding her, then lurched to her feet, using a wall for support when her body tried to tip the opposite direction.

"'M fine."

"Ye sure, lad?" Ah, the helping hand belonged to Barry from downstairs.

Phee nodded, then immediately regretted it when it felt like her brain sloshed against the inside of her forehead. "Just need to sleep. Thank you for your help. Oh, and Barry? Did your brother write back yet?" Several residents of the building came to Phee to dictate letters to their sweethearts or family and have the replies read aloud. Barry's brother usually replied within a month. She searched her aching head, trying to think of anything other than how much she bloody hurt. It had been six weeks since Barry's last letter.

"This afternoon. Thank ye for asking after it in your condition. I'll come around in a day or two if'n ye don' mind." Barry helped her unlock the door to her room when her hand scraped the key over the keyhole without sliding it in. "Here, lad. Ye rest now."

Throwing the lock behind her, she swayed, then caught herself against the wall. Out of habit, even in her injured state, she made a cursory sweep of the room to make sure everything was as she'd left it. A bed, four walls, and a plain but sturdy wood chair with a mismatched tufted footstool by the fire composed the living space.

Adam Hardwick was a simple man living a simple life on a very strict budget. But only for a little while longer.

After pulling the drapes closed, Phee slumped in the chair. A few pokes in the fireplace brought heat blazing to life, and the warmth hit her body like a shock. She reached to remove her hat and came away empty. That was right. Her lovely new hat either topped someone from the gang or had rolled into the gutter. What a waste. With slow, deliberate motions, Phee removed her single glove finger by finger so as not to ruin the fine leather more than it already was. Then she stared at it. What the hell would she do with one glove?

The trousers fell into a pile by the fire. They'd have to wait for their cleaning, because her head was threatening to fall off. One ear hadn't stopped ringing since the first blow. The shirt joined the trousers, leaving her in smalls and the linen wrap around her chest. Any other night loosening the linen would be a priority.

Not tonight. Tonight, her pillow held far more appeal than unbinding her breasts. If it weren't for distinctly plump nipples that made their presence known through thin shirts, she could have gotten away without binding altogether. Pulling a blanket over her shoulders, Phee fell into oblivion.

"Damned little fool." The words were rough, but the hands accompanying them were gentle as he smoothed her hair back from the place she'd been hit.

Cracking one eye open, Phee winced to see Cal standing over her. Mrs. Carver must have let him in, but there was no sign of her landlady now. The privileges of aristos, entering private homes by nothing more than the power of their names. Cal turned around and retrieved a lantern. Lighting the wick, he lowered the light to her face.

She slammed her eyes closed. "Bloody hell, Cal. Get that away from me."

"You need a doctor," he said.

Oh God, not a doctor. People on the street might not look past a skinny frame and male clothing, but an actual examination of her body would mean the end of everything. The end of Adam. "No doctor."

Cool air brushed her shoulders as Cal pulled the covers back, then paused.

Blast. The binding. Panic punched past the pain and the fog of sleep. Phee clutched at the blanket, trying to cover herself. Her head protested the movement.

"Already wrapped the ribs," she mumbled. "I'll be fine. Need to sleep. You didn't have to come out here."

"At least you managed that much," he grumbled. "Where else did they hit you? Any stab wounds? Cuts or bullet holes?"

"Just a cudgel. Knees to take me down. The head is the real problem. Falling off my shoulders might be a mercy. Move the light, will you?"

"For an injured man, you're awfully opinionated," Cal said.

"Calvin, move that bloody light out of my face. I'm alive. Now leave me alone and let me sleep."

"You can't mean to stay here?" His incredulous tone held so much horror, she almost laughed.

"Stay here. You mean, in my home?"

"This isn't a home, Puppy—it's a hovel. A single room where before now, you slept in relative safety."

"I am not going to argue our socioeconomic differences when it's the middle of the night and I feel like shit. Either go away or make yourself useful and stoke the fire."

A few moments later a flare of heat testified to Cal building the fire, but his silence told her he was pouting about it.

"What am I going to do with you, Puppy?" Cal thumped the chair down next to her bed, which made Phee close her eyes for a second as the noise reverberated through her skull.

"Judging by your tone, I'm guessing that leaving me to sleep is out of the question." The firelight made Cal's hair glow. Lady Amesbury's tipsy confession earlier had been an understatement. He wasn't pretty. He was beautiful. The halo effect was rather angelic, although his dark eyes under the heavy brows made her question if Cal's angel status was of the fallen variety.

With a sigh, Cal rested his face in his hands. "Fine. Sleep. I'm staying to make sure you wake tomorrow." Settling into the chair, Cal loosened his cravat and crossed his arms over his chest. Phee rolled her eyes, then winced. Damn, her head hurt.

Phee turned her head toward the wall, away from the light of the fire. Within moments, sleep claimed her, providing an escape from that dark gaze.

Cal kept his head cradled in his hands and stared at the shiny black toes of his boots until Adam's breath settled into the easy, heavy cadence of sleep. That he'd woken grumpy and mouthy was a relief. The thieves had beaten him but not broken that scrappy spirit.

Adam's pale complexion matched the linen covering his pillow, gone gray from too many washings. Even his freckles seemed pasty. The shock of red hair was the only color left to him except for the flickers of gold where firelight caught the tips of his eyelashes.

The wooden chair Cal sat in was unforgivingly uncomfortable. Numbness set in almost immediately. Shifting his weight helped, so he stretched his legs to prop his feet on the bed frame. Crossing his arms, Cal prepared for a long night, because no way in hell would he leave his friend alone in this room.

The intention to sleep didn't last. He kept replaying that moment when the scruffy boy had arrived. Higgins had answered the door as usual, but the lad's frantic message had echoed from the hall to where Cal had been relaxing after the night out. *Mr. Hardwick is hurt. Come quick!* His heart had stopped. He'd swear it.

All those missions and errands where he'd sent Puppy into dangerous areas of London tallied in his mind like a stack of tarot cards depicting a series of awful outcomes. This could have happened so much sooner. For all he knew, tonight's attack was the result of one of tonight's fact-gathering missions for the *Wilhelmina*.

His tailbone fell asleep, which was a new sensation. Who knew a tailbone could tingle like that? This chair was an atrocity. Shifting again, Cal hoped to find a miraculously comfortable position.

If Puppy had known Cal sat here worrying over him, he'd have had strong words to share. God knew he was chock-full of opinions. But if Ethan had lain in this bed, Cal would have worried too. Maybe not as much, because Ethan was built like a brick wall. Adam was finely built. Nearly delicate, really. In the flickering light, Cal stared at the bruises blooming over Adam's slim shoulders and angled brow. *Delicate* was the right word, and he felt protective, like he should be fighting off someone, but the attackers had already done their damage and scurried back to their hidey-holes.

Which left him with restless energy that wouldn't let him settle in for the night. Glancing around, Cal searched for something to do.

Like most tiny spaces, if one thing was out of place, the room looked ransacked. Trousers and hose lay in a crumpled heap before the hearth. One dirty glove rested on top, what remained of the pair he'd purchased earlier on Bond Street.

Cal lumbered out of the chair and gathered the discarded clothing. The hose were filthy but not torn. With a thorough laundering, they might be salvageable. He folded them neatly, then placed them on the footstool. The shirt could be mended but might still be destined for the scrap pile. The trousers were probably a loss. A seam on the side had given way, and he wrinkled his nose at the unidentifiable filth covering them. God only knew what he'd just gotten on his hands.

If these were his clothes, he'd burn them without thinking twice. But that wasn't his decision. Giving them a shake, he tried to dislodge the top layer of grime. A shower of dirt sprinkled onto his shoe. As he gingerly folded the trousers, a lump in the fabric shifted, then hit the floor, rolling to a stop next to his boot.

Plucking it from where it landed, he went to place the piece of scrap wood on top of the clothes but paused. Approximately four inches long and sanded smooth, the wood had been hollowed all the way through, with a wider fluted opening on one end. He cocked his head, turning it over in his hands, then checked where the object had fallen from.

The trousers revealed a pocket sewn inside the placket, with seams aligning perfectly to disguise the addition. He'd recognize Adam's tailoring anywhere. Cal slipped it in the pocket, then slid it out again. Sure enough, the wooden...whatever it was...fit snugly into the space Adam had created for it.

It looked like a penis with a wide opening on one end. There wasn't a better way to describe it. Despite their general filth, Cal held the trousers, slipping the carved wood into the pocket over and over, then held it up to the light from the lantern.

A choked noise from the bed made him glance over.

Adam was awake.

A shudder rippled over her body, whether from dread or pain, she didn't have time to determine.

"Hand me my shirt." She tucked the blanket under her arms, covering the chest bindings.

Cal pointed at the pile of clothing, still holding the pizzle she'd whittled last month. "That shirt? No way am I touching that again. It was disgusting enough the first time."

"Cal, I'm almost naked. Hand me a damn shirt. And put that down unless you want piss on your hands." Her head ached, it hurt to breathe, and this new development was pushing the evening into worst-nights-of-her-life territory.

Without another word, he set aside the wooden pizzle, then shrugged his coat down his arms and crossed the three steps it took to reach the bed. Gently, he laid the dark-blue garment over her shoulders, managing to avoid touching her as he did so, then took a seat on the chair he'd brought to the bedside.

"You don't need to say anything if you don't want to," he said.

The fabric smelled like him. That peculiar blend of spices that made her crave gingerbread, plus an added warmth from his body. It took everything in her to not indulge in a sniff of the collar as she slipped her arms through the holes and wrapped the coat around her.

She wasn't prepared to deal with this. Not right now. Not injured. Not while she felt naked and exposed, and he sat there polished and perfect. A jangle of what-ifs played through her head. What if he fired her or, worse, ended their friends because she was a liar? What if he told everyone a over a decade of struggle toward a better futu

She squeezed her eyes closed, wishing fruitlessly to wake from this nightmare. Through the tangled emotions, her practical nature asserted itself with one question that needed to be asked.

"If I'm fired, please let me know now. Once my wages are paid, you'll never have to see me again."

Cal jerked as if she'd slapped him. "Fired? Why the hell would I fire you? You have a position in my house for as long as you want it. No matter what all this means, you are my friend and a valuable employee."

That was something at least. Still, a large part of her wanted to run before he reconsidered and threw her out like yesterday's newspaper. After all, she'd lied to him for two years. If he learned this secret, how long would it be before he knew everything? That she'd not only taken her brother's identity but killed him as well. That it was an accident didn't matter. Not when the result was losing the person closest to her.

It might be better to run now and let him wonder. Let him think back in a few decades and ponder about whatever became of Adam Hardwick. She was good at running.

It was the overwhelming exhaustion the idea of starting over shere else brought that loosed the words.

isn't Adam Hardwick. I'm a woman. I'm hiding live as myself again."

fingers together in front of him and was before saying, "How can I help?"

v head is killing me, and talking makes wasn't more important than her need urs to recover from being beaten

in the street. Even though he was being sweet and remark-
ably Cal-like about the whole situation, she didn't appreciate
having to do this now. Answers to whatever questions he
might have could wait for when she felt like telling him more.
Friendship or not, she didn't owe him a full confessional
right this instant.

He cocked his head. "Can I stay if I stop talking?"

She was already slumping back down into bed, snuggling
beneath the layers of blanket and his coat. "Just be quiet. My
whole body hurts."

Blessed foggy peace was creeping around the edges of her
brain when he asked, "What do I call you now?"

"I'm still Puppy." With the next breath, she drifted away
under the cover of sleep, wrapped in the comforting smell of
gingerbread.

Chapter Seven

〜

$\mathcal{C}$al climbed from the carriage with a wince, taking a moment to stretch and loosen his aching muscles. Slumping in the world's most uncomfortable chair meant waking with a stiff neck and an even stiffer back. Not that he could complain about physical aches when Puppy was so obviously in worse condition. His mind was still reeling that Adam was actually an Eve.

He'd left shortly after a footman had arrived with a message from his father. Eastly wanted to discuss what Cal had thought of Violet Cuthbert last night at Vauxhall, and frankly, that was the last thing he wanted to think about right now. That conversation could easily be summed up—not interested.

But he knew his father. The note was a false courtesy, a sort of warning shot declaring that Eastly would be calling this morning, like it or not. So he'd left the footman to watch over Puppy and come home. He'd deal with his sire, then return to Shoreditch.

"Coffee, my lord." Higgins knew better than to phrase it as a question when he greeted Cal at the door.

"Thank you, Higgins. Coffee is definitely called for." There might not be enough coffee in all of England to counter the last twenty-four hours.

The library welcomed him with a soothing stillness. He wasn't a great bibliophile like Ethan, but there'd always been something peaceful about the atmosphere of the library.

A maid entered with a cart, dipped a curtsy, then left.

As he poured his first cup, Cal's mind circled around to Puppy. He'd sat awake for most of the night. She'd been restless, wincing and letting loose the occasional whimper in her sleep. As Cal waited for the next time his friend awoke needing a drink, he'd been left with nothing to do but observe.

They'd never slept near each other before except for the occasional midday nap on the pair of drawing room sofas. Adam always insisted on returning home to that tiny room no matter how late the hour of their escapades. That made sense now.

The coffee burned as it slid down his throat, so he set the cup down with a rattle and balanced it and the saucer on the arm of his favorite chair.

Curiosity had compelled Cal to stare at the lines of her face until something stirred within him that hadn't gone away with the rising sun. It had been a revelation to watch his friend at rest in the dim light of the meager fire in the grate.

Puppy wasn't ugly—but not likely to turn heads either. Taken as a whole, her square jaw fit nicely with her angular cheekbones. Angular everything, to be honest. Amidst all the sharp points reflecting in the firelight last night, her nose stood out as perfectly straight—obviously never broken.

Cal rubbed at the bumped bridge of his nose. The badly healed break was a reminder of a scuffle at Eton with a boy who'd called Cal a molly when he discovered his friendship with Lord Hopkins. He and Hopkins had only been friends, but people who called others names for reasons like that weren't often prone to logic. Such things weren't discussed openly at Eton, but they weren't uncommon. Cal knew a few men who, in those explorations, found home. And there were others who lived as authentically true to themselves as possible, even when society didn't endorse their choices. This was an area where Cal didn't care about society's disdain. Everyone deserved to live their life with dignity and honesty.

There could be many reasons behind her choice of disguise. Perhaps she preferred women lovers and felt more comfortable in a man's persona. Yet he had never seen Adam show interest in a woman. Or a man, for that matter.

As he puzzled through it, he tested another sip of coffee and found it cool enough to drink. Thank God.

One thing Puppy had said last night nagged at him. She'd said she was hiding until it was safe to live as herself again—which implied living as a woman. The fact that she'd said that while beaten and bruised wasn't lost on him. He'd wondered if the attack was random or the result of one of her information-gathering jaunts for him.

But a third option had occurred to Cal sometime in the wee hours of the morning. Especially given that she was already living in disguise when they met. There was a history of tension between her and her uncle, whom she never spoke of favorably. Her uncle could be behind this.

It was a mystery. And like a curious cat, his brain couldn't let it go.

Licking a drop of coffee from his lip brought to mind the time he'd spent staring at the full curve of Puppy's mouth while she slept. Too much time, if he were honest. As she dreamed, her body had given off a warmth that had changed the usual sandalwood Adam wore into something more personal, especially wrapped up in his coat. Her sandalwood and his spiced soap had combined into a scent that had sent a curious humming of interest under his skin.

Inconvenient ponderings for a man who'd spent years cleaning up his father's financial and social messes, only to be forced into marriage with a complete stranger. When would it end? The choices appeared limited. He could marry a woman who, last night at Vauxhall, had looked as unenthusiastic about their introduction as he'd been. Did she know about this bet and engagement already? Was that why she'd been so quiet and uncomfortable? Beyond a few monosyllabic answers, she hadn't seemed inclined to get to know him.

Or he could refuse to comply with this nonsensical plan of his father's and face complete ruination of everything he held dear.

There must be a better option.

Cal was filling his cup for the second time when Ethan sauntered into his library as if he owned the place.

"You look like shite," Ethan said.

"Did I send out a silent cry for help?" Cal asked.

"Aye, my friendship antennae tingled."

Cal smiled around another sip of coffee.

"Actually, Lottie isn' feeling well this mornin'. Too much champagne last night. Threatened tae cut off my bollocks when I proposed a shag. She's insisting I leave her alone tae die till at least noon. I decamped for my safety. Now, why do you look like something I should scrape off my boot? I never see you in your shirtsleeves. Where's your coat?"

Out of habit, the pair took their customary seats by the fireplace. The black coffee rippled through Cal's system, shaking off exhaustion with every sip.

"I left my coat with Puppy. Long story. Where to begin? On the way home last night, Puppy was robbed and beaten. No"—he motioned for Ethan to remain in his seat—"he will recover. But it isn't pretty. I stayed with him all night. The stubborn mule refuses to move from Shoreditch." He'd promised her he would keep her secret, and he would, even from Ethan, his closest friend.

"Bloody hell. What can I do tae help?" Ethan leaned his elbows on his knees, concern etched in the deep valley between his eyebrows.

"Not much at the moment. I haven't talked to Adam yet about the men responsible. This can't go unanswered, though." Cal ran a finger around the smooth porcelain rim of his cup while his brain scrambled every which way, playing through possible scenarios. The more he thought about it, the more convinced he became that the uncle from Northumberland would be all over the situation when they found the assailants. But on the off chance that this wasn't random or orchestrated by her uncle, Cal would accompany her on the next few trips to the docks. It wasn't unheard of for him to do so, but he'd been taking a more hands-off approach lately. No more. Not now that he knew there was a threat.

"Aye. He may be young and pasty, but he's ours," Ethan said.

Cal couldn't have said it better himself. "Exactly. Then my father sent a message that he planned to call, so the day is going to go to hell."

"I wonder what happened this time? Opera dancers or cards?" Ethan's posture relaxed as the conversation veered into familiar territory.

"In this instance, I already know. He summoned me yesterday afternoon, and I haven't had a moment alone with you since." Yesterday afternoon seemed like a lifetime ago. Pasting on a wry smile, he said, "It seems Eastly traded me for a horse." The look on Ethan's face almost made the circumstances comical. Almost.

"You'll be tellin' me the details of that. But do ye want tae check on Adam? Is he alone?"

"I left a footman and strict orders to send a message every hour." Which meant a message should have been due a quarter hour ago. Cal checked his watch. After snapping the cover closed, he tucked the timepiece in his waistcoat pocket.

"Your messenger is overdue, isn' he?" Ethan guessed.

Instead of answering, Cal strode to the doorway. "Higgins? Has Charles sent a message?"

Higgins shook his head. "Not yet, milord. I will bring it straightaway when it arrives."

Worry niggled at his brain, which was coming up with

worst-case scenarios. Cal closed the library door again but couldn't let go of the doorknob.

"You're goin' tae fret all morning until you get word. Why don' we pay the lad a visit? I'll join you. Although t'would be a shame tae miss Eastly's call." When Ethan shifted to rise with a conspiratorial grin, the chair protested with a creak.

The show of support made Cal chuckle. "I'd appreciate the company, thank you." He had yet to shave or change clothes, but Ethan was right. The worry wouldn't let up, and the last place Cal should be was lingering in this library, waiting for news. If it meant delaying dealing with the reality of his father for a few more hours, then he'd be grateful for the momentary distraction.

"We'll take my carriage," Ethan said as the front door closed behind them. Higgins had sniffed disapprovingly at their insistence that they'd walk to the stable and wait there, rather than in the comfort of the library.

"They're housed in the same mews. It will be just as fast to call mine."

"But yours has that shiny crest on the side, you pretentious knob-head. Mine won' draw as much attention." Ethan shot him a look that spoke volumes.

Cal hadn't thought of that. It shouldn't surprise him that Ethan had.

As they made their way through the tighter streets toward Puppy's neighborhood, even Ethan's understated equipage drew stares, and Cal was grateful he'd listened to the Scotsman.

"Isn't that your livery?" Ethan pointed his driving whip

toward a footman dressed in immaculate pale blue and silver, standing outside a shop.

"What the hell is Charles doing there? Puppy shouldn't be out and about. I gave strict orders to stay in bed."

Ethan's side-eyed glance matched his smirk as he parked the rig near the shop. "Perhaps the lad decided you weren' his ma, and got out of bed. Charles might be doin' his best tae keep up with 'im."

That didn't deserve an answer, because damn his eyes, Ethan was right and they both knew it.

When Cal approached the shop—a butcher shop, according to the signage—Charles stiffened, his posture poker straight.

"He's a stubborn cuss and wouldn't listen when you insisted he stay in bed, right, Charles?" Cal guessed.

Pink bloomed over the footman's cheeks. "I relayed your orders, milord. I also sent a messenger to Hill Street when we left to come here."

Ethan clapped a hand on Cal's shoulder, gently pushing him past the servant. As they continued toward the door, Ethan called to the footman, "Not tae worry, Charles. You did your best, I'm sure."

Puppy and a man one could assume to be the butcher by the bloody apron stood close together near a wood-slab counter. They paused their conversation when a bell announced Cal's entry to the shop.

"What are you doing here?" Puppy asked. Except it wasn't just Puppy now, was it? She wasn't Adam any longer. Not to him. Searching her face, he tried to find some indication that things were different now that he was in on the secret, but she acted as if nothing had happened. Nothing to see here, just another day of interrogating the butcher after being beaten and robbed. Lord, how did she do it?

"You look like hell—rather like someone who's been attacked and left for dead in the street mere hours ago." The words came out with a casual air, when he really wanted to ring a peal over his friend's broken head. "One would expect you to still be in bed recovering from your recent *head injury*."

The sarcasm was met with an eye roll exactly like the ones Emma gave him, ending in a wince. If Cal hadn't been so concerned and irritated with her, it would have been comical. As it was, the wince merely served to make his point.

"Surely getting a rasher of bacon or a link of sausage isn't more important than healing." The overwhelming smell of blood and raw meat turned Cal's stomach. How did someone with a head injury hold down their breakfast when that smell coated the air?

Unless she hadn't eaten breakfast. There'd been nothing but an apple and a hunk of cheese in the room. A room which had been devoid of any personal touches and had very few belongings. There'd been a tidy stack of clothes and a narrow table against the wall for accessories like hand-kerchiefs and gloves. Now that he thought of it, the hat stand had been empty.

"Where is your hat?" he asked.

"On the head of a thief, I imagine." She turned to the butcher. Clearly, further discussion could wait, and Cal had interrupted her conversation. Cal caught himself before he rolled his eyes as Puppy had just moments before.

"As I was saying, I need to talk to you about your son."

"Nelson? Aw, he's a good lad."

"I agree. You raised him well, Shaw. But are you aware of the crowd he's running with these days?"

Things began to make sense. Puppy had identified one of her attackers. Cal shot her a look, but her focus remained entirely on the butcher as she somehow exuded compassion and confrontation at once.

"What's this about, Mr. Hardwick?" Shaw punctuated the question with a slam of his cleaver, bisecting a slab of... something.

"Nelson was one of the crew that attacked me last night. Stripped me nearly naked and took everything." Puppy's voice grew clipped as she recounted the night in those few short words.

The butcher froze with the shiny blade hovering in mid-air. The space between his brows narrowed, resulting in one long fuzzy caterpillar-like eyebrow, before he let the knife fall once more, separating flesh from bone. Emotions flashed over his face so quickly, Cal couldn't fully identify them. Disbelief? Anger? Sadness? For a father to hear that his son had fallen in with violent criminals must create mixed feelings.

"I don't need my things returned," Puppy said. "But if it were my child, I would want to know. Nelson is better than this."

Before yesterday, Cal might have clapped a hand on Adam's shoulder as a silent show of support. But with myriad bruises covering her skin, a consoling hand may not be welcome—or appropriate, come to think of it. There might be another way to help, though. Cal stepped forward.

"If Mr. Hardwick claims your son is trustworthy, even after last night, then I am willing to find him a position with my staff."

The butcher's gaze flickered toward the window, where Charles's livery gleamed bright and out of place against the wood and stone buildings. Shaw might not know who Cal was, but he must recognize quality clothes and all they implied.

"I can't help the other lads in the crew. But if Hardwick cares for your son, perhaps we could find him a less criminal group of men to associate with." With several estates, surely there was a place for him at one of them. Perhaps mucking stables and cleaning livestock pens. It was what the little thief deserved.

"Shaw, this is my employer, the Earl of Carlyle. A position in his house could mean Nelson would be out of London for a time, but if that is what it takes to keep him from continuing down this path, it might be worth it," Puppy said.

Shaw grunted, wiping the cleaver on his dirty apron. "Let me think on it. I'll talk to the boy and the missus. I'm sorry you were hurt, Mr. Hardwick. You've never given us reason to wish you ill."

Stepping away from the counter, Cal swept an arm toward the street, letting her go first.

The redhead lasted until the shop door closed behind them before she rounded on Cal. "Why are you here? And leaving a liveried servant in my room? No offense, Charles." Puppy waved toward the footman. "Do you have any idea what a spectacle you've made?" She seemed to stop herself mid-sentence and drew a deep breath. When she spoke again, she measured the words between sharp inhales. Her ribs must be hurting. "I know your intention is to provide protection. Or a nanny, because you think me a child. But you painted a target on my back. Why not make a sign that says 'Has friends with money and influence' so I can attract every criminal element in the neighborhood?"

Just like that, frustration and worry boiled over. Leaning over so they were nearly nose to nose, Cal growled, "I told Charles to stay behind because you scared the shit out of me, and I needed to know there was someone here to help you." The Puppy's eyes sparked with gold flecks, likely from wanting to throttle him.

A large hand was inserted between their faces, gently compelling Cal to step away. "You bicker like an old married couple," Ethan said. "Cal, listen tae the lad's concerns. His safety has already been compromised once, and you flashin' coin makes him a bigger target. Some circumspection on your part wouldn' be amiss. Adam, take a breath and try tae be grateful you have people who care."

Puppy shot a look at Ethan. "Lord Amesbury, while I appreciate the sentiment, I can't help but notice this shiny new carriage, which only adds to the problem. Flashing coin and liveried footmen isn't the only sign of wealth we are dealing with right now."

Ethan raised a brow. "I talked him out of the rig with the coat of arms on it. But you're right. We should have taken a hack."

Cal sighed. This was more complicated than he'd thought. "I'm sorry Charles's presence made things worse. Let's get off the street and discuss this further." Placing a hand on Puppy's back, he nudged her toward Ethan's carriage. Through the layers of clothing, Cal could feel the subtle ridges of bone where shoulder blade cut toward spine in a delicate wing. Especially wearing his oversized coat, she appeared fragile. But she'd made herself into a scrappy survivor. It took a special person to pull off a masquerade of this magnitude.

Severing the contact as she climbed into Ethan's carriage was harder than it should have been. Hell and blast. Nothing good could come of this.

Chapter Eight

⟋

I wouldn't have pegged you for a coward."

Phee snapped her head around to stare at the library doorway, where Emma posed against the doorjamb, looking fresh as a daisy. "Coward? What are you talking about?"

"Our interlude at Vauxhall." She wiggled her brows suggestively, and it was all Phee could do not to roll her eyes. "Then you disappeared for over a week. What's a girl to think?"

Phee held her tongue, letting the silence grow.

Finally, Emma laughed. "I'm only teasing. But really, where were you?"

"Your brother didn't say anything?"

Emma shrugged, then moseyed into the room. Plucking books from the shelf at random, she glanced at the covers before shelving them again in the wrong places.

If Phee ventured a guess, Cal probably had mentioned something, but Emma hadn't listened. "If you paid attention to anything besides matters relating directly to yourself, you would know that I was attacked the night of Vauxhall. Beaten and robbed."

To her credit, Emma's concern appeared genuine when she whirled around. "Goodness! But you're all right now?"

"Right as rain and happy to be at work." Phee dismissed her, returning to the mail.

"You don't think Roxbury might have sent a few men to encourage your silence on what you saw that night, do you?"

Slowly, Phee faced her. "No, I don't believe your odious beau had anything to do with it. And frankly, if you believe him capable of such a thing, you should be running in the other direction."

Emma sagged a bit. It was on the tip of Phee's tongue to snap that she doubted Roxbury cared enough about Emma to exert himself to such an extent. Instead, she swallowed the remark and said, "Not everything is about you, Lady Emma."

"You don't like me, do you?" Emma asked.

"There's a difference between a person and their actions. I like you fine. But your actions are unlikable—not to mention selfish. Have you thought of how your behavior reflects on your family?"

Her short laugh lacked any humor. "As if my father cares a whit about my behavior. He couldn't be bothered to host or fund my Season. Not even a ball. Cal's handling my debut alone."

"I agree about Eastly—don't get me started there. But your brother is a different matter."

A few beats of silence followed before Emma turned and left without another word. There was no getting around it. Cal needed to know what Phee had witnessed that night.

The stack of correspondence crinkled in her fist.

They hadn't been alone since the attack and her confession. He and Lord Amesbury had visited her in Shoreditch several times—taking a hack, as suggested. With two men in her room, the small space had shrunk further, and she'd been acutely aware of the lack of accommodations for guests. She had only one chair, so they'd all stood awkwardly in the middle of the room for the entirety of the visits. When she'd suggested returning to work, Cal had insisted she heal for a few days first.

But he also hadn't left her alone. An out-of-uniform servant stood at her beck and call in the room or in the hall.

This mother-hen side of Cal's personality might be the thing to push her into a full-fledged emotional collapse. People didn't *take care* of her. Not like this. The last decade had been solitary overall. She'd taken Adam's place at school, then moved to London on her own. Now there was someone...there. Seeing to her needs. Protecting her.

It could drive a person to distraction. She was glad to take care of herself and return to work.

To make matters worse, during those nights lying in bed, acutely aware of a guard sleeping on a cot only a few feet away, she'd realized something. Once the sun set, the feeling of safety she'd enjoyed within those snug walls disappeared. The shadows and noises weren't familiar anymore. Everything became a bogeyman waiting to pounce, until her heart threatened to pound out of her chest. God help her, by the second night, she'd been grateful for the footman after the sun went down.

Sleep became an elusive beast until all she could think about was returning to work in Mayfair, with its polished facade of security. So not only did the care and attention unsettle her, but it made her feel safe—which only highlighted a previous lack she hadn't acknowledged until it hit her over the head. Literally. Damn it, she was going to have to thank Cal, and she wasn't looking forward to it. Eleven years of taking care of herself, and now this earl with a stubborn heart of gold charged in and *helped*. Even though he knew she'd lied to him for their entire friendship.

Cal might be right. Maybe she should find somewhere else to live. Lord, the man would be insufferable if she admitted that *and* thanked him for the guard.

Best keep to safer conversational grounds—like catching his sister tossing up her skirts in the bushes with a scoundrel. Lordy, life had gotten complicated lately. She rubbed a palm down her face and sighed.

Emma was right—she was being a coward. Just not in the way the girl thought. For the last two years, Phee's workday had usually begun in Cal's dressing room. They'd share a cup of coffee while he dressed and made plans for what they needed to accomplish. Would he even let her in the room now that he knew she was a woman? She didn't have the faintest idea what to do about any of this. Did they pretend that conversation hadn't happened? How long could she avoid being alone with him?

Sunlight illuminated the library in rectangles across the

carpet, with one shaft of light cutting across the desk. How long would he wait in his dressing room before he realized she wasn't coming upstairs? Phee reached for her watch, then patted the flat pocket. Ah yes. Robbed. No chain, no timepiece. So she paced, glancing at the mantel clock every other time she passed it.

Flopping in the desk chair, Phee closed her eyes and let the sun warm her.

Until it became too warm, because it was bloody summertime, and they designed cravats to strangle a person slowly. For a moment, she imagined wearing a light muslin gown. Not the ruffled pinafore and short skirts she'd worn the last time she'd been a girl in public. But a proper gown. Stays— even though they wouldn't do anything for her, lacking in breasts as she was—with a linen petticoat and light-weight fabric that showcased her delicate collarbones and shapely arms.

Those were two body parts she liked. Not that she actively disliked her other bits, but she looked forward to showcasing those in particular someday. She'd wear gowns, perhaps with clocked stockings and silky pink ribbon garters.

The cuff of her coat itched at her wrist.

Enough. He might turn her away at the door, but at least she would have tried to keep their normal routine. Phee stuffed the small stack of letters needing her attention in her coat pocket and opened the library door with slightly more force than required.

And ran right into Cal's chest.

"Careful, Puppy." His hands grasped her arms as he stepped back.

"Apologies, milord. I wasn't sure where we were meeting today."

He cocked his head. "You only call me milord when you're mad at me."

Phee closed her eyes and sighed. "I'm not mad at you."

He said over his shoulder, "Higgins, could you send in coffee please?" then moved past her to the desk. "We will figure it out, Puppy. In the meantime, there's work to be done. Have you heard from your dock urchins lately?"

Work. They could work. That was why she was here, after all.

"Frankie hasn't sent a message about the *Wilhelmina*, if that's what you're asking. But I could pay her a visit today and check in."

Cal stared out the window and ran a hand through his hair. Kingston hadn't tied it back yet, and Phee watched with a familiar ache in her chest as he dug in a pocket for a scrap of ribbon, then secured the long strands in a queue at his nape. She'd observed this same action hundreds of times. Once she'd asked why he didn't cut it, and he confessed that he'd initially kept it long to annoy his father, but now it was sheer vanity. The one way he refused to comply with fashion.

"We need to find that boat, Puppy. Investors are getting twitchy and looking to me for answers because I'm the one who set up this voyage and rallied everyone together. My coffers will be fine with this loss, but some...some will be devastated."

The coffee arrived, so she poured them each a cup. When she set his on the desk, the delicate clatter of cup and saucer against wood made him turn. He looked tired, with purpled skin under his chocolaty eyes. He obviously hadn't been sleeping well.

That made two of them.

Silence wasn't normal for them, but this morning they drank their coffee without further conversation. She kept her hands busy with the correspondence she'd found earlier. Piddly details, really. A note from the game warden in Northumberland regarding a poacher they'd caught. Two messages from contacts outside the city who vouched for the character of the Duke of Gaffney, who had asked for help with a financial project on his estate.

"Word is getting around about your partnership with Lord Amesbury. First working with Ethan, now Gaffney wants to begin a similar project. I wonder who's next?" Viscount Amesbury was crafting ale from his estate's hops and turning it into a retail business. The duke wanted to focus on cider. Not the rough scrumpy of some counties, but a reliable product to bottle and sell in Town.

"All we need is an Italian count with a vineyard, and we could be happily drunk for the rest of our days," he said.

"Know any Italian counts?"

"Can't think of any off the top of my head, but I'll be on the lookout."

It was a silly joke, and nothing of real consequence. Still, it felt like a piece of normal life to tease with him. A knot in her chest loosened. Maybe they'd find their way through it. Figure it out, like he'd said.

"It's not really me, anyway. They have the idea and the product. I just organize the finances and help with the paperwork side of things," Cal said. He stared at her for a moment with his arms crossed as he leaned on his desk. "Let's get out of here. We'll try to track down Frankie. See if there are any other leads we can pull. I don't think I'm any good for desk work today."

"You mean you'd rather not sit in the library avoiding looking at each other all afternoon?"

His hint of a smile was a mere quirk of lips instead of his usual grin, but for the moment they were in accord. "I don't want to say the wrong thing or pepper you with questions you don't feel like answering. But it's good to have you back, Puppy."

That smile, seeing Lord Calvin Carlyle, of all people, unsure of himself, unsettled her. She rose, then ran a hand down the front of her waistcoat. Violet jacquard silk today, with silver buttons she hadn't yet sold and replaced with wooden ones. "Let's get to work, then."

Once upon a time, Calvin had been a rather scrawny young man trying to determine if a barmaid named Linette fancied him. He'd stuttered into his glass of ale and counted under his breath to make sure he looked at her for more than a count of three but less than a count of seven—Thomas, the slightly older friend showing him the ropes, insisted that anything over a count of seven unsettled a girl, and they'd get their drinks thrown in their faces.

Sitting in a hack across from Puppy, their knees occasionally brushing as the carriage clattered over the uneven roads, Cal realized he was once again in unknown territory, like when he'd attempted to flirt with Linette—who hadn't thrown a drink at him. She'd cheerfully taught him how to kiss that night, and at the time he'd thought her lips were magical.

And now he was staring at Puppy's mouth. Again. For a much longer count than seven. Thank God she was facing the window instead of him. Her studied avoidance of looking in his direction allowed the summer sun coming in through the dirty glass to illuminate her face.

It was a face he'd seen nearly every day for two years, but somehow there were new details he'd noticed only this past week.

And God help him, but it was getting harder and harder to look away. There were the same familiar blue eyes with gold flecks, framed by ridiculously long eyelashes. The coppery lashes tended to disappear amid the freckles and Puppy's distracting grin. But with light on her face like this, it made those lash tips look like sunrays, in the way a child draws squiggly lines and random spikes when sketching sunlight in the corner of the paper.

"You're staring," she said, still looking out the window.

Cal cleared his throat. And here he'd thought she wouldn't notice. "Sorry. It's hard not to look for all the things I hadn't noticed before."

Finally, she faced him, arching a brow. "Such as?"

"You've never had to shave. You don't have an Adam's apple—which is ironic when you think about it."

When she bit her bottom lip to contain a smile, he had to close his eyes against the image. Her mouth was wrecking his equilibrium, and she didn't even know it. He shifted on the seat. "Which isn't definitive proof of anything, obviously. I'm just surprised I never noticed."

"People see what you tell them to see."

"How long have you lived as Adam?"

"Eleven years."

"Eleven? Good God. How have you managed it?" She was so casual while mentioning something utterly remarkable.

Puppy shrugged one shoulder. "I've avoided making friends for the most part. If no one is close enough to ask questions, life is easier. You're proof that deviating from that strategy was a bad idea."

"Ouch." He winced. "Rather brutal, don't you think?"

The look she gave him told him without words to stop feeling sorry for himself, but he rubbed at a phantom ache under his breastbone anyway for dramatic effect.

"Eleven years, Calvin. Over a decade, and then you came along. You were supposed to be a job. A steady stream of reliable income until I inherited. Then you charmed your way into my life, and look at us now."

"You make my charm sound like a bad thing. For the record, being charming is literally my most valuable skill."

The hack lurched to a stop in time for her to roll her eyes before she opened the door and jumped to the pavement. Holding the door open for him, she said, "You and I both know that's utter nonsense."

He grinned at her, then paid the hack driver. They were only a few streets from the river now, and the smell of the Thames in summer was overwhelming here in a way it wasn't in Mayfair. The stench dug into one's nose with foul blades until it overwhelmed the other senses, coating the tongue, filling his head. At his side, Puppy moved with the loose-limbed grace of someone comfortable in her environment as they wove through the throngs of people, animals, carts, and hacks.

"Does Frankie still frequent the same pub?" he asked. It had been a while since he'd accompanied Puppy on one of these jaunts to the docks, but with a possible threat against her, he couldn't in good conscience stay home.

"That's her territory. She and her group cover the area from the pub to the dock at the end of this street, and the span of one block in either direction."

"And if they stray from these specific streets?"

Puppy's mouth twisted with an emotion he couldn't name. "Then children start disappearing. Either gone altogether or roped into another gang."

His stomach rolled at the thought. "My own childhood wasn't idyllic, but that's abhorrent." At the pub, he opened the door and stepped back to let her enter first.

She shrugged. "No, that's London."

And she'd survived. Respect for this woman rose one more notch.

Inside the pub, a smoky haze hung in the air from lamps, customer's cheroots and pipes, and a kitchen in continual use. Being this close to the shipping epicenter of the docks made the pub a favorite place of theirs to meet the right people to exchange information. Its ale was decent, and the daily loaf was consistently good.

Puppy took a seat toward the edge of the room, and Cal followed suit. Within moments, a buxom barmaid sauntered over with a cheery grin.

"Mr. Hardwick, good ta see ye. Oh, and you've brought your pretty friend with ye. Haven' seen ye in a while, gov." She threw a saucy wink at Cal and he grinned.

"Hello, Peg. You're a lovely ray of sunshine as always. Do you have some of your delicious bread you could bring over?"

"And if Frankie is in the kitchen, could you send her our way?" Puppy asked.

Peggy shook her head. "Haven' seen the scamp since last night. Can I pass along a message?"

Puppy said, "Maybe you could help. We were hoping for word on the *Wilhelmina*."

The barmaid headed toward the kitchen and called over her shoulder, "I'll be back with yer loaf."

"Translation: the information isn't free, and the cost of our meal tripled," Puppy murmured.

"Let's hope the information is worth it."

Within moments, Peggy returned and set down a crusty loaf of bread and a crock of butter on a wood platter scarred with deep grooves from years of knives. She leaned an ample hip against the table and crossed her arms. It wasn't until Cal slipped a few coins across the table that she started talking.

"I got a letter yesterday, but the date was from a while ago. Ned says the storm off the Cape really tore up the ship. They limped into the nearest port. Were still there when he wrote it, but they might be headed home by now. I hope, anyway."

"Any lives lost?" Puppy asked.

"Three men went over during the late watch. One second

they were there, the next gone. The sea's a brutal bitch, Mr. Hardwick."

"I'm glad your Ned is safe, Peggy." Cal slathered a slice of bread with butter and handed it to Puppy.

"You're probably more worried about the cargo, ain't ye, gov?"

"I don't want to be insensitive to Ned's losses, but that's where my financial interest lies, yes." He offered a slice of bread to the barmaid as well, and she took it, picking out the soft center first and leaving the crust whole.

"Better tell yer money men not to get their hopes up. That's not the official word, mind ye. But Ned mentioned taking on water in the hold. That can't be good, right?"

A heavy sighed rolled out of him. "No, that's not good. I appreciate the news, Peg."

She dropped the crust, then brushed her hands off and returned to the bar.

Puppy rested her chin on her hands as she studied him. "This is more than the *Wilhelmina*. I've been with you when you got bad news on investments before. This reaction isn't like that."

Cal bit into his bread, then looked away from her. "What do you mean? I haven't even said anything."

"Exactly. You haven't said a word. Usually you'd have already made at least two jokes and be plotting a way to make up the loss. Numbers are toys to you, and you shuffle them around like game pieces."

"You know Eastly sunk a considerable investment into that ship. What you don't know is his current precarious financial position. I'd hoped the *Wilhelmina* would provide the answer."

Puppy, ever practical, got to the heart of the matter. "How bad is it?"

"He made a ridiculous wager. The forfeit is a princely sum he could have managed if this blasted ship had returned with cargo intact."

"Will they accept something else in forfeit? Some land? A hunting cottage somewhere? I hear you have a forest in Northumberland you aren't doing anything with."

Cal cleared his throat. "Remember Baron Rosehurst and his daughter from Vauxhall?"

"That's who Eastly bet with? How does his daughter fit into this?" She must have come to the right conclusion as she asked the question. "Damn, he's wanting his darling daughter to be a countess, isn't he?"

"Apparently. I don't know how Miss Cuthbert feels about the situation, but I am definitely against this plan. Which means I need to come up with a solution that doesn't involve paying for my father's poor judgment with my bachelorhood."

"Tell Eastly to marry her. Then she could be a marchioness. Or simply say no to all of it. If Eastly has to retreat to the Continent for a while to escape the debt, it might actually make things calmer for you."

"I suggested he marry her. Really, though, I wouldn't wish that fate on anyone. And I've considered leaving the debt in his hands, even if it means he decamps to the Continent. But there would be a scandal and talk about his financial instability, which would lead to questions about Emma's dowry. I can't do that to her. Not during her debut. She's made such a splash, but all that attention could turn sour in an instant with a scandal like this."

Puppy covered her face with her hands and groaned. "Oh God, I forgot. And this is the worst possible time. But while we're talking about ruining lives, and Emma's reputation, I need to tell you something."

"What's she done now?" he asked, sawing another slice of bread for himself. Since he'd taken care of the Roxbury situation, some of his worry over Emma had subsided. To his knowledge, she hadn't latched onto anyone new and inappropriate since.

"Roxbury. And more than once if the scene I saw at Vauxhall is any indication."

Cal froze, then snapped his gaze up to collide with hers. "Explain. Now. And leave nothing out, because that's a grave accusation to make, Puppy."

She sat up straight and folded her hands on the table in front of her. "On the night we went to Vauxhall, Emma and I did not encounter one another at the waterfall display as she claimed. I noticed she'd been gone for some time and left to find her. It took longer than expected. She and Roxbury were, ah, engaged. Willingly, and quite enthusiastically by the sound of it." She hastened to add, "I only mention it to reassure you that there didn't appear to be any force involved. Not to imply she's wanton—God, Cal, don't look at me like that." She slumped forward again, resting her face in her hands. "I don't enjoy telling you this. Murderous looks aren't helping."

"The murderous look is only partly for you," Cal said, gritting his teeth. Vauxhall was after his visit to Roxbury, but the timing didn't matter more than the seriousness of the accusation. "When you say *engaged*, exactly what do you mean? Be specific, because if I'm going to kill that bastard, I want to know exactly what he did."

Puppy grimaced. "No French letter. There's the possibility of pregnancy." She cast a worried look at his hand, and he glanced to see he had formed a fist and hadn't realized it.

"Roxbury is a dead man."

"If there is a baby, he'll be no use to you dead."

The expletive Cal spat out hit the air with a slap. "How could she allow this to happen with a man like that? Wait— they know you caught them. How did she react?"

Puppy stared over Cal's shoulder at the wall, and he knew then that he wouldn't like the answer. The bread he'd eaten weighed a ton in his gut as he waited for her to speak.

"She, uh, she kissed me. Then threatened to tell you I'd made unwelcome advances."

A rueful laugh that had nothing to do with humor escaped. "Of course she did. Because blackmail solves everything. That girl is too much like our father."

She smiled. "It wasn't a very good blackmail attempt. It backfired rather spectacularly, because here we are."

"Right." With his world falling apart, with Puppy by his side in a dark pub by the rank Thames. And somehow managing to laugh, even if it wasn't wholehearted. "Here we are."

Despite the many secrets between them—mostly on her side—he didn't want to be having this conversation with anyone else. It didn't stop his brain from circling around to his sister, though.

"What on earth is she thinking? I mean, if she wants to re-create the absolute hell of our parents' marriage, this is a damn fine way to do it." The Marquess and Marchioness of Eastly had done everything passionately. Wedded, bedded, fought, and betrayed each other—all at top volume, with full theatrical flair, and usually with witnesses. If his mother still lived, they'd probably be in the same poisonous pattern.

"There are similarities between Lord Devon Roxbury and Eastly, if you don't mind me saying so."

Cal grunted. She wasn't wrong. He'd have to pray a decent chap caught Emma's attention quickly. And clearly Roxbury didn't have any intention of holding to his side of their bargain. Puppy was right about one thing—if there was a baby, Roxbury would have to do his duty. Which meant Cal couldn't call him out. More's the pity. Getting to his feet, Cal plopped his hat on his head and handed the rest of the bread to Puppy.

"Let's get going. I have to write investors and prepare them for bad news." Granted, without knowing what percentage of cargo had been salvaged, there was no way to determine the full losses. If they were lucky, people might break even. But that would take tremendous luck, and luck wasn't something working in his favor lately.

Outside, Puppy handed off the loaf to the first urchin they saw, then climbed into the hack.

"Hill Street," Cal called to the driver.

Somehow, while the drive out to the docks had seemed to take a year, the ride to Mayfair was a blur of buildings growing steadily larger on wider streets as the smell of the Thames lessened the farther west they traveled. And through it all, Cal observed the woman across from him.

"You're staring again, Calvin."

A smile crept over his face. "Oh, I know."

A delicate pink stained her cheeks, but then she worked her jaw into that stubborn line he recognized, and stared at him in return. "Are we going to do this all the way back to your house?"

"I can't speak for you, but I'm enjoying the view."

She opened her mouth, then closed it, as if rethinking her words.

"If I'm making you uncomfortable, I'll find something else to do. But I enjoy looking at you."

"Because I'm suddenly a woman?"

"Because I'm realizing that I've been remiss in appreciating you properly on several fronts. You're quite extraordinary, and to overlook that for another minute would be tragic. Without the relationship you've built and maintained with Peggy, today's errand would have been a waste of time. The docks, Shoreditch, Almack's—you seem to find a place for yourself anywhere you go. I am guilty of underestimating you, Puppy. I thought I knew you, so I stopped paying attention." An idea occurred to him. "You don't have to take it if you don't want to. But I have a dare for you. Might be the hardest one yet." And God knew there had been quite a few absurd dares over the course of their friendship.

She raised her chin, but her lips quirked in a smile. "Harder than running along the rooflines above the pub that one time? I didn't think I'd make some of those jumps."

"And I swear my heart stopped until you landed safely. But yes. Harder than that."

"What's the challenge?"

"I dare you to give me one more piece of honesty...Tell me your name."

It took her a minute. A slow blink, then a deep breath that became a heavy sigh. "Ophelia. My name is Ophelia."

Chapter Nine

A dam's sister? So Adam is real?"

"Yes, Adam's sister."

A footman in pale-blue livery opened the door and waited for them to disembark. Cal hadn't even realized the carriage had stopped. Motioning for her to go first, he averted his eyes so he wouldn't give in to the urge to stare at her pert bum in those snug breeches as she stepped down to the pavement.

Getting new personal information from her was like pulling teeth from a chicken, as his childhood cook would have said. That phrase had never felt more appropriate.

"I'm going to finish a few pieces of correspondence in the drawing room before I go home for the day," she said.

When Cal handed his hat to Higgins, the butler said, "A young man by the name of Nelson Shaw arrived at the servants' entrance. Cook got one look at him and insisted on feeding him. We have him in the kitchen until you're ready to see him, milord."

So the butcher's son had decided to accept his offer of employment after all. "Put him in the library. I'll be there in a moment. Thank you, Higgins."

Exactly five minutes later, Cal made his entrance.

From the side, Nelson Shaw didn't look like a ruffian. If anything, he resembled a scared kid whose mama had combed his hair, then spit on her thumb to wipe the dirt off his face. His clothes were freshly pressed but fit him poorly as he stood at attention in the middle of the room, as if afraid to move a muscle.

The anxiety evident in Nelson's stiff posture and profile made Cal want to soften, but looks could be deceiving. Ophelia proved that. No matter how he appeared at the moment, Nelson had participated in the attack on her. Fresh anger brewed in his gut.

Had this nervous kid been the one to kick her ribs and stomach? Cal had seen the bruises himself, blossoming beneath the edge of the bandage around her torso. Had Nelson let her fall, watched her head smash against the cobblestones?

Maybe Nelson had kept some of her clothing for himself. With a critical eye, Cal examined what the young man wore. None of it looked familiar, which worked in the lad's favor. One thing Cal knew was clothes—particularly her clothes, since once upon a time they'd been in his own wardrobe. But no, these garments would make his tailor wince, although Nelson had made an effort for the interview.

Cal closed the door behind him with more force than necessary, announcing his presence. He hadn't thought it possible, but Nelson straightened further.

"We meet at last, Mr. Shaw. I've heard so much about you."

Cal took a seat behind his desk but refrained for the moment from waving Nelson to a chair. "Not all of it good."

A ruddy blush stained Nelson's cheeks, but he acknowledged the statement with a jerky nod.

"You are here today to discuss a position in my employ because of one reason, and one reason only. Even after your role in his attack, Mr. Hardwick vouched for you. He claims you're redeemable. Are you?"

"What? I mean, pardon, milord?" Nelson gulped. Goodness, the young man's voice cracked. For a moment, Cal felt sorry for him.

"Redeemable, young Nelson. Are you a good man who made a bad choice, or are you a thief taking advantage of Mr. Hardwick's kindness?"

"I'd like to think I'm a good man. Or at least, I could be."

Cal grunted and steepled his fingers under his chin. "We shall see, won't we? My offer of employment comes with one condition."

Hope lit Nelson's features. "Yes, milord?"

"I expect loyalty from my staff. By extension, that implies loyalty to my friends and family. Those that enter this house are under my protection. That would include Mr. Hardwick. You see where the dilemma lies, do you not?"

Nelson shifted slightly and stared at his shoes.

"Yes, I think you do see. If I take you on staff and you steal from me, I will see you prosecuted to the fullest extent of the law. They hang thieves, you know." A smooth chill wrapping around the words. Silence descended until Nelson cleared his throat and met Cal's gaze.

"I won't steal from you, milord."

Meeting his gaze took stones—he'd give him that. "And Mr. Hardwick? What about him? You've already stolen from him. How do you propose to make that right?"

Nelson opened his mouth but shut it again. With a frown, he finally asked, "How can I, milord?"

It felt like a hunter catching prey in a trap, and when Cal smiled, he made sure to show teeth. "Information. In this position, you will have a smart uniform, ample food, and a salary that contributes to your family significantly. In exchange for wearing my colors, you will tell me everything you know about the crew from your neighborhood." Cal eased out of his chair, rising to loom over his desk. Were he built like Ethan, intimidation would be easier. The broad and burly Scotsman would have this youngster pissing himself with one broody glower. "I want names. I want to know why you attacked my friend. Was it random or targeted? If targeted, you'll tell me why and who ordered it."

The intent turned out to be effective, even without Ethan's size. Nelson shuffled back a half step, keeping a wary eye on Cal, but gave a terse nod. "Understood, milord. I won't run with them no more. I won't need to with this job."

Cal moved around his desk to lean against the front, crossing his arms. "Don't cut ties entirely. Not yet. You must walk a fine line for a while. Obviously, I expect you to refrain from criminal activity. But you'll have to be close enough to hear and report to me if Mr. Hardwick becomes a target again. If you hear his name in any context, I expect a report."

"You want me to be a turncoat."

"I see we understand each other. As long as you and I are on the same side, you'll find your time here valuable. And should you find that a position in service isn't one you want to pursue long-term, I will write a reference for you in line with the man of character Mr. Hardwick believes you to be. Agreed?" Cal offered a hand, and after a brief hesitation, Nelson shook it.

"Agreed, milord."

"Good, then you and I should sit for a chat. Afterwards, I'll take you to Higgins. He will get your livery and assess where you'll fit best in the house." Waving his new double agent toward the fireplace, Cal took his customary chair.

Nelson paused in the air, hovering briefly over the seat.

"Second thoughts, lad?"

Nelson sat. "The crew," he began. "If they find out I've betrayed them, things won't go well for me or my family."

It was a valid point and showed forethought. It also made him think of Ophelia a short time before, when she explained territorial street gangs with a flippant *that's London*. He and young Nelson lived in very different versions of the same city.

"I have several properties across England, Scotland, and Wales. If you feel you or your family are in danger, please tell me. There are plenty of places to hide. Temporarily or permanently." Softening his tone, Cal said, "You're not making a deal with the devil. I understand I'm asking you to do something dangerous. My orders come from a deep desire to protect my friend. Your crew could have killed him." His throat closed over the word *killed*, making his voice crack. "I need details if I'm to make sure it doesn't happen again."

There must have been some measure of loyalty within Nelson, because the rigid line of his shoulders softened. "Understood, milord."

"Good. Let's have that talk, then, shall we?"

A half hour later Cal handed Nelson over to Higgins, then made his way upstairs to the portrait gallery, where he and Puppy fenced nearly every day. Not the use his forefathers had intended for the room, but certainly a more logical use of space than displaying paintings of dead people.

Lines of perfectly coiffed men and women looked down their noses from gilded frames. Their rows of golden perfection had intimidated him as a child, before he fully understood what a herd of degenerates they'd been. Sure, a few had been generally upstanding members of society. Or at least, their misdeeds hadn't made it into the family lore. The male ancestors in particular had possessed the moral fortitude of meringue—pretty on the outside, utterly empty beneath the decorative finish.

Running a hand over the plain waistcoat he'd chosen for the day's jaunt to the docks, Cal paused before the portrait of his mother. She fit right in with the others. Lovely. So utterly lovely. Maybe in the beginning, she'd been faithful. As the story went, his parents were a love match. Until they weren't. The spectacle of his parents had been exhausting to watch as a child and humiliating to deal with as a young man. The clearest memories from his childhood were of standing at the window, watching as servants loaded his mother's trunks onto a carriage again—sometimes only days after unpacking them amidst showering kisses and declarations of love for her family—and knowing no matter how obedient a boy he'd been, it wasn't enough for her to stay. Or to take him with her.

"She was beautiful. You look like her," Ophelia said from behind him.

Cal turned, oddly relieved to see her. "You're still here? I thought you'd gone for the day."

She shrugged a slim shoulder. "I got bored. Figured you might be too. Thought I'd stay and see if you'd indulge me in a match."

"Feel the need to be trounced, do you?"

"You always say that, and I always win." She grinned.

A bit of the tightness he'd been carrying in his chest unfurled with a laugh. Puppy, or rather, Ophelia, had a knack for doing that—making him laugh when he didn't think he could.

"Today might be the day I send you home with your tail between your legs. You never know."

"I'll believe that when I see it." She seemed relieved that he wasn't going to press her for more details after she'd shared her name. What she didn't realize was that over the course of the interview with Nelson, his priorities had shifted. Yes, he wanted to know her secrets. The why to all of this. But first, he had to find the words to warn this woman that despite her clever disguise, her uncle wanted her dead.

"Cal was right." Her voice cut through the empty room, punctuating the mess the intruders had left behind. Somehow, Milton had found her amidst the masses of the city.

That precious bubble of anonymity she'd constructed since leaving her uncle's house over a decade before, by keeping her head down at school, then during her years in London—*poof*. Gone. Just like that.

And she'd been so close. A few more months, and she could reclaim her life. Reclaim her honesty.

The attack wasn't random, Ophelia. Nelson claims an older man ordered it. Cal's words earlier that evening weren't ones she'd wanted to believe. The proof lay before her.

Phee scanned the room to make sure she was alone, then closed the door.

A man calling himself Smith paid cash. The gang's spy followed him to a room at the Clarendon. Mr. Smith registered under the name Milton Keating. If Nelson spoke the truth—and how could he pull such a credible lie out of nothing?—Uncle Milton had somehow figured out where she lived. Not only that, but he'd visited the offices of Hapsburg Life and Property Insurance on three occasions during this trip to Town. It would appear Milton had taken out a life-insurance policy on Adam. With mere months before the birthday that would remove the family fortune from her uncle's reach, he'd taken action to collect on his investment. It all came down to money.

Money. Phee charged toward the bed, with its bits of ticking and strips of blankets piled into a messy heap. "Please, please, please," she breathed in a chant. There, pressed between the wall and the side of the bed, was the small pillow she cuddled close every night. Miraculously, the seams were intact. Wrapping her arms around it, she squeezed until a muted crinkle within the stuffing provided reassurance. They hadn't found her nest egg. Tears pricked at the corner of her eyes as she slumped onto the edge of the bed, clinging to the one thing that mattered within the chaos of the room.

How had he tracked her?

Nothing on paper tied her to this address. When she needed a bank, she traveled to the farthest corner of London from where she laid her head at night. The measly quarterly pittance from her parents' estate was always paid out in person from a solicitor in Cheapside that she knew served Milton's interests over hers. Fat lot of good those protective measures did her.

A piece of paper stuck to her boot, and she bent to pick it up. They'd even shredded John's latest letter. At least it had been happy news—Vicar Arcott had rallied after her visit and grew stronger each day. She threw the bits of paper into the fireplace.

Phee carefully righted the broken footstool, its slashed cushion bleeding stuffing onto the floor. Cramming the bits of fluff into the gaping fabric hole might be a lost cause, but she tried for about fifteen seconds before setting it aside. Pieces of cotton and feathers drifted onto the toe of one boot, pale against black leather.

Cal had told her, but she hadn't wanted to believe. Not while feeling vulnerable and exposed after sharing another piece of herself with him. After each revealed truth, they seemed to have a period when they scrambled to reclaim a sense of normality. Being in the pub today had been another piece of blessed routine—he hadn't accompanied her lately, but he used to canvass the neighborhoods with her all the time. The light flirting in the hack on the way to Mayfair was certainly new, and she didn't know what to do with it. But that was an issue for a different day.

Now this. Information showing the robbery wasn't a random act of violence. Accepting it meant accepting that her charade was truly over, short of her goal. Yet to ignore the evidence of her destroyed room would require a level of self-delusion even she couldn't muster.

She plucked two pieces of a torn waistcoat from the floor. They'd even stolen wooden buttons.

A gentle tap at her door made her sniff, then swipe at her eyes with the back of a hand.

"Mr. Hardwick?" Mrs. Carver's voice came from the other side. The landlady's tone said it all. Adam Hardwick was getting evicted.

Dread settled heavy in her limbs as she flipped the latch and opened the door, still clutching the pillow in her other fist.

Mrs. Carver's face softened with sympathy. "I'm sorry, Mr. Hardwick." The landlady pulled a few coins from her apron pocket and held them out.

Phee nodded, knowing what came next.

"Here's the rest of this week's rent returned to you. You're a good lad. I don't know what kind of trouble you've gotten yourself into, but it's not trouble I want on my doorstep. Gather your things. I'll need you gone by nightfall."

Phee squeezed out a breath and tightened her hold on the pillow. The faint crinkle soothed the panic tickling the edges of her brain. "I understand. Thank you, Mrs. Carver."

She would be fine. No, this wasn't ideal. But she was not without resources. She just needed to survive until the end of the year. Straightening her chin to stand as tall as possible, Phee closed the door and surveyed the room once more.

This time she'd go somewhere her uncle couldn't reach her—perhaps to the seashore—and leave Adam's name behind a little early. A plan formed from spinning thoughts while she sifted through the room in search of something salvageable.

The town would need to be within a reasonable distance from London, since she'd have to collect her quarterly allowance one more time. Perhaps she need only pretend to be Adam for that one meeting. The idea of finally shedding her brother's name felt odd. Not quite the dark heft of grief, but not the lightness of relief either.

Under the bed, the corner of a miniature caught the light of the lantern. Beyond that, miraculously intact, lay the small sewing kit she used to alter her clothing. Smoothing dirt from the tiny painting's frame, Phee studied the faces caught by a rather subpar artist. Her parents had been good people. So good, perhaps, that they hadn't believed others capable of the depravity Uncle Milton held within his pinkie finger. Such blind trust to leave him with the final say in the amount of her allowance.

The whole situation made her blood boil, but being furious with her dead parents felt disloyal to the early memories she held of them. Guilt hit with predictable precision. She swallowed it down from habit, tucking it away as neatly as she pocketed the small portrait into her coat.

"So that's it, then. A pillow, a sewing kit, and a miniature." Pathetic, really. Everything else would be fuel for warmth or perhaps passed around as scraps to the other residents of the building. Maybe they could use the bits and pieces as patches for their clothes or a quilt. Some good might come of the mess that way.

The familiar faded wallpaper of the hallway greeted her for the last time when she stepped out of the room. Mrs. Carver took the key she proffered, then clasped Phee's hands. "Be well, lad."

"Thank you." A thought occurred to her, cutting through the numbness she'd pulled around herself like a cloak. Her neighbor would receive another letter soon and not have any way of reading it. The thought cracked the calm she'd fabricated. "When you see Barry next, could you tell him I'm sorry I won't be here to read his correspondence anymore? I hope he can find someone else to help him keep in touch with his brother."

"I'll tell him. Best get along before it gets dark, Mr. Hardwick." The nudge was gentle, but there nonetheless.

Quick as that, she was homeless.

An hour later, if Higgins was surprised to see Phee on the doorstep, he didn't let on. "Mr. Hardwick."

"Hello again, Higgins. Is his lordship home?"

"I'm afraid Lord Carlyle and Lady Emma have stepped out for the evening."

So this would not be a quick goodbye, then a walk to the nearest posting house. She could simply leave a note and move on with her life. But on this entire planet, there were three people who knew Ophelia was alive: Vicar Arcott, John, and Cal. Even if he didn't know all the details. Walking away with no more than a letter sounded like an awful, cowardly way to leave things. He'd taken her under his wing and offered friendship when she'd been completely alone.

The fresh memory of her destroyed belongings, clearly meant as a threat to intimidate, flashed through her mind. Cal's feelings weren't more important than her safety. However, Cal owed her wages, and frankly, she needed every coin she could get if she was going to successfully move and hide for the next few months. Money provided a solid reason to say goodbye in person, when logically she should be fleeing the city and abandoning every connection and friendship.

"Do you mind if I wait in the library?"

Instead of answering, Higgins puckered his brow in a tiny gesture she might have missed were she not paying attention. The butler glanced at the pillow. "Perhaps you'd prefer to wait in a bedroom and address your business with him on the morrow? You know a chamber remains prepared for you at all times on Lord Carlyle's order. The family likely won't return until very late."

God, if Higgins softened his voice further, Phee would cry. The unexpected kindness caused her eyes to burn with unshed emotion. "I look that bad off, do I?"

The butler straightened, all business once more. "I am hardly one to pass judgment, Mr. Hardwick. If you choose to wait in the library, you are free to do so. I'm simply doing my duty by reminding you that Lord Carlyle has made it clear you will always have a place here."

Blinking to clear her eyes, Phee adjusted the pillow under her arm. "Thank you, Higgins. If you wouldn't mind sending notice when his lordship arrives home, I'll take that offer of a room."

"Of course."

A footman led her up the stairs and down a familiar hallway. "Are you sure we're going the right way? Isn't this the family wing?" They passed the heavy wooden door to Cal's room, then stopped at the end of the hall before a set of similar doors.

"No mistake, Mr. Hardwick." The servant opened the room to show a chamber three times the size of the room she'd been renting, with a door ajar on the far wall showing an additional dressing chamber.

Typical Cal. Generous to the point of excess, providing a soft place to land after a day of emotional turns and surprises. Standing in this lush chamber, with its carved wood mantel and grand bed piled with luxurious linens, it hit her that for the moment at least, she was safe.

Her knees went soft until a chair caught her. Wrapping her arms around the pillow and hugging it to her chest tighter, Phee leaned her head back.

It hadn't been the worst day of her life. But the bar for that was rather high.

Phee swallowed around a hiccuping sob and squeezed her eyes closed. God, she'd been so close to her goal, and now this. Starting over from scratch again. Goodbyes. Death threats.

Rubbing a fist over her eyes, she scrubbed away tears. There would be time to cry later. After Cal returned from yet another night of socializing with all the other glittering, pretty people. After she left him behind. And she'd certainly cry once she'd climbed aboard the mail coach and "Adam" disappeared from London.

What she'd give to find out how large the insurance policy was. How much was she worth to Milton? Before today, she'd have used the pennies allotted for her allowance as a metric. Clearly, she was worth more dead than alive.

A tear escaped, so she wicked her cheek dry on the shoulder of her coat.

Later. There would be time to cry later.

Chapter Ten

*M*r. Hardwick is upstairs, milord. We showed him to his room." The butler took their outerwear, then paused while Emma kissed Cal's cheek and climbed the stairs to her room. "Lord Eastly stopped by as well, and per your orders I turned him away. Again." With a low voice, Higgins said, "I believe something might have happened with young Mr. Hardwick. He carried a pillow. Most odd."

"Thank you, Higgins." Cal handed his hat and gloves to the butler and ran a hand through his hair. When he snagged on the ribbon holding his queue, he slipped it free and tucked it in his pocket while he climbed the stairs two at a time.

A knock on the door at the end of the hall went un-answered. He glanced at his pocket watch and grimaced. It was late—or terribly early, depending on one's perspective. But Higgins suspected something might be wrong, and Cal trusted Higgins's read on most situations. Ophelia hadn't listened to his protests when she left for Shoreditch earlier.

He'd insisted she stay here for her safety, but she'd refused. Obstinate woman.

He stood there for a moment, considering the options. It was late and she might be asleep already. Lord knew he was tired after a long day. Between the interview with Nelson, fencing with Ophelia while pretending they hadn't flirted in the hack, and their conversation about her uncle, it had been rather anticlimactic to return to work.

But that was the reality of his life, and it was far from the glamorous, laughing facade he put on for society. No matter what else was falling apart around him, there were still books to balance, columns of numbers to provide some level of certainty. There was comfort in the black-and-white finality of sums.

Taking Emma out tonight had been nerve-racking, watching for clues to her behavior he'd missed before. Some hint at the secrets she kept. When Roxbury hadn't shown up to the event, she'd pouted but eventually enjoyed herself.

In short, he was exhausted. But Higgins thought Ophelia needed help, and for once she'd come to him.

With his brain whipping through a list of worst-case scenarios, he opened the door. All was dark within, the fireplace down to glowing embers, but the bed didn't have the expected lump of a sleeping body under the blankets. When he lit a lamp, he spotted Ophelia in the overstuffed armchair, cuddling a pillow to her chest like a child with a favorite toy.

The light didn't disturb her sleep, so he perched on the bench at the foot of the bed and took a moment to gather his thoughts.

Today he'd crossed that invisible line from admiring to admitting it aloud. Flirting, even. Not that she'd really acknowledged it before leaving the carriage. And once inside the house, she'd pretended that taut moment in the hack when they'd openly stared at one another hadn't happened.

She slept with full lips slightly parted, but her hands clutched at the pillow with white knuckles. Even at rest, she wasn't relaxed, and it killed him.

With her head turned to the side, the firelight illuminated the pink shell of her ear and the delicate blue veins of her eyelids. This woman with her secrets deserved the chance to truly rest, and he hated to wake her.

But tangled in the protective feelings were less altruistic desires.

If he could, he'd trace the regal angles of her face with his lips. He wanted to discover her confidences one by one as she offered them up like sweet treats. He'd indulge in her if she allowed it.

During their match this afternoon, she'd removed her coat and bent over to place it in the corner, and he'd nearly swallowed his tongue. She had a perfectly heart-shaped arse, and the fact that he'd never noticed before made him wonder about his eyesight. That gentle flare at the hip made his fingers itch to explore and see what other curves she hid.

There had been something in her gaze this morning—yesterday now, given the hour. Something that woke his desire after a long, cold hibernation. The tension in that hack hinted that perhaps she wasn't someone who preferred female partners. Or not exclusively, at any rate.

Of course, he could be wrong about all of this. Maybe she

didn't want to change their relationship. Or maybe she didn't know how to cross that bridge from friendship to more. And given her masquerade and her uncle, maybe now simply wasn't the time.

Not knowing what his next move should be was new territory, and frankly, nothing about this was fun. In the face of attraction, he usually only needed to say yes or no, then set the parameters of the relationship—and there were always limits. With a father who couldn't keep track of his numerous by-blows as an example, Cal was extremely picky about his lovers. During those encounters he'd focused on the numerous ways to please a partner without risking a child.

In the quiet of this room, every one of those ways crossed his mind. This attraction was blasted uncomfortable. As if a floodgate had opened now that he'd seen his friend in a different light, he couldn't close his mind to all the things about her that he'd missed before now. And damned if he didn't want to just stand there mooning over her like a lovesick suitor.

She must have licked her lips as she dreamed, or fallen asleep right before he got home, because her plump bottom lip shone wet and enticing.

Yet something had happened to bring her here tonight. There was likely a price on her head, and here he was wondering if she'd let him kiss her. Climbing to his feet, he crossed to the chair.

"Ophelia, wake up." Not so much as a flicker of a copper-tipped eyelash. How long had it been since she answered to her name? "Adam," he tried, louder this time.

It hit him in that heartbeat between her sleep and awareness that if she didn't share this attraction he was navigating, their friendship could get extremely awkward, very fast. He could have misread everything this morning.

Damn, he needed to get a grip on himself. Crossing his arms over his chest, he nudged the toe of her boot. "If you need to sleep, there's a perfectly comfortable bed right over there, and nightshirts in the dressing room."

Ophelia grunted as she came awake, and he refused to be charmed by the sound.

"What's happened?" he asked.

She blinked, rubbing a palm over her face. "Landlady evicted me. I went home and the place had been tossed. I don't know how they got in, but they destroyed everything. Well"—she smiled weakly—"almost everything."

A cacophony of emotions exploded in Cal's chest, then crept up his throat. Closing his eyes for a second, he tried to make sense of them all.

Fear. "I told you there was a threat. What if you'd been there when they got in?"

Anger. Thrusting fingers through the long strands of his hair, he shoved the mass off his face and paced a step or two, only to whirl around and return to where he'd started. She didn't have much to begin with. How dare they destroy her things?

Then, blast it all, satisfaction slithered through to rear its ugly head. "You can move in here, obviously. I've been asking you to for a while." Cal gestured around the room. "Whatever you need. It's yours for as long as you want to stay."

Puppy, damn her stubborn hide, shook her head. "Thank you for the offer, but no. I came to say goodbye, collect my wages, and tender my resignation."

The words hit him like ice from a champagne bucket. "Resignation? Now you're talking nonsense."

She lifted a shoulder in a half shrug. "My uncle found me. That's obvious. I only need to make it to the end of the year. I'll slip off to a small village somewhere. Make it harder for him to track me this time."

"That's the most ridiculous thing I've ever heard," Cal snapped. "If he's found you once, he'll find you again."

"Thanks for the vote of confidence. I feel so very safe now." She rolled her eyes. "I'll take on another name. Only come to London to collect my allowance."

That was a small comfort. At least she had some sort of plan.

"But you're going to leave? Just like that? Casually end our friendship and quit your job? Toss a wave over your shoulder, then go live under an assumed identity?" Cal added a dramatic hand flip in case the point wasn't clear. A part of his brain stood removed from the situation, wondering what exactly he was doing. Reminding him that he looked ridiculous. That part of his brain grew quieter with each pounding heartbeat as the emotions he'd been grappling with since her attack spilled over.

In response, Puppy thumped her head against the padded chair back. "It isn't like that. You're adding connotations to this. Am I quitting? Yes. Because it's rather hard to deal with my duties here if I'm not living in London. And if I stay, I'll wind up dead. Although, if you'd like me to be an *actual* steward to that forest you refuse to let me do a damn thing with, then by all means, keep paying me a ridiculous wage to oversee a copse of trees in the middle of bloody nowhere. But we both know I'm not a steward, and I can't carry out my duties long-distance. This doesn't have to be the end of our friendship. I can visit when I collect my allowance."

Just like Cal's mother visited in between lovers. Mother would be home long enough to reignite hope that perhaps this time she'd stay. In all fairness, her departure usually coincided with his father finding a distraction with another married woman or a servant and starting the whole brutal process over again. Always in competition, those two. Seeing who could hurt the other worse, flouncing off in a fit of theatrics with zero regard for how their abandonment affected Emma and Cal, who wondered each time if their parent would ever return. Cal wouldn't let his heart wander into that kind of unstable territory again.

"I don't want you to go." The words tore out of him.

"There's no reason for me to stay," she said.

"Ouch." Cal recoiled, rubbing his chest. "Warn a gent next time you take a swipe, will you?"

"Don't take it like that," Puppy huffed. "I don't see any reason to stay in London. You've welcomed me into your life, and I appreciate that. I do. I appreciate your"—she stumbled—"friendship. More than you know." Her voice softened. "But I don't have anything in London besides you."

Maybe it was the late hour. Or the wine at dinner and the brandy after. Or that feeling of someone else he cared for leaving him behind, but he didn't bother to temper his reply. "Aren't I enough?" Honesty sounded an awful lot like begging, but there it was. "I can keep you safe. Hire guards to protect you—"

She lurched from the chair to stand so close their chests nearly touched. It took every bit of his self-control to not close that gap. He wanted to feel her. And yet her expression gave no indication of physical desire. Frankly, the woman looked like she'd happily wring his neck. At least she was talking to him and not marching out the door.

"I've been evicted because my landlady doesn't want these problems at her door. What makes you think I'd bring them here and expect you to handle them?"

"Because handling problems is what I do." His voice rose with the tension roiling inside him.

"I won't be another one of your problems," Puppy said, matching his volume.

The space between their bodies disappeared, and he breathed in her sandalwood heat until she filled his head. When he spoke, it was quieter, which only made the crack in his voice that much more obvious. "You could never be a problem."

She melted against him when he cupped her jaw, brushing the corner of her mouth with his thumb. God, her lips were so pink and plump, and *right there*.

"I wish you'd let me help. You've been alone for so long, but you don't have to be anymore. Trust me. Please."

Phee recoiled from the gently spoken words. Trust him? She did...to a point. But wouldn't she have to tell him everything at some point? Which meant answering questions about Adam and that day on the pond. There was no way he'd look at her with such sweet vulnerability on his face if he knew.

Flashes of memory assaulted her with images of pink water and Adam's pale face, eyes wide open, as if dying young had surprised him too. The chair caught her when her calves bumped against it, toppling her away from Cal.

"You should leave." The words scraped through a tight throat, while anxiety threatened to dislodge dinner from her stomach. Lord, she might be sick all over his perfectly polished leather shoes. Of course they were polished and perfect, just like the rest of him. The very opposite of her, with her one remaining suit of clothes, battered pillow, and two personal possessions.

Although it wouldn't hide anything, Phee covered her face with her hands. The urge to tell him everything nearly overwhelmed her. To get it over with and purge every damning secret. He'd let her leave then, without a fuss. Accepting a liar was one thing. But a murderer?

However, this was Calvin. She sneaked a peek up at him standing there with hands on his hips and a fall of hair nearly hiding his disgruntled expression. This man's generous nature sometimes overrode common sense. What if he tried to help? It would be nothing for him to wave his magic wands of money and connections and make it all better. Like assigning a footman to guard her while she slept, but on a larger scale.

"Get some rest. We can talk in the morning if you wish. There are just as many ways to run off when the sun rises," Cal said gruffly.

The door latch closed with a gentle *snick* as he left the room.

She ran her fingers through her short curls and sighed out a gusty exhale. Lordy, what a day. Beyond the glow of the lantern, the bed beckoned.

Staying the night wouldn't change things in the long run. Besides, one place she'd be safe from Milton's henchmen was Cal's house, with its legion of footmen and the regular patrols outside protecting the residents of Mayfair.

Crossing to the window, she flicked the curtain open barely enough to peer into the night. Along the street, gas lamps illuminated tiny circles of pavement in otherwise inky darkness. No silhouetted men loitered in any of those dots of light, but that proved nothing.

Maybe things would look clearer tomorrow. Because to be wholly honest, she didn't want to leave London. Not really. Feeling tired and frayed around the edges like this made the available options appear limited. Sleep might help. For now, she was safe.

She plucked her pillow from where it had fallen on the floor, and the pound notes inside crinkled with a soothing reminder of her life's savings. After pulling back the blankets, she sat on the edge of the mattress and removed her boots. With that move, it became official, in her mind at least, that she'd stay for the night. After carefully folding her clothing, Phee snuffed the lamp.

The bindings around her chest had become a familiar pressure over the years. Sleeping in them wouldn't be a problem, especially when exhaustion pulled at her limbs.

A down-filled pillow dipped under her head, and she cocooned herself in smooth linens and the comforting weight of blankets over bare legs. Sleep should come quickly.

Except it didn't.

When she closed her eyes, her brain settled on one thing: he'd nearly kissed her. And she'd wanted him to. His pupils had taken over the warm chocolate of his eyes when he brushed a thumb over her bottom lip. Cal's spicy scent had filled her head, even as she'd realized his breathing was as unsteady as hers.

As she rolled to her side and tucked the blankets into the crook of her neck, an ache in her chest grew with each new thought spinning in her head.

She'd never kissed a man.

When she and Adam turned thirteen, Uncle Milton had sent Adam to boarding school, then arranged a marriage for her to Sir Potter—who'd been seventy if a day, and some kind of business associate.

That was when she cut off all her hair and tried to run away.

When Milton found her, he locked her up until she agreed to marry Sir Potter. She stayed in that room for eight days, living on scraps the chambermaids slipped to her when they made their rounds.

Adam came home from school on the ninth day for a scheduled break.

He died on the tenth day after he picked the lock and sneaked them from the house to plot their escape. With the blind hope of children, they'd decided to stow away on a ship to America and start a new life.

Claiming grief, she avoided Milton until it was time to take her brother's place at school.

That day by the pond, she'd dressed in her brother's sopping wet clothes and stolen his future. In reality, she'd never really been a woman. A girl, yes. And that had nearly been the end of her. Since then, womanhood had been something she'd dreamed of, while keeping it firmly in the land of "someday." With Cal's near kiss lingering as a tingle where he'd touched her, it looked like someday was arriving earlier than expected.

The most beautiful man in London wanted to kiss...her. Which begged the question *why*. And why now? She'd been wrestling with this attraction to Cal for two years. Like looking directly into the sun, it could only hurt to study her feelings when she couldn't allow them free reign. The self-denial had been a near constant torment, although one she'd grown accustomed to.

Yet he'd almost kissed her.

Why? All the clamor in her head quieted under that one word. None of this made sense. A public relationship with "Adam" would be a tremendous risk for Cal, so why flirt in the hack or nearly kiss her tonight?

With a huff, Phee flopped onto her back. The dark canopy above the bed offered a better view than the water-stained, chipped plaster ceiling of her rented room, or the wooden interior of a mail coach.

What she really wanted to do was charge into his room and demand answers. But what if she'd misunderstood? What if he hadn't considered kissing her? The physical signs she'd read as desire might have been irritation or anger. It wasn't like she knew what the hell she was doing, after all.

But what if she was right, and he wanted to kiss her? It could be glorious. It could be the beginning of something wonderful.

Or it could ruin him if anyone found out about them. He'd been appalled at everyone laughing about the marquess's-mini-member jokes and discussing his love life—how much worse would it be when he couldn't defend himself without exposing her secrets?

And all this was pure conjecture, because she could be wrong about everything. He hadn't actually kissed her.

But he wanted to. Probably.

She swore into the dark room, loud and colorful with the flavor of the gutter she'd lived in until today. After flipping the covers off, she stomped to the chair and shoved her legs into her breeches, then threw on her shirt. The floor chilled the bottoms of her feet, but she ignored her boots and flung the bedroom door open before she could think better of it. Only one man had answers to her questions. Sifting through all the things floating around in her brain might be too much, but this one thing, she could do.

A knock at the door was the last thing he'd expected. Cinching the tie on his banyan, he set aside the brandy he'd poured after dealing with the maddening woman across the hall.

The door swung open, and Ophelia charged in, looking

ready to fight, with her serious eyes, stubborn jaw, and tight mouth. Cal braced himself for the next round and hoped like the devil it would end better than the conversation in her room. It was nearly impossible to not feel raw and exposed after literally begging, then being thrown out on his ear.

"Did you nearly kiss me? If so, I need to know why. Because the math doesn't add up. Us, I mean. Why risk it? Why start something with me?" She gestured between herself and Cal with such a confused look, Cal wanted to either laugh or cuddle her. He wasn't sure which, or if either would be welcome.

"The math works perfectly. And yes, I wanted to kiss you." He let it go at that to see where she would take the conversation next. Ophelia's coppery-red brows scrunched, and she shifted from one foot to another. One bare foot to another. He smiled at how wonderfully intimate it was to have her standing barefoot in his room in the wee hours of the morning. Even if she was there to quarrel.

"My, your toes are long." They were as delicately boned as the rest of her.

"What? Oh, yes. I got teased about them as a child. I can pick up a pencil with my toes, you know." She shook her head. "Which is entirely off topic. I'm struggling to wrap my head around this, Cal."

He inched forward. The need to follow through, to touch her, thrummed in his fingertips, but she might not want that. Cocking his head, he tried to dissect the emotions flitting across Ophelia's face. "Which part is confusing? Is it that you're pretending to be a man and I still find you attractive?"

She swallowed loudly. Hesitated, then said, "I mean, yes, that is a shock. But it's more that you're all this"—she threw her hand out to indicate Cal's general person—"and I'm all this." This time gesturing toward herself.

"Is this a self-confidence issue, or are you questioning my ability to see beyond your—admittedly very clever—disguise?"

She wrinkled her nose. "Both? I understand you liking Adam. But being attracted to me as Ophelia is...unexpected."

Separate from his new feelings toward the woman, Cal could see her point. Objectively, she wasn't classically beautiful. But only if you didn't pay attention. Now that his eyes were open to her unique appeal, he couldn't see anything but beauty. "Not to be a total arse and answer your questions with questions, but I'd like to know something. What do you see when you look at me?"

They stared at one another while Cal's pulse thudded in his ears.

"Um, you have a mirror. You know what you look like."

"That's not what I asked. What do *you* see?" Cal reached out one finger to touch Ophelia's chest near her heart. Under his finger, her chest rose, then fell on a breath before she answered.

"My friend." She closed her eyes and seemed to come to a decision, because when she opened them, her voice didn't shake anymore. "You're smart. Most people don't realize how intelligent you are. And you're funny. Not the kind of funny that makes others the joke. But humor that comes from genuine wit." Spots of pink flagged her cheeks. "I...I like it when you need a shave and your beard stubble shows so many colors. I've tried to count how many colors are in your beard, but I'm scared you'll catch me staring." Hesitating, she raised a hand, then swept one finger across his evening scruff from his cheek to his chin.

The words—maybe not an agreement that she wanted his kisses, but certainly an acknowledgment of awareness— sent his heart pounding madly. Brushing a finger over the voluptuous curve of her bottom lip, he smiled when her thick lashes fluttered closed. However, he had a point to make here. "Now ask me what I see when I look at you."

Her eyes flew open so wide, the copper lashes nearly touched her brows. "I don't really want to."

Cal leaned forward until their noses nearly touched. "Ask me."

Her breath huffed, warm and sweet on his face, and he couldn't resist dropping a kiss on the tip of her nose. It was an adorable nose, after all.

She rolled her eyes, parroting the question. "Fine. What do you see when you look at me?"

Between them, she rested her hands on his chest, but she clenched them into fists, as if preparing to block an attack. Whoever had taught this woman that words could be weapons deserved to be shot at dawn.

Smoothing his fingers along her cheekbones, then down to her pointed chin, he tried to soothe with both his touch and his words.

"Like you, I see a friend. A survivor. A woman who will make something of herself through sheer stubbornness. And I see color." Cal couldn't help smiling, because there was no better way to describe her. "You brighten every room you enter. When the light catches on your hair, I see shades of red and gold I didn't know existed."

"I hate my hair."

"No interrupting, Puppy," he chided, taking shameless advantage of how close she stood to kiss her temple. One short curl brushed his nose, while another stood straight up. "I appreciate that you're honest in everything you can be. Even with hard topics like my sister's bad decisions. Put an épée in your hands, and you'll beat me nine times out of ten, and for some reason I find that incredibly attractive. And I can't stop staring at your lips. They dominate your face and inspire thoughts I never expected to have about you." Her gaze settled on his mouth, which he took as an encouraging sign when her lips were a scant inch away. "Yes, I think about kissing you. It's a recent development, I admit, but once the idea entered my head, I've thought of little else. Does my vision sound like how you'd describe yourself?"

"Not really, no."

"But do you stand by what you said about me?"

"Of course. Everything I said is true."

"Is it? Perhaps I see myself differently. Perhaps I see my looks as a burden, not an asset." That piece of honesty stung. "If I choose to believe you, to accept your words, they become true for *us*." Cal waited a beat to see if she followed what he said. "If you choose to believe me when I say I desire you, it becomes real for *us*. And then, the math—as you put it—works fine. In fact, it means we're equals. Friends with a mutual attraction, albeit under unusual circumstances."

She finally looked him in the eye, and for the briefest of seconds her face lit, a smile twitching at her lips. But that lasted only an instant before Ophelia seemed to catch herself. Shaking her head, she stepped away. "In no version of reality are you and I equals."

It felt like a rejection, hitting him sharp enough to steal his breath. Although he opened his mouth to call out, he waited when she paused with her hand on the door. She glanced over her shoulder, and with heartbreaking vulnerability, he saw everything play across her face—the desire and the fear waging war within her.

She'd been hiding for over a decade, and the street where she'd lived wasn't safe anymore. All those words he'd wanted to say died on a sigh. Asking her to handle all of that, plus his feelings for her—out of nowhere—wasn't fair.

He might want to save her, but that didn't automatically mean she needed saving.

The bedroom door closed, leaving him alone again.

Chapter Eleven

~

Creeping out in the middle of the night like a thief would have been a better idea. Phee took another sip of coffee and tried to ignore the tension in the breakfast room. The sunny-yellow striped wallpaper acted as a cheerfully ironic backdrop to their uncomfortable silence.

Cal set his cup aside with a clatter that jarred her from her thoughts. With a jerk of his head, he sent the servants from the room. Wooden doors clicked shut, leaving them alone, two seats apart, with a pot of coffee between them on the table and a whole lot of unfinished business hanging in the air. "So, this is awkward."

After their talk in his bedroom, she'd lain awake staring at that canopy, mulling over something he'd said. *You're honest in everything you can be.* That was how he saw her, and God knew that was how she wanted to live her life. He already knew she was a woman and that Milton wanted her dead. Telling him her story didn't necessarily mean confessing details about Adam's death. Those were her demons to wrestle, not his.

Taking a steadying breath, she gathered her courage. "My brother, Adam, called me Phee."

He took a moment before replying. "Good, so we are going to talk about it. And where is Adam these days?"

"The same place he's been for the last eleven years. In a graveyard in Northumberland, six feet under a headstone with my name on it."

Cal paused midswipe while spreading butter on his toast. "Let's start at the beginning, if you don't mind. Walk me through it. I want to help, but I need to know what you're dealing with."

Pouring another round of coffee into their cups kept her busy long enough to find the beginning in her mind. The coffee urn wobbled, but she managed to get every drop into the cups and not on the table's glossy finish. Small victory, that.

"Adam and I were orphans. My family tree is scraggly, and Mother's oldest brother was the only relative who could take us. Milton is a businessman, so I assume my parents thought their fortune would be in capable hands until we inherited."

"The bit about coming into your money at twenty-five is the truth, then."

"I tell the truth when I can." She nibbled on a toast point. "Milton didn't want children and hated taking on someone else's. We were an inconvenience. At least, that's what he told us over and over, but I think he enjoyed having easy targets. He's not a pleasant man." A kind understatement.

"As soon as we turned thirteen, Milton sent Adam to school and arranged a marriage for me to a geriatric business associate."

Cal placed the knife and toast on his plate with carefully measured movements that hinted at his emotions. He got very precise when trying to maintain his composure. It was something she'd seen often with his father and sister, but never directed at her. Sure enough, the betraying twitch of his left eye showed his inner struggle. "Thirteen? Is that even legal?"

"Shockingly, yes. In protest, I hacked all my hair off, dressed in my brother's clothes, and bolted. Didn't get far before Milton caught up with me. When Adam came home a few days later for a school break, we managed to sneak out to the pond. We were planning to run away together, you see, and were figuring out the details of how to go about it. The pond was *our* place. That was the day Adam drowned."

Because she'd been fussing and acting like a brat. A bite of breakfast stuck in her throat. With a shaky hand, she lifted her cup once more to wash down the food and guilt.

Adam had attempted to tease her out of her mood, and she'd swatted his chest. Not hard. But hard enough to unbalance him. She'd tried to grab his hand but missed, and over he went.

There were rocks in the shallows. Boulders that could, and did, split a head open.

The coffee turned bitter in her mouth, and she nearly spit it out.

"I'm sorry. You saw it, then," he said.

"Yes. I ran for help." She struggled to form the words. Talking about this was not something she did. Not ever. "Vicar Arcott and his son, John, came. The vicar knew about my runaway attempt. This grand charade was all his idea, actually—to swap clothes with my brother. He falsified the death record, and we buried Adam under my headstone."

"Thus avoiding marriage to an old lecher."

She managed a nod. Some said the truth would set you free. Feeling free would be a lovely change from this iron-heavy grief. "I took his place at school. Became my brother in every way I could."

Cal slowly chewed a bite of sausage. "And now Milton wants Adam dead before he inherits."

She shoved her plate aside, all appetite gone. "Vicar Arcott mentioned that Milton has made some poor business decisions recently. I think he needs money. Which makes sense if our theory about the insurance policy is correct."

"So darling Uncle Milton gets your inheritance and the insurance money when you die. I'd really love to punch him in the throat."

She giggled at the very Cal-like threat, then clapped a hand over her mouth. For an instant they shared a look that had nothing to do with the conversation, and everything to do with that surprisingly girlish noise.

The corners of his eyes crinkled in a familiar grin. "You laugh, but I would. I could take him."

Phee leaned back in her chair, crossing her arms. This teasing was familiar territory, easing light into the darkness that had crept in during their conversation. Tilting her head, she squinted. "I don't know. He would probably fight dirty."

Cal wiped his mouth with a serviette and rose from his seat. "I still say I could take him." He paused next to her chair and propped his rather spectacular behind on the polished table beside her elbow. Crossing his arms in a mirror of her posture, he studied her. "You're rather incredible, do you know that? Keeping a secret of this magnitude for this long is impressive. And the solutions you devised are rather clever as well."

Her blush burned her skin as it crept from her chest to her face. The curse of being a redhead. "You mean my pizzle pocket."

"Your—" He couldn't finish the words before dissolving into laughter. Finally, he wheezed, "Is that what you call it?"

Straightening, Phee asked rather indignantly, "How else am I supposed to piss standing up?"

Cal covered his face with his hands as a snort escaped. After a moment, he smoothed his hair off his face and threaded his fingers together behind his head, still chuckling. Goodness, he was made entirely of long lines and trim muscles. Kingston hadn't confined Cal's hair to an orderly queue this morning. Probably because it was still damp from bathing. She liked it this way—loose and a bit wild, hanging past his shoulders. The strands caught the light streaming through the window, giving him a glow she should be used to by now. But no, there was still a funny flip in her stomach at the sight he made.

The spicy scent of him teased her nose, and a craving

for gingerbread hit her with a fierceness that made her mouth water.

"I still can't believe you call it a pizzle pocket. But I'm glad I found it that night. Even if it has made you distracting as hell." His grin flashed, then faded, as if he couldn't tear his gaze from her face. "It made me pay attention to all the things I missed before now."

Phee fidgeted in her seat under the frank appraisal, rolling a fork between her fingers to watch the tines flash in the morning sun streaming through the window. "People see what you tell them to see."

"Yes, they do. I'm sorry I didn't see you earlier, Phee."

Hearing her name on his lips brought her head up. Like it had last night, the world around them narrowed to only the two of them. The sound of his breath, slow and measured, filled the space between them.

One would think his eyes, being such a dark brown, would be just that—brown. But there were flecks of gold and green in there too. Like the rest of him, unable to be simple or monochromatic. There were always more layers to Cal. More color. More insight. More intelligence behind the humor.

It was hard not to fall face-first into the temptation he offered. Friendship, trust, the promise of kisses. An ally. Heady stuff. "I have a hard time believing everything you said last night. Fully, I mean," she said.

Slowly, as if approaching an animal who would shy, he brought a finger to her bottom lip as he had the night before, barely grazing her skin. "Your secret is safe. I won't tell anyone else. But I don't know how I've spent two years looking at these extravagant lips of yours without wanting to kiss them."

If he were a spider, this would be his web, and she would be caught. Nervous, Phee licked her lips and accidentally caught the tip of his finger with her tongue. His breath stopped altogether, and the blacks of his eyes flared. Cal held her gaze as he spread the moisture over her bottom lip, then brought that same finger to his mouth. Phee forgot to breathe as he sucked the very tip of his finger, then straightened.

His voice rumbled, rough and uneven. "I need to make a few calls. Promise me you won't run away today. Please?"

A jumble of desire and confusion stole her ability to speak, so she nodded, then stared at his back as he left the room.

He'd called her Phee.

There was no way he could ride in this condition. A cock-stand and a saddle seemed like an unwise combination. Cal managed to make it out of the breakfast room before he drew a full breath.

Holy hell, if this was what having Ophelia—Phee—under his roof would be like, he'd strain a groin muscle within a week. Leaning against the wall, Cal folded his hands in front of the bulge in his breeches and closed his eyes.

Think of Prinny naked on a frigid day. His stomach gave a roll. *Count kittens. Something.* He imagined a basket with a lid, and fluffy kittens climbing out of the basket one by one. Twitching whiskers, baring wicked-sharp claws, and swishing puffy tails.

It took seven kittens for his breeches problem to sort itself.

It said something about the current condition of his life that finding out one of his best friends was actually a woman wasn't the most complicated situation on his plate today. Miss Violet Cuthbert must be dealt with, and frankly, he dreaded addressing that whole mess. Given this newfound—he glanced at his deflating placket—attraction to the friend formerly known as Adam, entering into any kind of agreement with Miss Cuthbert was out of the question. And the sooner he informed Miss Cuthbert of that, the better.

There must be a way to work around his father; he just needed to find it. Cal ran a hand through his hair. Hell and blast, he hadn't secured it off his face yet. Patting his pockets, he finally found a slip of ribbon and tied his hair at the nape. There. Presentable enough to break an engagement he'd never agreed to in the first place.

The baron and his daughter lived in a newer townhome in Portman Square. A perfectly respectable address, with a grim-faced butler and slightly worn-looking maids that scurried out of his way as he entered the drawing room.

The room's décor reflected the height of the Egyptian craze from a few years earlier, complete with strange animal-print patterns and a sarcophagus in the corner. Bringing a sarcophagus into style was something he'd never understood. It would be like drinking tea and eating biscuits off the top of Granddad's tomb. Why anyone thought that was a good idea was beyond him. Maybe it made him a snob, but there was such a thing as trying too hard to be fashionable.

Miss Cuthbert appeared at odds with her environment. She sat on a settee covered in faux—God, he hoped it was faux—zebra print with legs painted to look like gilded paws. *Why not hooves?* She seemed like your average debutante, like any other you'd see in Almack's on a Wednesday night. Blond ringlets, a sheer fichu to lend modesty to her day gown—because a true lady allowed the good bits out only after dark.

Phee didn't seem to have much in the way of those bits, and it was hard to not compare the two women. Miss Cuthbert rose when he entered, and blushed prettily when he bowed over her hand—those well-covered but still obvious bits on display when she dipped her curtsy.

Ophelia had never curtsied that he'd seen, and she said words like *cock* and laughed without restraint. Miss Cuthbert, for all her English-rose charms, held no interest for him.

"Would you care for some tea, milord? I saw clouds in the distance and fear it may rain. I always find a warm beverage staves off the incoming damp."

No, Miss Cuthbert would probably die before saying *cock* or whittling a wooden penis for herself. In fact, she'd probably marry exactly whom her father told her to. Unlike Phee, who'd upended her life in her fight for some semblance of freedom.

His mind wandered back to his house. What was Phee up to? Had she gone to the library to find work to do? After all, she'd promised not to run. And decade-long masquerade aside, Cal trusted her to keep her word.

"Tea?" Miss Cuthbert asked again, pulling him from his thoughts.

"No thank you, Miss Cuthbert. I don't plan to stay long. And frankly, I abhor tea. Terribly un-British of me, I know."

"What prompts your visit today, milord?"

Jumping right into it, then. "Are you aware of the bet our fathers made?"

For the first time since he arrived, he detected a crack in her polish. She twisted her lips and inhaled with a rather dramatic flare of the nostrils. "Yes. I'm aware."

"Miss Cuthbert, I'll be blunt. I'm not going to marry you, and frankly, I think my father is grossly irresponsible for making such a wager in the first place."

She sagged like a rag doll. "Oh, thank God." Pretense and social niceties disappeared. "So what do we do? Our fathers are set on this plan of theirs, in case you hadn't noticed."

"I've refused entry to Eastly for the last week and ignored his messages, but he has trouble hearing the word *no*. Avoiding him until he goes away has never been an effective long-term plan."

She rose to pace the length of the room, which left him standing until she chose to sit again. Occasionally holding his gaze with a direct stare, she apparently expected him to think of something brilliant to save them from marriage to one another. Shifting from one foot to the other, he placed his hands behind his back as she paced.

"What do you think will pacify the baron? If we can make him happy, we might find a solution."

"He wants me married. I love my father, but he's a bit of a

social climber. He wants a title for me. Securing an earl was quite the feat, and he's been crowing about it for days. Already calls me Countess in private, if you can believe it."

Not if Cal had anything to say about it. "And what do you want?"

She paused and stared blankly for a moment. "No one has ever asked me that. It sounds silly, and it might be a schoolgirl fantasy, but I want to feel that instant spark when I meet my husband. No offense intended, but I don't feel that spark of interest for you." She looked him up and down, then shrugged one shoulder. "In the end, I'll do my duty. I know not to push Father too far. You're handsome, so things could be worse. But if I chose for myself? I want starlight and poetry, and a fever in my veins."

God help him. A week ago, he'd have said that sounded like a condition best treated by a medical professional. But when a simple breakfast with a friend gave him a cockstand, it would be hypocritical to scoff at her rhapsodizing. "You want a love match."

"Not that it matters. I know my role. I'll marry whom my father dictates. You're in a position to change Father's mind, not I."

What a muddle. Two grown adults pacifying two mule-headed old men, with the livelihood of everyone who depended on him on the line. "If we can find you a husband—a titled husband you care for—will that satisfy the baron? If we meet Rosehurst's end goal and I have a hand in it, would he accept that, do you think?"

She flounced onto the zebra sofa, her gown settling around her once more in a flutter of muslin. "I think so. I'll give you all the credit in the role of matchmaker. But whoever he is, he has to be titled to satisfy Father."

"And recite poetry," he teased with a smile, taking a seat.

With a hesitant nod, she agreed. "It would be better if he wrote his own verse, but I'll accept a man who quotes Byron. You don't quote Byron, do you?"

"Not a word. Sorry." He wasn't sorry.

The most efficient way to matchmake would be to gather several potential suitors in one place. Miss Cuthbert must have been making the rounds of Season events, but if she hadn't felt that spark with anyone, she might need extended exposure to form an attachment. A house party, perhaps? The idea caused the familiar stir of excitement he felt when he found the solution to a problem.

A house party meant Phee would be out of Town and far from her murderous uncle, which would mean everyone could breathe easier. It would also get Emma away from Roxbury for a few weeks, since the rat clearly wasn't honoring their agreement. Perhaps Emma would find a match for herself while he found an appropriate husband for his not-exactly fiancée.

Rising once more, this time with an exit in mind, he made a bow and said, "I'll be in touch within a couple days. But I'm thinking a house party full of eligible bachelors might be in order."

With a pert smile, she offered her hand for a kiss, and he played the part.

Her hand smelled of rose water, which made his nose itch. Sandalwood might have ruined rose water for him forever.

A sneeze escaped as soon as the Cuthberts' butler closed

the door behind him. Maybe it was the rose water. Then again, it could have been dust from the sarcophagus in the corner. Was the décor more *en vogue* if the dead guy was still inside? Had he just sneezed dead-man dust?

He didn't want to know.

Chapter Twelve

Charles, the footman, accompanied Phee to visit her old employer, the secondhand-clothes seller. As they rode through the streets in a hired hack, she flinched at every unexpected noise. By the time they arrived at the clothing stall, her hands were clammy and sweat pooled along her spine. She glanced at Charles. "I'm jumping at shadows. This entire business is unnerving. Thank you for being here."

"Anyone would be nervous, Mr. Hardwick. There's no harm in being careful," he said.

She forced herself to leave the hack and pretend that she wasn't as twitchy as a horse ready to bolt. Straightening her shoulders, Phee surveyed the crowded street to get her bearings. Milton had made her cower in the past. Giving him that power in the present was unconscionable. It wouldn't help anyone if she took unneeded risks, though, so Charles monitored the entrance to the stall while she made her purchases.

The stall provided enough of the wardrobe basics to get her through. Even though she knew she'd gotten a fair price, her gut twisted as each coin left her palm. There were a few lovely pieces in the bundle under her arm. If nothing else, the alterations would keep her occupied.

Back in her room, Jenny the maid cleaned out the grate in the fireplace, sweeping the ashes into a bucket. "Good morning, Mr. Hardwick. I'll finish in two shakes of a lamb's tail. Lady Emma didn't want to be disturbed, but perhaps she will let me in once I'm done here."

Glancing at the clock on the mantel, Phee frowned at the late hour. "When does Lady Emma usually rise for the day?"

"Oh, she's been up. Ate breakfast and so on, but she's resting now. Her maid asked that no one disturb the poor thing," Jenny chattered. "We're worried about her downstairs. She's been spending more days than usual in her room with headaches. The rigorous schedule of a Season might be too much for her delicate constitution."

"I'm sorry to hear that." Being an employee in the house meant the servants spoke freely in front of her. At times like this, it meant Phee heard information Cal might not. A warning instinct buzzed at her nape. Since when did Emma have a delicate constitution? Clearly, Cal wasn't aware of these headaches, otherwise he'd be hovering over his sister and not flirting with Phee in the breakfast room.

After setting the bundle of clothing on the bench at the foot of her bed, Phee left the room. A simple inquiry to another maid in the hall led her to the correct door. Emma's lady's maid answered her knock.

Phee donned an innocent smile. "I've been asked to fetch gloves for Lady Emma."

If Emma was within, Phee would claim she'd misunderstood her task, then bid the maid good day. But within moments, she stood in the hallway, holding a pair of kidskin gloves trimmed with a row of fine silver and mother-of-pearl buttons.

Emma wasn't inside the room. She'd sneaked out, lied to the staff, and left her maid at home to cover for her. No doubt this wasn't the first time either, if the servants had noticed a pattern. Slapping the gloves against her thigh, Phee returned to her room. She tossed the gloves on a small table by the door, then opened the curtains to let the light in.

Emma's determined focus on misbehavior would worry anyone. Why wouldn't the girl see sense? Everyone knew Roxbury's reputation. Cal was throwing everything he had toward ensuring the success of his sister's debut. A million girls in this country would kill to have the opportunities Emma took for granted. That silly chit threw it all away.

But then, Cal might have stumbled upon this information himself if not for Phee's circumstances distracting him. Lord, what a muddle.

Pulling the first waistcoat from the bundle of clothes, she sank into the chair, opened the sewing kit, and got to work while her brain spun.

The changes of the last few days were happening so fast, it made her feel as if she were continually catching her breath.

The threat of Uncle Milton had Phee twitching at shadows and on edge.

Cal suddenly knew her secrets, and she wasn't used to *anyone* knowing her business. Damn the man. After over a decade of successfully pretending to be Adam, a wooden dick had felled her charade. Dicks ruined everything.

Even Nelson's new position in the house made her wary. What if he found proof of her secret like Cal had? Nelson's job meant spying for them and passing along Milton's plans for her. But what if Milton got to Nelson too? It might not be hard to flip a turncoat for the other side. Nelson was a good kid; she firmly believed that. But he'd already participated in the wrong plans once, so it would be unwise to trust blindly. With loyalty for sale, there was no guarantee Cal offered the highest price. Nelson was their closest tie to information on Milton's next move. Cal was her closest tie to Nelson, thanks to his decision to employ the lad.

The small metal scissors slipped, cutting into the precious brocade silk instead of snipping the fine thread of the seam. She sighed, then set aside the waistcoat before she could damage it further. Altering clothing required meticulous attention to detail. An endeavor that required her full focus. Something she lacked as her brain skittered from thought to thought.

Usually, when she needed a soothing, repetitive motion, she whittled. As hobbies went, it was a far cry from embroidery and watercolors, but useful if one's life revolved around impersonating a man. The number of wooden cocks she'd made over the years was rather impressive. Oil, then wax sealed the wood when she finished, but even with that, a wooden pizzle didn't have a long life.

They tended to absorb odors. Nasty things, but a necessary evil. When she made a new one, the old made excellent kindling.

It took only a quick trip down the stairs to ask for the supplies needed. She could have pulled the cord in her room and summoned someone, but having servants at her beck and call felt strange. Higgins provided a scrap piece of wood and a penknife, and Phee retreated once more to her room.

The repetitive motion of blade against wood, the sound of the knife cutting through the grain soothed her. Yes, this was what she needed. Her shoulders eased, and she settled into a familiar rhythm, leaving her thoughts to mull over the matters at hand. Perhaps today it wouldn't be a pizzle. Being in hiding meant no social obligations, which meant she wouldn't need to use the pizzle she still had.

The knife dug into the wood, cutting its way into a new pattern. She could make anything she wanted for once. Maybe she'd carve a bird, with wings open, flying free.

With their spy in place, it stood to reason that remaining within Cal's house would be safest, but part of her wanted to fly like the bird she would coax from this wood. Maybe she'd go to the Outer Hebrides. Or Kent. Kent might be a better idea.

Lord Amesbury would take her on as an employee at his estate. She didn't know a damn thing about sheep or hops or crafting ale, but she could learn. Ethan and Lottie would assist if she asked. All she had to do was knock on their door.

But she'd promised Cal she wouldn't run away today. Honoring the spirit of their agreement would mean waiting to take action until he came home. Although waiting didn't come easy to her. Allowing anyone a voice in her plans was such a foreign concept, it left her feeling adrift, with no idea of what came next.

She'd chosen to trust Cal, and trust him she would. But if need be, she could still run.

Some promises must be broken—especially when it came to her safety. The emergency exit plan to speak to Ethan about a position in Kent or simply head for the coast was tucked like an ace up her sleeve. As long as an escape plan existed, she could wait.

For now.

In her hands, the bird took shape, channeling her nerves into something useful. Phee held it out in front of her, examining it from different angles. The details would take time, but creating something different with her hands was a unique challenge.

The clock chimed, indicating it was nearly the hour to change into evening clothes—not that she could, since she wore the only clothing that fit—when the sound of Cal's door closing filtered down the hall to her room. She'd see him at dinner in a while. The last time they'd discussed schedules, he had mentioned a rout Emma wanted to attend this evening.

The wood and penknife in her hand weren't enough to distract her for long. After all, the latest misadventures of Emma weren't something she could keep to herself. Not for another minute. Emma may not be her problem, but Cal's sense of responsibility regarding his sister went deep.

Without further thought, Phee darted across the hall and opened his door.

The wrong door, it turned out. This wasn't Cal's dressing room but his bedroom. During their morning meetings in his room, he'd always been at least partially covered by the time she arrived. This? His arse was a thing of beauty. She sagged against the door on knees gone wobbly, closing herself into the room while Cal wiped a soapy sponge across his chest, then dipped it into a small basin of water. A squeak escaped—a reaction to seeing him in the altogether or a polite alert to her presence, she'd never know.

The dips on the sides of his tight bum were absolutely enthralling. Her arse didn't look like that.

Phee didn't know where to look first. Every fevered imagining she'd indulged in while alone, in which she'd ruminated on her friend's extraordinary beauty, hadn't come close to reality. Before now she'd thought she possessed a pretty lively imagination. Lordy, had she been wrong.

He looked over his shoulder, eyes widening, then shuttered whatever emotion might have been there. Instead, he grinned as if he stood nude in front of her every day. "Here to wash my back, Phee?"

"I'm sorry. I didn't knock. Um, I'll turn around. Or return later." She started to do that and even had her hand on the doorknob, when the sound of splashing stopped her.

"No need. You're here now. Hand me that banyan, will you?" Cal stepped from the basin and bent over to towel his legs. Sweet lord above. His movements were without modesty or self-consciousness, and she couldn't stare hard enough. Everything was on display. Every. Thing.

Covering him might constitute a crime, but she needed to do it if her pulse had any hope of calming. A velvet brocade banyan was draped over the end of the bed, within reach, so she held it out.

"I'm sorry. I heard you come home, and didn't think." She couldn't take her eyes off him as he walked toward her. Everywhere she looked there were sleek muscles and graceful lines, the likes of which she'd seen only on marble statues. Cal moved as if he knew what every muscle was doing at any given second and had complete control of his body. Goodness, to have that kind of inherent grace.

Offering the dressing gown with one hand, she covered her eyes with the other. Shutting her eyes seemed to be the best way to avoid temptation, but it only narrowed her senses to the steady cadence of his breath and the warm spicy scent coming off all that bare skin. Perhaps it was his soap that reminded her of gingerbread, and not a cologne.

With him invading almost every sense, nearly two years of ruthless self-control unraveled like a runaway spool of thread. In a moment he'd dress, covering all that perfection, and that would be a damn shame. Biting her lip, Phee threw modesty to the wind and peeked through her fingers.

Even though he took the gown, Cal held it to his side instead of covering himself. He angled his head with the same smile he'd given her this morning. "You're staring, Ophelia."

Caught. She dropped her hand. "I'm trying not to. But it's quite hard."

With a raised brow he glanced down. "Not yet, but it'll get there if you keep looking at me like that."

Well, now she had to look. Her eyes widened, and Cal laughed, but there was a tinge to it she couldn't identify.

"You'll look at me naked but wouldn't let me kiss you last

night." He shrugged into the dressing gown, leaving the sash loose at his sides.

"I was sure you'd regret kissing me once you thought it over the next day," she confessed, a bit breathless.

"Well, it's now the next day, and I'm standing here with the beginnings of a cockstand from looking at you and seeing how you look at me. What does that tell you?"

She gathered what little composure remained. "I should leave you to bathe, and you can come to my room when you're dressed again."

Cal took a step closer. "Are you scared?"

His comment hit the nail on the head, but she shook her head. The brow he arched told her he didn't believe her any more than she did.

Of course she was scared. The heat suffusing her bones was testimony enough to the danger Cal posed to her control.

What would happen when he realized there wasn't much beneath the facade of Adam? When he peeled off her cravat and waistcoat and saw for himself that she didn't know how to act like the society ladies he was used to? She didn't walk, talk, or think with genteel sensibilities.

There was so much more to consider here than a mere kiss.

If she gave in to this attraction, it would only complicate things. Not only their friendship within these walls but how they acted when out in society. That was a massive risk for Cal. And what about her job? If their friendship changed to romance, she couldn't imagine a man would be thrilled with the idea of his lover sprinting down dark lanes, digging out secrets in alleyways, and shepherding her flock of pint-sized informants.

But she ached for him. After two years of denying her feelings, the opportunity to let them out now felt freeing— allowing them to fly like the bird she'd carved today.

A heavy heat settled low in her belly, enticing her to give in and taste what he offered.

Even if it was only once. Even once was a risk, though.

"What if someone sees us kissing? Everyone thinks I'm a man. Have you thought about that?"

"We'll be careful outside the house. My servants are well paid and loyal."

"It's still a risk," she said, but the protest sounded thin as her body swayed closer.

"What if I dared you to kiss me?" he teased.

She'd wanted him forever, and here he was daring her— practically begging her—to take a risk on them. How was anyone supposed to resist that?

"You're right. I want you, and it scares the devil out of me." One step forward brought his erection against her belly and made his breath hiss between his teeth.

"I dare you to do it anyway."

"I'll take that dare."

Kissing him turned out to be as natural as breathing. As simple as meeting him halfway, because he reached for her too. The taste of him rolled through her, coffee and brandy.

Cal filled her senses with the heady scents of yuletide sweets, wrapping around her as effectively as the drape of velvet covering his skin. She swept her hands up his neck to pluck the ribbon from his queue so his hair fell around them like a soft curtain. If she was going to indulge in this fantasy she'd played out so often in her mind, she wanted everything. Hair down, bare skin, and Cal quivering under her fingertips.

He groaned into her mouth, a desperate sound that released a flood between her thighs and made her rub shamelessly against the hard ridge between them.

"Sweet Jesus, Phee," he gasped before she wrapped his hair in a fist and pulled him closer. They could talk later. For once, she had no desire to hear his commentary. At the base of her spine, one of his hands clutched her jacket, tugging until she shrugged out of it.

Everywhere she touched she encountered the bare skin of her fantasies, and it was absolutely glorious. His jaw scratched at her palm with prickly evening whiskers until even the nerves of her finger pads were more alive than they'd ever been. No wonder people liked kissing so much. This was amazing. Why did people *stop* kissing if it felt like this?

When his hands rounded over her bottom and lifted her body higher against him, she gasped "Yes" before wrapping her legs around his hips. Tongues tangled and teeth scraped tender flesh, until the only thing her body knew was him and this overwhelming need they'd created.

This kiss twisted their relationship into something new. Every touch they'd shared, every joke and conversation they'd held through facial expressions alone over the course of their friendship—everything came together. She *knew* him, and now she knew his taste. It sank into her pores as his tongue licked into her mouth, and it still wasn't enough.

The carved wooden post of his bed pressed against her back, pinning Phee between the unyielding frame and

Cal. His large hands palmed her hips, tightening her legs around his waist, until she clung to him as desperately as he clung to her. One of his hands pushed under her shirt, and when he encountered the linen binding her breasts, he growled.

Sliding down his body to stand on shaky legs, she whipped the shirt over her head. With an intense focus, he brushed a hand over the linen strips, looking for the end. For a moment, the idea of him seeing her bare breasts sent a spike of worry through her. There wasn't much there, but that had always worked in her favor until this exact moment.

Worrying was nonsense. No, she wasn't built for curves. But—she reached down and wrapped a hand around his cock—Cal didn't appear to mind. He gulped as if swallowing his own breath, then covered her hand with his, moving them together along his length while his other hand tugged at her binding.

"Later, when I'm thinking about this and get hard all over again, it's going to be remembering how amazing your hand feels that will make me come." His voice was as ragged as his breathing, and it sent a rush of power through her.

Holding him like this made everything between her legs ache. This had escalated so far beyond a kiss, but she was having a difficult time regretting that right now. He pulsed in her hand as they stroked together.

The size of him, the steely hardness covered in silky skin, was nothing like the wood imitations she'd created over the years. "You know what I'm realizing?"

"I don't know, but you have my full and undivided attention," he said, groaning on a shuddery sigh when her palm caressed the plump head, then slid down to the tawny curls at the base of his sex.

"I don't want this to be a onetime kiss."

"Thank fucking God for that."

She giggled and he swallowed the sound with a kiss.

"Pardon, milord." The bedroom door closed, and they froze, then looked toward the empty doorway.

Panting, Phee asked, "Was that Kingston?"

Cal eased away enough to give her room to bend down and grab her shirt off the floor, but once the shirt was in place, he ran a hand down her arm and held her hand. Lordy, he looked delicious, all tumbled and flushed and breathing as if he'd run a race.

But his valet had proved all her fears to be valid.

"I told you I'd handle it, and I will. I promise. Trust me, Phee."

She knew her eyes were huge, but it was hard not to worry. "You're nearly naked, and he thinks I'm a man. Except he saw my bindings, so he might think I'm a woman. I don't know which is worse." She pressed a hand against her belly to quell the rolling sensation there.

Cal shook his head. "Even if the staff thinks—" Some of her panic must have shown in her face, because he finished with a simple "I'll deal with it." He cradled her jaw and kissed her again, slowly, as if savoring her. "Because I plan to spend a lot of time kissing you, Ophelia Hardwick."

A tap against the door made Cal mutter an expletive as he dropped a kiss on the top of her head. He cinched the tie of his banyan closed, and she darted for the door to his dressing room. In the doorway, she glanced back, and he threw her a wink.

Fine, she'd trust him. As she slipped out into the hall, she heard Cal speaking to Kingston.

Once in her room, she collapsed against the door with jelly knees while her heart thundered in her ears. Lordy.

"I don't think we're just friends anymore."

Chapter Thirteen

❧

*H*aving Phee at his breakfast table might be the best part of his day. Even when he'd thought of her as Adam, there'd been a satisfaction in feeding his friend. Today's bit of primal gloating had nothing to do with charity and everything to do with having the woman who dominated his thoughts under his roof. Not in his bed—although after last night, he had high hopes—but in his home. Available to talk to, accessible enough to barge into his room at all hours.

Unfortunately, she wasn't the only one who barged into his room. The conversation with Kingston had centered around discretion and privacy. It had been more difficult than expected to protect Phee's secret. Kingston thought she was a man, which meant everything now depended on his valet having the character to keep his mouth shut about the Earl of Carlyle's sexual proclivities. If word got out, this was something that could destroy Cal—and by extension,

Emma—more effectively than anything his father had ever done.

Yet he couldn't regret the risk as she sat drinking coffee with adorably blurry eyes, blinking her way into facing the day. The breakfast room doors were closed, and they were alone. So with ears alert for the sound of footsteps in the hall, Cal stopped beside her chair and quickly kissed the spot of skin between her linen cravat and the red curls behind her ear. A shiver rippled over her and he nearly smiled.

Except something wasn't right. He sniffed the side of her neck, this time without romantic intent. "You smell wrong. And you're wearing the same clothes. Again." He reared back, questioning with a tilt of his head.

She shrugged, taking another sip of coffee. "The thieves stole my scent. Until I can get everything altered, these are my only clothes. The maids have been wonderful about laundering them, though. Your staff is exceptional."

Cal slumped into the seat beside her. Here he was worrying about reputations and lusting after her, while Phee wore the same clothes each day because she had *nothing* and her life was in danger. "Well, damn. I should have realized. How can I help?"

The gold slivers in her blue eyes were particularly bright in the morning, especially when she smiled at self-absorbed earls. "I'm fine for now. It might be a few days until I get everything altered, but I should have some pieces finished by tonight. I didn't buy evening clothes, so it's a blessing my social calendar is nonexistent."

Cal shifted in his seat, then rose to peruse the offerings

on the sideboard. "About that. You need evening clothes. I have to throw a house party at Lakeview. It gets us away from your uncle, and I have one more debutante to marry off, thanks to my father. Miss Cuthbert needs a husband."

A pause. "Why is Violet Cuthbert still your problem?"

He winced and added another slice of bacon to his plate, then resumed his seat. "It's just the latest in a long line of Eastly's problems I have to fix. I'll handle it, I promise." He picked up her hand and kissed the top of her fingers, then released her so they could eat.

"That's the second time you've said that in less than twelve hours."

A dull thud started at his temple. "Miss Cuthbert and I agree that our fathers' bet was a terrible idea. So I'll find her another husband. Easy solution."

She rolled her eyes and shook her head. "Do you have a list of potential bachelors?"

There was his practical friend. "Yes. I'm also hoping one of them will turn Emma's head. Marry off both debutantes, hide you from your murderous uncle, and we can all live happily ever after. Our life sounds like a stage farce." Cal tried to grab an abandoned piece of bacon from her plate, but she swatted at his fingers testily.

"And I need an evening coat for this?" She knit her brows in skepticism.

"Unless you want to confess to everyone that you're a woman, yes. But in that event, you'll need a gown. You would look lovely in green or copper."

Phee rubbed a palm over her face. "Fine. I'll find

something." She grimaced and said, "Damn, I forgot. I meant to tell you yesterday. I have more Emma news."

Alarms went off in his head, and he suddenly wished he could retreat to bed for a day or two. Preferably with Phee. "What's she done now?"

"She's been sneaking out during the day. I can't be sure she's meeting Roxbury, but it makes sense. I found out yesterday. I'm sorry, I meant to say something but then got distracted, and—"

Cal groaned and tilted back in his chair to stare at the swirls in the ceiling plaster. "The women in my life are destroying my sanity. One by one, you ladies will be the death of me." He shot her a glance, but she ignored his theatrics.

Midchew, she paused and looked at him. "What? I hope you weren't anticipating sympathy. I'm waiting for you to finish whining. Drink another cup of coffee. Everything looks better after coffee."

Given her need to stay out of sight, Phee had plenty of time to assemble a guest list, send invitations, and coordinate with the staff in place at Lakeview. At least it gave her something to do besides sew and stew over the situation with Miss Cuthbert.

Fortunately, an invitation from Lord Calvin Carlyle was a rare and precious commodity, and this one coincided with the highest temperatures of summer. No one in their right mind wanted to stay in the stench of London during the hot months, but with Parliament still in session and not likely to break anytime soon, people were jumping at any excuse to escape to the country. Even for an event that was essentially a game where the grand prize happened to be a pair of blond debutantes with questionable taste in men.

She remembered feeling an affinity for Miss Cuthbert at Vauxhall. But the way Calvin's father and hers had winked and nudged their way through the introductions, fully expecting Cal to fall at the little blonde's feet, sparked useless flames of jealousy now.

Phee shrugged off the unpleasant feeling. Cal had promised he had it handled, and she believed him. The jealousy was one more indication that it was too late to keep her heart from getting deeply involved in this budding romance between Cal and herself. She didn't know what to do about that. Before now, they'd been close friends. Hell, he was her best friend. It stood to reason that if their feelings turned romantic, they wouldn't be lukewarm. Their newfound attraction for one another seemed as deep as their friendly affection had been. Unfortunately, that meant there was more at stake if everything went sideways. She'd lose a friend and a potential lover—and just when she was getting used to the idea of wanting a lover.

Two years of daydreaming about Cal was one thing. Getting pulled into empty rooms and kissed senseless by the man was another beast altogether. He showed affection unreservedly, but each time he kissed her, she worried they'd be caught. She worried that her feelings were barreling past friendship and into love.

They'd shared countless stolen kisses and frantic touches.

The taste of him and the sound of his voice, rough with desire, had been imprinted in her mind forever. But for every stolen moment, there was an interruption or an obligation pulling him away. While she was stuck hiding in this posh town house, Emma's social schedule whirled on, and Cal needed to be there for it. Given Emma's recent choices, Cal was on high alert.

Not that it would make much difference in the end. Emma would make whatever bullheaded and ill-advised decisions she wanted, with little regard for anyone else.

Every day, worry lines dug their way around Cal's mouth. It was hard not to feel guilty when fear for her safety because of Milton only added to his burden. Yet the opportunities to remove some of that load were few and far between.

Two nights ago, Cal had fallen asleep beside her in bed. She'd been a heavy sleeper all her life, and now she cursed that fact. Even the presence of a man in her bed wasn't enough to wake her. So they'd slept.

When she awoke cradled against his shoulder—his bare, warm, smooth shoulder—disorientation made her jerk before her brain caught up with the situation. Kingston's knock at the door interrupted Cal reaching for her. The valet hadn't looked at her when he reported that there'd been an attempted break-in overnight. The kitchen door had sustained damage, and the servants were all aflutter.

Cal didn't visit her last night. However, Kingston sent Jenny the maid to her room this morning with a freshly starched cravat. Phee took that as a sign that the valet would keep what he'd seen to himself. She ran a finger over the smooth linen around her throat. The man worked miracles with cloth and starch.

A knock on the library door interrupted her musings. "Enter."

Nelson slipped into the room. He held out a slip of paper. "A message arrived for you, Mr. Hardwick. One of the neighborhood kids dropped it off. I told them you weren't here but I'd pass it along if I found out where you were."

Phee took the paper and read the uneven pencil scrawl. *No boat news.* "Thank you, Nelson." The lad lingered instead of leaving, so she cocked her head. "Is there anything else?"

"Is his lordship here?"

"No. Would you like me to relay a message?"

"I'm not sure." Nelson seemed quite young as he twitched in his livery and ran a nervous hand through his hair.

Phee set aside the note. "Nelson, does this have anything to do with my uncle? Do you have information to share?"

His shoulders slumped on an exhale, and he nodded. "The break-in the other night? That was a test run. I didn't know about it, or I'd have said something, I swear. The boys are comin' back tonight. They have orders— ugly ones. Your uncle wants to collect on that insurance something fierce, Mr. Hardwick. They know Lord Carlyle is hiding you. I'm supposed to let them in the servants' entrance and clear a path to your room. I don't know what to do."

Icy dread settled in Phee's belly. Of course Milton realized she was here. With the right ears listening on the right corners, he'd know Adam Hardwick to be a particular friend of Lord Calvin Carlyle, in addition to an employee of the house. The dirty paper on the desk with news of the *Wilhelmina* was proof that several people in London knew where to reach Adam.

"Thank you for telling me." The thud of her heartbeat pulsed in her ears, but remembering one thing calmed her: Calvin's resources outmatched Milton's, no matter how much her uncle had stolen from her inheritance. "Tonight, you say?"

Nelson nodded. "Midnight."

"When Lord Carlyle gets home, let's determine a plan. Thank you for warning me. You just saved my life." She offered her hand. Nelson's was warm and clammy. Phee smiled, trying to reassure him without words that he'd done the right thing. "We will talk soon. Until then, resume your duties."

A half hour later, Cal strolled in from his ride with Ethan. When he entered the library, she looked up from her work in time to see his face light as he caught sight of her at her desk. Try as she might, the greeting she offered didn't feel true. The smile slipped from his face, and those grooves around his mouth deepened. "What's wrong?"

"Nelson was here. Milton ordered an attack for tonight. The orders are to bring them to my room. At least they're planning to kill me themselves and don't expect Nelson to do it." She bit the sentences off, knowing with each statement she snatched away the fragile feeling of safety they'd been enjoying. It pained her to watch the happy glow seep out of him. As if she'd personally stolen his joy.

"You need to leave for Lakeview," he said. "They can't hurt you if you're not here."

"And abandon you to deal with them? What if you're injured instead?" Milton was ruthless and proving to be more so with every piece of news they received.

Cal gently cupped her face. She liked it when he did that, when he showed her with his body that she was his sole focus in that moment—nothing else mattered but them. The chocolate depths of his eyes, rimmed by inky lashes, anchored her, replacing the twist of emotions hammering inside her chest with a calm that grew with every breath. "I could not live with myself if they hurt you again. Not when I knew the attack was coming. Please, Ophelia." He placed a tender kiss at the corner of her eye, then her cheekbone, then the corner of her mouth. "Think of it as traveling ahead to finalize house-party details."

"It's two weeks early."

"Then I'll follow in a day or so, and we will have two blessed weeks alone. Just the two of us, endless acres of wood paths to wander, and so many rooms to steal kisses in, your head will spin. And if I'm lucky, a very large bed you'll consider letting me into."

Phee arched a brow but turned to kiss his palm. "Fine, I'll go. You should talk to Nelson. I think he needs some reassurance. I'll be upstairs packing. Oh, and this arrived." She slid the slip of paper across the desk to him. "The *Wilhelmina* remains a mystery. No new information from Frankie. I can go poke around before I leave for Lakeview. One more trip to the waterfront won't hurt. Frankie and the kids might not be talking to the right people, so who knows—"

Cal interrupted her with a hard kiss. "The *Wilhelmina* isn't as important as your safety."

Phee grumbled, "I'd rather feel useful than hide. But I suppose you're right. I'll go pack."

"I'll join you as soon as I've spoken with Nelson."

In her room, she gathered her meager wardrobe, then folded everything neatly on the bed with her sewing kit atop the pile.

The maid arrived with a small traveling trunk for her things. "His lordship sent this up. Said you're leaving us today, Mr. Hardwick?"

"Yes, for a little while. Thank you, Jenny."

Phee sank to the edge of the mattress. Fretting over Milton was useless, so she'd worry about Lakeview instead. She was flexible like that. Phee chuckled to herself at the dark humor.

The picture Cal had painted of their next two weeks at his country house sounded idyllic. They'd have so much more privacy. Fewer interruptions. Less need to hide, with an entire estate to wander, far from prying eyes. While she was eager to take their kisses further, doubt slithered in, marring the anticipation.

Being Adam had become comfortable, and leaving that behind, even in private with only Cal, was a big step. She stood and tried to view herself with fresh eyes in the tall oval looking glass.

It had been years since she'd seen herself like this— all at once in a mirror, instead of the reflection of a shop window. Phee canted her head. Did she even look like Adam? He might have filled out. Men often did as they aged. Perhaps by now, they wouldn't have been so alike.

In fact, she'd been terrified of getting older. The boys at school spoke of girls getting breasts, as if their chests had magically appeared one day. She'd checked each morning, in case a bosom had attached itself to her while she slept, thus destroying her disguise. Breasts never came, and eventually she stopped waiting for them. Her body was her body, and there was no changing it. The idea of sharing it, though, gave her mixed emotions. Sex with Cal? Yes, please. Cal seeing her naked? Nerve-racking.

With the practice of someone who'd moved far too many times in her adult life, Phee packed her few possessions into the trunk with efficient movements, securing her sewing kit inside a satin pocket in the lining, along with the miniature of her parents. Against the dark-brown leather of the luggage, her hands were pale, scarred, and calloused. Beneath her male clothing, her muscles had lines and dips, honed by hours of fencing and living a life of work instead of leisure. She'd used those muscles this morning in a match with Cal—which he'd nearly won, because she got distracted by the clear desire on his face while they fenced. How remarkable that crossing swords with her seemed to make him want her more.

No, she might not be a fainting violet, but her body served her well.

Violet. Phee scrunched her face. Jealousy did her no favors.

There were more important things to worry about. She snapped the latch of the trunk closed with more force than needed.

Cal had asked her to trust him to deal with Violet Cuthbert, and it certainly hadn't been *Violet's* bed he'd slept in the other night, or *Violet's* bed he'd share at Lakeview. Now that he'd brought that up, the thought wouldn't leave her head. Not that she minded. Imagining them in bed was a pleasant thing to obsess over, especially given the other options.

But so much of it was beyond her control. Letting Cal swoop in and save the day felt odd, and hiding inside this house instead of earning her keep felt even odder. Her hands clenched and released at her sides, over and over, so she sat beside the window with her bird carving. The details were coming together now, and gouging out grooves of feathers gave her hands something to do.

"You really do have the strangest hobbies." Cal's voice came from the doorway. Phee glanced up with a smile.

"What are you making?" He pushed off the doorway and closed the door behind him.

"I thought I'd try something different." She held up the piece, with its open wings and sturdy little wood body. "Is everything settled with Nelson?" With the tip of her blade she followed a line down the wood, then tilted her head, examining it from the side.

"It's beautiful. Why a bird?"

Phee shrugged a bit sheepishly. "Because I wanted to fly away."

Cal reached out, and she handed the piece to him. Tracing the detailed wings, he said, "What about now? Do you still want to fly away?"

"Sometimes. Less so in the last few days. Don't take it personally. I've been running a lot longer than I've been staying with you."

"Or kissing me." He said it casually, but she heard the underlying question as he returned the carving.

Phee nodded. "Kissing you changed things, yes. And if we share a bed at Lakeview, it will change things even more. We should probably talk about what comes next."

Cal squatted in front of her chair and ran his long-fingered hands over her thighs in a casual caress that sent her blood humming. "I want a relationship, Phee. I hope you do too. You're right. We should talk."

She set aside the penknife and bird, then tucked an escaped piece of hair behind his ear. "How is this going to work, Cal? I've been to too many events as Adam to suddenly don a dress and fool everyone. And I can't live openly as a woman until the end of the year—assuming I live that long. We'd be sneaking around for months if we take this beyond Lakeview."

"You've been by my side nearly every day for two years. We're friends, and I hope lovers. Let's deal with issues as they come, working together like we always have."

She kissed the corner of his mouth, where late-day bristles were rough under her lips. "Together, then. In every way. But it will be my first time, and I expect us to take measures to avoid pregnancy. I'm already on the run from a murderous uncle—we don't need to add an unexpected baby and turn all this into a melodrama."

He settled on his heels but kept his hands on her thighs. "With half siblings scattered throughout the country, and probably the Continent, I have always worried about pregnancy. So I appreciate you wanting to take measures."

She bit her lip, and his gaze focused on her mouth. Talking

about being in bed with him had her ready to strip down and dive under the covers. "I wish I wasn't leaving. I wish we could climb in that bed over there and stay for days. I missed you last night." She caressed the skin above his cravat and felt his rough swallow under her touch.

"We hadn't spoken about sharing a bed, and when Kingston woke us, I realized I might have overstepped. And trust me, Phee, I wish you weren't going anywhere." Although his expression was hot, his hand was gentle as he traced a line from her cheekbone down to her mouth.

She blinked slowly, clearing some of the scrambling effect that look had on her. "Unless you hid everything from me, you haven't taken a lover in a while. Why me? Why us?"

The look he gave her would have melted her petticoats had she been wearing any. As it was, her skin tingled within her breeches. "Because it's you. Because you're in my blood, and I don't ever want you to leave. And because for the first time, I see my future sitting right in front of me." He leaned back with a comical wince. "But there's something we have to fix first." Reaching into his pocket, Cal withdrew a small bottle.

The sound she made was somewhere between a coo and a gasp at the sight of the familiar label. The small bottle of sandalwood scent was an expense she'd agonized over until finally justifying it as a onetime indulgence. Phee turned her chin to the side so he could dab a little behind her ears. "Thank you. It's a rather masculine scent, but I love it."

Cal nuzzled her neck. "Masculine, feminine—doesn't

matter. It's your scent. And that's the important thing." He sighed against her skin. "Now you smell right."

"Come to my bed at Lakeview," she breathed as he nibbled a line along her jaw.

"The second I arrive. I promise. But first we need to get you out of here and safe."

Chapter Fourteen

*L*akeview was a full day's travel from London, but the
day was nearly over. Phee and his servants would overnight at an inn along the way, then arrive the next day. Cal
watched the traveling coach rumble down the street from his
library window.

She'd asked the question that lingered in his mind as
well. What kind of future did they have? Sure, they might
continue as they'd began, once they'd dealt with the threat
of her uncle. They could be "bachelor friends" who lived
together as companions. They certainly wouldn't be alone in
that designation.

Kingston, thus far, had kept mute on the subject, but
eventually another servant would find them embracing. Or
they'd come across proof that Adam Hardwick was not what
he seemed. No matter how much he paid his staff or how
loyal they were, keeping Phee's secret would be like holding

water in their hands—eventually, something would leak out and make a mess.

All that assumed there would be a future. That Milton would be in custody or otherwise neutralized and she'd be safe. Everything else remained uncertain. Any version of a future between them came with questions. Big questions.

But he wanted her. Amidst all that unknown, that was something Cal knew down to his bones. Their turn toward romance deviated from every norm and broke every rule of proper discourse.

And he didn't give a damn.

He, the one who spent so much of his time handling the scandals of others, minimizing the damage, was barreling forward with Phee, heedless of how things might look to outsiders.

This could easily explode in his face.

Higgins cleared his throat from the doorway. "Milord, the Marquess of Eastly is asking to see you."

Cal didn't turn from the window, although her carriage was long gone. He'd been staring into the distance, mooning like a green lad, and hadn't noticed his father's coach arrive.

"I'm not at home to my father at the moment. Thank you, Higgins."

"Very good, milord."

The door closed, leaving Cal alone once more. Hell and blast. The weight of his father's expectations squeezed another bit of happiness from him.

With a deliberate exhale, he released the worry and his shoulders relaxed. In the end, it wouldn't matter. Miss

Cuthbert wasn't going to marry him, and they'd already devised a plan to work around their fathers.

This ridiculous situation with Miss Cuthbert nagged at him, and he knew it bothered Phee. He'd asked her to trust him. Things were well in hand. He would juggle this, like a dozen scandals and irresponsible bets made by his father before. Phee had bigger things to worry about than Eastly's poor judgment. Like staying alive.

There were still unwanted visitors to deal with later that night, and he'd need help. With Father's carriage at the front of the house, evasive maneuvers were called for. Cal darted across the hall, used a servants' passage to get to the rear of the house, then took the narrow staircase down to the kitchen. A friendly wave to Cook, then he slipped out the kitchen to the garden. Cal's staff had installed a thick iron lock, glistening shiny and solid against the newly scarred wood door. A gate led to the lane between his house and Ethan's, where another similar gate opened to his friend's property.

Sure, they could involve Bow Street. But that would mean an official inquiry, interviews with Phee—which he didn't think she'd want to give—and more time than he had available. Besides, authorities were a bit of an overkill when you had a best friend conveniently built like a bull.

This wouldn't be the first time he and Amesbury had taken care of things their way.

Slipping into the Amesbury home was essentially the same process as getting out of his, but in reverse. A cheeky wave and blown kiss toward their cook—which earned him an apricot tart straight from the oven—and then a maid told him the couple were in their library. Out in the hall, Cal stomped his boots to echo off the marble tile, pasted on a smile, and called out, "Incoming visitor! Cover your bits!"

Thankfully, the lovebirds appeared to be enjoying a rare moment of leaving their clothes in place. At least, he thought so until he saw the book in Lottie's hand.

"Your book is upside down, Lottie. Hate to interrupt your wedded bliss, but I have a situation."

"We've missed you at breakfast these last few days," she said, casually turning the novel in her hands over.

"Sorry, I've been eating with Adam." The name felt wrong on his tongue, but there was no helping it. "There's been another threat, so he's gone to Lakeview early. My spy made himself useful today. He says they'll attack at midnight. Ethan, I need your help."

Over the next hour they concocted a plan. Direct, to the point. Nelson would let the men in, thus securing the foot-man's position in the crew as an inside man. The rest of the staff would have strict orders to stay in their rooms, no matter what they heard. The last thing Cal needed was injured innocent bystanders if things went sideways. Milton's hired crew would have a clear path to Phee's room, where Ethan and Cal would be waiting.

From there, it would take weapons, brute strength, surprise, and a prayer that luck would be on their side. Whatever happened, Cal would do anything necessary to secure Phee's safety.

That night, as Ethan and Cal lay in wait, a tap on the door made them tense. Nelson slipped into the unlit room. "Stand down, milords. They sent a boy with a message. One of the lads watching the house saw Mr. Hardwick's travel carriage. The crew knows he ain't here, but they lost his route once he passed Hyde Park."

Beside Cal, Ethan sagged against the wall. "Damn. No fight tonight, then, aye?"

"No, milord," Nelson said.

Which meant the threat remained. Cal relaxed his fists and sighed. He hadn't realized how much he'd looked forward to sending a message to Milton tonight. They could contact the man directly—if they could find him—but that would mean surrendering the element of surprise. Surprise might be their only true advantage, Ethan's brute size notwithstanding.

"Thank you, Nelson. You've done well," Cal said.

Ethan clapped a hand on his shoulder, then left the room, moving on silent feet through the dark.

Returning to his own room held little appeal, so Cal settled into Phee's bed. The linens smelled like her. Wrapping himself in her scent was the next best thing to having her there. Sleep would be elusive, but he had to believe the outriders would protect her.

The carriage rolled to a stop at the front entrance of Lakeview, a relatively new Georgian house surrounded by rolling lawns ending along the shore of the requisite lake. Lush woodlands encircled the entire estate. The house party would be lovely.

"Hobby, please drive around to the servants' entrance. Thank you!" she called to the coachman. The stones of the driveway crunched under the wheels as they bypassed the impressive arched front doors and made their way around the side of the house to a less ornate portal.

Cal would have a fit if he knew she made a habit of using the servants' entrance. But unlike Cal, Phee couldn't ignore her status as a nobody. Besides, she wasn't here as a guest. Officially, she'd arrived early to oversee the house-party plans, but the staff wouldn't take well to her meddling in a situation they had well in hand.

Phee grabbed her small traveling trunk, donned her new hat, and rang the side bell.

A handsome footman opened the door, holding an apple and chewing a giant bite. Wordlessly, he stepped aside and gestured for her to enter with a jerk of his head. Quite the different greeting on this side of the house.

Mrs. Hodges, a cheerfully efficient woman Cal claimed managed the house with the force of a velvet-covered hammer, met Phee in the kitchen. "Well, you're just a scrap of a thing, aren't you?" she said. "Let's get you something to eat before you settle into your room. I can't imagine you ate anything decent on the road."

Actually, the breakfast at the inn that morning had been fantastic. Nevertheless, at the offer of food, her stomach growled, letting loose a gurgle at least three other people in the room heard, judging by their smirks. "That would be welcome, thank you."

A short time later, Mrs. Hodges led her down the hall, the keys of her chatelaine clinking with each step.

"His lordship sent instructions. This will be your room." She opened a door.

Phee's eyes went wide, taking in everything. "This is beautiful," she said. An understatement. Light-green toile wallpaper acted as a backdrop to the finely carved furniture. A mint-green velvet canopy covered the bed and contrasted with the crisp white linen counterpane. The idea of keeping anything larger than a cravat white made her shudder. A vase of fresh flowers sat beside the bed, and another graced the small table next to a delicate chair near the fireplace. It was by far the loveliest room she'd ever seen, and she was terrified to touch anything for fear of smudging, breaking, or otherwise marring the perfection of it all.

Mrs. Hodges rocked on her heels with a satisfied smile. "Isn't it, though? You're the first to stay in it since Lord Carlyle has owned the property. You must be a close friend to warrant a room in the family wing." She shot Phee a speculative look.

"I will thank his lordship for the great honor." What else should she say? Cal, being Cal, wanted to be kind but hadn't considered how it would look belowstairs. It was the footmen-in-full-livery-in-Shoreditch situation all over again.

"Well," Mrs. Hodges said. "Get yourself settled. When you're ready, ask someone to bring you to the yellow drawing room. I'll meet you there to go over details about this house party."

"Thank you, Mrs. Hodges."

The door closed behind the housekeeper, and Phee let the trunk fall with a thud. A door on the wall stood open to a separate dressing room complete with delicate furniture painted white with gilded details. This was a lady's room. A pair of armoires stood ready to hold luxurious gowns, silky petticoats, and satin slippers. With a slightly manic giggle, Phee dragged her tiny traveling trunk into the dressing room and plopped it unceremoniously on the floor.

"Utterly ridiculous," she muttered.

Unpacking would take all of three minutes, so she'd do it later. Instead, she washed with clean water from the ceramic pitcher on the washstand and dabbed on the sandalwood scent Cal had given her. Every time she held the tiny bottle, it made her smile.

As expected, the staff helped her find the yellow drawing room. Mrs. Hodges had the situation under control and only needed Phee to add insight as to the specific people invited and pass along snippets of gossip that might be helpful in accommodating their distinct personalities and needs. Mrs. Hodges made notes in a small diary in her lap.

"I know it's a lot of extra people underfoot, but his lordship tried to keep the guest list small," Phee said.

"We've handled worse under shorter notice. Thank you, Mr. Hardwick. I notice one couple missing from the list. Viscount and Viscountess Amesbury. Are we expecting them?"

"Alas, no. Duties at Woodrest keep them from joining us. They asked me to send their regards to you and the staff."

"They're kind to think of us. Now, would you prefer to dine at country hours or London hours this evening?"

The housekeeper meant well, but she'd shoved food at

Chapter Fifteen

The carriage containing Cal's trunks and Kingston was far behind him, but Cal had been too eager to keep pace with it. Last night he'd dozed long enough to greet the dawn, then set out for Lakeview. Murphy, his gray gelding, lived for long distances and had been more than happy to travel beyond the well-manicured parks near Mayfair.

He and Phee would have two weeks to themselves before Emma arrived—weeks in which his sister would be living in their father's household, much to her dismay. Asking the marquess to be responsible for anyone other than himself might be begging for trouble, but the man *was* their father. Expecting him to parent his own child shouldn't be out of the question. Eastly now knew about the need to keep Emma from Roxbury, but only with broad strokes of information. No father wanted to hear about his daughter bumping fun bits with inappropriate men.

Eastly had tried to steer the conversation to Rosehurst and his daughter, but Cal held firm with the initial delay tactic of waiting on the *Wilhelmina*.

If he could have outridden his worries, he'd have spurred Murphy until his hooves left the ground altogether and they flew over the packed dirt. As it was, Cal rode ahead with one thought in mind—Phee.

Now he stood in the doorway to her chambers, unable to tear his gaze from the sight of her. Never in his wildest dreams did he expect to find her waiting in bed for him. At rest, her face relaxed, making her sharp features appear softer. Bedding piled around her, framing the creamy pale expanse of skin with its enticing freckles peeking through the wide, open neck of the thin lawn shirt that had slipped off a shoulder and clung to the tip of one breast. She looked like a pixie resting amidst clouds.

Cal wiped a palm over his face and blew out a breath. Dear Lord, she had freckles all over her chest. Like little sweet spices scattered across a feast, and he was ravenous.

He possessed enough presence of mind to turn the key in the lock on her door before shrugging out of his coat and unwinding the cravat from his throat. The carpet swallowed the sound of his steps.

Sitting on the edge of the mattress, he pulled his boots off. The shifting of the bed under his weight didn't stir her at all, but she let out a tiny snore that made him smile.

When she asked him to come to her bed as soon as he arrived, he hadn't expected that promise to be quite so literal.

In her place, he'd love for her to wake him with kisses. Crawling on all fours across the covers, he stretched out beside her. He trailed his mouth over her shoulder, inhaling her familiar warm sandalwood scent. With sweeping fingers, he tugged the hem of the shirt up until an adorable freckle at her waist shaped like Scotland caught his attention. It needed a kiss.

Any second now she'd come awake, sleepy and smiling. His cock hung heavy in his breeches, and he could hardly wait for her to come apart in his arms. Logically, it hadn't been long enough since he'd held Phee to feel this desperately starved for her, but it took a massive effort to restrain himself from falling upon her like some kind of slavering beast.

Dragging his lips up her belly, he pushed the shirt over the ridges of her ribs. God, she was perfect. Small breasts with dusky nipples and cinnamon freckle sprinkles. Desire coiled like a spring, prepared to release as soon as she was ready. Sucking one nipple, he closed his eyes.

Utter bliss. If her skin was this soft on her breasts, he could only imagine the velvet perfection she hid between her thighs. Damn, he'd missed her.

The punch didn't register right away. First, his eyeball rolled back in its socket. Then the pain and pressure battled for dominance in response to the single hit Phee landed to his face.

Howling in pain, he rolled off her, clutching his face. "Shit, Ophelia!"

Phee jerked to sitting, instantly awake. Horror dawned on her face. "Oh God, did I hit you?"

Cal paused midwhimper to stare out of the eye that didn't feel like a throbbing mass of ouch. "You didn't mean to?"

"No, of course not. It must have been a reflex. Let me see." She peeled one of his hands off his face and winced. "On second thought, cover that." She gently replaced his hand and patted it for good measure. "We need to get a steak on your eye."

"Just give me a minute. That's quite the right hook you have." Cal blinked experimentally before deciding he wouldn't be doing that again anytime soon. Damn, his face hurt. "I thought we were in agreement, but if you've changed your mind and don't want me in your bed, I'll respect that."

"I want you here. But maybe don't try to wake me up like that until I'm used to sharing a bed with you, all right?"

Cal winced. "Fair. That's fair. I'm sorry. I didn't think." Even her lightest touch on his cheekbone made his breath hiss. "You should have joined me at Gentleman Jackson's."

She shrugged, seemingly unconcerned that her shirt hung off one shoulder, nearly putting that delicious breast on display. The sight was almost enough to distract him from the pain in his face. Almost. "Sometimes the fights are bare-chested, otherwise I'd have been right there beside you."

Someday this would be a funny story. They'd laugh about it and joke about how he should have known better than to sneak up on a scrapper like Phee. He shot her a one-eyed leer. "You're right. You'd cause a riot. I'm certainly enjoying the view, love."

Not even trying to hide how he stared, Cal held out a hand toward her. Without hesitation, Phee twined her fingers with his, giving him a crooked smile.

"We both know there isn't much to see here. Prinny has a better set of breasts than I do."

"I beg to differ. My face aches like a son of a bitch, but I'm still hard as a pike looking at you, and you aren't even naked. All I see are freckles I want to trace with my tongue. Nipples I need to suck until you moan—preferably without you blackening my other eye, thank you. You're perfect."

Phee cocked her head. "Are you trying to start something again, milord?"

Tugging her hand closer to where he sprawled, Cal grinned, ignoring the throb of his face. "Miss Hardwick, I think it's safe to say I'll always be starting something with you."

"But what about your eye?" It was a half-hearted protest at best, as she left her puddle of blankets to kneel beside him. Holy hell, she wasn't wearing anything but the shirt.

"I can see fine out of one eye. Come here and let me taste you. Please."

She laid a gentle kiss on his aching cheek, then rested on her heels. He swept a palm from her hip, then under her shirt to cup one breast. Even though she arched into his touch, Phee shook her head.

"You're incorrigible. That eye needs attention far more than your cock does." With a teasing wink, she straddled his waist and ran a hand over his chest. "Let's get you taken care of. We have all the time in the world for the rest." Phee wiggled against the tent in his breeches, apparently just for the fun of torturing him, then crawled off the end of the bed.

Indulging in an unobstructed view of her miles of leg and flashes of a pert behind, Cal groaned. Sure, this encounter hadn't gone the way he'd imagined. At. All. But goodness, she was all limbs. Soon enough, those legs would wrap around him, and the wait would be worth it.

Predictably, the cook fussed and made tutting noises over Cal, with enough sideways glances toward Phee that she suspected his explanation of "a friendly bout of boxing gone awry" would entertain everyone belowstairs.

She hadn't meant to hit him. In fact, she didn't have a memory of doing so. After thinking over little else all day, she'd deduced that after years of being on guard, her body defended first and would ask questions later. Cal had successfully joined her in her room in London, but he had done nothing other than sleep next to her. It would take time to adjust to having a man touching her.

And she wanted him to touch her.

The sun was gone by the time a knock at the door sounded. A shiver of excitement rippled under her skin, leaving a tingle in its wake and a grin on her face. Waiting had been nerve-racking. Now that he was here, trepidation vanished and anticipation filled her. She clambered out of bed and opened the door.

Cal stood, tall and handsome as ever, but for a black eye. He'd stripped to breeches, a shirt, and boots, with his hair hanging free. Holding out two towels and his banyan, he said, "Want to go on an adventure?"

Phee leaned against the doorframe. "Am I going to get naked during this adventure?"

"God, I hope so." His lopsided grin sent butterflies loose in her belly. "Put this on. Let's go."

Lifting the wide collar of the robe to her nose, she breathed deep. It smelled like him and made her wonder if any part of him would taste like gingerbread.

"This way." He took her hand and led with confident steps through the quiet corridor, down a dark staircase, and through a door into the night.

They'd walked for several minutes through inky darkness when a subtle flash of light winked between the trees. As they stepped through the line of elms, the light flashed again as the moon overhead shone on the lake. Cal set the towels on a rock and began tugging off his boots.

"You swim, right?" he asked.

A glance over her shoulder showed the lake, placid and waiting, reflecting moonlight. "I haven't in years."

Her meaning didn't take long to sink in. He slumped over. "Hell and blast, of course, you'd avoid lakes and such after what happened. I'm sorry."

She touched his shoulder gently to stop his self-flagellation. The silvery light off the water held her attention. "Just give me a minute."

This was the closest she'd been to any body of water besides the Thames since the accident. Since she lived in London, the river was nigh unavoidable, so she'd gotten used to it. Besides, the stench of the Thames, with its floating layer of disgusting debris from humanity, was a far cry from this serene scene. This resembled the pond in Northumberland.

The pond had been the place where her entire plan had

been born. The one she'd clung to for years meant boarding a great ship and crossing an ocean, bound for a new life. She and Adam had created that plan, and it had always felt imperative to see it through for him. If she didn't get over this aversion to water, the crossing to America or the Continent would be utter hell. But given the new relationship with Cal, would she even get that far? She might never have to face the Atlantic, and frankly, she didn't know how to feel about that. With him sitting so close, that sea voyage seemed further away than ever. A problem for another day.

Phee cleared her throat. "I can manage a swim. If you'd wanted to row out there, it would be a different story. No small boats. Not after Adam." Not after she'd pushed him and sent him toppling. Phee shoved the thought down. "The water looks inviting. Let's do it."

Cal studied her but didn't move otherwise. "You're sure?"

She nodded, toeing off her shoes.

"If that's the case, then strip." With a wink, he pulled off his shirt, letting it billow onto the ground, then stood and unbuttoned his breeches.

Not to be outdone, Phee dredged up her earlier excitement and bravado from this afternoon, when she'd thought nothing of sitting in front of him nearly undressed. That bold, confident version of herself was someone she longed to be all the time. So she let the banyan join his clothes on the ground and fingered the hem of her nightshirt as she stared at him.

Lordy, his kind of beauty shouldn't be available to mere mortals. Yet he stood, immobile, looking at her too. Really looking. Not glancing over to give his usual flippant comment, then going about his merry way. No, Cal's gaze was nothing short of hot. Hungry enough to light an answering fire within her.

Phee quirked a smile. The lake water would probably sizzle when it hit their skin from the heat of his expression alone. "No one's ever looked at me like you are right now."

"Then they've never really seen you. If you're more comfortable with the shirt, then leave it on. Once it gets wet, it will be sheer anyway," he teased, holding out a hand.

Phee inched the hem higher on her legs, enjoying how his gaze focused on each new inch of skin. There was nowhere she'd rather be, and no one else she'd choose to share this night with. It might take time to get comfortable being naked with him, but even as Cal stood before her so confidently, he didn't push beyond what she wanted to give. With a deep breath, she drew the shirt over her head and let it fall to the ground.

Cool water lapped at his ankles, the silty bottom squishing beneath his toes as he led her into the lake. Every time he came home to Lakeview, he swam. It had become his private ritual over the years, and bringing Phee along tonight felt right. They stopped when the water reached her breasts, and the rhythmic waves against her body entranced him. He wanted to kiss right there, where the water made her skin wet and shiny like a pearl.

"Did you swim here as a boy?" she asked, distracting him from the sight she made.

"No." He shook his head. "I won Lakeview in a game of cards during my misspent youth. Maybe that's why it's my favorite property. Father has never visited, and Mother was already dead."

"So it's unentailed and entirely yours. From everything you've said about your childhood, I can see why you wouldn't want those memories here."

Cal glanced toward the trees and the house well beyond them. "This place doesn't have those ghosts. It's peaceful." He gestured toward an inlet partially hidden behind a willow at the water's edge. "Want to swim? I'll race you."

The strokes came as second nature, and soon he whipped through the water with ease, Phee keeping pace beside him. Putting on a burst of speed, she shot forward, showing that same competitive spirit she brought to their fencing matches.

Soon she pulled ahead. An arm's length. A torso ahead now. She was quick, cutting through the water with those long limbs.

The edge of the lake drew closer with each breath, each stroke. Out of the corner of his eye, the willow tree appeared, trailing its branches over the water. He reached out a hand and caught her calf and yanked.

Phee surfaced, sputtering and swearing. "Damned dirty cheat!"

His laugh echoed off the lake until her hands slapped his chest, then rested against him. "Cheat? Never. We're behind the willow. You won."

Wicking water drops from her eyes, Phee looked back. The line of her neck enchanted him as thoroughly as the feel of her waist under his hand. Wet, naked skin pressed against him, and he didn't care one whit who'd won the race.

"You admit defeat?"

"I do. You swim like a fish." He panted, slightly out of breath. A pleasant burning in his lungs let him know the exercise had been welcome. Like a congratulatory handshake to his muscles for a job well done.

"Are you actually a selkie?" He skimmed his fingers along her spine. The soft lake bottom touched his feet as she bobbed off to find her footing, taking her heat with her. A protest died on his tongue when she backed toward shore, baring more of her body as she moved. With every step, the water level slid lower along her skin.

The tops of her breasts shone wet under the moon. Then nipples. Then her ribs. Then an adorable dip of a belly button. She stared at him, then at his waist, and raised a brow in challenge. The minx knew exactly what she did to him. Cal watched her with a predatory focus as goose bumps raised along her skin.

"Don't selkies lure men to their deaths?"

He grinned, and she responded by flashing her own white teeth in the moonlight. "That might be a siren you're thinking of. Either way, the thought applies. Wet and naked is an excellent look for you, Miss Hardwick."

Phee flicked drops of water from her eyes. Short curls stuck up from her head like twisted hedgehog quills, and he wanted to sink his fingers into them while he devoured every inch of her.

"Either you're deluded, or you're trying to seduce me." She threw a flirtatious look over her shoulder as she inched closer to shore. The waves lapped under the curve of her bottom now. With deliberate casualness, she stretched her arms overhead, and he couldn't wait anymore.

Water splashed around his legs as he joined her in the shallows. When the heat of her finally pressed against his front, a sigh escaped them both, and she pulled his lips to her neck.

They were of one mind then, because his entire focus had narrowed to tasting her, burying himself in her until neither remembered how it felt to exist alone.

Her small breasts made him ache. They fit perfectly in his palms as he tugged her nipples between his fingers. She was warm against his lips. The fresh bite of lake water and the earthy tang of sandalwood teased his nose. "I'm a bit obsessed with your nipples."

"They're nipples. Literally every person on the planet has a pair."

"Yes, but yours are perfect." He rolled the tips between his fingers as if to punctuate the statement, and her breath shuddered. "They're darker, like your lips. Incredibly responsive." With only a fingertip, he traced a circle around each areola, and the skin puckered even more. "And when they're tight like this, they look like they're begging for attention. Begging for my hands. For my mouth." Grazing the slope of her shoulder with his lips, he slid one hand along the front of her belly toward the nest of russet curls.

Water licked along her slit in a wet little flick against his finger when he found her clitoris. She quivered, pressing tighter against the hardness of him. A low, rumbling moan worked up his throat when she pushed against his fingers, showing him with her hips exactly where she wanted his touch. Good. The best lovemaking required both people to give and take. He wanted her to show him what she needed.

"God, Phee, I've missed you." The confession tore from him, welling from deep inside, where he hadn't intended to let her go. But she'd burrowed in nonetheless, and now he didn't want her to leave. He explored her puffy, slick folds, then slid a finger into her. She whimpered and he groaned at the tight heat.

There were few things he could offer that he hadn't already shared with someone else. Except tonight. He could give her this, now, and know it would be theirs alone. "How do you feel about sex outdoors?"

She tilted her head as if thinking it over, though he suspected it was to give him better access to nibble and suck along her shoulder. Every time he did, more goose bumps rippled over her skin and he smiled. Damn, her body responded so beautifully. Inside her hot quim, he hooked his finger, pressing against the spongy area he knew would feel good. Her knees buckled, but he caught her against him.

"I can see the appeal. It's quiet." She panted between the words, then let loose a breathy moan when he added another finger to her tight passage. "Secluded. No servants about."

"I've never made love outdoors. I want to give you as many of my firsts as I can." Her hips moved in time with his fingers.

The other hand plucked her nipple, then he brushed his palm over the tender flesh, tracing his fingers over the taut skin of the prettiest breast he'd ever seen. She shivered, then groaned his name like a prayer.

Phee reached between their bodies and wrapped her fingers around him. "Now. Please, Cal. I need you."

"Thank God." He turned her around and cupped her bottom when she hopped and brought her legs around his waist. The hard line of his erection met the warm slit of her body, and he nearly spent right then. If he had to recite limericks or the lineage he'd been forced to memorize from *Debrett's Peerage*, he would—anything to make sure this wouldn't be over before it had truly begun.

Phee clung to him, pressing their slick chests together while her tongue battled his, gasping as if coming up for air after holding her breath underwater. With a roll of her hips, she settled her heated center over his cock.

The first Earl of Carlyle, Henry Battenmore, gifted the title by Queen Elizabeth on August 25, 1598…

Water splashed in cool droplets against his legs as he got them the rest of the way to shore with more speed than grace. When he laid her on the bank, Cal took a second to take in the picture she made. Long limbs, creamy skin, and that thatch of curls where she'd soaked the top of his dick a moment before.

"You're sure?" he had to ask, even as he prayed she wouldn't say no.

A disbelieving laugh shook her chest. "Calvin, get inside me." A frown cut her laughter short. "Unless *you* aren't sure. If you're having second thoughts—"

His mouth stopped the flow of words and doubt, and he let his body answer her question. Reaching down to guide himself into her inch by amazing inch, Cal held her gaze, held his breath, and tried to hold time still even as his body shook.

Bloody hell, he was having sex with Phee. God, she felt good. Slick and tight and *right*.

Resting on his elbows, he tried to hold his weight off her slender frame, but Phee was having none of it. She sank her hands into his hair and pulled him down for a kiss, then wrapped her legs around him and squeezed until he was fully inside her.

With every stroke, she welcomed him with another flood of silky wet heat, and Cal's eyes nearly rolled back in his head. Skin on skin, moans, and breathy words of encouragement echoed off the lake. Her name became a chant on his lips as they stared into each other's eyes. She tugged his head down until their foreheads touched.

"Good?" she murmured.

"Better than good." Understatement of the century, but all he could manage when his bollocks were this tight. Pressing against her nub, he rocked deep until her breathing stopped altogether for several beats. There. That was what she needed to topple over the edge before him, because damn, he couldn't wait much longer.

Her hands didn't rest, clutching the muscles of his arse with every thrust, then along his spine until they anchored again in his hair.

When she broke, she arched, squeezing his cock until he saw stars and claiming him as thoroughly as he claimed her.

"I'm too close," he managed, slipping from her body at the last minute. He trembled, then groaned when she stroked him once, twice, before he spilled on the grass.

"So that's what all the fuss is about. Sex, I mean." Warm breath fanned over his ear. He chuckled against her shoulder, then kissed it, too exhausted for more than that. She turned and he caught her smile—wide and happy and satisfied. "I'm glad it was you."

Later, after another bout of lovemaking under the stars, exploratory and by turns tender and frantic, they swam to where they'd left their clothing. And when he tugged her into his room instead of opening the door to hers, she didn't argue.

Chapter Sixteen

ardon me, milord. Lady Emma has arrived, and I'm
afraid she's in a state of distress."

Cal cracked open one lid. Kingston stood by the door,
pointedly *not* looking at the occupants of the bed. Glancing
over at Phee, Cal got an eyeful of pert breasts and creamy
skin his valet didn't have any business seeing. Throwing the
blanket to cover her, Cal rubbed his eyes.

"What time is it?"

"Three in the afternoon, milord. I brought a pot of
coffee, since I believed a restorative of some kind might be
warranted." Kingston cleared his throat delicately. "I took
the liberty of bringing more than one cup."

They'd taken a nap after a spontaneous afternoon romp
between the sheets. To be fair, he and Phee had hardly left
the room for two weeks. "Restorative before dealing with my
sister? That bad, is it?"

"She is less than happy, milord." Kingston, king of the understatement. "Shall I bring the cart in?"

"Please." Cal donned the robe draped over a chair nearby. Behind him, Phee didn't stir. That woman could sleep through anything. But he'd bet on her coming awake once she smelled coffee. The bedroom door opened, and his valet pushed a cart into the room. Coffee and small bite-sized things triggered Cal's stomach to gurgle happily in anticipation.

His valet didn't meet his gaze as he fussed with items on the cart that didn't need adjustment.

Cal lowered his voice in case Phee woke. "Kingston, I know you saw her. I have no choice but to trust in your loyalty and discretion in this matter."

Kingston straightened and finally looked him in the eye. "You can rely on me, milord. In the future, shall I bring two cups with your morning coffee tray?"

A smile kicked up one corner of Cal's mouth. "I'm sure she would appreciate that." Kingston nodded and turned but stopped when Cal said, "Kingston? By holding your tongue, you are protecting someone precious to me. And she has a damn good reason for having this secret."

Another nod, then he left. Cal poured his coffee, then another for Phee, adding cream until it turned the shade she preferred. He blew on the surface, then took a sip before carrying the cups to the bed. The room smelled like them, like warm sex and fresh coffee. If Emma wasn't waiting for him—mid-meltdown, by the sounds of it—he'd love to wake Phee in a way that would guarantee more time in bed. Over the past two weeks, he'd learned the trick to waking her without triggering a defensive panic. Once he said her name a few times—just enough to make her eyelashes flutter as she surfaced from dreams—it was safe to approach the fair maiden with the wicked right hook.

He hated to go. Guests would arrive tomorrow, and then official host duties would interrupt their current habit of whiling the days away, lost in one another, sans clothing.

She wouldn't like that his valet knew her secret, which made Cal hesitant to tell her. After all, it wasn't as if they could do anything about it. Kingston would be either honest or not. But he hadn't said anything when he'd thought she was a man, and that was rather more salacious gossip. Cal trusted him with his own secrets, but entrusting anyone with Phee's was a weightier thing. He pushed the worry aside and shelved it with everything else he couldn't do a blasted thing about.

He could, however, wake his lover with coffee and then go deal with his sister. "Phee, time to wake up."

Without opening her eyes, she scrunched her face and rolled over, stealing his pillow in the process. Unbelievably adorable. But then, nearly everything she did made him smile. Amidst the many things he juggled at the moment—his father, Emma and her Season, Miss Cuthbert, this house party—Phee was the only thing he found complete joy in.

"Fine, then I'm stealing your coffee." The threat wasn't serious, as the better part of a pot remained on the cart.

She slept on. With a shrug, Cal drained his cup, then dumped the coffee he'd poured for her into his own cup. No coffee left behind. Especially when there were sisters to deal with.

Being a gentleman, though, he moved the cart to her

side of the bed so she'd see the offering when she awoke. He dashed off a quick note—*Emma arrived. Off handling her. Please eat*—and drew a heart at the bottom on a whim, then threw on clothes and went to face his sister's histrionics.

When she awoke, it was to a pot of warm coffee and enough bite-sized nibbles to satisfy the appetite she and Cal had created before they'd passed out in postcoital bliss. A clock on the mantel chimed half past three.

With a lazy stretch, she poured herself a cup and read the note beside the coffeepot.

Damn. Emma was home.

It would take only a moment to dress. Moving to stand before the oval mirror, she donned a shirt and turned sideways to examine her reflection. The pads of her fingers slipped under the fabric and skimmed along her taut belly. Thanks to regular meals, her bones didn't jut out at each joint like they used to, and her breasts and bum had tiny curves to them. Fine. The chest curve was minuscule. More nipple than anything.

No matter her overall frame, the heart shape of her bottom was something she'd always liked. She smiled. This might be as plump as she'd ever get, but the thought didn't bother her as it once would have. For years she'd been trapped in a tug-of-war with herself—feeling grateful that she could pass as a boy, while despairing because she didn't look like the women in paintings and sculptures. She might not have honest-to-God cleavage, but her bum was rather spectacular, her legs were long, and her arms were strong.

A pair of breeches lay on the floor nearby where they'd been abandoned earlier. Those would do until it was time to change for dinner. Tying her cravat in the mirror, she smoothed the linen around her throat and slipped into her coat.

Odd that she'd stepped into her brother's shoes over a decade before, but only now did it truly feel like a costume. After a couple of weeks of being wholly herself behind closed doors, suddenly pretending to be her brother felt nearly impossible. The coat was too tight across the shoulders, the cravat made her chin itch, and she couldn't moon over her lover like a ninny when she wore these clothes. Months of maintaining the lie loomed ahead of her before—well. Who knew what would happen then. Her stomach clenched at the thought. No matter how tempting the treats on the cart, she couldn't eat a bite.

Downstairs, it was easy enough to find the siblings. One need only follow the volume of Emma's diatribe. Phee hadn't lived with them long, but she'd learned to navigate Cal's sister purely by tone of voice. Right now, Emma was irate. Past the point of reason and apparently blaming Cal for whatever had upset her.

Common sense and self-preservation urged Phee to turn around and walk the other way. When Emma used that tone, nothing good came of it. There would be flouncing, and no one would leave the conversation happy.

Phee hovered outside the drawing room, wondering if

joining them was the wisest course of action or if she should leave them to their little family drama—after all, it wasn't her place to intrude. Yet it felt more and more like her place was next to Cal.

The door flew open and Emma burst through—red-faced, tears streaming down her cheeks, with one hand clamped over her mouth. Phee stepped aside, providing clear passage for the dramatic exit. The girl didn't get far before she lurched to a stop and grabbed a ceramic vase from a table. The perfectly formed conical shape echoed the sound of her retching, magnifying the noise in a way Emma would surely find mortifying when she remembered the incident.

Phee rushed forward before she thought it through, running a soothing hand over Emma's back as she was sick. "Cal! I need a drink for your sister, please."

Emma shuddered, head still over the foul vase. "I'm fine. Just travel sickness from the carriage."

The girl was awfully blasé about vomiting into a priceless piece of porcelain in the front hall.

"Maybe you should rest in your room until you feel more the thing," Cal said, approaching them with a worried frown.

Wiping her mouth with her hand, Emma nodded. A greenish cast to her usual peaches-and-cream skin lingered. "I'll do that." She set the vase aside and climbed the stairs to the family wing without looking back.

Phee and Cal both eyed the vase. She shot him a look, and he wrinkled his nose.

"I'll do it." She rolled her eyes. "When I return, perhaps you can tell me why she was so upset."

"You don't need to clean my sister's sick. You aren't a

servant." Grimacing, he held the vase out at arm's length. "Where are we taking it?"

"Rubbish pile would be best, I think. In the garden."

"As to why Emma was so distraught—she discovered Roxbury took money to stay away from her. All hell broke loose. Claims I'm ruining her life, et cetera."

"You paid off Roxbury? When did that happen?"

He shrugged. "A few weeks ago. Before Vauxhall, so we know he didn't honor his side of the agreement. The money was his idea. I didn't like it, but it seemed expedient at the time."

The idea of someone demanding money to leave a woman alone struck her as icky in every way. At least it hadn't been Cal's idea. But Lordy. "You're awful calm about Emma's fit."

"You should have seen our mother. Emma needs to step it up if she wants to impress me. Although this"—he nodded toward the vase—"was a nice touch."

An hour later, Emma bounced into the morning room, all smiles once more. Any trace of her earlier illness and the fit about Roxbury appeared to be in the past. Cal took the mercurial change in stride, but Phee couldn't help wondering at the shift. No matter how many side-eyed glances Phee gave her, the girl's cheerful demeanor stayed in place.

Maybe her sickness *had* been a lingering travel ailment.

Phee shook her head. It didn't matter. At the end of the day, Lady Emma wasn't her problem. This party wasn't her responsibility. She wasn't the mistress of Lakeview.

After selecting a book from the library, she retreated to her room. The lush chambers were familiar now. The massive bed and a charming view of the surrounding fields were designed to cradle a lady in the lap of luxury, but today it was wasted on her. No matter how hard she tried to focus on the book, her mind wandered until she finally set it aside and paced the thick carpet.

Between Emma's presence in the house and the imminent arrival of guests, Phee might be stuck in her own bed for the foreseeable future. If nothing else, she and Cal would need to be extremely circumspect. Even knowing what could happen if people thought the Earl of Carlyle and his employee were lovers, spending her nights apart from him made her want to pout and stomp her foot like a child.

And therein lay the problem. The ease with which she'd fallen into this romance should frighten her—but the fact that it didn't was a concern of its own. In no time at all, he'd moved from being an important part of her life to being the center. Which, given the way her life usually went, could lead only to disaster. Everyone important died or betrayed her. Except maybe the vicar. But that logical fact had no place in this mess of emotions.

For two blessed weeks the rest of the world, her future, Milton, everything had disappeared. Nothing else had mattered, and it had been so lovely to relax. To enjoy Cal. Now reality roared again, clanging louder after the peaceful reprieve. Everything seemed so far out of her control, and thinking of all the unknowns made panic bubble inside her as she considered her options.

Returning to London meant walking into danger. Running off to another village and changing her name meant leaving Cal. And she wasn't ready to do that. Not yet.

These weeks had been a gift. Regretting Cal would be impossible, even if it meant she walked away with a broken heart at the end of all this. And there very well could be an end, although she didn't want to think about that. Cal talked as if they would be together in the future, but how could that work?

The only sure shot at happiness within her reach would be to curl up with him in the big bed behind her and let the world disappear again. During those times she'd discovered pieces of herself she'd thought out of touch forever. The man acted like a truth serum, forcing her to be honest and wholly herself, rather than exist within her brother's persona. But honesty and vulnerability went hand in hand. Without a facade, she had nothing to hide behind.

He'd changed everything. Or perhaps he'd merely been present for the change. After all, he'd witnessed her shedding Adam's clothes and held her as she'd taken those initial steps to embrace the woman she could be. And he'd done it while making her feel safe. Safety was the ultimate luxury. Was it any wonder her heart had tumbled into his hands—whether he knew it or not? Such a quick slide it had been from friend to lover to beloved.

Staring out at the bucolic scenery, Phee waited until the unease gave way to clarity. Even if she didn't know what the future held, even if she had no right to sleep in the family wing of this grand house, she would take her happiness where she found it.

And right now, she found it with Cal.

Baron Rosehurst and Miss Cuthbert were the first guests to arrive. As soon as the baron stepped through the front doors, he craned his neck about, gawking at the soaring ceiling and grand sweeping staircase, then said in an echoing voice, "This will all be yours, Violet. Take note of the staff and household practices. It's your job to make them better."

Oh God. So that was how this was going to go. Cal's cheeks felt as immovable as steel, unable to muster a polite smile. To her credit, Miss Cuthbert closed her eyes in clear mortification before saying calmly, "Nothing is settled. Such talk is inappropriate, Father. Lord Carlyle is our host. I am merely a guest in his home." Turning to Cal, she said, "Which is lovely, milord. I apologize for my father's comments. He's tired from traveling. I have no doubt your staff are efficient and will ensure everyone's stay is comfortable."

Well, if nothing else, that pretty speech saved Miss Cuthbert from damp sheets on her bed. The baron might not be so lucky, and frankly, Cal wouldn't blame his staff one bit if they let the standards slide a bit in that bedchamber.

He returned Miss Cuthbert's efforts with a grateful smile, then offered a tight nod to her sire. "Baron Rosehurst, welcome to Lakeview. I hope you'll enjoy your *brief* stay in my home."

If he could get through this house party without strangling Rosehurst, he'd count himself—and the baron—lucky.

Over the next three hours the center hall of Lakeview became a bustling hub of barely controlled chaos with servants scurrying about and guests greeting one another. At one point a petite fluffy dog joined the fray, and for the life of him, he had no idea whom it belonged to.

He kept checking the stairs, hoping Phee would make an appearance, but it would seem Adam Hardwick intended to keep a low profile. Or she'd gone into hiding entirely. Not that he blamed her. Dealing with Rosehurst and his daughter for the next weeks wouldn't be fun for her.

If he had his way, he'd cart Phee to his room and lock the door against everyone else in this house. But if he did that, he'd never fulfill his promise to Miss Cuthbert. And then someone would have to deal with his father's harebrained bet, and he'd never marry off his headstrong sister.

Smile. Make a joke. Don't step on the yippy little dog. "Whose dog is this?" he asked the room at large. A maid stepped forward and saved the animal from getting trampled.

He still didn't know whom it belonged to.

No matter. He blew out a breath.

Only one guest hadn't arrived—the reclusive Duke of Gaffney, his best chance at a match for Miss Cuthbert. If it hadn't been for their budding business dealings and the promise of face-to-face talks, Cal never could have gotten Gaffney to Lakeview.

The soft poet heart of Lord Hornsby might appeal to Miss Cuthbert, but Gaffney's ducal coronet would satisfy the baron. Hell, it would satisfy any papa with sense.

He'd instructed his staff to seat Miss Cuthbert between the

two lords at dinner each night. With any luck, one of them would spark a mutual attraction.

Lords Warrick and Ainsley were extra insurance, in case the poet or the higher title didn't stick. Both men were in their prime, handsome, charming, intelligent, and amusing. Surely one of them would interest Miss Cuthbert. And if not her, perhaps Emma.

The hard part of planning this had been finding other women that would be enjoyable company for the party, without distracting from the appeal of his sister and Miss Cuthbert. As crass as that sounded, it served his interests to shine a light on them, and inviting competition didn't make sense. Miss Georgina Lowden and Miss Lillian Fitzwilliam fit the bill perfectly. Miss Georgina was a quiet woman who did her damnedest to blend into the wallpaper at every social occasion but came from an old family. Miss Lillian had been out for several Seasons but hadn't brought a suitor to scratch—possibly because of her social-climbing mother and a rather brusque personality.

Through the doorway, he spied a carriage with a ducal crest on the door. Meeting the duke at the top of the stairs, Cal offered a warm handshake. "Gaffney, so glad you could make it."

The newest duke in the realm shook his hand and returned the smile with one of his own. "Carlyle. Thank you for giving me a reason to avoid London for a while longer," he said, showcasing a charming dimple. Yes indeed, the ladies would love him.

"Come inside. Your room is ready, but if you choose, there's some excellent brandy in the library. I've had Cook procure some of our local hard cider with you in mind, as well. Perfect on a hot day like today."

If Miss Cuthbert didn't turn on the charm this evening at dinner, Cal might have to take drastic measures. Lock her in a closet with each eligible bachelor or something. Because come hell or high water, he would not be marrying the baron's daughter.

Chapter Seventeen

*M*iss Lillian Fitzwilliam must possess a soft spot for awkward, pasty-skinned redheads. That, or this was all a rather cruel joke. No one at the dinner table could overlook Miss Lillian's rather outrageous flirtation with Adam Hardwick. Which dashed Phee's hopes of passing the house party in relative anonymity. Everyone eyed Adam Hardwick with speculation, and she couldn't blame them.

Cal appeared to find the whole thing hilarious, and the one ray of happiness in this dinner so far had been watching him try not to choke on his wine while stifling his laughter. No doubt she'd hear about it later. Anticipation warmed her belly. Because there would be a *later*. He'd whispered a promise when they'd crossed paths before dinner, and her pinkie finger had tingled after he'd brushed it.

Thinking about the things she planned to do with Cal later that night while a woman rested her rather impressive bosom on Phee's arm felt dirty—and not in a fun way. At least

Miss Lillian was friendly. Which struck her as odd, since prior to this house party, during the few social occasions where they'd met—usually because Cal had finagled an extra invitation—Miss Lillian had seemed a trifle rude and generally not very likable.

"Tell me, Mr. Hardwick. How long have you been in London? I thought I'd met all the notable men, but I don't recall seeing you before this year." Her smile was pure coquette, and Phee had to give her credit—Miss Lillian didn't look silly with the expression. Phee would look like she suffered from bowel issues if she attempted a simper like that.

"After school, I came to London. I didn't move about in society much until Lord Carlyle hired me." Surely, the gentle reminder of Adam Hardwick's status as an employee of their host would cool the flirtatious line of questioning.

"I do love a man who is not afraid to make his own way in the world," she said. "It would have been so easy to simply be a gentleman of leisure while awaiting your inheritance, but you chose to work. To build connections and friendships with your peers and earn your living. That's admirable."

How the hell had her inheritance become a topic of discussion? On Phee's left, Miss Georgina Lowden gave her a wide-eyed look. Miss Georgina picked up her wineglass and drank with a focus that held its own commentary, as if the only way to ensure she didn't say the wrong thing was to keep her mouth busy. If Phee had any confidence that alcohol would help the situation, she'd happily join her.

"Miss Lillian, I am not sure what you've heard, but I don't feel comfortable discussing my personal finances with anyone."

Miss Lillian waved aside the objection with a flutter of her hand and a sweep of her lashes. "I apologize, Mr. Hardwick. That was poorly done of me. Mother made a dossier for all the guests, and I thought your story fascinating. I didn't mean to make you uncomfortable with my admiration." The guest placed a hand over Phee's fingers, covering the death grip Phee had on her butter knife.

Cal's eyes were suspiciously bright.

Do something. She raised an expectant brow.

He cleared his throat. "Miss Lillian, I'm sorry to see your mother absent this evening."

"Thank you for asking after her, milord. Mother doesn't travel happily, I'm afraid. It's usually a day or so before she finds her equilibrium after spending hours in a carriage."

And yet here Miss Lillian sat without a maid or chaperone. Granted, she'd been out for several years. Still. Between the lack of chaperone and her comment about having a dossier on each guest, Miss Lillian's goals were obvious. She'd set out to snag herself a husband, no matter what.

Miss Lillian's mother could probably investigate for the Home Office if she'd found information on Adam Hardwick's modest inheritance. While the money—assuming Milton hadn't gotten his hands on all of it—ensured an eventual lifetime of comfort, it would never be enough to fund a lifestyle like those enjoyed by the people at this table.

As soon as possible, Phee reclaimed her hand and the knife she needed to cut the next bite of delicious pheasant. When Miss Lillian shifted away, Phee rested that hand in her lap, thus removing the opportunity for the woman to rest her breasts on Phee's forearm again.

Lordy. It would be easier to hide upstairs and avoid the house party altogether.

Across the table, Lady Emma abruptly shoved her chair back and hurried from the room. When several moments passed and she didn't return, an instinct tingled at her nape, and Phee rose as well.

"Pardon me, Miss Lillian. Miss Georgina." Phee brought her wineglass with her as she left the table in case her hunch was correct.

Sure enough, Lady Emma had made it as far as the library doors before spilling her dinner into yet another vase of flowers. This supposed traveling sickness would be tremendously hard on the porcelain if she kept on like this, but it wouldn't be kind to see what type of excuse the girl would give this time.

Instead, Phee waited until the retching finished, then held out the glass of wine. "Here, milady. Rinse your mouth out."

Emma didn't look at her but did as instructed. Hazarding a guess, Phee murmured, "It gets better, you know. A few weeks in. For most women, anyway."

Emma's panicked look confirmed everything. "You can't tell Cal."

A heavy sigh rolled out of Phee. "Not this again." She held out a hand to ward off Emma's protestations. "You need to tell him yourself. Have you told Roxbury?"

Tears welled in Emma's eyes, and she suddenly seemed far younger than eighteen. If anyone saw Emma crying, there'd be no stopping the rumor mill. Glancing over her shoulder for witnesses, Phee pushed against the library door and hustled Emma inside. She settled the girl in a chair and handed her a handkerchief.

Instead of dabbing at her tears, Emma let them fall while she twisted the linen square around her hand until the tips of her fingers turned pink, then white. "I called on him two weeks ago. He's refused to see me since."

Phee sat, then rested her elbows on her knees. "I take it things didn't go well."

When Emma shook her head, blond ringlets bounced about her ears. Although she opened her mouth, her chin quivered too hard for words to form. Fresh tears pooled, and she gave an indelicate sniffle.

"He said I couldn't prove it's his," Lady Emma finally managed, then squeezed her eyes shut.

Phee muttered a curse.

"He said he loved me." The words wobbled with a shaky breath.

"I'm sorry." Shouting *I told you so* wouldn't be helpful and frankly would be like kicking a puppy. But damn it, Emma had been warned.

Lady Emma straightened, then scrubbed her face with the handkerchief as if she could wipe off emotions as well as tears. "May I ask, Mr. Hardwick—are all men lying bastards, or only the ones I've met?" A heavy pause fell between them.

"Honestly, I've met my fair share of bastards. But there are fine men too. Your brother is one of them."

A glimmer of a smile broke through Lady Emma's gloom.

"You're right. Cal is a good one. And you seem to be as well. Thank you for listening. And thank you for your discretion, Adam. May I call you Adam?"

Phee nodded.

"Then you shall call me Emma. Anyone who shares secrets should be on a first-name basis, don't you think?"

"Emma it is, then. Are you returning to the dining room?"

She wrinkled her nose. "Could you tell them I was overcome by the heat or something?"

Phee rose and offered her hand. "I can do that. Let's get you settled for the night, and I'll prevaricate the best I can with the guests."

In the hall they handed over the vase of flowers with apologies to a maid, then climbed the sprawling giant staircase. At Emma's door, Phee dipped her head in a bow.

"Please break the news to your brother soon."

The blond ringlets bounced again when Emma nodded, but worry burrowed a groove between her brows. "You're right. I know you're right. But at the moment, I want to sleep."

"Good night, then." If Phee didn't return to the party, Cal would worry. She trudged downstairs, her evening shoes padding on the steps. From the sounds of it, the ladies had retreated to the drawing room, which meant the men would be drinking and telling tall tales in the game room.

Phee stopped outside the door, listening for a moment to the muffled din of voices coming from the room. Assuming the persona of her brother took effort today, but she managed. Worries over Emma would have to wait. Right now, she needed to be Adam Hardwick.

It didn't used to be this hard to lie to everyone.

The role of host grated at Cal, and it was only day one of this damned party. When Phee entered the room, a ripple of awareness skittered along his spine.

The men lounged about the room with glasses of port or brandy. Some played billiards; others simply sat and smoked cigars. A cloud of smoke hovered over the room, and Cal tried not to wrinkle his nose. The carpets and drapes would need a thorough airing after this. Such a nasty habit.

In the past, he probably wouldn't have questioned the rather frank discussion going on around him. Although the men spoke of the women, there was a definite lack of commentary regarding Emma—probably out of respect for him—so for that he could be grateful.

Lord Warrick made the shape of an hourglass with his hands, then cupped imaginary breasts in front of himself, which sent the baron cackling. The cruder comments— mostly from Ainsley and Warrick—stopped when Cal said, "The more you talk about women's bits, the less convinced I am that you've ever actually seen any for yourself. A real man doesn't need to boast."

The others laughed uncomfortably but changed the topic, and that had to suffice.

Across the room, Phee shifted in her chair. How did this sound to her? And had he ever done worse in her presence?

None of these men would say such things if they knew a lady was present.

Granted, no one said anything completely reprehensible. But the drastic difference between their polished manners at the dinner table not a half hour before and the faces they showed each other in private made him wish every woman at this house party could see these men with the masks of gentility off before committing herself to marriage.

Over at the bar, Phee poured a glass of brandy, then found a seat at the edge of the room. She didn't sip at the drink but seemed content in her role of silent onlooker.

He caught her eye. In a silent conversation, she raised a brow, then looked deliberately at the door.

Yes, he'd love nothing more than to go upstairs and escape from their guests. Cal wrinkled his nose.

No, love. Can't escape.

She pouted her bottom lip, then looked away.

Lord Hornsby sat on the sofa near her, cradling a book in his lap. Occasionally a burst of laughter from the other guests would cause him to look up and offer a vague smile to the room in general before returning to the book.

Hornsby had a strong nose and decent jaw. Brows that were nearly black made a nice contrast to the light-brown hair in need of a trim. Not a bad-looking fellow at all, and he had a peaceful reserve about him. Perhaps a man like Hornsby was exactly what Emma needed—someone to act as an anchor when she flitted to the heights of fancy and emotion. The book of poetry in his hands—assuming Cal read the spine correctly from this distance—implied he might be a suitable match for Miss Cuthbert. A solid option for either lady.

Because his body seemed hyperaware of hers, Cal noticed when Phee took a sip of the brandy. Her first drink since arriving.

Warrick and Ainsley were telling tall tales to the baron,

trying to outdo one another in their blatant lies, and Cal hoped he wouldn't have to rein them in again. So far, they'd kept things respectable enough. Barely.

Ainsley said, "Hornsby, my good man. You're a handsome fellow. Surely you have your share of stories to tell us."

Hornsby gave them that slight smile again. "Hate to disappoint, but I'm not much for London. The country suits me well enough."

Hmm, if Hornsby didn't like London, he might not be ideal for Emma. Cal would point Miss Cuthbert in that direction, then. No matter. There were options aplenty.

Gaffney still seemed a solid choice for Miss Cuthbert too. Lord knew the baron would have to be content with a duke in the family, a fact that gave Cal a sure path out of this mess. Not only had all Phee's initial reports about his reputation been clean but Gaffney rose in Cal's esteem by ignoring Ainsley and Warrick altogether in favor of playing billiards.

Cal cocked his head and studied the duke as he took a draw on his snifter of brandy. Gaffney would do nicely, and facilitating a match between him and Miss Cuthbert might even solidify the budding business relationship between himself and the duke. Cal wandered over and picked up a cue. "Care for company? I've been looking forward to talking with you, your grace."

"By all means. Let's play." Gaffney waved him closer and set up the table.

Across the room, Phee set her mostly full glass on a tray and murmured something to Hornsby. She was making her escape. Meanwhile, he and the other men would join the ladies shortly, then while away the hours, pretending to be impressed by pianoforte performances or recitations of poetry.

Cal would rather sleep. Preferably with Phee beside him. He couldn't help watching her pert heart-shaped arse as she left him to deal with the social niceties.

"Do you want to go first, or shall I?" Gaffney asked, pulling him from his thoughts.

Cal drained his glass and set it aside. "Rank over beauty. You first."

The duke grinned and lined up a shot.

"Speaking of beauty, have you had a chance to talk to Miss Violet Cuthbert yet?" Cal asked, and cast one last look at the door. To think, if not for this role as host, he could leave right now and have Phee moaning within minutes.

Instead, he was playing matchmaker, holding a stick and balls.

Chapter Eighteen

*A*rchery had been a horrible idea.

"Mr. Hardwick? Show me again how to draw the bow. You're so accomplished at this." Miss Lillian's attention hadn't wavered since dinner the night before.

Phee drew a deep breath and prayed for patience, then got a lungful of the woman's lavender perfume. Many women favored lavender, but her opinion hadn't changed since childhood. It smelled like cat piss. That she managed to stop her instinctive lip curl was nearly miraculous.

"Maintain a firm wrist. Be strong through the arm and shoulder," Phee instructed, stepping away to examine her overall form.

Miss Lillian made another attempt, but she either was tremendously bad at this or was being disingenuous about the whole exercise. "Perhaps if you stand behind me and place my arms properly, I will grasp your meaning."

Sweet Lord. Phee sighed and did as requested. The

obvious ploy combined with the noxious perfume and too many nights in a row of limited sleep meant Phee's tolerance measured at an all-time low. Last night she'd bowed out early, then tossed and turned until Cal crawled into bed next to her, slightly tipsy from too many glasses of wine and brandy while talking to Gaffney about his cider operation. They'd cuddled together like a pile of puppies, wrapped in limbs and languid pillow talk in the darkness, an experience that struck her as more intimate than coming together in a passionate frenzy. That, they'd done this morning. Phee smiled at the memory.

Once Miss Lillian stood in the cradle of her arms, it was a bit startling how small she turned out to be. For such a big personality, Lillian came in an awfully tiny package. Phee towered over her by at least six inches—a detail Miss Lillian noticed and appreciated, if the coy eyelash fluttering gave any indication.

Aligning the angle of the other woman's elbow just so, Phee grasped Miss Lillian's wrist and reminded her, "Hold firm. Make your body a series of straight, strong lines."

Together they released the arrow, both holding their breath as it flew in a graceful arc to hit the straw target for the first time that afternoon.

"I hit it!" crowed Miss Lillian. "All thanks to you, Mr. Hardwick. Although I believe that's the first time a man has ever told me to make my body a straight line. Don't men like curves?"

Damn. Right when Phee was nearly enjoying the triumph of Lillian's achievement, the lady had to turn it into a flirtatious comment. Pretty words took too much effort, and she was done.

"Miss Lillian, please understand that I mean no offense. But of all the men in this house, why are you trying to charm me? There's a duke, an earl, three viscounts—several of whom I'm sure would appreciate your attention and flirt in return." Not Cal, obviously. But Lillian might have a legitimate shot at Hornsby. He'd been sneaking glances at the lady when the party decamped to the side lawn for archery.

Miss Lillian tilted her head, studying some distant point beyond the target. When she turned to Phee and spoke, some of the illusion disappeared. No more playing the coquette; she was finally without artifice.

"You seem to embrace a direct approach, so I shall answer in kind. I spoke the truth at dinner last night. Your story is fascinating. Tragic and romantic. You've made a life for yourself, which shows strength and character. Truly, Mr. Hardwick, you underestimate your appeal. You have kind eyes and a remarkable smile. Besides, without a title, your future wife is likely to never be at the center of the London Season again. I've been out for three years, and frankly, I've had enough."

Phee rocked on her heels. Blunt Lillian was far more likable. The honesty softened Phee's feelings toward the woman. Everyone deserved a chance to be happy. "Thank you for your kind words. I must tell you, though, that my affections are engaged elsewhere." When Lillian's expression fell and her cheeks laced with pink, Phee hastened to add, "However, Lord Hornsby might be worth your attention. Old family, and

I've never heard a bad word spoken about him. Last night he mentioned preferring his country estate. Persuading him to avoid London might be a simple thing."

Miss Lillian eyed the man in question several target lanes away. Phee pressed the point. "See how strong his arms are? He's a striking fellow. Say the word and I can change your seating assignment at dinner. Or you can go now and ask him for archery advice."

"But he's speaking with Lady Emma. Why would he pay attention to me instead?"

"I'll take care of Lady Emma. Would you like to talk to him?"

Miss Lillian lifted her chin, appearing to draw determination around her like a cloak. "Yes, please. I would appreciate a proper introduction to Lord Hornsby."

"In that case, come with me." Phee dared a friendly wink and offered her arm.

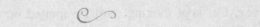

Miss Lillian appeared to be moving on from her infatuation with Adam Hardwick, thanks to some deft maneuvering by his lady. Cal eyed the pair as they began an animated discussion with Hornsby and Emma. Making it seem like the most natural thing in the world, Phee and Emma split off from the group, leaving Hornsby and Miss Lillian to the archery and their conversation.

As Phee and his sister walked off, arm in arm, they seemed at ease with one another, smiling and chatting as they wandered across the grass, greeting guests. Cal had seen his sister flirt, and Emma wasn't flirting with Phee, so at some point they must have struck up a friendship. Frankly, he didn't know what he'd do if Emma *had* been flirting. If nothing else, it would have been terribly awkward, all things considered.

Analyzing the relationship between his sister and the woman who'd invaded every area of his heart struck him as rather ridiculous. Cal grinned as he stuffed arrows into the quiver. The situation appealed to his overdeveloped sense of the absurd. Someday their children would ask how they'd met, and they'd have quite the story.

His hands froze, and he looked up, searching for Phee among the guests milling about on the lawn. That was where this was going, wasn't it? Marriage. A life together. Maybe even children. Even though he had no idea how they'd manage it, the dream of that future settled into his bones with a certainty he'd never known before. With his feelings teetering toward beautiful but scary and unfamiliar permanency, Cal kept looking until he spotted her still standing near Emma.

How the hell had she bamboozled everyone for *years*? The breeches she wore clung to slender thighs and molded around a delicious bottom designed to fit perfectly in his hands. The cut of her coat hid her upper body, but he knew her breasts were tender mouthfuls. He'd called her a selkie their first night at the lake, but he'd been wrong. She was a siren, and he was so damned lucky he'd heard her call.

She and Emma were still in conversation when he approached.

"Not him?" Phee asked.

"He seems like a lovely man. It would be awful to ruin that," Emma said.

Cal missed the context, but with his fingers twitching to touch Phee inappropriately until she melted and made that delicious purring sound... well. Explanations could wait.

"Puppy, could you come with me, please?" He held his hand out for her to take before catching himself and turning the gesture into an awkward wave, as if sweeping his arm toward the house had been his intention all along.

"Certainly. If you'll excuse us, Emma." Phee bowed slightly, then turned toward the house with him. "What's the rush?" she hissed.

"You're too delectable for words, and I need to bury myself inside you until you clamp around my cock and make me see stars. Any objections?"

"Not a one. Walk faster."

They made it as far as the side entrance of the house before the joy bubble burst. Baron Rosehurst and his daughter approached, making their first appearance of the day. It had been a relief to not have to deal with the baron over his bacon this morning. Beside him, Phee stiffened.

"Lord Carlyle, well met. Leaving the archery field so soon?" The baron's overly familiar jolliness felt forced, and Miss Cuthbert pasted on a false smile. It was obvious they'd been bickering, and Cal wanted nothing more than to leave them to it.

"Something rather pressing came up, I'm afraid. But please join the others and enjoy." Cal refused to slow and encourage conversation. "Miss Cuthbert, might I suggest asking the Duke of Gaffney for assistance with your quiver and bow?

He should join the party shortly and won't steer you wrong. You'll be trouncing the others in no time."

Once inside the house, Phee turned toward the stairs that led to their rooms, but Cal redirected her with a hand low on her back. "Too far away. Library."

The heavy oak door slammed closed like a thunderclap under the weight of their bodies crashing together. Their first kiss clashed teeth and lips, with tongues tasting gasped words of encouragement. Keeping one hand against the door, Cal used his other to fumble for the buttons on Phee's breeches.

The only thought driving him was getting inside her immediately. Desperation overrode finesse, but when he sank two fingers into the curls between her legs, the heat of her welcomed him. Pillowy lower lips wrapped around his fingers, and they moaned together.

"So wet, love," he managed to say.

"More," Phee demanded, riding his fingers.

The logistics made him swear. "This would be so much easier if you were in a gown." She froze, and he could practically hear her brain whirring. Hell and blast. First running into the baron, and now he stuck his foot in his mouth. The mood could take only so much before it broke entirely.

He rushed to reassure her. "But then I couldn't lust over these long legs and perfect arse all morning. The boots will take a bit to get off, though."

Phee latched her lips onto the side of his neck for an open-mouthed nibble that sent his knees trembling. "Easy enough to fix that," she said against his rabbiting pulse, then turned and pressed her bum against Cal's bulging placket.

Dragging her breeches down her thighs, Cal murmured, "Bless you, gorgeous woman." His buttons gave way, and within seconds their groans mingled.

With their hands against the door, they set a pace ruthless in its efficiency. Her body drenching his, Cal wished he could strip her bare to enjoy the long lines of her arching before him. The slapping sound of them coming together matched the pounding of his heartbeat. Every noise she made as she met him thrust for thrust flung them closer to a finish line they both needed.

Releasing one of her hands, he sank his fingers into her damp curls and nearly came when he felt where their bodies joined. The wet slide of him diving into those tender folds was the most erotic thing he'd ever felt. It looked even better. Intimate and slightly obscene in the most delicious way.

He circled and flicked with the pad of his finger the way she liked, painting her clitoris with the slickness they'd made. As if flying apart one layer at a time, she shuddered, peeling away artifice and manners, until all that remained was the two of them wallowing in sensation.

Tremors racked her body. Her head rested against the wood door as if it were too heavy for her neck. Breath escaped her in whimpered gasps as Cal rode out her orgasm, shaking when her body milked him with her pleasure. Burying his face in the side of her neck, he slapped a palm against the door and thrust once, then twice before following her into oblivion. With his knees locked behind hers, they stayed pressed against the oak as they regained their breath. Her body was warm and languid around his cock, and he'd never felt anything so right in his entire life.

Abruptly, she turned her head and hissed, "You're still inside me."

He kissed her cheek. "You feel amazing."

Phee wiggled away, pulling on her breeches with jerky movements. "No, you didn't pull out, and we didn't use a French letter."

Her meaning slammed into him, but instead of panic, a wave of calm washed over his heart. Which proved once and for all there weren't any lingering doubts about his feelings. He loved Phee. Strong, resilient, complicated Ophelia owned his heart, for better or for worse. Watching her grow with their child and raising a family together didn't scare him in the least.

But the timing couldn't be worse, and she'd never said a word about children except to ask him to take precautions. Which he'd failed to do. "*Fuck.*"

"Yes. That's exactly what just happened."

Shaking his head, Cal scrambled for words. "No, that was more than—well, yes, but—" And to think, he'd once thought himself smooth with women. Phee undid him on every level. He sighed and tried again. "I'm sorry. You asked that I minimize the risk of a baby, and I didn't do that. The last thing I want to do is put you in a position where you feel trapped with me."

She tilted her head and gave him a quizzical look he couldn't interpret. "You're not upset?"

"No, love. Besides, it was my fault. Whatever happens, we handle together." He smoothed the groove between her eyebrows until the lines softened.

"All right. We handle it together."

She kissed him, light but lingering, and Cal sank his fingers into her fiery puff of hair, holding her close for another moment. "I love you. Whatever happens in our future, I welcome it if you're by my side."

For the rest of his days, he would remember the smile that crept over her face. It started in her eyes before finally lifting her cheeks and curving her mouth. "I love you too. I want a future with you," she said.

They sank together against the door in a kiss. Several minutes later, she murmured, "We should return to your guests. Are you sure there isn't something I could be doing to help? It feels odd to not have a job while I'm here."

And have her tangled in the middle of all this? She had enough of her own worries. "No, love. Take this time to relax."

Putting themselves to rights took a moment or two, but in the end, they were both presentable—although the color of Phee's cheeks was like a flag declaring her freshly tumbled, and he couldn't stop smiling. As long as they didn't meet anyone in the halls on their way out of the house, they should be fine. Cal squeezed her hand, then let go as he opened the door.

Rotten luck or poor timing sent the two men on the other side of the wood tumbling into the room at that exact moment. If they hadn't been embracing, they'd been on the verge.

Ainsley and Warrick sprang apart, then froze as they took in the sight he and Phee made. Standing too close, flushed, the smell of sex in the air—it was fairly obvious these two men weren't the only ones who'd thought the library would be perfect for a tryst.

A smile spread over Lord Ainsley's face. "Sorry to intrude, gentlemen." Ainsley winked and then exchanged a grin with Warrick.

While Cal considered ways to handle this, Phee made the choice for him.

"Think nothing of it. Good day, milords," she said, neither confirming nor denying anything.

Out in the hall, Cal nodded a greeting at Miss Georgina, who chose that moment to scamper, pink-cheeked, from a drawing room three doors away.

"Think they'll say anything?" Phee whispered once Miss Georgina had disappeared down the corridor.

"Warrick and Ainsley? They were clearly planning to use the room for the same purpose. One would hope they'd provide discretion and expect it in return."

The door to the same drawing room Miss Georgina had left opened again, and Gaffney slipped out, running a hand through his hair.

Cal and Phee shared a look. "The number of eligible bachelors at this party is dwindling rapidly," she said.

Which meant his options for getting out of the mess were dwindling as well. Bloody hell.

Chapter Nineteen

Right at this moment, Cal and the Duke of Gaffney were in the library, and she hadn't been invited. Since Phee was the one who'd done the legwork to look into Gaffney's business proposal, being excluded stung. When she'd said as much, Cal had brushed a hand over her hair and said, "It's nothing personal, love. Go enjoy the day with the guests. You're here to relax, not work."

It was awfully close to patting her on the head, and she'd nearly hissed and bitten his hand like a feral cat. Her temper seemed to shorten the longer this house party lasted.

Phee stopped under the branches of a giant elm and looked out over the lawn. Guests milled about in the sun near the lakeshore. Another few hours of scheduled activities, and she should be able to escape to her room. Not that sitting held much appeal when she really needed something to *do*. Genteel relaxation didn't feel natural to her.

At least the mornings had normalcy, which made everything else a little easier. The daily fencing match with Cal was the highlight of this party as far as she was concerned. Now that she'd figured out his newest tricks, the balance of power had settled back to where it should be. Meaning she usually won. For a while there it had taken only a wink and a suggestive flick of his tongue to destroy her focus.

However, once they finished fencing, Phee had to share Cal with the rest of the guests.

The visitors at Lakeview had fallen into predictable habits of their own. The men gathered in a pack, like wolves. You rarely saw one without at least two others for company, as if they were afraid to wander alone and find themselves in the parson's snare. They weren't wrong, given the purpose of the party. The ladies spent their time in pairs or peaceful solitude.

Miss Georgina often found a corner with a book. She seemed to be a sweet enough girl, although difficult to get to know. When the other women were around, she didn't participate too much. Phee suspected she might be painfully shy.

After witnessing the young woman and the Duke of Gaffney leaving the drawing room the other day, Phee paid more attention to the pair. If Gaffney lingered nearby, Miss Georgina blushed and stammered over her words. They were adorable but nearly painful to watch with their awkwardness. Clearly something was happening there.

Phee wanted to smooth things over and spark a conversation with them so they'd relax. But every time the urge struck her, she reminded herself that she was not the hostess;

it wasn't her job to ensure everyone enjoyed their time at Lakeview.

Lord Hornsby and Miss Lillian walked side by side, elbows occasionally brushing as they meandered toward the lake. Miss Lillian's parasol hid their faces from the others who were already near the water's edge, but Phee had an unobstructed view of how close he dared lean as they conversed.

A sound to her left alerted Phee to Cal and Gaffney leaving the house, still in conversation. When Cal looked up, he waved her over, so she pushed away from the tree and wandered in that direction. Since she was still a bit sore about being left out of the meeting, Phee didn't want to appear eager, so she trailed casually behind them as they made their way toward the lake.

Down by the shore, Emma laughed at something Warrick said, then invited Hornsby and Miss Lillian over toward their small group.

As a hostess, Emma was a natural—at least, when her pregnancy wasn't inducing her to vomit into household decorative objects. Eventually, Emma would have to come clean to Cal. Every day Phee asked her to, and every day Emma claimed this would be the day she confessed her condition to her brother. But by the time they said good night, Emma still hadn't found the right moment. Phee had reported to Cal about his sister in the past, but this? This would change Emma's life forever, and she needed to tell him herself.

Cal might want to marry off his sister to someone at this party, but that grew less likely by the day. Emma possessed enough of a conscience to realize that duping a perfectly nice gentleman and foisting off another man's child might not be the best way to handle her life. Which left the girl with limited options.

At some point over the last ten days at Lakeview, she and Emma had become friends. Sort of. Having never had a female friend before, Phee wasn't sure. The honesty between them was rather one-sided. But Emma came to Phee when she needed help or an excuse to get out of an activity.

Emma was different during their conversations. The humor and wit she showed reminded Phee of Cal, but they came out only when Emma stopped trying so hard to fulfill the diamond of the Season label. Did she occasionally act like a spoiled brat in need of a spanking? Absolutely.

But since Phee had discovered the truth about Emma's condition, the girl had opened up. Parlor games in the evening allowed some couples to pair off under the guise of playing and left the unmatched guests with time on their hands. She and Emma often kept one another company.

The sweetness Cal's sister revealed in those conversations came as a surprise. Sometimes it was painfully obvious how young Emma was. The girl had made poor decisions with Roxbury, but one couldn't deny the unfairness of him leaving her alone to deal with the very adult consequences.

Not knowing how to help had kept Phee awake late into the night over the past week, despite Cal's thorough efforts to exhaust her. Although sexual satisfaction and contentment hummed through her veins, and the man of her dreams slept beside her, heavy and warm, making their sheets smell like his spicy scent, she'd tossed and turned and worried through the hours. A bloody shame, when she should be wallowing in their orgasms and then slipping into blissful dreams before creeping back to her room in the wee hours of the morning.

Keeping their relationship secret grew more difficult by the day, and Phee occasionally wanted to intervene when one of the ladies flirted with him—never mind that there wasn't any danger of another guest distracting his attention from her. But it was the principle of the thing.

Cal loved her. She loved him. The future was unsure, but they'd discover it together. If she ever doubted that, she need only remember their frantic lovemaking in the library and the potential consequences. They'd been careful since then, but God knew it only took once.

Maybe this wanting to publicly claim him was a natural side effect of suppressing herself for all these years. A couple of weeks of being allowed free rein, and now her femininity felt a bit feral—out of control and prowling under her skin, demanding an escape from the guise of her brother's persona.

The urge was particularly strong when dealing with the obnoxious baron. Rosehurst gravitated toward rudeness to begin with and compounded that character flaw by prancing around the house as if he owned the place. More than once Phee held her tongue while Cal gently but firmly put the man in his place, and Miss Cuthbert apologized for her father's behavior. Cal had said he would handle it, but damn it, Phee wished Violet would get on with her part of the plan and snag another man.

This afternoon at the lake was supposed to be a picnic. On the lawn near the shore, footmen arranged chairs and tables laden with crisp white linens and an impressive array of food and drink. It was essentially an outdoor tea, complete with fluffed pillows on the chaise.

The aristocracy were strange folks.

In her youth, a day at the lake had meant minimal clothes, splashing water, and squealing children who ended the afternoon pink from the sun. Now, apparently, they needed cut crystal and bone china to make a proper outing.

Phee straightened her cravat and tugged her hat down to shade her eyes against the blazing sun in question. The last things she needed were more freckles by the end of the day, thank you. And Lordy, what she'd give to be cool in a light muslin gown like the one Emma wore. A breeze under the hem and only a dress and chemise rather than all these layers sounded like heaven. She sighed. Soon. Not today. But soon. Winter—just when she would be grateful for the layers and the tall boots. Oh, irony. Thou art an evil bitch.

Tufts of white clouds floated like bits of cotton in a sky so pure blue, she wished for a wild moment that she possessed the ability to capture the scene on canvas. A light breeze saved the day from being oppressively hot and lifted the fine curls at her nape.

Cal's smile caught her, blinding white and intimate when she approached where he and Gaffney stood. Asking how the meeting went would have to wait, but Cal had to know that conversation was coming. Her enthusiasm for hearing about Gaffney's business venture fizzled into a cold lump of dread as several servants rowed around the willow tree in wooden boats gleaming with fresh coats of paint. The women along the shore clapped at the prospect of being on the water, and the men began joking and bragging about their prowess with oars.

No way in hell was Phee getting in a boat. A rickety, wooden, easily tipped or sunk boat—not an option. No matter how many layers of paint they'd slapped on the hull or how shiny the brass hardware securing the oars, each dinghy transformed in her mind into a faded gray wood boat with oars that splintered your palms. Those oars had turned a dark inky brown from her bloody hands after she'd managed to drag Adam back into the boat.

Only Cal appeared to notice Phee shaking her head. He reached out a hand and laid it on her shoulder. "Adam, if you'd like to remain on shore, I'll stay with you."

She blew out a breath. "Thank you, I'd prefer that."

He moved closer and whispered, "I'm sorry. Mrs. Hodges changed the outing, and I didn't know until now. We were supposed to play croquet, damn it."

Removing herself to a comfortable chair seemed wise while he found the last few stragglers places in the boats. A footman offered a glass of champagne—perfectly chilled, naturally. It wouldn't do for the Earl of Carlyle to serve tepid champagne.

Considering she'd been battling panic moments before, this was the best possible outcome. Phee smiled her thanks to the footman and took a deep drink. With a seat in the shade and servants on hand to tend to any needs that may arise, her day had just turned around. Best of all, she wasn't getting on a boat anytime soon.

One by one, the boats full of guests launched with a

sturdy footman in the bow, in case the gentlemen's boasts were empty and someone needed assistance returning to shore.

Cal was handing the last lady into a dinghy when a footman arrived, slightly out of breath. "Pardon me, milord," the servant said. The men leaned their heads together and lowered their voices.

It was a minute thing. Had she been paying less attention or not possessed the knowledge of a close friend and lover, Phee would have missed it. His eyes went blank. Not polite. Not cool or distant. Cal wasn't angry or scared—just suddenly empty. Devoid of emotion.

He sent one more wave to the boat, then launched the guests with a nudge of his boot and walked toward the house with the footman. Not a glance back or a word to anyone else—Cal's gaze stayed firmly fixed ahead and composed.

A quarter of an hour, then a half hour passed while Phee observed the guests' antics on the lake from the safety of the shore. They frolicked happily, occasionally splashing each other with oars or slapping the water with a hand to bellows of laughter and squeals.

Concern made Phee feel each of those minutes like a month. Something was wrong. Cal had excluded her from the meeting with Gaffney, then hadn't invited her along to deal with whatever was happening now. For nearly two years she'd been the one he went to when he needed help fixing something. Sure, this month had been light on work, but certainly that was only due to safety concerns. A private business meeting was one matter. After all, she wasn't privy to every business conversation he had. But anything that made him abandon his guests was something she should help deal with.

What if Roxbury had shown up? The rotter couldn't be the one to tell Cal about Emma's baby. Containing the news would be impossible if their host throttling Lord Roxbury became the highlight of this house party. Rationalizing the need to follow wasn't hard.

Of course, she could be overreacting to a piddly minor event. There might be a servant matter to deal with or some such lord-of-the-manor thing. In which case, slipping away for a few minutes of privacy while the others were on the lake would be a better way to pass the time than quaffing champagne on the grass.

Phee set aside her champagne flute and rose. There, that wasn't so hard. She had perfectly valid reasons to follow Cal.

At the house, a male voice came from the direction of a drawing room off the main hall. Curious. Someone uninvited had arrived. Lordy, Roxbury must be here. Cal would be irate. Emma was on the lake, so there might be time to deal with her ex-lover before the guests returned.

Now that she was closer to the drawing room door, which stood open by several inches, she could identify the voice. It was the marquess who'd called, not Roxbury. That didn't strike her as preferable, given the Violet situation. Cocking her head—as if that would somehow help the men's voices carry more clearly—she tried to follow the conversation.

Out by the lake on Cal's first night here, he'd said Eastly had never been to Lakeview. That this was a home without ghosts or bad memories. After years without an invitation, the marquess had to know he wasn't welcome, and the tone of the voices wasn't exactly friendly. Impotent irritation made Phee's lip curl as she grasped the door handle.

Eastly's voice slithered around the polished wood doorframe, at once cajoling and demanding—as if he knew he wouldn't be denied but wanted Cal to feel good about caving to his wishes. She'd heard the tone before, and usually it meant Cal would do his best to comply. "The baron has been more than patient, Son. He's bought a special license. Time to be done with it. Violet is under your roof. Marry the girl and she can be in your bed too, if she isn't already. Not a hardship at all, eh? Your fiancée is a fancy little piece. The perfect countess, if I say so myself."

A bark of laughter she'd heard countless times over the years made her stomach sink. "A rushed wedding invokes scandal, and no countess of mine will have scandal attached to her."

Phee's chest went hollow. A dead space. Cal's words—not a denial, and not surprised that Eastly still expected him to marry Violet Cuthbert—echoed off the walls of her ribs, taking chunks from her heart.

Son of a bitch, he'd said he'd handle it.

He'd said he loved her.

He'd promised this would come to nothing, but evidently he hadn't made that clear to his own bloody *father*. And God knew Eastly always got what he wanted. Cal never denied the man anything, just walked behind him, cleaning his messes and paying off people left and right. Hell, she'd delivered those payments more than once. Even now, after professing his love for the hundredth time when she'd left his bed this morning, he stood in that room *not* telling Eastly to take those wedding plans to the devil.

No countess of mine will have scandal attached to her.

That eliminated Phee as an option, now didn't it? He'd spoken of a future, but had he ever actually mentioned marriage?

It didn't take long to search her memories. Happy, joy-filled memories, with promises she'd cherished and held close to her heart. He'd never mentioned marriage. Not once.

Lordy, she'd been taken in by the oldest trick in the book—that future he talked of wasn't marriage. He wanted a mistress. A secret relationship, where she'd spend the rest of her life hiding, as she had for so long already.

One by one the emotions she'd entrusted to Cal withered into a deadened lump, like a flower that dared bloom too early, only to succumb to frost. Air stalled in her lungs, and she was afraid that if she drew in a deep enough breath, it would become a wail. Not the whimpering tears of a broken heart, but the battle cry of a lover betrayed.

What had she expected? That the rich and powerful Earl of Carlyle would—what? Marry a nobody like Ophelia Hardwick? Had she truly thought the man who spent his time finding new ways to make money and suppressing his family's scandals would marry *her* when he could save his father's hide for the umpteenth time and gain a healthy dowry to boot?

Hell, Phee didn't even technically exist on paper. How ludicrous to think for even a second he might wait for her to inherit, then marry her once she'd assumed a new name.

The hand on the doorknob curled into a tight fist until the

tendons in her forearms protested with a sharp ache. She'd trusted blindly, for the first time in years, believing everything he told her. Somehow, he'd even maneuvered *Phee* into planning a house party for the woman Eastly wanted him to marry.

How dare he.

Out of the cold remains of her heart, a thick hedge of thorns grew around where she'd once been soft and vulnerable. Maybe he hadn't lied outright, but there could be no doubt he'd omitted, manipulated, and played her for a fool.

Despite the fury roiling in her, a sob broke through. She slapped a hand over her mouth to stifle the sound. He wouldn't see her cry. Phee's vulnerability and softness weren't his to witness anymore.

In fact, he wouldn't know she'd discovered the truth until she was damn good and ready to tell him. Two could withhold information. The thought settled deep into her new blessedly numb state.

Since the day of the accident that killed her brother, she'd lived by a plan. Phee needed to retreat to that place in her head where claiming her inheritance and disappearing were the most important things. No more beautiful earls who looked like fallen angels and lulled her into believing she could live a fantasy.

If ever there'd been a time that called for action, this was it. When she finished with Cal, she'd be free.

Piece by piece, like a puzzle coming together, a new plan formed. One that would not only help her but prove to Cal once and for all that the street scrapper he'd sent to investigate his problems could solve her own problems, thank you very much. The brilliance of it made her lips curl in a twisted imitation of a smile.

The dull thuds of her footfalls echoed off the fine marble tile as she made her way out of the house. At the lake, the boats were returning to shore, and servants bustled about in their fine livery, as if caring for the pampered guests was the only thing in the world that mattered. As luck would have it, Miss Cuthbert's boat pulled to shore when Phee joined the party with studied casualness. Pasting on a cheerful smile, Phee offered her hand to Miss Cuthbert as she disembarked.

"I hear felicitations are in order. The Marquess of Eastly is at the house and let slip about your understanding with Lord Carlyle."

Miss Cuthbert stared down at her feet. "Thank you, Mr. Hardwick. Our fathers arranged the match."

There'd been no misunderstanding, then. A tiny seed of fragile hope she didn't even know she had been sheltering died. Phee offered a shallow bow. "Best wishes on your wedding, Miss Cuthbert." Phee let go of the dainty gloved hand as quickly as possible and turned to the occupants of the next boat. "Lady Emma, might I have a word?"

Emma dimpled prettily. "Of course, Mr. Hardwick. Shall we walk?"

They strolled side by side away from the party, following the curving shore of the lake. Phee clasped her hands behind her back and said, "There's much I want to say, but by talking to you now, I am trusting you. Are you trustworthy, Emma?"

Emma's fingers worried at the edge of her glove. "You're

privy to my biggest secret. Except for Roxbury, and possibly my maid, you are the only one who knows. We might be bound by secrets, you and I."

The success of the next step of Phee's plan relied on Emma being a willing participant. "I haven't shared my secrets with you. I'd like to rectify that now."

Emma tilted her head. "I'm listening."

The guests of the house party were well behind them, with the lawn swallowing the sharp, trilling scales of laughter and rumbling conversation. Phee glanced over her shoulder, but no one seemed to care that they'd wandered off on their own. "I've been impersonating my brother, waiting until he would have been old enough to inherit."

A small shard of her conscience warned that there'd be no going back after this. That this path would change everything forever.

Emma's eyed widened. "You aren't Adam Hardwick?"

"My name is Ophelia. You may call me Phee in private if you wish." Phee forced herself to stand still as that information settled across Emma's face and the irrevocable truth was laid bare.

If she'd thought Emma's eyes were wide before, they were nothing compared to the expression the girl wore now. Slowly, a blinding grin made her mouth gape open. "*No.* You—you're a *woman*? Does Cal know?"

Phee's ears burned, and she cursed her redheaded complexion. "Yes." She cleared her throat. "He knows."

Emma giggled. "Ah, that's how it is? Who'd have thought it from my brother, of all people? Lord Anti-Scandal is certainly comfortable with a friendly bit of hypocrisy, isn't he?" Her glee faded when Phee didn't smile in return. "Wait, what's he done?"

"He promised he wasn't marrying Violet Cuthbert, but it appears he didn't inform Eastly or Miss Cuthbert. Your father is in the drawing room right now, pushing for Cal to use the special license Rosehurst brought with him." Phee wicked away a welling tear. Damn it, the last thing she needed to do was start crying now. This was the time for fighting, not wallowing.

"Why must men be awful liars?" Emma rubbed Phee's arm sympathetically. "I'm so sorry. We're both dealing with heartbreak, then."

Phee nodded toward Emma's belly, where the girl's hand rested. "Do you know what you'll do yet?"

Golden curls bounced against her cheeks when she shook her head. "No. I need the impossible—a husband who won't mind the pregnancy. Preferably someone I can tolerate."

Phee drew in a deep breath. No, there'd be no going back. But the only things behind her were lies, and she had to do *something*. Given the choice between letting pain consume her or rallying a battle cry in response to this betrayal, her path was clear.

Time to enact the plan.

"On paper, I'm a man. We could help each other. Marry me."

Chapter Twenty

❧

For better or worse, Phee and Emma were in this together—and would say so in front of witnesses as soon as possible. But first, they had to deal with Emma's father.

Emma went into the house first, making sure Phee could meet with her father without having to deal with Cal. "Leave most of the talking to me," Emma said before they entered the same drawing room, where a lifetime of heartbeats before, Phee had overheard the marquess and Cal talking. Eastly smiled when Emma entered, and gave her a hearty buss on the cheek in welcome.

"Hello, beautiful girl," he said.

"Good afternoon, Papa. I—we, rather—have something to discuss with you. May we sit a moment?" Emma had turned on her charm full force, with dimples on display and her sweetest tone of voice to showcase her genteel training and social graces. Over her head, Eastly shot Phee a questioning look.

They sat, Emma beside her father, and Phee on the nearest chair. Emma didn't waste time. "Papa, we'd like a special license so we may wed as soon as possible."

No wonder the man lost his bets—he wouldn't be able to bluff if his life depended on it. Eastly's confusion over the diamond of the Season wishing to marry a nobody like Adam Hardwick was so apparent, Phee nearly snickered.

Emma pressed on. "You see, Papa, Adam will come into his fortune when he weds, so he's not without prospects. And of course, my dowry is generous, because you're the best father in all the world." She patted Eastly's hand. That might have been laying it on a bit thick, but the marquess smiled indulgently, so what did Phee know?

"Darling, you can have any man you want. But you can't marry a mere land steward, even if he has a fortune waiting for him. Why, I have it on good authority that the new Duke of Gaffney is at this party. Cast your net there instead."

"Adam is my friend, Papa. I want to marry him. And I'm afraid time is of the essence." With a rather pointed look at her father, she rested a hand on her still-flat belly.

The marquess stared at her hand, his face growing redder as the silence stretched between them. He turned to Phee with an expression that promised not only murder but a slow death. "You did this."

Phee schooled her features into a polite and nonconfrontational expression. "No, milord. The babe's not mine. But as Emma said, we are friends. I will accept responsibility."

"Who's the father?" he demanded.

"I won't tell you that. It's only important to know Adam is stepping in where the father would not," Emma said. A current of steel infused her voice, and Phee couldn't help but be proud of her. She'd grown out of being that girl who'd kissed Phee at Vauxhall and then tried to use it as blackmail. Although Emma's knack for lying her pretty tail off was certainly coming in handy now.

The marquess rested his elbows on his knees in a posture so reminiscent of Cal, it sent an unwelcome pang of longing through Phee. He stared at his hands as he asked, "You're sure?"

Whom the question was directed toward remained unclear, so both Phee and Emma answered, "Yes."

"The baby will have a father, my reputation shall be saved, and Adam will gain the inheritance left by his parents. It's all rather tidy, actually."

Eastly sighed. "Very well. I'll leave right now and return with a license. Lucky for us, the archbishop is visiting the area this month."

"Thank you, milord," Phee said. "We have one other request to make in connection with this." Phee shot a look at Emma, who nodded encouragingly. "Lord Carlyle will not look favorably on the match. But, milord, since you are head of your house and have given your consent, yours is the only opinion I care about. We ask that you not say anything about this to Lord Carlyle or anyone else until it is done. When we say our vows, he may find out along with everyone else."

A glimmer of amusement appeared in the marquess's expression. Emma had been right to suggest Phee appeal to her father's place as head of the family and his love of secrets.

"I will hold my tongue and call on the archbishop." Eastly stood, smoothing the front of his waistcoat, and tugged his coat into place. "Mr. Hardwick, I believe I owe you my thanks for helping my Emma-girl." He held out his hand, and Phee stood to shake it. The older man's grip was firm, but his hands were soft. "Welcome to the family."

As soon as the front doors closed behind him, Emma grinned. "We did it!"

Phee let herself relax a little. "That's that, I guess." Having never had a girlfriend before, she didn't know what happened next. Did they hug? Squeal? This relationship was a mystery.

"You have no idea what to do now that we have the plan in motion, do you?" Emma asked.

Phee huffed out a laugh. "Is it that obvious? Normally, I'd talk through the next stages with Cal, but if I see your brother, I might spit in his eye." Or punch him—on purpose this time.

"Cal isn't normally one to play fast and loose with a girl's affections. I would never have pegged him for a bounder. But you're right. Clearly, he protested but didn't actually cry off if Miss Cuthbert and Rosehurst are still expecting her to become the new countess. I love my brother, but you deserve better." Emma took one of Phee's hands and squeezed.

Phee tried to smile, but it wobbled, and tears threatened. "I think I'll go lock myself in my room for the rest of the day. If anyone asks, tell them I got too much sun and felt unwell."

"I will. Try to rest. We have a lot ahead of us. The hardest part of this plan might be keeping the details to ourselves until it's done," Emma said.

"No one would believe us if they knew the full truth."

Phee was at the door when Emma said, "I can never thank you enough for helping me."

"We're helping each other." With one last smile at her new friend and soon-to-be sort-of wife, Phee escaped to her room.

Hours later, Phee's eyes were puffy from crying. Each time she blinked, it felt as if her eyelids were moving at a snail's pace, and the spiky clumps of her lashes wanted to tangle together. The focused anger hadn't lasted long enough to result in a smug feeling of satisfaction at seeing her machinations play out or to grant her the peace to nap. Instead, she'd sprawled in the chair by the fireplace, having taken off only her cravat, coat, and waistcoat before collapsing into a sobbing heap.

On the other side of the wall, the faint murmur of voices in the hall warned that Cal was retiring for the night. Any other night, she would slip out and meet him at the door. She would kiss that beautiful smile and feel like the luckiest person in the world, even if she could be a lover only in secret.

She couldn't face him. Not yet. Not without yelling, begging to know *why*, or confessing to the things she'd put into motion. When the doorknob turned, she glanced over to make sure the brass key stayed in the lock where she'd left it.

"Adam?" A pause. Phee bit her lip. Anyone could hear him call down the corridor, so of course he'd call her Adam. Their relationship was one big lie. "Are you awake? Emma said you weren't feeling well. I've hardly seen you all day. Please let me in."

Phee stayed in the chair, watching the door, listening to

the voice that had been the root of her fantasies for so long. *No countess of mine will have scandal attached to her.*

She'd loved him well. To the best of her abilities. She'd loved him to the point of sometimes wondering if she'd kept any love for herself, or if she'd poured everything into him.

Well, now she knew. There'd been plenty reserved for herself, and it was hers alone. No one else could touch it. Even though the loss hurt, at the end of the day she didn't need him to love her. Especially not if it meant sacrificing her self-respect. She deserved to be loved out in the open, not hidden away like a shameful secret.

The sounds from the hall quieted. Eventually, even the usual house noises of doors opening and servants murmuring faded.

Cal didn't fall asleep easily, usually wanting to talk through the day. It was something she'd teased him about, because he'd once said that Emma couldn't rest until she'd expelled everything on her mind. The siblings were so alike in some ways. Like his sister's, Cal's body needed to wind down like a pocket watch, expending all his energy until there was nothing left to run on.

Phee glanced at the clock. Hell, he probably hadn't even undressed yet. Cal liked to end the night with a brandy in the chair by the hearth—even during the summer, when there wasn't always a fire.

That was one example from thousands of things she knew about him. Intimate facts like schedules and preferences. Paying attention—no, reveling in those personal details— had been easy when she'd tricked herself into believing their relationship would last.

Such a gullible fool she was. The exhaustion and despair Phee had wrapped around herself earlier disappeared as fury awoke, rolling through her in a hot wave. The rage burned away reason and logic and any lingering tenderness toward him.

She'd given Cal her body. Her heart. Her trust. What was it he'd said in the library, when he'd confessed his love? *Whatever happens, we handle together.*

Meanwhile, Cal—despite his protestations—had been engaged to an heiress the entire time. Phee and Cal hadn't handled anything together. He'd kept her in the dark and fed her lies.

Lies she'd gobbled up, because they'd come with affection she'd been missing her entire life. It had been unwise to trust anyone other than herself, and she'd *known* that. All those years on her own should have made Phee immune to the sting of betrayal.

But damn it, they were supposed to love each other. Each time they'd come together, Phee had believed Cal gave as much as she did—an equal exchange of devotion. Maybe he'd only been taking.

When he'd called through the door, parts of her had responded like they always did, warming and softening in expectation of what usually came next. Logic and self-preservation declared their affair was over, but her traitorous body hadn't embraced that knowledge yet. Hell, Phee might always crave him. Crossing her legs did nothing to cool the heat that gathered at her core.

If nothing else, she deserved to say goodbye as she saw fit. And if this would be her last chance to touch him, to own his body for a few final moments, Phee would do whatever she wanted, and to hell with the consequences.

It was her turn to take.

The door slammed against the wall when she stormed into his bedroom and interrupted his pacing. Sure enough, he remained fully dressed, with a snifter of brandy on the small table between the chairs by the fireplace.

"Phee? Are you all right—" She cut off his words with a kiss, sinking her fingers into the long strands of his hair—he liked it when she held him like that.

She knew, because she'd been paying attention. Wanting to please him. Wanting to believe the fantasy that he loved her. God, she'd believed he'd fallen as she had. Silly girl.

"Do you want me? Do you want this?" she demanded.

"I always want you, Phee. Are you all right? I missed you at dinner—"

There were better uses for his mouth. Her tongue and teeth chastised him, showing without words that this wasn't the time to talk. Tugging the hem of her shirt up her thighs, she rucked the fabric over her torso, then pulled it off. Catching on to her urgency, Cal's hands tore at her binding until he palmed her breasts, pinching her nipples between his fingers with a low groan.

Frantic hands made quick work of opening the placket on his breeches to free the hardness pushing against the buttons. She had to give him credit; Cal was always ready for her. Of course, she'd believed it was because he loved *her*, not just bed sport.

But with the perfect Miss Cuthbert available, Ophelia was obviously nothing more than someone to pass the time with until a respectable *lady* warmed his bed—wed and legally bound.

Phee sure as hell wasn't feeling ladylike at the moment. His girth swelled as she worked her grip along his cock, then dropped to her knees. Holding Cal's gaze, she swallowed him deep and shuddered with satisfaction when he cursed and grabbed one of the ornately carved posts of his bed frame for balance.

At the mercy of her hands and tongue, his body became her plaything. But Phee knew the game now, and it was high time the rules changed in her favor. Cal might not realize it yet, but this encounter wasn't for him. And she'd make damn sure he remembered it for the rest of his life.

Phee's heels dug into her bottom, and a cool breeze from an open window beaded her nipples into tight peaks. Cal's fingers clenched in her hair, then caressed a line across her cheekbone.

As if she meant something to him. As if she was special.

Well, she wasn't the one he'd been negotiating an engagement with. Phee added the soft scrape of her teeth—which, judging by his low groan, only heightened his pleasure; he'd entirely missed the implied threat.

Shivery goose bumps followed in the wake of his fingertips along her skin, and she hated him for it. Hated that part of her still wanted him, despite everything.

Determined to find her pleasure first, Phee shoved her hand down her breeches and speared two fingers into the curls between her thighs. The slick response from her body coated the epicenter of nerves at the top of her slit. Working her mouth on him and her fingers in herself, a jolt of dark pleasure pierced Phee when Cal's eyes rolled back and his thighs tensed under her hands.

A perfect lady like Miss Cuthbert would probably be horrified at the idea of sucking a cock. Phee dug her fingers into the hard muscle of Cal's perfect bum and took him even deeper.

Lucky for Cal, Phee wasn't a lady. Maybe for a few precious days or weeks she'd dared dream of being his wife, but now she knew better. This gilded life wasn't for her. If she wanted happiness in her world, Phee would make it herself. She had to claim any good fortune as her own and take what she wanted.

Right now she wanted Cal.

Just one more time.

At her mercy, chanting her name, completely undone.

No way in hell would she let him come first, and he was close. Gentling her rhythm, she licked, lapping at him like an icy treat, until the hard line of his thighs softened under her hand as she coaxed him from the edge. The fingers in her breeches stayed in place until the now-familiar tingling began at her toes, then traveled up her calves.

It wouldn't be long now. Mere moments left to taste him. Smell him. Hear that growl she'd only ever heard from Cal while in bed.

His breath scissored in and out in time with the suction of her mouth. Bittersweet satisfaction inflamed her arousal when Cal breathed her name on each exhale and it sounded like a benediction. "Phee, Phee, my God, Phee..."

Climaxes came in so many forms. This one tore through her with brutal efficiency, curling her toes and severing her last contact with the man she'd loved. Still loved, damn him, but that was her problem. On unsteady legs, she got to her feet, shaking like a newborn calf. Cal reached for her, eyes still glazed with desire, but she stopped him with a finger to his lips—the same finger that was still coated with her slickness.

Between one labored breath and the next, Cal sucked the finger into his mouth, closing his eyes on a moan to savor her flavor. A ribbon of desire flickered back to life, pushing past the pain, but she snuffed it out.

Ignoring the chill creeping over her bare torso, Phee stepped close, until the tips of her breasts brushed against his coat. Except for his open breeches and tousled hair, Cal looked ready to walk into any fine drawing room in the country.

Her finger slipped from his mouth as she turned and donned her shirt.

"Phee? Where are you going?" Bless him, he looked so bewildered that for a moment her anger wavered. The temptation to ask for an explanation clawed at her brittle control.

Yet even if there were perfectly logical reasons, he'd been playing someone false. After hearing him with Eastly, Phee knew it had been her. He'd made her the other woman. And that? That, she couldn't forgive.

Thank God it was only a handful of steps to the door. She could fake a confident swagger that long. Her long legs, unhindered by skirts and shod in tall black leather boots, allowed her to walk anywhere she chose. Even out of his life.

It wasn't a hardship to glance over her shoulder and

indulge in one last look to admire his perfect beauty. Even a liar could be gorgeous. She sneered. "That was for me. If you want an orgasm, ask your fiancée to take care of you."

"What? Phee, what are you talking—"

She cut his protestations short with a sweep of her hand. "No. This is where we end."

Chapter Twenty-One

*C*al would rather not delve into whatever circumstances had led to the archbishop owing his father a favor. It could have been anything.

Eastly summoned him to the drawing room—which annoyed Cal to no end, because this was his blasted house—and there stood Phee and Emma and an older man he didn't recognize. Phee's boots shined with a high gloss, and her hair had been ruthlessly subdued with pomade. Purple smudges under her eyes told him she'd slept as little as he had. Emma clutched a nosegay of flowers to match her pink dress trimmed in Brussels lace.

"Son, this is Vicar Norton. He's here to officiate. We are witnesses." Eastly leaned close and whispered, "She's in the family way. Young Hardwick is stepping up. Smile and give your blessing. Now."

What the hell? Cal bit his lip to stop his instinctive protest. Emma was pregnant and marrying the woman he loved. The absurd impossibility of it tore through him like a cannon-ball, destroying the last remnants of certainty he'd clung to, believing he might be able to explain to Phee today.

Last night, when she'd rocked his world off its axis as per usual, he'd barely been able to comprehend the parting volley she'd shot over her shoulder. It didn't take a genius to figure out that Phee had overheard the meeting with Father yesterday.

In this very drawing room, Cal had prevaricated, side-stepped, and danced along the line of outright lying to buy Miss Cuthbert a little more time to pull off their scheme. He should have simply shut down the conversation. Then perhaps Cal wouldn't be standing in the middle of an unfolding emotional hellscape in which he lost Phee forever.

To his bloody sister, of all people. Cal stared at the couple, looking for a clue that Emma knew the truth about Adam Hardwick. If she did, she played her part beautifully. With dimples out in full force, Emma beamed at her redheaded husband-to-be.

For the first time, Cal's efforts to fix one of Eastly's scandals had failed spectacularly. Yet his first inclination wasn't to salvage Father's reputation or regroup and change the plan. The only thing concerning him right now was going on right in front of him.

The vicar spoke. "Dearly beloved, we are gathered together here in the sight of God..."

A cold sweat broke out along Cal's spine, and the points of his collar scraped against the underside of his jaw. For the first time since standing before a mirror at the age of fourteen and admiring the fit of a well-made suit of clothes, all Cal wanted to do was loosen the cravat so he could fucking breathe.

Everything about this was wrong. Somehow Emma had learned she was pregnant yet hadn't said a word to him. Since her first skinned knee, she'd always come to him when in trouble. But not this time. To add insult to injury, she'd confided in Phee, and Phee hadn't told him either. Now his lover stood before a man of the church, making vows before God.

And not only was Cal not the groom, but Phee wasn't even the bride.

During the last twenty-four hours, his life had spiraled out of his control, and Cal didn't know how to fix it.

Phee knew he'd failed to handle the Violet situation, and Cal didn't have words that weren't excuses. He wanted so desperately to explain that Eastly was like an explosive device—he must be handled delicately to avoid a tantrum that would inevitably make the situation far worse. Unfortunately, Cal should have realized Phee was capable of blowing things up too. Now she was clearly not open to further conversation, since she was busy getting married.

"Therefore, if any man can show any just cause why they may not lawfully be joined together, let him now speak or else hereafter forever hold his peace." The vicar paused for dramatic effect.

Emma shot him a glare, promising hell to pay if he tried to intervene. Clasping his hands behind his back, Cal couldn't look away from the picture they made standing before Vicar Norton. If Cal hadn't been paying attention, he might have missed Emma's wink to Phee.

That was a relief, at least. With that playful, friendly wink, he knew Phee had shared her secret. That look had been one of shared conspirators, not lovers.

Then, there. Only a flicker, but Phee glanced his way. As if worried he would protest the marriage—which would require Cal to reveal her secret in front of Eastly and a vicar. The trust they'd built was truly gone if she thought he would betray her.

Vicar Norton announced them man and wife, and that was that. Before God and everything. With the deed done, the vicar shook everyone's hand, wished the couple a long and happy life together, then departed.

Impeccably awful timing securely in place, his father elbowed him. "You're next, Son."

Cal closed his eyes and wished he could will himself back to bed, where he'd awake with Phee pressed snugly against his side and discover the past twenty-four hours had been a nightmare.

When Cal opened his eyes, the reality remained unchanged, and Eastly still stood there with his never-ending expectations of compliance. But why shouldn't Father anticipate Cal's obedience? It wasn't as if Cal greeted each new disaster with a smile, but there had always been a willingness on his part. Years of this pattern—in both his and Father's roles—had created one reliable point of stability in their family. Fixing everything proved time and again that Cal was useful. That he held value in a relationship where he otherwise never received affirmation, despite his achievements.

Phee and Emma wore twin looks of censure, as if to remind

him of every misstep in this latest effort he'd bungled. Cal sighed, suddenly too old and tired to fake cheer.

"Father, I'll only say this once, so pay attention. I am not marrying Violet Cuthbert. The whole purpose of this house party was to find a match that would satisfy Rosehurst and get you out of your latest debacle."

"Judging by your father's shocked expression, you should have made your wishes on the matter clear sooner." Phee's statement would be mistaken for polite commentary by anyone who didn't know better. If Cal stood close enough, he'd probably feel her vibrating with restrained rage.

Sighing, Cal slumped into the nearest chair and buried his face in his hands. So that was how this was going to happen. With witnesses. "I promised I would handle it, and I have been trying to do that. You had enough to worry about with your uncle—who is still a threat. And thanks to this marriage, my sister is now in danger as well."

Emma stepped closer to Phee, as if forming a wall of solidarity. The battle lines couldn't be clearer. He was the enemy.

"*Friends* don't hide things from one another, Lord Carlyle. No matter their intention," Phee said.

Lord, she'd used his title. Another piece of his battered heart broke off and turned to dust. A spike of anger flickered to life amidst the pain. "Speaking of hiding things, when were you two going to say something about Emma's condition?"

His sister bit her lip and looked away. Something that might have been guilt crossed Phee's face before disappearing behind a hard, composed mask. "That wasn't my news to share. As to Milton, if his goal was to eliminate me before I could inherit, that's now moot. I'm married; I've fulfilled the terms of my parents' will."

"And the insurance policy?"

"If he paid for it out of the estate, then I'll have the power to cancel it."

There was the quick mind he'd relied on for the last two years. Losing her as a lover was gutting. Losing her as an employee would have lasting repercussions too. Cal shook his head. A dull throb thrummed at his temple.

"All right, but this doesn't end when you notify the solicitor of your marriage. If you think Milton will just shrug and slink off when he finds you've outmaneuvered him, you're delusional. The threat remains."

Eastly cleared his throat. "Murderous uncles, pregnant daughters, and barons with the power to destroy us. It's quite the party you're having, Son. We'd best hope your machinations are effective, because if Miss Cuthbert doesn't catch the eye of someone during this visit, there will be no saving us." On the list of things sustaining his father's existence, drama ranked high, along with opera singers and other men's wives. With typical flair, the marquess delivered that dire prediction-cum-threat, then swept from the room.

Everyone observed his departure, then looked at one another in silence for a moment. Exhaustion made Cal's feet feel like he wore lead-lined boots as he rose. "You could have warned me about the marriage."

"For someone so comfortable misleading the people in his life, you might want to check your position right now," Phee said.

"I asked you to trust me. I *needed* you to trust me." The words came out sounding strangled. Phee's mouth tightened into a hard line.

"And I needed you to be an honest partner. You wouldn't have kept Adam in the dark. Before this last month, you would've not only included me but expected me to help you," she said.

Ouch. She was right. He would have told Adam everything and pulled him into the details. But Phee? He'd treated her like someone he could pat on the head while saying, *There, there, I'll fix it.* She'd said *partner* and he'd failed there too. "You're right, Phee. I hate that you're right, but you are. As usual." Cal turned to Emma. "And you should have told me, brat."

Emma nodded. "I know, but I was scared. Besides, you don't have to fix everything, big brother." With a grimace, she added, "I suppose we go tell everyone else now. Not that I'm really in the mood to celebrate."

"Are the vases in danger again?" Phee asked, quirking her lips.

Emma laughed. "I don't think so. But that could change at any moment. Stand at the ready, Phee. I might need you."

Hearing Phee's real name from Emma made Cal smile. Phee had one more friend who knew and would keep her secret, and knowing she wouldn't be alone was a relief. "I'm glad you know the truth, Emma."

"That Adam is actually Phee? Of course I do. Now, I may not want any champagne, but I have the fiercest craving for rhubarb tart. Do you think we could convince Cook to make some?"

"You're the bride. You get what you want." Phee offered her arm.

"One moment." Emma fluffed the linen of Phee's cravat. "There. Can't have you appearing less than perfect when we tell everyone you've caught me."

Phee laughed and shook her head. "Very wifely of you."

They slipped out the door together, leaving Cal no choice but to watch them go, then swear profusely into the empty room.

"The tension between you and my brother is so thick, it would choke a goat. Also, you're pale as a sheet," Emma hissed. "I think the better question is, Do *you* need a vase?"

Phee pulled in a steadying breath. "Facing him was harder than expected."

"You handled yourself beautifully when face-to-face with him, though. And again, I can't thank you enough." Emma squeezed Phee's arm in a sort of side-body hug.

"We are helping each other. And as we said, we will deal with the future together." Echoing the words Cal had said to her in the library made Phee wince. In the grand scheme of things, her and Cal's brief stint as lovers would be a mere blip compared to the years ahead of her. Eventually, she might think of this time at Lakeview as nothing more than a lovely visit to the countryside. But right now, she hurt. Like vinegar on a wound, thoughts of being with Cal made her ache.

Since overhearing the conversation with the marquess

yesterday, Phee had discovered a spectrum of pain. A sting, a throb, crippling agony—all unique and Cal's fault.

Except, with the first step of her plan executed and Cal's reaction played out for her to see, Phee had to wonder if there'd been another way. An explanation that would have satisfied her or exonerated him.

A hiccup of breath threatened tears if she explored that line of thought further. No. It was done. Anger kept her going right now. There'd be a time to set that anger aside and grieve everything, but showing him the full extent of her pain wouldn't happen—and certainly not in the public rooms of his grand house, swarming with guests.

The murmur of voices filtered down the corridor from the breakfast room, where the late risers were beginning their day.

Phee had already died a thousand deaths and gotten married before they'd even drunk their first cup of tea. Straightening her shoulders, she nodded to Emma. "Let's get this over with."

"It will be all right. You'll see. I'll do my society-darling bit and smile a lot, and we will get through this. They'll expect us to disappear after breakfast, then you can spend a few hours alone if you want to."

What a bloody depressing wedding day. It hit her then. "Emma, I'm sorry. Here I'm focused on my disaster with Cal, and I haven't once thought about what you're giving up. This isn't the wedding day you dreamed of, nor am I the groom you wanted."

Emma's dimples flashed, although the smile didn't reach her eyes. "Both of us gained and lost in this arrangement. Not to mention the potential eternal damnation for taking vows under false pretenses."

Phee wrapped an arm around her shoulders and squeezed. "For what it's worth, you're a beautiful bride. I'd like to think God understands the situation."

When they entered the breakfast room arm in arm and announced their marriage, there was a moment of shocked silence. Miss Lillian was the first to stand and offer her well-wishes, then the others followed. Most of the congratulations sounded genuine, if skeptical. Everyone knew Lady Emma Carlyle had married beneath her. Phee shook hands, accepted the good-natured teasing from the men, and counted the minutes until she could retreat to her room.

The worst of it would come later, when any suspicions about the hasty marriage would be confirmed as news of the baby spread. By then, she and Emma would be long gone from London. For now, it would be the wedding itself that would set tongues wagging.

Perhaps the political climate would distract from Lady Emma's unexpected match. With Queen Caroline essentially on trial and fighting to keep her title, the papers were busy with those salacious details. Mr. Nobody Hardwick marrying the daughter of a marquess should not warrant much more than a simple announcement. They could hope, anyway.

Servants rushed to provide champagne for the impromptu celebration. Raising a flute, Phee toasted Emma. "To the most beautiful bride in England."

The sparkling wine slid cool and fizzy down her throat, washing away the unease of the morning. In its wake, resolve settled in her heart. She didn't want to live the rest of her life remembering what it felt like to be held—she wanted to *be* held, and safe, and loved by someone who saw her beauty the way she did now. At the moment, it seemed impossible to imagine such a thing with anyone but Cal, but if Adam's death had taught her one thing, it was that Phee could endure far more than she thought. So while she couldn't picture it now, she knew someday she'd have love, safety, and a life that made her happy. And Emma deserved the same.

Chapter Twenty-Two

❧

A special license, eh?" Milton's solicitor looked over the half-moons of his spectacles and raised unruly silver brows at Phee. "You found a girl with money, then." He studied the document closer. "The Marquess of Eastly's chit? My, my, you are coming up in the world, Mr. Hardwick."

Phee bit her tongue and did her best to maintain a benign expression. "I'm sure we will be very happy." That should be innocuous enough. Every word during a visit to the solicitor handling her parents' estate—and by extension, her uncle's—would get back to Milton. After all, this same solicitor had drafted the marriage contracts for a thirteen-year-old girl and hadn't raised a fuss. Closing this chapter of her life would be a relief. Plus, she'd never again have to set foot in this office, which smelled of musty onions and moldy books.

"It appears all is in order. You've fulfilled the terms of your parents' will, and funds will be available to you as laid out in their last wishes. Given your young age, you'll want to keep your uncle on the accounts to oversee the transition period," the solicitor said, as if it were a foregone conclusion. That the solicitor's first inclination was to keep Milton in charge only confirmed his loyalties.

"Absolutely not. Effective immediately, I'm taking full control of my inheritance. Should questions arise, I have the resources and counsel of the Marquess of Eastly and my brother by marriage, the Earl of Carlyle."

Name-dropping her new connections had a satisfying effect on the solicitor, who drooped slightly but nodded. Not only that, but she'd managed to say Cal's title without choking. In light of everything, Phee counted that as progress.

After this there'd be a visit to a different solicitor—one Phee knew from her former position with Cal. Although it pained her to admit Cal was right about anything at the moment, he'd been right about Milton. To expect her uncle to tuck his tail between his legs and scamper off was unrealistic. Protecting Emma and the baby needed to be the top priority. That meant a will of her own with provision for Emma and her rather excessive dowry with a solicitor she could trust.

Thankfully, the next solicitor was easier to deal with and had the added benefits of not being a snitch to her uncle or of smelling like onions. The last order of business on the agenda was to call on the offices of Hapsburg Life and Property. If Phee's accounts had paid for a life-insurance policy, then she owned said policy. God forbid, but if something did happen to her, Phee didn't want Milton benefiting from her death.

Finally, a hackney deposited her in front of Cal's address.

The whitewashed edifice of his townhome loomed over the street. Black cornices framed the windows like concerned eyebrows, so the house looked like it judged all who passed by. Strange that she'd never noticed the effect before now. Knowing the awkward silence awaiting Phee in that house made her want to tell the hack driver to take her anywhere else.

Cal's decision to stay behind at Lakeview had bought Phee and Emma some peace, but things between the three of them had been chilly since his return home. Everyone tried to remain civil, but frankly, Phee couldn't wait to move. Eastly hadn't been forthcoming with an offer to stay with him. So until Milton's fingers were officially removed from Phee's banking, she and Emma were keeping rooms on Hill Street, where they shared brutally tense dinners with Cal every night.

In the gold drawing room, Emma sprawled rather inelegantly on a chaise, idly flipping through the most recent copy of *La Belle Assemblée*. Phee grinned. Marriage to Emma—as unorthodox and platonic as it was—had been a bit of a revelation. Her new friend made an entertaining companion, and with the fear for her future gone, Emma's excitement about the baby grew each day. Having a female friendship was foreign but surprisingly fun.

With all the pregnancy talk between them, it had been a relief when Phee's courses arrived right on schedule. One less potential scandal for the Earl of Carlyle to deal with—not that he'd done that great a job with the last few.

When the door closed behind Phee, Emma didn't look up. Instead, she turned the magazine around to show an illustration of a gown and said, "Do you think this style would mask my condition for a while longer? Waistlines are tightening and lowering right when mine is expanding. It's dreadfully unfair."

Phee squinted at the drawing. "Lady Amesbury swears by Madame Bouvier's designs. If you visit her shop, she could probably create something like that but with room for the baby."

Emma flipped the magazine around and tilted her head to the side as if considering. "Madame Bouvier made my wardrobe for the Season. I might visit her again. You don't mind if I get a few new gowns?"

"It's your money—why would I care what you do with it? Besides, you'll need clothing for your confinement. All I ask is that we pay our bills promptly. We won't live on credit. I... can't. Not after living with the poorest of London. People deserve to be paid for their work promptly."

"I've never thought of credit that way before. But I hear what you are saying. You really don't mind me buying a new wardrobe? People will say Mr. Hardwick overindulges his new wife," Emma teased.

"Well, we both know he does nothing else with his new wife. The poor girl deserves to feel pretty," Phee said dryly.

"Being married to you is better than I thought it would be." Emma grinned.

"I'm glad you think so, because we should talk about what's next. Uncle Milton is probably even now being told that my money is beyond his reach. Shockingly, the account was healthier than I expected. Unfortunately, his solicitor knows you came with a generous dowry, since that is hardly a secret. We are a tempting target for Milton's ire at the moment, and I have no idea what he will do."

"With the legalities observed, we should publish the marriage notice in the *Times*. Otherwise it looks like we're ashamed of the connection or hiding something," Emma said.

Phee dropped into the nearest chair. "Agreed. On the topic of hiding—do you still want to leave Town before you start to show?"

"I think that's best, yes. You've already done your part. My baby will be legitimate. We should move towards fulfilling my end of the bargain. So—" Emma took a deep breath as if bracing for impact. "To that end, perhaps you should get a few things from Madame Bouvier as well."

Unease seized Phee, even though Emma had a point. Years of dreaming about a hypothetical someday, and suddenly that someday was a now.

"Surely Madame Bouvier has a few things on hand." Emma nodded toward Phee's clothes. "You're handy with a needle. We'll buy something premade and alter it."

Phee tried to imagine owning a gown. Fitting it to her adult body. Feeling pretty in her clothes, versus ensuring she didn't look like herself. Would she be comfortable in a dress, or would it feel like a costume, like her cravats did now? Those weeks with Cal had changed her, destroying the ease Phee had once found within Adam's persona. At the idea of a beautiful dress, a bubble of hopeful happiness settled uncomfortably in her chest alongside her broken heart. Phee rubbed at her breastbone and turned to stare out the window as she mentally walked through the next steps of their plan.

Emma must have misinterpreted her silence, because she

pushed the topic. "Isn't that the point? My baby gets a legal father, and you finally live as a woman."

The details of the plan essentially boiled down to what most of her plans over the years had—run and start over elsewhere. Present herself to new acquaintances as if the new lie were truth and wait for the lie to feel real. Phee sighed, exhaustion pulling at her—the kind of tiredness that a nap wouldn't fix. Aches were her constant companions these days, along with that shattered feeling, as if her emotions were shards of glass rattling together, chipping at each other and doing no good except to cause more damage. She turned to Emma.

"Not to sound mercenary, but we need all the money in the bank first. Sums of this size take time, and the will's paperwork must be processed properly. Then we can move and enact the next stage of the plan."

Emma nodded. "I still think you should choose a gown or two when I get mine."

"Fine." Phee rolled her eyes. "I'll see what they have on hand. Something made for a particularly tall, flat-chested child, maybe."

"The height will be the hardest element," Emma said. "Your legs are miles long, aren't they? I'm quite jealous of that."

Phee shot her a dubious look.

"I'm serious. You have these endless, graceful limbs. Everything about me is short. Soon I'll be as round as I am tall. I understand you may not have a lot of experience with extolling your wiles." Emma's sarcasm rang clear and made Phee snort despite the serious subject. "But you're unique.

Long and lean, like a racehorse. And we know how men adore those."

Phee pressed her palms to heated cheeks. "Is this what having girlfriends is like? We talk about our bodies and dresses and men in far too intimate detail?"

"Never fear that I'll press for intimate details about the men in your life." Emma shuddered and curled her lip. "There are things I don't want to know about my brother. Besides, I am not ready to make nice yet—he treated you abominably and deserves to suffer. But essentially, yes. Few topics are off limits. If it makes you more comfortable, I can belch and scratch myself like a man. Or throw up in another handy piece of porcelain. My body is a never-ending delight of bodily functions these days."

Phee grinned. The pregnancy sickness had been the great leveler for Emma. A bit of humility did the girl some good, but Phee wouldn't say so aloud. Besides, Emma had already figured it out.

Girding her proverbial loins, Phee stood and smoothed her turquoise damask silk waistcoat. "How about we visit the modiste now?"

"You mean, before my brother returns from his ride, and you two stare at each other across the dining table like a couple ninnies?"

"Precisely."

Cal stepped aside to allow another footman, burdened with a trunk, access to the line of carriages waiting in the street.

Neighbors all around them suddenly seemed to feel a need for fresh air as one by one, doors opened and people wandered out for a curiously sloth-like promenade along the street. Out of sheer perversity, Cal made eye contact and called out a cheerful greeting to every one of them. *Yes*, he wanted to say. *I see you. You aren't as sly as you believe. And your fascination with my sister and my lover moving out of the house is not subtle.*

This was hell. Over the last few weeks, Phee wouldn't look at him for longer than a moment or two, and Emma hadn't spoken to Cal about anything of importance since her wedding day. Dinners were torturous hours of small talk and cutting silence.

He tamped down the frustration before it could boil over and lead him to snap at the curious bystanders. These neighbors had no way of knowing it was his lover leaving him. They'd stare harder if they knew Phee had once warmed his bed and stolen his heart and that Emma was pregnant.

Yet against all odds, somehow the secrets remained safe. No one knew—so no one acknowledged his pain, and Cal couldn't help resenting that. Which was illogical. Especially when he tried so hard all the damn time to maintain privacy.

Standing on the pavement with the sun warming his un-covered head, it occurred to him that he witnessed everyone else's problems and ultimately found the solutions for them. But no one witnessed his messes. No one handled his prob-lems. The two people who knew the details of this situation were overseeing the last stages of loading these carriages so they could leave.

Not that Cal necessarily wanted to live under the same

roof as Phee. Fine, a masochistic part of him did. Because even if she hated him, at least she would be safe while she hated him. Seeing her caused a physical pain in his chest, and yet he ached for that moment when she appeared. Cal drank her in, savoring the sight because he knew he'd have mere seconds to do so.

As if on cue, Phee's voice drifted through the doorway, and Cal turned to steal a look.

"Thank you, Nelson. This trunk stays with our carriage, not mixed with the rest of the luggage."

The throaty timbre of her voice managed to both soothe and rile him. Phee stepped out the door and hopped lightly down to the street level, ignoring Cal entirely. Her waistcoat was apple green today. One he'd ordered with her in mind and then feigned a distaste for once it arrived. In the weeks since they'd left for Lakeview, she hadn't cut her hair, and the sun played with the fluff of curls, creating colors he didn't think had names yet, because they existed only in her.

Phee turned, caught him staring. These last few weeks, he'd made a habit of looking away, but now he didn't. Not when there were precious few minutes left to soak her in. After a brief hesitation, Phee straightened her shoulders, as if preparing for some monumental task, then approached him with brisk strides. Cal stepped forward to meet her, but she stopped several feet away, out of reach in so many ways.

"I know none of this is easy, but I need you to remember one thing. Don't believe everything you read in the papers."

His confusion must be plain on his face, but instead of explaining, she turned and left him staring after her. Curse him as a dog, but he couldn't resist enjoying the sway of her little heart-shaped arse as she left him wanting for the thousandth time in recent weeks.

Sure, Phee had withheld knowledge of Emma's pregnancy, but his indignation over that no longer felt so righteous. Not after he'd put her in the position of watching him play matchmaker to avoid marrying someone else—all because he hadn't told his father to hang from the beginning. In fact, given his stellar track record for handling scandals, Cal had bungled things rather spectacularly. The accusation that he'd have handled it all differently if she'd still been Adam haunted him.

Cal couldn't miss the feeling of déjà vu. There were so many instances from his childhood when he'd stood helpless as his mother loaded the carriages, leaving pain and tears in her wake as she chased her happiness or fled another betrayal from her husband. Cal hadn't been enough of a reason for her to stay, and the hopelessness beating at his chest suggested not much had changed.

The emotion seemed to be his constant companion now. The pile of things he'd managed to ruin would crush an elephant at this point.

Emma had made one awful choice after another, all under his oblivious nose. Only Phee had seen everything and recognized a problem. Cal hadn't had a hand in protecting Emma or her reputation.

Phee's danger with Milton? Cal might have gotten her out of Town, but in the end, Phee had dealt with that too. All along, Phee had proved herself to be the best possible partner and friend to him, and he'd been too bullheaded to acknowledge when things weren't well in hand.

In the end, everything had gone to hell despite Cal's best efforts. The baron had demanded payment. Rosehurst was done waiting.

Everything was changing, and none of it for the better. The days when Cal and Adam could sit in the library drinking brandy and speaking honestly about problems were long gone. Phee's quick mind and willingness to dive into solving a situation had been priceless, and he'd squandered it. He missed his lover, but above all, Cal missed their friendship.

And damn if Phee wasn't the prettiest thing he'd ever seen, with her legs showcased in snug breeches and boots.

A movement to his right interrupted his shameless ogling.

Ethan arrived and surveyed the carefully orchestrated chaos with crossed arms. "Moving day, aye?"

Cal tried to answer, but the words stuck until he cleared his throat. "Yes. Emma and…Adam are taking a wedding trip. They've picked some tiny village by the sea to settle in for the time being. Newlyweds and their privacy, you know."

The weight of Ethan's gaze made the side of his face prickle, but Cal resolutely stared forward, refusing to look from the carriages, the trunks, and one redhead who directed it all.

"I don' understand all of what's happening here. But you look like you need a friend. You dine with us tonight," Ethan said.

"I don't think—"

"What part of that sounded like a choice?" Ethan interrupted.

Cal gave a huff of weak laughter. "Fine. I'll be lousy company. You can't say you weren't warned."

Ethan clapped a hand on Cal's shoulder. "I'll tell Lottie tae use the old china so I can throw things at your hard head if you get out of hand."

The first genuine smile of the day crossed Cal's face. "Fine." Tonight he'd dine and mope. And tomorrow he had an appointment with Eastly to discuss Rosehurst and his daughter.

Miss Cuthbert had made friends at the house party but had not enticed a lover. The party hadn't been a total matchmaking failure. As of this week, a few other women at the party were engaged. Miss Lillian Fitzwilliam and Lord Hornsby's whirlwind romance was the talk of society. And Miss Georgina had somehow landed Gaffney. How the hell that had happened, Cal had no idea. He'd gently quizzed Gaffney during their meetings at Lakeview, but his grace hadn't been forthcoming with personal information. The woman was mousy, quiet, and apparently irresistible to the young duke. And of course, the whole *ton* knew about Emma's marriage to the unlikely Adam Hardwick.

Cal had failed. Spectacularly. He'd failed Emma. He'd failed Violet. But most of all, he'd failed Phee.

In every way. No wonder she showed no signs of forgiving him anytime soon.

On the street, Phee pointed toward a carriage, saying something to Nelson. The sun in her hair had been so beautiful he'd failed to notice the shadows under her eyes. The hollows beneath her cheekbones were carved deeper, making her appear sharp and gaunt, but highlighted her ridiculously pouty lips. God, he missed her.

Beside the carriage, Nelson said something that made her smile, and Cal lost his breath.

Nodding a goodbye to Ethan, he fixed a neutral expression on his face and retreated inside. The house would be empty soon, and being alone suddenly seemed like the worst possible punishment.

Chapter Twenty-Three

❦

"You grew up here?" Emma's face pressed against the glass of the carriage window, making her words echo with a tinny quality.

"Near here, yes. The manor house is down that lane and then through the woods, past the pond. According to Nelson, Milton is in London. Or he was as of two weeks ago. So we should be safe to visit Vicar Arcott, then leave Warford before anyone knows we're here." The familiar houses of the village appeared, then disappeared in succession outside her window. After the first night on the road, they'd broken off from the caravan of carriages and sent the others on toward their rented house in Olread Cove, while she and Emma had continued to Northumberland. Not only was the whole caravan of luggage not needed in Warford, but there was zero chance of such a spectacle being overlooked in the village. One carriage was far more stealthy, all things considered.

In John's last letter he'd claimed Vicar Arcott was weak

but continued to improve, despite all odds. John also reported his engagement to Daisy, the baker's daughter.

"They're not expecting us, but I don't think we need to stay long," Phee said.

Finally, the church with its tidy graveyard and snug vicarage came into view.

Vicar Arcott himself answered their knock. In that moment, she was a little girl again, faced with the one adult who always had a hug for her. He opened the door, stood shocked for a heartbeat, then opened his arms, as he always had.

"You have no idea how wonderful it is to see you up and walking again," Phee said into his chest. He was still frail and likely always would be. Her arms easily wrapped around his torso. But saints be praised, he stood there under his own strength.

"Darling girl, you look tired. I didn't expect you." Arcott pulled away enough to examine her face with a concerned frown. Then he looked over her shoulder. "And you brought a friend."

Phee turned to Emma. "This is Lady Emma Carlyle, now Lady Emma Hardwick." She glanced at Arcott. "She knows everything, but the staff does not."

Vicar Arcott eyed them, then the fine traveling carriage. "You'd best come inside," he said in a low voice.

Phee directed the coachman and groom to where they could water and rest the horses behind the vicarage, then sent them on to the tavern in the village for their supper.

Inside, the cottage remained exactly as she remembered it. Gratitude that she could stand here one more time, when she'd been so sure the visit in May would be her last, made tears pool. For once they were happy ones. Turning to Emma, she said, "This is the closest I have to a home. I learned my sums and my letters at that table." She pointed to the scarred wood where a plate and glass remained from the vicar's last meal, with a dark cloth serviette folded neatly beside them.

Emma's eyes were wide as she took in everything. It was a far cry from the London townhome on Hill Street. The entire house would fit inside Emma's bedchamber, but Phee couldn't be prouder to share it with her.

"This is where I came from. And the vicar is the finest man you'll ever meet." Phee hugged the older man with one arm around his waist, overwhelmed at seeing him again.

"Are you hungry? Mrs. Courtland left a pie, and I can put the kettle on." Without waiting for an answer, the vicar shuffled toward the hearth, kettle in hand.

Emma opened her mouth, but Phee cut her off. "Mrs. Courtland makes the best pies. You don't want to miss the opportunity to taste one. Vicar, let me do that. I'll make the tea. Take a seat and get to know Emma."

Once he'd served the pies, bursting with late-summer berries and encased in a flaky crust like only Mrs. Courtland could make, Phee poured tea for everyone and finally joined them at the table.

"Where's John?" she asked.

"Finishing the lessons at the schoolhouse. He'll be home late." Arcott turned to Emma. "He's marrying soon. A girl he's been sweet on for an age."

Emma nodded, but she looked a little lost, as if slightly out of her depth outside a posh drawing room. Phee smiled, then closed her eyes in bliss when the first bite of pie hit her tongue.

Following her lead, Emma took a bite, then made a happy little moan before covering her mouth with her hand. "Sorry, that wasn't a ladylike sound. This pie is perfect, though, isn't it?" Her cheeks blushed a vibrant pink as she took another bite.

"I told you. Mrs. Courtland's pies can't be missed." Phee reached over and covered Arcott's gnarled fingers with hers. "Vicar, I have a favor to ask. I'm afraid I need your help one last time."

"Is it time for Adam to finally be at peace, then?"

"Yes." Her throat tightened around the word. "We won't publish the death notice quite yet. But it's time. Emma needed help, so she will be Adam's widow."

Arcott's eyes filled with tears, and his fingers shook when he turned his hand over to squeeze hers. "What shall your new name be, child?"

Phee smiled. She'd thought long and hard about this. "Fiona. Then I can still be Phee. Same last name, I think. A distant cousin, if we can do that."

He nodded. "You'll need a baptism record. I'll take care of it."

"Thank you. I'm sorry to ask you to lie again."

"This will bring us full circle. I took your place in the world, but now I can give you another." The teacup rattled in the saucer when he set it down. "Go visit your brother while I find the right record book."

The chairs scraped against the floor when they rose, then Phee held the door open for Emma.

Early evening sunlight dappled the leaves overhead as they wove through the headstones in the graveyard. At the right marker, they stopped, and Emma hugged herself at the sight. "Doesn't it disturb you to see your own name in stone like that?"

Phee sighed. "It hurts more to not see his. It'll actually be a relief when this is over and I can visit a headstone with Adam's name." Reaching out, she trailed a hand over the curved rock face, sweeping at a bit of moss that clung to the *O* in Ophelia.

"I don't know how you did it, Phee. You're remarkable," Emma said.

Phee knelt and rested her hand on the grass atop the grave, the ever-present grief for her brother welling to the surface. "No," she whispered. "I survived. That's all. We do what we must. I miss him, though. I wish you could have known Adam."

Emma placed a hand on Phee's shoulder. "I knew a version of him. And next, I get to meet Fiona."

As Phee looked up at her, backlit as she was by the sun, the resemblance to Cal was strong, and it added another layer of ache to her chest. "Please, God, let this be my last name change."

Vicar Arcott was a man of his word and, thankfully, was willing to falsify records one more time. An hour later she kissed him goodbye, and he pressed a slice of pie into Emma's eager hands at the carriage door. "Don't stay in the village. Milton will get word if you do, especially with this fancy rig," he said.

"I know. We'll stop for the night closer to the coast." Phee wrapped her arms around him one last time and closed her eyes for a moment. Needing to say everything in case this turned out to be the last time she saw him, she pulled away and looked him in the eye. "Thank you for everything. I love you. I wish you'd been my father."

He swallowed roughly. "You've always been mine. Sometimes God brings us children that don't share our blood. Come home when you can, my darling girl."

One more hug, and then they took their leave. They'd need to push hard to get as much distance as possible between them and Warford before nightfall. She knew from experience that Milton had spies everywhere.

"I'm going to look ridiculous," Phee grumbled, even as she continued sewing neat stitches in a perfect row.

"No," Emma said. "You will look lovely. What's going to look ridiculous is your hair. And that's why God made bonnets. Has it always poufed like that?"

"Yes, unfortunately. As a child I had ringlets. But no matter what I did, it always became a tangled rat's nest by the end of the day. Honestly, I think dealing with my hair at a longer length will be what I hate most about living as a woman again." Phee snipped the thread. "There. Can you help me into it?" They were at their fifth inn, taking a deliberately leisurely approach toward the tiny seaside village of Olread Cove. They'd arrive at the leased house the following day.

During the interminable days of travel, Phee and Emma

kept their hands busy by making alterations they'd marked and pinned together the evening before.

Seeing the grave again, this time so close to the end of her charade, had left Phee unsettled. Sleep had been poor, and a fidgety unease made her jumpy. What if she wasn't ready for the next step? What if she couldn't unlearn the pieces of her brother she'd adopted? The walk, the manner of speaking—none of that was right for a lady. Layers of binding, a shirt, jacket, waistcoat, and cravat had been an armor of sorts, protecting her from the reality of being alone in the world.

The sounds of the bustling inn drifted through the wooden-plank floor as they removed her men's garments and she donned the gown. They'd done some version of this to fit the dresses each evening, but as Emma helped her with the pins and tapes, Phee knew. The gown was ready.

The fine chemise, gossamer thin and trimmed in delicate lace, was the prettiest thing she had ever owned. She couldn't help but think of how Cal would react if he saw it. The thought brought a pang, so she stuffed it down. He'd become part of her past. This was the time for creating a future.

Tomorrow they would tell the coachman that Adam's cousin Fiona had arrived during the night and Adam had set off early ahead of them. Then the charade would begin. The coachman and other staff would return to London as soon as they arrived in Olread Cove, and no one would be the wiser that Adam wasn't waiting at the cottage like they said.

A petticoat trimmed in embroidered green silk leaves peeked out beneath the gathered hem of the skirt. She had no shoes to match, but she'd found a pair of walking boots at a used clothing stall during their travels.

The sturdy little boots made her feel better. They felt solid on her feet, like her tall boots had, and in a way this ladylike footwear straddled two worlds. The old existence of breeches and cravats, and her new reality of skirts and fripperies.

"What made you pick this copper shade?" Emma asked.

Because Cal had once told her she'd look lovely in copper or green, and no matter how hard she tried, Phee couldn't forget a single moment of their time together. "I thought the shade would suit me," she lied.

Using the windowpane, the women stood side by side and studied their reflections.

"The Widow Hardwick and her cousin by marriage Miss Fiona Hardwick," Emma said, imitating the tone of Higgins announcing visitors.

Phee lost her voice, overcome by the picture they made. Except for her hair, she looked like a sophisticated young lady.

"Stop staring at your duck fluff, Phee. You have all the time in the world to grow it out now."

And Emma was right. Wasn't that the damnedest thing.

It had been ten days since he'd heard her voice, and Cal might go mad during the lifetime ahead of him filled with this awful silence. Not that he'd expected Phee to reach out with news, but Emma hadn't written either. At his desk, Cal pushed aside the contracts for Gaffney's cider operation, the message he'd received from the captain of the *Wilhelmina* this morning, and the ledgers awaiting his attention. It hadn't been good news for the investors, and unfortunately, Eastly wouldn't see a single penny back. That was the nature of investments—some worked out, and some failed. But this failure killed any hope of Eastly paying his way out of the Rosehurst pickle.

Yet none of those burdens weighed as heavily as the absence of Emma and Phee. He pulled out a sheet of paper.

Dear Emma,   *October 5, 1820*

The house seems empty without you here, chattering while sprawled on your favorite chaise in the gold drawing room. Perhaps once you're settled in your new house, I could send it to you. Think of it as a belated wedding gift. It may make you feel more at home. Although I admit, I hope you'll return to London after the baby is born.

Have you considered names? Are you feeling better? I hope the travel wasn't too much for you.

I know you're mad at me about everything that happened at Lakeview, but I pray you'll write anyway.

Love,
Cal

He hesitated, then sighed. No one said he'd have to mail every letter he wrote. And damn, he missed talking to Phee. Out came another sheet of paper, and although she'd never read it, he began to write.

Dear Phee,   *October 5, 1820*

You talk in your sleep. Did I ever tell you that?
My bed is too quiet without you.

Pouring out his heart was cathartic in a way. Like lancing a wound, although that was a disgusting comparison. But then, his feelings at the moment weren't exactly pretty either. He didn't have poetry to offer the one who'd stolen his heart and his sister. So the letter became honest and messy and didn't make him look good—he sounded pathetic and broken without her. But putting on his mask hadn't been the point.

He read it over, signed it with a flourish, then promptly crumpled it in his fist and threw it in the rubbish bin by the desk. The stack of ledgers sat as silent witnesses to his foolishness. Beyond the door, Higgins's voice rumbled an order to another servant. The few steps from the desk to the door were tiny procrastinations, but Cal welcomed any excuse to put off his next task.

"Higgins? Could you send up a pot of coffee? I have a long night ahead of me, I'm afraid."

The butler dipped his head in a shallow bow. "Yes, milord. I'll notify Cook."

"Thank you." Cal stood awkwardly, not quite leaning in the doorway but not having any reason to linger either.

"Will there be anything else, milord?" Higgins asked.

Cal sighed. "No. I'm putting off dealing with my father." The admission slipped out, and he couldn't call it back.

"In that case, I'll have Cook add cake to the tray." Higgins turned, but Cal would have sworn he saw a hint of a smile on the old retainer's face.

At least now he'd get cake. There was always a silver lining. Cal turned toward the massive mahogany desk. The ledgers waited exactly where he'd left them. He was rather hoping they'd grow legs and run off, but no such excuse presented itself.

Time to get to work. Because in that stack of ledgers was the answer to his troubles. He hoped. Even with the loss of the *Wilhelmina* investment, somewhere in those columns of numbers must be the solution to paying his father's debt with something besides Cal's bachelorhood.

He sat, wishing for the hundredth time that he'd chosen a more comfortable desk chair. It would be a long night, or week, or however long it took him to find a way to save the estate.

The baron's good will was at an end.

Chapter Twenty-Four

~

Dear Phee,   *October 5, 1820*

You talk in your sleep. Did I ever tell you that? My bed is too quiet without you.

It may make me a sentimental fool, but the day you left, I stole your pillow and refuse to let the maids touch it. Feel free to laugh at the mental image of me comforting myself with a musty pillow. If I sniff deep enough, there are still traces of sandalwood, and finding those final bits of you in my bed seems to be the only way I sleep these days.

Truth be told, I haven't slept well since the last time we were together. As much as the memory brings me pain, I have to admit that you were perfect in your execution of revenge. Just like

*during our countless fencing matches, your attack
was effective, focused, and brutal. You're remarkable, but then I knew that.*

I knew that, and I still made a hash of us.

*Because of my misplaced confidence in my own
ability to juggle the world—at the expense of our
relationship, I've lost you forever.*

I'm never mailing this—

Phee stopped reading. The paper's crinkled lines told a
story of being crumpled into a ball. If he'd thrown this away
after writing it as a sort of personal journal entry, then she
didn't have any place reading it.

And yet.

Dear Phee.

This letter belonged to her. Whether or not he'd meant to
mail it, she held it in her hands now.

*I'm never mailing this, so I can speak freely. The
Wilhelmina finally arrived in port this week. Crew
is in good spirits, but the cargo is a complete
loss. I find myself identifying with the ship as I
deal with distraught investors—my father being
chief among them. Like the Wilhelmina, I'm alive,
but empty.*

*I love you. That wasn't a lie. I think I've loved
you since that night in your old room, watching
the firelight play across your features, terrified*

*for you. Unfortunately, I'm still terrified for you.
Nelson's connections with your uncle's ruffians
report that Milton has gone silent. I could write
you another letter, updating you on the report,
but what would I say? "I'm sorry I ruined us,
but I love you, and even though your uncle is
not making any additional threats, his silence is
telling?"*

*So, I say nothing, and I wait, and I hope that
where you are, the halls ring with your laughter,
and there's a pillow that smells like you. I wish it
rested beside mine.*

A tear snaked down Phee's cheek before she dashed
it away.

Damn the man. And damn whoever had gone against his
wishes and mailed a letter she was never supposed to read.

Despite the vicious thoughts, Phee carefully smoothed the
paper, then refolded it.

Outside her bedroom window, cool air carried the loamy
smell of green earth and the tang of salt spray from the sea that
crashed at the base of the cliff where the house perched.

The chair in this ray of sunshine had become Phee's
favorite place in the house. Each night the low rhythm of
the waves lulled her to sleep through this window. In the
mornings, Phee drank her coffee in this chair, and every day
offered a different view. Sometimes fog rolled in and she
listened to the gulls cry. Other mornings brought brilliant
early sun sparkling off the water.

When they'd arrived at the house, they'd sent the servants

back to London, then hired their own staff from the town. Providing immediate employment in a rural place like Olread Cove not only met their needs but quickly ingratiated them with the locals.

The villagers had no reason to believe they weren't the Widow Hardwick and her cousin by marriage Miss Fiona Hardwick. Emma wanted to keep whispers to a minimum, so she'd left her honorific behind in Mayfair.

Now they'd settle into a quiet life until the baby came, then Emma would decide what she wanted to do next. Phee had promised to stay through the birth before choosing where she'd go. Watching the sea each day, as breathtaking as it was, only reinforced her desire to not spend a great deal of time on a boat. The Continent might be the place for her, instead of America.

Phee turned from the open window, searching for the wrap she'd discarded earlier. A flash of blue caught her eye from under the book she'd read that morning. After slinging the dark wool over her shoulders, Phee tugged on a pair of kidskin gloves and went downstairs. "I'm going on a walk," she called to whoever might be listening. Emma, the cook, and the maid had been in the kitchen the last time she'd checked.

Salt air slapped Phee's cheeks as she pulled the heavy wood-plank door closed behind her. She gave the iron handle an extra yank to ensure it stayed closed, as the door sometimes stuck in the doorjamb and didn't latch properly after a day of rain.

Tugging on her bonnet as she walked, she tied the ribbons under her chin. Truth be told, she missed the hats she used to wear with male clothing. A bonnet covered her baby-duck-fluff hair, which resisted all efforts of taming as it grew, but it still seemed like playing dress-up. Wearing a dress felt more natural now, but the bonnets? Not so much.

The favorite walking path she'd found wound around the top edge of the cliff, then led down a rocky slope to the beach where Phee collected shells and colorful glass worn smooth by the water. No doubt the breeze would ensure any wisps of hair uncovered by her bonnet stayed vertical for the rest of the day, but this restlessness within her surpassed vanity.

Gravel shifted beneath her feet as she deliberately lengthened her stride, walking as she had when she'd been living her brother's life. Emma had been working with Phee to change her walk, but for a moment, Phee wanted the familiar. The easy.

Cal's letter had been simultaneously hurtful and beautiful. Bad luck that she'd get that missive today of all days. She'd thought she was ready to leave the past behind, and then Cal's penmanship had snagged her calm into a tangle, and now she wasn't sure she could do the one thing on her agenda.

Phee had to send the death notice to the *Times*. The final piece of letting Adam go. Her steps quickened until she ran, heading toward the cliff edge as if chased by a literal ghost instead of a figurative one.

Adam had been gone for over a decade, yet sending a letter to the *Times* felt like a death of another kind. She and Emma had decided, after their visit to the gravestone outside the Arcotts' home, that Adam deserved a headstone. A marker with his name, commemorating his life, short as it had been. Even if the death date was wrong, Adam's name belonged in stone next to the other in Warford, beside the vicarage. To those in London who cared, Adam Hardwick would die tragically young, which was nothing but the truth.

A tear wet her cheek, although Phee didn't remember crying again. She dashed at it, inadvertently wiping her face with the letter from Cal, which was still clutched in her hand. Holding the paper to her nose, she tried to catch a whiff of his spicy gingerbread scent, like he'd confessed to searching for sandalwood on his pillow.

No such luck. For some reason, that brought another tear to her eye.

Cal's sweet letter, pretty apology, and declarations of love were for Ophelia.

Crossing her arms across her middle, she stared out at restless waves. All that remained of Ophelia was a headstone in a graveyard in Northumberland. She'd become someone new. Again.

Like it or not, she would be Fiona now, and she must move forward. That meant some things had to stay in the past.

No countess of mine will have scandal attached to her.

Opening her fist, Phee let the paper flutter in her palm, hovering and falling until it caught the wind and took off. Like a tiny kite, the paper rode an air current, lifting and floating with a freedom she envied. Finally, the letter to a woman who no longer existed floated over the cliff edge and disappeared into the waves below.

Unless Cal showed up on their doorstep to make those proclamations to her face, there was nothing to be done. A letter was lovely, but at the end of the day, they were words he hadn't meant to send. Empty words.

Just like names were words, and a death notice didn't make Adam more dead. Phee took in a deep breath of salt air and straightened her shoulders. Maybe today she would get that death notice written after all.

Adam needed to die. Only then could Phee truly live.

Dear Emma,   *October 12, 1820*

Another week of silence from my baby sister, and I have no choice but to assume you have yet to forgive me for what happened. Is this some kind of sisterhood you two have formed? If so, I'm glad Phee has you in her corner.

Please don't feel caught between us. If given the chance to do everything over, I'd definitely make different choices.

I'd treat Phee like a partner. I'd spend more time planning a future with her than dealing with our father.

I'd have told you that Roxbury demanded payment to leave you alone. I would do many things differently.

Thank you for being a better friend to Phee than I was.

Tell the baby—whom I've decided to call Mortimer Hildegard unless you write back and tell me otherwise—Uncle Cal loves him. He loves you too, brat.

Sincerely,
Cal

Dear Emma,   *October 20, 1820*

How is little Mortimer Hildegard? Is he/she kicking yet? I remember our mother's joy when she felt you stirring in her womb. Her eyes would light, and she loved to hold my hand to her belly to see if I could sense you moving. I couldn't until the last month. Then your constant tossing and turning would make her entire stomach roll and shift, and it gave my young brain nightmares. So, thanks for that.

I wanted to let you know that I've come to a decision. Father didn't overstate his circumstances. I've looked over the books, checked every avenue, and ran through financial scenarios until I'm falling asleep at my desk and dreaming of dancing columns of numbers. Unless he sells everything unentailed and lives with strict discipline (ha!) at the family seat for the next few years, paying the debt to the baron will be impossible. There's one

clear path that will save the estate and serve the tenants. I have to marry Violet Cuthbert.
It will be a Christmas wedding.

Cal

The pen hovered over the page for so long, ink dripped from the tip and fell to the paper with a splat. He wanted to ask how Phee was. If they were comfortable, if the villagers were friendly. And then he wanted to ask about Phee again. If she was happy. If she laughed, or if she moped about like he did.

When he'd visited a couple of days before, Miss Cuthbert hadn't been any happier with the news than he was. Especially since he'd arrived in her drawing room looking like a grieving wreck. After he explained that the one he loved had married another, Miss Cuthbert patted his hand and suggested they make the best of it. The baron had been thrilled that the Earl of Carlyle had come to call—and all that implied—so he'd been happy to make himself scarce from the Egyptian-themed drawing room. The sarcophagus looked on disapprovingly when Cal and Miss Cuthbert spoke honestly about the situation.

Despite the Season and the house party, she didn't have a beau who'd caught her eye. They agreed that perhaps a friendly marriage would do, since high passion clearly wasn't working out for either of them. When they'd first met, Miss Cuthbert had told him she would do her duty, and that was what it came down to.

They were pawns to their fathers. And in the baron's

defense, it was a brilliant marriage for his daughter. It wasn't egotistical to say so. If Cal were a better son, he'd be content with a beautiful blond wife.

But he missed Phee. He didn't want blond curves. He wanted red curls on the pillow, finely made bones, her contagious laugh, and easy friendship.

The sand he threw on the ink scattered across his desk, but it was hard to care. Standing to stare out the window, Cal shoved his hands in his pockets. The trees along the street were vibrant with color, but he'd become so gray inside, their hues seemed garish. Soon the weather would turn cold and wet, with a biting wind that cut through even the sturdiest clothes. In his current condition, Cal would blend right in.

The glass reflected a sight that made his lip curl. Blond hair hung lank around a face half covered with stubble. Kingston had despaired and threatened to quit, but Cal had consoled him with a promise that he wouldn't go out in society again like this. Which gave Cal the perfect reason to decline every invitation—he'd promised his valet.

In fact, Cal had rarely left the library in the last two weeks. The staff tiptoed around as if afraid of spooking their master, who'd clearly gone feral, and a disturbing smell permeated the room that he was afraid might be *him*.

From the doorway, Higgins cleared his throat. "These arrived via messenger from your solicitor, milord."

Cal glanced over his shoulder. Higgins held a brown leather satchel. Probably the wedding contracts. "Set it on the chair. And post this letter to my sister. Thank you, Higgins."

Cal faced the window again, taking in the view but seeing nothing.

Higgins cleared his throat. "May I get you anything, milord? Coffee? A tray of food? Cook would love to send some of her ginger cakes, I'm sure."

"No, thank you." A leaf skittered by on the pavement, propelled by a breeze as it trailed along Hill Street. Down the lane, a child's laughter echoed off the stone buildings. Cal felt no more connected to the world beyond the windowpane than to the one inside his house. As if he'd separated from his body and now remained blessedly numb. Numbness had to be better than hollow pain.

The door closed, and the library fell quiet once more. Ethan had called earlier in the day, but Cal had put him off, needing to write the letter to his sister before he lost the nerve. Something about telling Emma, and by extension, Phee, made the situation too real. Here in his library, hiding from the world, he could pretend his engagement was hypothetical or another tall tale he'd share over brandy. *Remember that time Eastly traded me for a horse, and I outmaneuvered him?*

Once that letter was posted, it would all be real. He would marry Violet Cuthbert so the lives and properties of his father's tenants would continue undisturbed, and Eastly would gain a racehorse he didn't know what to do with. The idiocy of it all was so overwhelming yet melded rather perfectly with this undeniably depressive turn his life had taken.

When the wood door rasped against the floor again, Cal sighed. The servants were concerned; he understood that. But this hovering about him like a bunch of nursemaids needed to stop. "What now, Higgins?"

"My husband is worried about you, which is inconvenient

for me. And when it's inconvenient for me, it becomes your problem." Lottie didn't wait for an invitation. She sailed in on a lemon-scented breeze, then took a seat by his fireplace. Cal couldn't help but straighten his posture when she snapped, "Take a seat, Calvin. If you wanted sweetness and light, you shouldn't have turned away Ethan this morning. Now you have to deal with me, and I have enough on my plate without worrying about your pretty little head as well. Sit."

He sat. The path of least resistance was often the smarter option with Lady Amesbury.

"You look like hell, you haven't seen Ethan in days, and everyone is concerned for you. Ring for brandy or coffee or whatever will get you talking. Because this is ridiculous." She motioned toward Cal's general person.

Higgins entered with a cart. He must have scuttled off for refreshments the minute Lady Amesbury arrived. Never mind that the master of the blasted house had left strict instructions barring visitors. Lottie's smile and murmured thanks to his butler confirmed his suspicions. They were plotting against him, but Cal couldn't make himself care beyond a faint stirring of indignation.

Pouring with a serene expression, she handed him a cup and saucer, then bit into a small frosted ginger cake. She settled deeper into the chair. "Now, talk."

Cal took a sip of the coffee. Like everything else recently, it inspired neither appreciation nor satisfaction. It was just brown bean water that helped him stay alert until he could retire for the day and stare at his bedroom ceiling. "I'm fine," he lied.

Her snort wasn't delicate or amused. "Try again, but make an attempt at honesty this time."

The cake didn't tempt him in the least, but he took a bite to avoid answering for a few seconds. Words gathered in his throat, turning the sweet treat to ash. "I'm getting married."

Lottie froze with her fork halfway to her mouth. "I beg your pardon? To whom? And how did we not know you were courting?"

"Violet Cuthbert, daughter of Baron Rosehurst. My father traded me for a horse. Ethan might have told you about that a few months ago. Well, it's come down to it. I can't escape the situation."

If Lottie rolled her eyes any harder, they'd stick, and she'd be staring at her own brain forever. "Calvin, darling. Yes, you're beautiful, but I also know you're uncommonly intelligent. Others might not give you credit for that, but I know. You are *not* a damsel in distress, so stop acting like it."

"What are you talking about?" Cal's question was automatic, but her statement stung. All his life, he'd garnered praise for his looks—something entirely out of his control. Not once had he gained notoriety for competently handling his family's affairs or making his own fortune on the Exchange and through investments.

"You're handsome, titled, rich, and wickedly smart. Stop standing on the sideline of your own life and take charge, for God's sake. Your father is an arse and a grown man. His consequences are his, and the natural result of his actions. Those problems are only yours to deal with if you take that responsibility on yourself." Lottie's voice was firm, her focus on him unshakable, and for a moment, Cal envied Ethan. To have such a partner in your life, an equal and a fighter, must be amazing. That Phee had been all those things wasn't lost on him.

"It's my *father*. He'll be ruined if I don't do this."

She made a dismissive noise in his general direction, then took a sip from her cup. "Nonsense. The Eastly title has the entailed estate, which will provide an income if he doesn't make an utter hash of it. Even if he sells off literally everything else, he will still be head and shoulders ahead of the average British citizen. To whine about his lot only shows what a spoiled brat he is."

Cal's chuckle sounded rusty, but it felt good to laugh. Lottie had a point, and as usual, she happily speared anyone's argument with an arsenal of logic.

Unfortunately, she was also acutely observant. She narrowed her eyes. "This level of grime and sloth isn't due to your father's latest misfortune. There's a woman involved. Who is she?"

All the fight seeped from him, and he slumped in the chair. His chest went tight, and Cal wondered for a moment if breath would simply stop under the weight of his emotions. "You remember Adam Hardwick?"

She blinked. "I didn't know your interests leaned that direction. But if that's where your heart lies, I see the problem. Being in love with your brother-in-law is problematic at best."

"Adam was a twin. His sister, Ophelia—Phee—took his place when he died." He couldn't say more, because saying her name aloud made his heart race.

Lottie cocked her head, considering. "That explains so much. I wonder why I didn't see it."

"People see what you tell them to see. At least, that's what Phee says."

"Let me guess—Emma is with child, and your Miss Hardwick stepped in to help?"

Cal nodded. "After I ruined everything. She's well out of reach now. A relationship is impossible. It doesn't really matter if I marry Violet Cuthbert or the onion seller on the corner. If I can't marry who I want, I might as well save my father. Again, and for the last time."

"I understand you're distressed and wallowing, Cal. And truly, this is the most epic wallowing I've seen outside Drury Lane. But you're talking nonsense." Lottie wiped her fingers on a cloth serviette, with dainty motions that were at odds with her tone.

"It's not nonsense. This is my life, and it's a disaster."

"Let me ask you something. Are Emma and your Miss Hardwick in love? Or at least lovers?"

Cal blinked. "Not that I know of."

"Then what is stopping you from living with them and having a relationship while she plays the part of Adam in public?"

"You mean besides the fact that it's a scandal waiting to happen?"

"So? Speaking as a former scandal, I can tell you it isn't that bad when you're with the right person."

That hadn't been his experience. As a child he'd dealt with the whispers, the drama. Boys at Eton had been merciless with their tormenting. Developing a carefree facade had been vital to his survival. If you pretended none of it mattered, it stole the fun out of it, and the boys eventually found other targets. In reality, each barb only reminded him of the truth—his parents didn't care. He and Emma weren't enough reason to be civil or to live separate lives so their relationship wasn't constantly under discussion by all of society.

As an adult, he'd done what he could—and sometimes more than he should—to protect Emma from the lasting consequences of their parents' choices. Given her the best chances at a good match. Tried to handle everything, until he felt like a performer he'd once seen at a traveling fair who'd managed to juggle a knife, a ball, and a shoe from a child in the crowd.

"If anyone is qualified at handling scandals, it's you. You've been training your entire life for this, and here you are, pouting in your library, instead of doing whatever you need to do to get into her good graces."

"I won't ever have heirs." The protestation sounded weak, but a lightening in the pressure near his heart felt an awful lot like hope.

Lottie shrugged. "Everything entailed reverts to the crown. Our new king could use the boost in his coffers. You know his divorce from Queen Caroline must be bleeding him dry. If the earldom means more to you than Miss Hardwick, you don't deserve her, anyway."

Cal felt his mouth go slack. "You make it sound simple."

Lottie reached for the leather satchel Higgins had brought in earlier. Reading the note attached, she arched a brow. "Wedding contracts, I assume?"

He nodded.

"It is simple. Burn them. Then go get your woman and tell her you'll do absolutely anything to live out the rest of your days with her. Pass along my condolences to Miss Cuthbert on the loss of her handsome fiancé." Lottie kissed his forehead in a sisterly gesture that struck him as both sweet and patronizing. "And next time my husband calls, please don't turn him away. You are surrounded by people who love you and want to help you, if only you'll let us."

Lottie set the leather satchel, heavy with papers, in his lap. The door closed behind her, leaving Cal and the tempting flames crackling in the hearth.

Chapter Twenty-Five

A fter a night of tossing and turning, examining Lottie's words from every angle, Cal finally came to a decision as dawn broke across the rooftops of London. With the resolution, he felt at peace for the first time in weeks. The solution had been simple, just as Lottie had said. Sometimes it took an outside perspective to help when one found himself stuck in a pit of his own making.

A handsome face was currency for his father, who'd always encouraged Cal to marry someone highborn, rich, and connected. Eastly himself had been using his looks to get what he wanted for his entire life.

Unfortunately, the marquess's willingness to take advantage of those around him didn't have a bottom. The more Cal gave, the more Eastly would take. It was simple math, and the sum would never be in Cal's favor if he continued to do his father's bidding.

At some point, there had to be an end to it all. He

desperately hoped Phee would be at the center of that happiness, but even if she never forgave him, Cal had to try. One thing was certain: playing his father's games would never lead to anything good.

After that bit of soul searching, he'd slept like the dead until Kingston woke him with coffee and a gentle reminder of the time. The coffee scalded his throat as he dressed in a hurry, bypassing his usual morning rituals.

Searching for a ribbon to tie back his hair, Cal opened the drawer in the table beside his bed. A piece of wood rolled forward and clunked against his knuckles.

Lifting it slowly, Cal caught his breath.

She'd left him the bird. Each feather was carved with exquisite detail, capturing the beauty of flight with wings outstretched. Before Lakeview, Phee had confessed that she'd carved a bird because she wanted to fly away.

And she had, hadn't she? Phee had flown. She'd found a way to be free.

He was the one in a cage.

But no more. Cal brushed a finger over the polished wood, then placed it on the table.

He had an engagement to break and a life to reclaim.

At the Rosehurst home, Miss Violet Cuthbert sat on the same awful zebra-striped chaise where she'd been when he'd visited her the first time. Admittedly, she was pretty as a picture, reading the paper with her gown draping around her as she sat in a beam of sunlight streaming through the window. When the butler announced Cal, she jumped to her feet and met him in the middle of the room.

That was a far more eager greeting than he'd expected.

"Good morning, Miss Cuthbert. I wish I'd called under better circumstances, but I'm afraid I come bearing unpleasant news." He grasped her fingers between them and looked her in the eye. "A gentleman never breaks an engagement, but I've discovered I'm less of a gentleman than I believed. You deserve a perfect match, and we both know I am not he—and you're not mine. I've realized I am not willing to settle for less than happiness, and neither should you. I'm sorry, but I can't and won't marry you. Our fathers will have to find another solution to their wager."

Miss Cuthbert shook her head, sending corkscrew curls swinging every which way. Cal's stomach sank. Given how open they'd been about their lack of attachment, this was upsetting her far more than he'd expected. Perhaps she feared that Rosehurst would be impossible to deal with about this.

"Any way I can facilitate your happiness, I will. I'll make introductions, get you invited to the highest functions. Whatever I can do."

"You're being so brave, presenting such a strong face. Milord, I'd never expect our engagement to go forward when your family has been dealt such horrible news. I read about it in the *Times*. I don't know how you're maintaining your composure after such a loss. I only knew him through you, and I'm overwhelmed by how tragic it is." With that impassioned declaration, Miss Cuthbert's eyes went glassy blue with tears.

She was nearly crying, and Cal had no idea what the devil she was talking about.

"You read about it in the *Times*?"

"Oh dear. You haven't seen it?" With a flutter of hands and swirling skirts, she gathered the paper from the chaise and flipped pages until she found what she was looking for and thrust the newssheet at Cal. "Here. I wish they'd given him more print space, especially given his connection to a noble family."

Deaths

Mr. Adam Hardwick, age 24, recently of London, died Monday of last week while on his wedding trip with his new bride, The Lady Emma Hardwick, at his side. His body was interred in the village of Warford, Northumberland, with services officiated by Rev. Charles Arcott. Mr. Hardwick leaves behind his loving wife to grieve his loss.

"They'd only just married," Miss Cuthbert said in a broken whisper.

Cal's knees were having a hard time supporting his body, so he let her guide him to sit on the ghastly zebra chaise. She sank beside him, patting his arm while he clutched the paper and read the words over and over.

Dead and buried. Gone. A tear slipped down his cheek and his nose went stuffy. Phee couldn't be gone. Surely, the world wouldn't be so cruel. Maybe it was silly, but Cal thought for sure that some part of him would sense it if Phee died. She'd taken so much of him with her, he'd have felt it if she'd simply ceased to exist.

Absolutely gutting. She couldn't be gone.

Don't believe everything you read in the papers. That was what she'd said.

Sanity and logic rushed in, drying his tears as he narrowed his eyes at the small print. If Phee had died and been buried already in Northumberland, there was no way in hell he'd find out by reading about it in someone else's copy of the *Times*. Emma would have written or sent a messenger.

None of this made sense. Even knowing the words weren't true, Cal couldn't stop reading the notice over and over. He'd probably recite it in his sleep during nightmares for the rest of his life.

"It's only natural to be so distressed," Miss Cuthbert said soothingly. "He was your dear friend and brother by marriage. This must have been quite a shock."

"Yes," Cal parroted. "Quite a shock." That would forever remain in his mind as the understatement of the century. Gathering his thoughts, Cal set the paper aside and covered Miss Cuthbert's fingers where they rested on his forearm. "I don't know when I will return to London, but I can provide written introductions to all the best hostesses. It's not much, but I'd like to help you achieve your dream of a love match."

Miss Cuthbert squeezed his fingers. "Lord Carlyle, through all of this engagement nonsense, you've been a friend to me. I don't look forward to dealing with my father's disappointment, but I think this may be an opportunity for an honest discussion about the match I want." She shrugged. "Who knows? This might be what forces my father to listen to me about my future."

He smiled. "I hope the baron hears you and understands. You deserve more than apathy from a spouse. I hate to leave you like this and am very sorry to go back on my word. But I hope you understand that I have to go."

"Your sister needs you, Lord Carlyle. Go to her." A residual tear broke free of her bottom lashes as she nodded, sending those curls flying about again, but she wiped it away with a bright smile.

Cal donned his hat. "Goodbye, Miss Cuthbert. I hope the next time we meet it will be during happier times."

Out on the street, Cal swung up onto Murphy and nudged him toward home. Phee was on the other side of the country yet had still managed to save his hide today. She'd even sent a sign with her whittled bird, whether that had been her intention or not.

One interview done, one more to go before he would be free to fly away too. The charade of Adam's death must be maintained during the visit with Eastly, but Cal would take that particular meeting in his own territory.

He brought Murphy around an apple seller's cart, then dodged a small dog yipping at a boy with a red ball. The gelding was a solid mount, capable of finding the best path through a crowded street. A lucky thing, because with a mind full of travel plans, the upcoming meeting with Eastly, and the memory of that awful moment when he'd seen the death notice, Cal's focus wasn't on the street.

A groom took Murphy when Cal arrived at home. Cal glanced at his pocket watch, then climbed the steps to his door two at a time. Father would arrive in an hour. That left barely enough time to confer with Kingston regarding packing and tie up a few loose ends before they set out for the coast.

Endless days of travel loomed ahead, but at least he'd see Phee again. He had to believe that newspaper announcement was false. Anything else would be beyond imagining.

Perhaps by the time he reached Olread Cove, he would have some idea of what to say. Apologies seemed inadequate given the events that had taken place.

When the appointment with Eastly rolled around, Cal was ready to have an end to this disastrous bet and all future feelings of obligation.

Higgins announced his father's arrival as Cal sat in the drawing room reading the death notice in the *Times* for the thousandth time. "Show him to the library. I'll be there momentarily. After my father takes his leave, please tell Nelson I'd like to see him. Thank you."

As a child, Cal had never seen his father working in the library. That had been a place for drinking with his cronies, not going over estate business. Eastly wouldn't make the connection, because he wasn't what one would call a deep thinker, but Cal wanted to end this in the library. Although not a bibliophile, he appreciated the room as his place of work. And he'd sacrificed sleep over this past week doing that work, right at that desk, attempting to figure out a solution to his father's irresponsible behavior. It seemed fitting, then, that this would be where Cal delivered his verdict.

"Good morning, Father. Thank you for meeting me so early." Well on noon now, but given Eastly's puffy face and red eyes, he'd been out late. Not a surprise. Cal didn't shake his hand or dispense niceties. With determined strides, he went to his desk and gathered the stack of ledgers. "You may take these with you when you go. I have all the information I need from them." Cal handed off the books, then leaned against the desk, crossing his arms over his chest and his legs at the ankles. "Essentially, the paths for getting out of the situation you find yourself in are limited but not impossible."

Eastly stared at the ledgers as if he'd never seen them before. "Where did you get these?"

"I took them from your desk last week. Now I'm returning them. Try to keep up, as I don't have much time to devote to this today. Let's discuss your options. As I see it, you can renegotiate the terms of the bet with Rosehurst. Perhaps refuse the horse and he will forgive the financial debt, then you both go on your merry way. That's the best-case scenario. If Rosehurst insists on payment, you'll need to sell the unentailed properties. With the loss of the *Wilhelmina*'s cargo, there isn't a viable option for paying this debt without heavy liquidation on your part. Living with an allowance and practicing economies will allow the coffers to heal with time. If you like, I can manage your finances and investments, and with a little luck you'll be comfortable sooner. However, I'll only do that if you agree to a personal budget. The first time you exceed your allowance, I'm throwing the whole thing in your lap and walking away. If at any point the tenants suffer due to your ineptitude, I'll wrest away full control of the estate's finances, and if you don't like it, you can take me to court." An empty threat when Eastly would probably win that lawsuit, but a court proceeding would be messy. Disastrously scandalous to the family, because every last one of Eastly's secrets would be published in the gossip rags when Cal tried to establish the marquess's incompetency.

His father blinked, then donned his persuasion mask. "Now, Son, I don't know why you went to all this trouble. Once you and Violet marry, this entire conversation is moot."

"I'm not marrying Miss Cuthbert. I said that at Lakeview. You fail to realize that my marital status is not currency for you to spend. My eligibility as a bachelor is not something you can trade on. I've cleaned your messes for long enough. That ends now. I'll help manage the finances of the estate, because there are people who depend on us for their livelihood—but only if you live within an allowance."

"I'm a grown man, not some green lad. Allowance, indeed," his father huffed.

Cal shrugged, a blessed emotional disconnect he'd never had before sliding into place. He had more important priorities now. In the end, Eastly would make his own decisions, and Cal would protect their tenants. With any luck, he and his father wouldn't be at cross-purposes. "That's entirely your choice. I can't force you to see reason. Just like you can't force me to marry Miss Cuthbert. My life is my own. I won't be stepping in to save your hide anymore."

His father stared at the stack of ledgers in his hands. "Sell everything?"

"The properties, yes. You aren't to the point where you need to strip the house of furnishings. But if you expect to weather this, you must liquidate your assets and regroup. Now—" Cal clapped his hands once and straightened. "I must be going. You might have seen in the paper that Emma is now a widow. I'll be leaving to go to her within the hour. While a latent thread of paternal love might inspire a desire to see her, I must insist you let me handle this initial time of grief. She will write when she's ready for your visit. I may not see you for a time, so be well, Father. If you want to take me up on my offer of financial management, send a note around to Higgins, and he will get word to me. Good day." They'd never been much for familial gestures of affection, so Cal squeezed his father's shoulder as he walked by, then left his sire standing in the middle of the library.

"Son?" Eastly called when Cal reached the doorway.

"Yes, Father?" He turned.

"Are you quite serious?" Eastly appeared a bit mystified by the whole conversation, and Cal smiled with unexpected sympathy. It would be a shock to suddenly have to face consequences at such an advanced age.

"Quite serious. Get word to Higgins if you need me. But now I must go." Whatever Eastly did was his decision. As he'd said, he was a grown man—and no longer Cal's problem.

In the hall Cal met the butler. "I trust you to see him out when he's ready. Could you send Nelson to the gold drawing room? And do you know if Kingston has finished packing?"

"Kingston is nearly finished, milord. I'll send in Nelson."

Once Cal determined that there was no news from Milton, he would be on his way. A tiny voice in his mind worried that the newspaper announcement might be true. He firmed his jaw and shook his head. Those doubts would cripple him if he considered them for too long. No, Phee would be fine. She was healthy, living in Olread Cove, and soon he'd see her and indulge them both in a thorough grovel.

He had a lady to win—and in the process, he would find out what on earth she was up to.

Chapter Twenty-Six

$\mathcal{I}$f she'd known beating the hell out of something would be this intensely satisfying, Phee would have learned to bake earlier.

"You must be gentler with the dough, Miss Fiona," Mrs. Shephard began, only to have her words cut off by the solid *whack* of the rolling pin hitting an unsuspecting lump of pastry.

"This is why the last attempt resembled modeling clay, Phee." Emma used less tact, but she didn't appear as concerned as their cook.

Phee shot Emma a grumpy look. "Do you want pie or not?"

"A truly exceptional pie is all in the crust. One needs a soft touch to achieve that perfect flake." Bless Mrs. Shephard— she was still trying to teach them a few kitchen basics. The woman had the patience of a saint and the tact of a diplomat.

Emma sighed, blowing a curl out of her face. "Mrs.

Shephard, let's leave that dough to Phee's tender ministrations, and we can roll out a fresh bit of pastry. I haven't been able to think of anything for the last three days except pie, and I'll go mad if I don't have some today." She rubbed at the curve of her belly. By their calculations, there were another four months left of her pregnancy. The cravings had hit in earnest this week, shortly after the unrelenting nausea had abated. The baby wanted pie, so the baby would get pie.

Phee stared at the misshapen disk of pastry dough despondently. "Starting over might be for the best. This batch is a lost cause, I think."

Emma patted Phee's hand that still gripped the rolling pin. "I understand. In your place, I would need to flatten something too. You go ahead and imagine that's my brother's face and kill the dough."

Mrs. Shephard rocked on her heels. "Ah, it's a man, is it? I should have known."

"I received a letter from my brother. He's getting married. And Phee—" Emma jumped when Phee hit the dough with the rolling pin again. "I mean, *we* are not pleased with the news."

"Well then, here." Mrs. Shephard grated sugar off a cone onto the dough in front of Phee. "Knead that in, Miss Fiona. Sprinkle, fold, press, and again. Some kinds of dough take a beating, and maybe that's what you need to do today. Let's see if we can salvage this. Sweeten and knead, there's a girl. Mrs. Hardwick, come over here and we will attempt a crust again." With kind but determined tugs, the cook removed the rolling pin from Phee's grasp and placed it by the canister of flour.

Phee set into a rhythm, letting her hands work while her mind wandered. Grate the sugar, sprinkle it on the dough, then fold over and do it again.

Cal was marrying Violet. That no-good son of a bitch. After all those claims that he would get out of it. He'd bent to Eastly, like always.

And that beautiful letter he'd written and someone else had sent. Those words haunted her. She dreamed of him showing up and saying what was in that letter. He'd been *her Cal* in that letter, and he'd thrown it away. But then, so had she. Tossing the only love letter she'd ever received off a cliff was an impulsive move she'd almost immediately regretted.

If Cal married, there would be no more declarations of love and longing. Not that her recent behavior encouraged such declarations, but seeing him move on so soon made her heart ache.

She couldn't deny now that a part of her had hoped he'd come. Hoped he'd apologize and fight for her. For them. In that fantasy, he told Eastly to hang and married Phee instead.

A tear slipped down her cheek, then splashed on the dough.

Phee rubbed at the ache under her breastbone, leaving a trail of flour on her apron. When she glanced up, Emma and Mrs. Shephard didn't try to hide their concern. That pressure in her chest built until Phee confessed with a gasp, "It hurts."

Just that. Tears fell, whether or not she wanted them to. Her shoulders shook, and for a moment Phee feared she'd shudder into a pile of emotional, tear-soaked bits— that this would be what broke her. That fatalistic thought sparked the anger all over again, because *how dare he try to break her*.

Of course, Cal didn't know Phee lived as a woman now. That with the death notice and headstone for her brother, she'd set herself free. In fact, Cal didn't know much of anything, and there was so much she wished she could share with him. The midwife said Emma and the baby were healthy. Their coffers were full after Emma received Adam's life-insurance policy and inheritance. They had outmaneuvered Milton and hadn't heard a peep from him.

Logically, the good in this new life outweighed the bad. But nothing felt logical at the moment. All Phee had were feelings of loss, and they were big enough to crush her under their weight.

The other two women stepped forward. Emma wrapped her in a hug while Mrs. Shephard rubbed a soothing circle on Phee's back and murmured noises about the uselessness of men and the benefits of salt water in dough.

"You were hoping he'd see sense and follow us, weren't you?" Emma asked.

Phee couldn't muster much beyond a nod and sniffle. "I know it's ridiculous when we never even hinted he'd be welcome here. I gave him no reason to hope. But... *Violet Cuthbert*."

"You deserve better, Miss Fiona. Especially after this hard year," Mrs. Shephard said. For a second, Phee was confused. Ah, the story they'd told the staff. On top of the death of her "cousin" Adam, Fiona had recently recovered from a fever that had forced a physician to shave her head. Another lie.

Phee offered a watery smile to the cook. "I'm sorry I cried all over the dough."

Mrs. Shepherd shrugged. "A little salt water never hurt nothing. How about you ladies take tea in the parlor, and I'll finish this crust. Quick as a wink, it will be ready for the oven. Baking lessons can wait for another day."

Polly, the maid of all work, ducked her head through the kitchen doorway. "Sorry to interrupt, missus. There's a gentleman come to call. A *handsome* one." Her eyes were wide as saucers.

A prickle began at Phee's nape. "Does he have long blond hair?"

Polly nodded so hard, her cap shifted on her head and she grabbed to catch it. "Looks like a storybook prince, he does."

Emma snorted, then covered the laugh with one floury hand. "You said you wanted him to follow us, Phee."

"But... now? When I'm covered in flour, and my hair is a disaster, and I've been crying over his sorry hide?" Phee brushed her hands on her apron, as if that would make a difference. "Your brother is impossible." A thought made her freeze. "Polly, is he alone? Or is there a blond woman with him?" Phee glared at Emma. "If he brought Violet, so help me God, I will bloody the parlor floor with his carcass and not regret it."

"Brought a valet who's nearly as handsome as he is, but no lady," Polly said with a grin.

Washing her hands, Phee scrubbed at the white paste the dough left between her fingers. "Damn it, Calvin."

"That's more like it." Emma grinned, swiping her palms

over Phee's cheeks to clear stray flour and tears. "Want me to go in first? Or would you like a few minutes with him in private?"

Phee hesitated, then looked at her apron and simple day dress. "Can you give me a bit to change and feel presentable?"

"Of course. I suggest the copper gown. It does marvelous things to the color in your cheeks." Emma popped a slice of spiced apple from the bowl on the counter into her mouth and waved as she left the kitchen.

Mrs. Shephard eyed Phee with a small smile. "The copper gown looks lovely on you."

Well, at least her wardrobe choice was sorted. Phee skirted down the narrow servants' hallway toward the rear of the house, where a stairwell would take her to the second-floor bedrooms.

She'd almost made it to her chamber when she bumped into a hard chest. "Oh, pardon me! Kingston?" Phee froze at the sight of the tall valet.

Kingston knew of her relationship with his master, but whether that meant he'd realized she was female, Phee didn't know.

Not until now, at any rate.

He bowed. "I'm happy to see you are alive and well, Miss Hardwick. The servants worried when we saw the *Times*."

Inexplicably, tears rose to her eyes again. She hadn't thought anyone would care about Adam's death notice beyond her uncle and Calvin—who wouldn't believe it, anyway. "Thank you, Kingston. I, ah, was in the kitchen. I'm a bit of a mess and need to change before I greet his lordship."

Kingston studied her for a moment until the silence made her shift from one foot to the other. "May I, miss?" He gestured toward her head.

"May you what?"

Kingston cleared his throat. "Would you like assistance styling your hair once you've changed gowns, miss?"

She bit into her bottom lip to stave off more tears at the kindness. "I would appreciate that. I'm afraid I don't know what to do with it as it grows longer. Give me a few minutes to change?"

He nodded in a shallow bow. "I'll gather supplies and meet you in the hall outside your door. Which chamber is yours?"

"Just there." She pointed. "I'll see you momentarily, then."

Thankfully, the copper gown was freshly washed and pressed. It had become her favorite and always made her feel sensual and beautiful. The deep scooped neckline showcased her collarbones and creamy skin, and the skirt swished when she walked.

Washing her face and hands in the small porcelain basin took only a moment, then changing gowns took a few more. When a lady's maid would have been required, she and Emma helped each other, but Phee had deliberately chosen a wardrobe she could don without assistance. They were living quietly here, with minimal staff. The lower a profile they kept, the better, until the timeline of their arrival and the baby's age blurred in the memories of the locals and their acquaintances in London.

She opened the door to find Kingston waiting in the hall, as promised.

"May I, miss? We can leave the door open to observe the proprieties."

She did just that, touched that he would think of her comfort and reputation. The man had adapted to the news with remarkable grace. Unless it wasn't news at all.

Phee took a seat at the vanity table, and he set to work combing her curls. "Kingston, how long have you known?"

He met her eyes in the mirror. "Awhile, miss. His lordship swore me to secrecy when I discovered, and you can trust I'll hold my tongue now. Lord Carlyle would hate me saying so, but he's been grieving the loss of you something awful. Did you get the letter?"

"You're the one who posted it?"

"I know I overstepped, but I thought you should have it. Now, as to your hair. Until it gets longer and has some weight to it, you'll need a product like this." In the mirror, he held up a small jar of pomade. "Whereas men use enough to slick the hair down, you only need a little on your fingers. Then you either shape the curls like this," he instructed, working some kind of magic that turned her fluff into an honest-to-God curl, "or you can form waves with your fingers instead of individual ringlet curls. With your bone structure, you'll wear either style well, but it depends on how much time you have to devote to your toilette. For today's purposes, we shall keep it simple."

"I'll be damned," she muttered, staring at the result. The valet's wizardry distracted her from the flurry of nerves tickling her stomach at the thought of seeing Cal again.

Kingston laughed under his breath.

"You're a miracle worker." Gone was the baby-duck fluff.

No, she didn't miraculously have a pile of thick hair, but she had a style instead of puffy ginger chaos. Finger waves, with a side part, and small curls framed her features.

"Do you have any rouge, or kohl for your lashes? You're a trifle pale. And there's only one chance to make a first impression. We want you to feel your best when his lordship begs to get you back, after all. That is the point, yes?"

If he was here to beg, then yes. Phee placed a hand over her racing heart. Cal was here. In the house. Without Violet bloody Cuthbert. The ire over that last letter battled with her nerves and won. Phee firmed her jaw. If he was going to beg, then she'd look like a queen while he did it. "I have a pot of rouge Emma gave me, but I rarely use it." She opened a drawer. Like the others in the vanity table, it was nearly empty of fripperies. The memory of slipping her carved bird into Cal's bedroom table surfaced. Had he found it yet? Had he connected what it meant—that she'd chosen freedom and hoped he would too?

The little black ceramic pot with gilt lettering rolled when she tried to grab it. "Here."

As if he did this every day, Kingston dabbed a bit of the cream on her cheeks and lips, gently blending it until she looked healthy and not like someone who could believably lie about nearly dying from a fever within the last few months.

The one time she'd played with the stuff, her outcome had been nowhere near as attractive. The valet surveyed her from head to toe.

"There. You'll do nicely." He handed her the pot of rouge. "If I may be so bold, miss? His lordship is a good man. But a bit of groveling wouldn't be amiss, I think." With that, he left for the guest room where Polly would have directed him to put Cal's things.

Phee smiled at the now-empty doorway, then tucked the rouge pot into its drawer. The mirror reflected an image that had her raising her chin and smoothing a hand over the front of her gown. Kingston seemed to think Cal had come here to reconcile. If Cal was still engaged to be married, surely his valet would have said as much.

Downstairs, Phee paused outside the parlor. The low rumble of Cal's and Emma's voices reached through the closed door. Goose bumps rose on her skin at the sound of him. Even though she couldn't make out the words, he refreshed a part of her that had withered in his absence, like a flower without rain or sun.

She closed her eyes and tried to steady her breathing. Damned red hair meant every emotion showed on her complexion, in blushes and blotchy skin. She might as well share her feelings on a sign around her neck. Fear. Anxiety. Anger. Desire.

Lordy, the desire surprised her. The way it unfurled within Phee at the sound of his voice, like a lazy cat stretching in a windowsill sunbeam. It would take every ounce of her self-control to not throw herself into his arms the minute he apologized.

Please, God, let him apologize.

"Let the groveling commence," she murmured.

Since Cal had rolled through Olread Cove and found the correct house, ghastly nerves about seeing Phee again had tied him in knots, along with an undeniable desperation to finally be in the same room with her.

Standing in the parlor of the snug cottage was surreal, but he still hadn't seen Phee. For one heart-stopping moment, he thought he heard her voice from somewhere in the house. A few seconds later, Emma entered the parlor and walked right into his arms.

"You came. I'm so glad," she said.

The hug restored a piece of his calm. Cal rested his cheek on the top of her head. "How's little Mortimer Hildegard?"

Emma stepped away, rolling her eyes. "He wants pie. A lot of pie." Her expression turned serious as she studied him. Not as a sister but as an adult and equal. It hit him all at once that his baby sister was growing up. "You'll need to beg her, you know. She's alive, despite what you may have read in the *Times*. I'm assuming that's why you're here."

He smiled, but it felt like a twisted thing on his face instead of an expression of joy. "Don't misunderstand. I love seeing you happy and healthy. But yes, I'm here for Phee."

And then in she walked, so utterly lovely that she stole all the air left in his lungs.

"See, brother mine? I told you—alive and well," Emma said.

"Phee." He breathed her name like a prayer. The way he used to say it in bed. Intimate, and with a touch of reverence. As if there could be any other way to speak to her after weeks without the warmth from her flame-red hair and joyful laughter.

By God, she made his knees weak. The gown she wore exposed delicious skin, showcasing elegant arms and the curving lines of delicate collarbones. Phee told him once in bed that she liked them, and the bones had fascinated him ever since. He wanted to simultaneously worship her and do filthy, earthy, sexual things with her until neither of them possessed any doubt who he belonged to.

The features he'd traced over and over in his mind were composed and distant, while the mere sight of Phee threatened to undo him.

"Hello, Cal. We weren't expecting you. Don't you have a wedding to plan? Or is your role to simply do what they say?" The words cut, but he was glad for it. Mad meant she cared. He could handle anger and hurt and anything else Phee threw at him—as long as it wasn't apathy.

"I deserve that." Clearing his throat, he fidgeted with the brim of his hat so he wouldn't reach for her. "I'm not marrying Violet Cuthbert." The carefully prepared speech he'd memorized over the days of travel disintegrated in his brain as he stared at her. "You look amazing, Phee. Beautiful as ever."

"And I look like an egg. Spherical and wobbly," Emma said beside him. He glanced her way to see her rolling her eyes good-naturedly. "No, Brother. Don't attempt to compliment me. I'll leave you two to catch up." She winked at Cal, then closed the door behind her.

Silence fell in the snug parlor.

Phee wrapped her arms around herself and gave him a wide berth, stopping in front of the window. Beyond her shoulder, Cal couldn't see anything worth watching. The packed-dirt lane in front of the house was empty except for a dusty traveling carriage rattling down the street slowly, taking its time over the rutted roadway. Olread Cove was a peaceful village.

She turned to face him. "You look like hell."

He rubbed a palm over the short beard Kingston claimed made him appear unkempt. Cal thought it lent him a vaguely piratical look. "You don't like it?"

There was no hiding the dark circles under his eyes and a new gauntness to his cheeks, though. These past few weeks had held little sleep and even less appetite.

A frown knit her brows together. "I'm not talking about the beard. You really look awful. Are you sick? Is that why the sudden change of heart about Miss Cuthbert? If you've come all this way to drop dead on my floor, I will pitch your corpse off the nearest cliff. Don't think I won't."

Cal's laugh grated roughly as if rusty from disuse. "Aw, Phee, you care." He covered his heart and winked.

She rolled her eyes, but a quirk at the corner of her mouth made him hope. "Why are you here, Calvin?"

Like a snuffed candle, the lightness in his chest died, and he remembered how it had felt to read that newspaper announcement. "I needed to see for myself that you were alive and well. I knew logically that if you'd d-died..." He stuttered over the word, then gulped and tried again. "If you'd died, Emma would tell me. But I had to see you." There was no reason to prevaricate, not after coming all this way. "I had to tell you in person that I love you. I'm miserable without you. I don't want to have a life apart from you. And whatever that looks like—wherever you want to live, under

whatever name you choose—I want to be part of it. I came
to beg, Ophelia."

She blinked. "My name is Fiona now. Fiona Hardwick."

"Still Phee, then. Just a different spelling."

"It's the closest I could come to living under my own
name." Her bittersweet smile made him itch to hold her. It
didn't escape him that she offered no comment or reply to
his declaration of love. He'd have loved if she'd fallen into
his arms and forgiven all, but that wasn't realistic.

Phee had been through hell and back, and he hadn't been
here for it. In the grand scheme of things, Cal's feelings
weren't bigger than the task she'd undertaken to change her
name and claim her future.

Stepping toward her, Cal held out a hand. "Nice to meet
you, Fiona. I remember reading somewhere that Fiona means
fair. The perfect name for a beautiful woman."

He didn't sense a softening in her posture until she finally
shook his hand. That battered flicker of hope in his soul grew
ever so slightly. Touching Phee again sent every nerve in his
arm tingling.

The grip of her handshake was tight enough to hurt when
she said, "If all you want is a mistress, you can climb into
that fancy carriage and drive right into hell."

"I don't want a mistress, Phee. Where did you get that
idea?"

She released his hand and spun away, hugging herself.
After pacing a few feet, she whirled on him and flung her
hands in the air. "You spoke of a future with me but never
marriage, then talked of marrying someone else, you bacon-
brained princock!"

God, he'd missed her. Daring her wrath, he crossed to where she stood, and traced a finger over one curl resting against her cheek. "You will never have to doubt my love and commitment to you. Not a mistress, my love. You don't ever need to hide again."

Those eyes he'd dreamed of for the past weeks studied him. "Let's go for a walk. During which you will tell me everything, beginning with your intentions. Perhaps then we can see where we stand."

Cal donned his hat and reached for the caped cloak he'd draped over a nearby chair. Phee opened the cupboard and removed a wool wrap.

Offering his arm to her, he said, "Miss Hardwick, would you care to show me your favorite place to ramble?"

"My favorite walking path follows the cliff edge. I suggest you choose your words carefully, or I'll push you over."

Cal snagged one of her hands before she could cover it with a leather glove. Raising her hand to his lips, he pressed a firm kiss to her skin, then breathed her in. Warm sandalwood, with a trace of sugar. He could eat her up—for hours. Days, if she'd let him. "I've missed you, Phee."

"I missed you too." Her voice shook. For the moment, that vulnerability was enough. It was a promising start, at least. No matter how long it took to win her back, he'd be here for it—but they could start with a walk and occasional death threats.

Outside, they picked their way along the gravel path through a garden and past a wooden gate toward the green expanse of land that cut off abruptly at the cliff. A cool breeze ruffled the curls on her uncovered head. Cal tucked her hand between his arm and body and angled himself to block most of the wind whipping off the water.

"Winter here will be brutal, I imagine," he said.

"I expect so. But the house is sturdy and seems to hold the heat well. We have enough firewood to carry us through till spring. This will do nicely until Emma decides where she wants to live with the baby."

"I'll get used to it," Cal said.

She raised a brow at him in query.

He shrugged, hugging her hand tighter to his body. "Where you go, I go. Unless you tell me you don't love me or want me, I will stay wherever you are."

"Your life is in London and at Lakeview."

He stopped, pulling her to a halt with him. "The only life I want is with you. Everything else is negotiable. Besides, I think we can both agree that I handle my life better with you by my side helping me."

"Then why did you tell your father you wouldn't marry a woman with scandal in her past? Why did you woo me while everyone thought you were promised to Violet?"

The hurt in her voice tore a hole in him, but it was a valid question. "When did I tell Eastly I wouldn't marry—wait, was that in the drawing room when he arrived at Lakeview?" Things clicked together in his memory, and he thought he'd be sick. Phee let go of him and continued down the path, but her silence was answer enough.

"I wish I had a justifiable answer," he called, following her toward the cliff. "I was stalling for time and grasping at reasons to put him off. God, what you must have thought." Cal reached where she'd stopped at the edge. "Love, I'm so sorry. I was prevaricating—like I always do, because my entire life, I've juggled my parents' scandals and handled the fallout."

"Why didn't you tell Eastly no? Tell the baron no. Hell, tell everyone no."

He rolled his shoulders. Not a shrug so much as a physical release of the truth. "I thought I'd handle it, like I handled dozens of problems before this. Not only were the stakes higher this time but my priority should have been to you. Instead of bringing you in like I would have before, I tried to shelter you from the ugliness of it all. You deserve more than that, Phee. You deserve a partner. I should have told Eastly to go to hell. I have now, not that it helps anything with us."

He grasped one of her hands and urged Phee to turn, needing to see her face. While he'd hoped to see forgiveness softening the hard line of her jaw, her eyes still sparked with anger.

"And the decision to marry Miss Cuthbert anyway? We received your letter today."

Cal winced. If he'd been one day earlier, he could have spared her the hurt of reading what he'd written while in the throes of a hopeless depression. "I'm sorry. I wasn't in a good place. After word of the losses with the *Wilhelmina*, my last hope for Eastly's finances died. I pored over the estate books, and the only way he can pay this debt is to sell everything unentailed, then live on a budget for a few years."

She snorted, then covered the sound with her hand.

He shot her a knowing look. "Exactly. We both know

that's unlikely. You were gone and hated me. So I though
I'd be useful if not happy."

Phee tugged her hand free, then walked to a narrow path
at the cliff edge. "What changed?"

The question was nearly lost to the wind as she descended
a rocky trail toward what Cal assumed would be a beach
below. She hadn't shoved him over the edge yet, so a
legitimate trail was a good sign.

"Lottie barged in and called me a damsel in distress." He
caught the lilting song of her laugh on the breeze, and it made
him smile. "Sometimes I think when someone is in a pit, they
forget there's a world beyond their view. They stop trying to
get out of that hole and tell themselves the dark is normal.'
Cal clambered down the path to join her at the bottom. "I
was deep in the pit, Phee. Stopped sleeping. Moped about
barking at people like some misanthrope. Lottie did everything short of throwing a bucket of water on me to snap me
out of it."

"What happens the next time Eastly has a problem?
Because you know there *will* be a next time." She tightened
the heavy wrap around her shoulders and crossed her arms.
Offering one hand, Cal held his breath until she reached
her hand out. Their fingers intertwined, knowing exactly
where to fall to knit together, as he closed the distance
between them.

"We both know I'm undoing years of habit. My first
instinct will probably be to rescue him again. But I can't
do that. I have offered to take over the finances, but I
doubt he will cede control. I should warn you, I come with
potential scandal. I threatened to declare Eastly incompetent

if he made the tenants do without. I hope it won't come to that."

Phee's gaze searched his face. What she looked for, he didn't know, but he drank in the sight of her, the feel of her under his fingers. "So Eastly's options are to liquidate assets, give you the purse strings, or face a massive scandal in court?"

"It's about time, don't you think? I hope he makes the right choice, but I won't hold his hand through it. I have other priorities now. My allegiance to Eastly overrode my honesty with you, and I promise upon my soul that will never happen again. Can you forgive me, Phee? Will you love me? Because I love you. I choose you. And I'll keep choosing you every day." He cradled her cheek, brushing his thumb over her lower lip.

She said nothing, but after an eternity of heartbeats, Phee leaned into his touch, turning to kiss his palm. The hope inside him transformed into budding desire. When she closed her eyes, the thick fall of her lashes brushed his fingers.

Gently, giving her time to protest, Cal brought her face closer, until the pillowy softness of her lips opened beneath his mouth.

A promise, a declaration, a vow of a kiss.

"I love you too," she murmured against his lips.

"Way to make me wait for it, Phee," he teased. She nipped his bottom lip in reply. What began as a sweet gesture of love and teasing transformed in an instant into something far more carnal.

"God, I've missed you," he managed before diving in for another taste.

She stilled under his hands, then pulled back. For one awful moment, he feared she'd step away. Instead, a sly smile crept across her face, lighting her eyes and curving those phenomenal lips, gone raspberry pink and shiny from his kiss.

"How do you feel about sex outdoors?"

Chapter Twenty-Seven

e

$\mathcal{H}$e laughed, and there it was. That spark that made Cal truly special. It wasn't merely his good looks that made her heart stutter. It was *him*. The quick mind, the jokes waiting on the tip of his tongue, the deep well of kindness Cal guarded with humor lest everyone take advantage of his soft heart.

"My feelings fall firmly in the pro column. Especially with water nearby, Madame Siren. But first..." He released her to pat beneath his cloak and removed his pocket watch. Carefully unhooking the clasp, Cal removed the watch from his waistcoat, then shook something into his palm that had been threaded on the chain.

Sparkling, gold, and blinding in the sunlight. "Is that..."

"Will you marry me, Phee? Be my friend and my lover, and wake up every day beside me for the rest of our lives. Here, London, peaceful, messy—I don't care as long as you're beside me. There's no one for me but you, and I hope you feel the same way." His eyes were hopeful, full of love for her.

Phee could only nod through the surprise. The sapphire-and-diamond ring slipped past her knuckle to nest right where it would stay for the rest of her days. Words finally formed. "I have to ask. Why wasn't this gorgeous ring protected in a box?"

"And ruin the line of my coat?" he asked with a dramatically appalled gasp.

Her laughter disappeared under his kiss. Within seconds, Phee's body went soft and needy. They backed together toward the cliff face, until she was pinned between the unmoving hardness of Cal and the rocks.

The full press of his body against her made her sigh. Lordy, he felt amazing. One of Cal's hands skimmed from her waist to grip her thigh, then wrapped her leg around his hip. Impatient, she slid a hand between them and sent a long stroke down the rigid length of his erection, then set to work opening the placket of his breeches.

The hand at her thigh slipped under her skirt, finding the skin above her garter, and then the swollen ache at her core.

He grinned against her lips. "Told you a dress makes this easier." The laughter in his voice felt like coming home. Finally. She'd missed him. Missed feeling connected with him, missed being on his side. Them against the world, unstoppable together.

Her hand stroked his length as he slid a finger into the slick heat of her. He grunted a curse, but it sounded like praise.

"I need you inside me," she said.

"Not yet." It would ruin the knees of his breeches, but Cal didn't seem to care when he knelt before her and kissed his way from her knee to thigh, then higher.

The press of the rock behind her didn't matter; the bite of the wind on her leg only made the skin under his fingers and mouth tingle more as the nerves came alive.

He sucked at the pulsing top of her slit, abrading her skin deliciously with his beard, then soothing the sensation with his tongue. Phee's breathing devolved into short, sharp exhales before turning into a keening cry when he slid a finger into her again. Lordy, she was close.

"Now, Cal. I want you inside me when I go over the edge."

The hot puff of his breath warmed her lips when he rose and kissed her. With eager hands, Cal tugged her bodice down until chilly air and anticipation puckered her nipples. A shiver rippled through Phee's body right to her toes as Cal hauled her higher against his body and claimed one tight nipple. He settled the wide, blunt head of his cock at her entrance, and they both groaned in relief as their bodies connected.

Cal's voice was a low, ragged rumble in her ear. "It feels like it's been forever since I was inside you."

"It *has* been forever," she panted.

Now that he filled her to the hilt, Cal didn't let go of her, even to thrust. So the movements were tiny, building a pressure between them as he rocked the base of his sex against that nub at the top of her slit. When his teeth tugged the hard point of her nipple, the tension built in that now familiar climb toward climax.

Control unraveled while everything within Phee tightened.

She was aware of only his teeth on her skin, and where their bodies joined.

Cal groaned his encouragement, leaving her breast only long enough to mutter a guttural "Fuck, Phee" before following her over the edge to bliss in a hot rush.

She could have stayed there all day, soft-kneed, pressed against the rocky face of a cliff, if not for a cry above them.

"Miss Hardwick! Miss Hardwick, come quick!" Polly's voice drifted down to where they stood.

Cal's face echoed Phee's concern at that cry.

"That doesn't sound good," Phee said.

"No, it doesn't."

"I'll be up in a moment, Polly! Wait there," Phee called from the deepening twilight shadows, shaking her skirts into place. She tugged at her bodice while Cal put his clothes to rights.

"Hurry! Miss Emma is alone with that man, and it doesn't feel right." The maid sounded genuinely worried, and by the time they crested the top of the trail to the cliff edge, slightly out of breath, Polly looked to be near tears.

"Who's with Emma?" Phee and Cal asked at the same time.

"An older gent in a carriage came to call. Seemed nice enough, so I let him wait in the parlor. Emma joined him, but something is wrong. I can feel it here." Polly pressed a fist to her belly.

An older gentleman? Phee looked at Cal as an awful possibility occurred to her. Without another word, they took off running toward the house. The lawn seemed an endless expanse of green. Phee cut to the right because the kitchen door was closer than the front entrance.

"Could you have been followed?" Phee whispered to Cal as they slipped into the hall beyond the kitchen.

"Nelson says the crew hasn't heard from Milton in weeks. What if I led him right to you?" Cal said.

Outside the open door to the parlor, they paused, being as quiet as possible.

Emma's voice rang clear. "I'm not discussing my late husband with you. Adam spoke of you, and never fondly. Please leave."

Milton's reply disappeared amidst a ringing in Phee's ears. That voice. For a moment she was a child again, helpless against his vile words. Trembling weakened her thighs, then moved through her torso until her stomach threatened to eject everything she'd eaten today.

Cal wrapped an arm around her waist in a warm, firm line of support. "You don't have to go in there. I can get Emma out of the room and take care of it."

She shook her head. "He's my dragon to slay, not yours."

Reaching for her left hand, Cal kissed the finger where his ring rested. "If you want to go in alone, I'll be right here waiting. But it might be better if he doesn't catch sight of you. No matter what, please remember you're not his ward anymore. You're a countess—or nearly, anyway. Milton can't take a blasted thing from you."

Phee drew a calming breath, and her head filled with the delicious mix of Cal's spicy scent mingled with her sandalwood oil. The smell grounded her as Phee wrestled through the awful memories. A tear slipped down her cheek, unchecked.

Life with Uncle Milton had been a torture by a thousand

verbal cuts. Phee clenched her fists, wishing she could physically fight through the words filling her head.

> *Stupid girl.*
> *Ugly little rat.*
> *Who would want you? I'll have to pay someone to take you off my hands.*

Saying such things to a child was unconscionable. Milton was rotten to the core—like a piece of fruit you bit into, then spit out before your tongue registered what your teeth had already discovered.

Turning to bury her nose in Cal's shoulder, Phee breathed in his calming presence as he held her, offering silent support as she struggled. The memories began to repeat, and Phee ground her teeth, answering each lie with truth.

> ~~*Stupid girl.*~~
> *No, I'm smart and loved.*
> ~~*Ugly little rat.*~~
> *No, I'm valuable and not vulnerable.*
> *I survived. I thrived.*

Clenching her hand until the new ring dug into her palm, Phee focused on that pinch. The unfamiliar band of gold represented one irrefutable fact. Phee had won. In the end, she was happy and healthy, while Milton chased financial phantoms to save his own hide or feed his greed.

These days, Phee looked in the mirror and loved who she'd become. She was an East End scrapper engaged to a

West End earl, with a life ahead of her filled to the brim with laughter, friendship, and love.

"Doing a little better?" Cal whispered.

She nodded.

"Are you going in, or am I?" he asked.

Logic clawed to the surface and Phee sighed. What she wouldn't give to rub her happiness in Milton's face. To show him that no matter how hard he'd tried to destroy her, she'd won. But letting Milton know she'd survived would only cause problems. He could dispute the validity of her upcoming marriage. He could cause issues with her inheritance in court or challenge the legitimacy of Emma's baby. Everything would fall apart if Milton knew Ophelia was alive.

Phee squeezed Cal's hand. "I'll go to my room. Please get rid of him."

She'd crept past the door to the parlor when they heard it. Raised voices and Emma's cry of "Don't touch me!" were cause enough for alarm. But then Emma made a sound that sent both Phee and Cal running for the door. Self-preservation be damned—Emma was in trouble.

They barged into the room in time to see Uncle Milton slump against the heavy wood writing desk. A trail of blood smeared in his wake as he listed to the side. Emma stood frozen with one hand over her mouth, stifling her cries, and the other hand still outstretched.

No doubt it had been self-defense, but Emma had pushed him. Thankfully, Cal's sister appeared unharmed, although pale.

In a daze, Phee walked toward the man softening on the

floor as if his bones had turned to jelly. Years of knowing exactly what his hands could do kept her from getting too close. Phee crouched just out of arm's reach and cocked her head to meet his hazy stare.

There. A brief flash of recognition.

"Ophelia..." His lips formed the name on his last exhale. The chest under his fashionable caped greatcoat stopped moving. One moment passed, then another. With shaking fingers, Phee reached out and closed his eyelids. He'd known at the end, but the victory felt hollow.

Phee rose and turned to see Cal with his arms around his sister. "I didn't mean to," Emma repeated every few seconds.

"I know. You defended yourself. Nothing more." Cal ran a soothing hand over her hair as Emma clutched his coat lapels with bone-white fingers.

"He was furious that we'd removed him from the accounts, and the life insurance paid to me instead of him. Kept saying I had no right to it. When he grabbed my arm, I jerked away. Then he came after me again. All I did was push him."

Those last words rang through Phee with a familiar clarity. The child within her, who carried the scars from Adam's accident, heard and recognized the pain in Emma's words. Phee hadn't meant to land a lethal blow when she'd pushed her brother in that rowboat all those years ago. Adam had tripped, then toppled overboard and met a rock. Milton had stumbled into the corner of a piece of furniture that weighed more than the average man. Neither Phee nor Emma had had any way of knowing what would happen. Yet they'd each been left with the same awful result.

An odd warmth seeped into Phee's limbs, sending a shiver skittering over her skin as she connected and compared events, analyzing them in a new way. Phee wrapped her arms around her friends, tucking her face in the crook of Emma's neck, which was damp from a river of tears. "Emma, it was an accident."

"But he's dead," Emma sniffled.

Phee spared a glance at the body on the floor. "Yes, and good riddance. Listen, this was an accident. But I know that's not much comfort right now. I've been where you are." This, Phee's deepest secret, could irrevocably change how they saw her. But her experience might help Emma weather the situation.

Phee tightened her hug around them both, then released them and stepped back. "I understand how you're feeling. Adam drowned in an accident. I'd been throwing a fit, and he'd played the jester, trying to make me laugh, as brothers do." She and Emma exchanged a look at Cal's expense, but Phee's smile was short-lived. "I shoved him. Only a little, but he wasn't expecting it. Adam fell overboard. A boulder under the water did the rest. I've spent years carrying guilt over killing my brother." Emma reached out her hand, and Phee took it gratefully. "I don't tell you this to minimize what you're feeling or distract you from what happened. But I hope you understand I don't blame you. This was an accident. If you need to talk, I'm here. We've supported each other through a lot so far. Perhaps we can help each other through this too."

No, the guilt wouldn't magically disappear. Grief over Adam would always be there in some form. Grief was what the living carried to honor their ghosts. But maybe walking with someone else through the same trauma would help Phee to work through her own. Then perhaps she could remember Adam and all he'd meant to her without guilt discoloring the memories.

Phee wiped her eyes dry and glanced at Cal. He wasn't staring at her in horror or disgust. Instead, he watched her with compassion and love.

Drying her face on the shoulder of Cal's coat, Emma said, "What do we do with him? The body, I mean?"

All three of them eyed the man on the floor.

Cal spoke first. "We could call the authorities. It was an accident, after all."

"The whole point of us living here is to escape notice," Phee said. "Can we move him? Make it look like the fall happened elsewhere."

Cal rubbed a palm over his face, but she spied a smile brewing. "Maybe somewhere that will show his true character to the world?"

Emma raised her chin and glared at Milton. "People should know how vile he was. He made Phee's life hell as a child and tried to kill her as an adult. Plus, he just tried to attack a pregnant woman."

"So we move him?" Cal asked. Phee and Emma nodded. "Give me a few minutes. I'll send Milton's staff on to the village, then get my coach." Cal slipped out the door, closing it securely with a click of the latch.

"Not my fault?" Emma asked in a shaky voice.

"Not your fault," Phee answered firmly, reminding them both as she squeezed Emma's hand.

A few minutes later Cal returned. "Milton's staff are heading to the posting house for the night. Either they'll hear word through the village in the morning, or we will have to be convincing actors and claim he left at some point. Let's get him into my carriage. I'm driving."

The sun had set, but the stars weren't out yet to guide their way. Under the cover of encroaching darkness, they shuffled Milton's body onto a velvet bench seat, talking a bit too loudly about him finding a bed at the inn, in case Polly lingered nearby.

"He never could hold his brandy," Phee declared to any servants who might be listening.

Emma shoved a newspaper under Milton's head. "Blood stains something awful, and Milton is not worth ruining this carriage."

The whole rig rocked as Cal climbed onto the driver's seat.

With the heart of the village only a mile off, this shouldn't take long. But as they wove through the streets, Emma and Phee exchanged a look.

"Do you know where he's going?" Emma asked. Phee shook her head.

After several minutes, the carriage rolled to a stop, and Cal opened the door.

It wasn't a stretch to find the right place to dump a body. One only needed to know what to look for to find the local house of ill repute. And when in doubt, ask someone on the street. The village was small, but with a busy port, it was sure to have accommodations for men who'd been at sea for God only knew how long.

Cal would never forget that scene in the parlor. Poor Emma. Poor Phee. Another thing to tie the women together. God willing, the future would give them happier opportunities to bond. He loved that they were friends now, since soon they'd be sisters by marriage.

Phee's expression as she'd confessed to accidentally killing Adam would break Cal's heart each time he remembered it. She'd been prepared for him to shun her. It was obvious in the defensive lift of her chin and the board-straight posture. Her confession had the air of one going to an executioner.

Later, he'd be able to hold her. Provide comfort. Eventually, Cal hoped she'd have such unshakable faith in him, it would never cross her mind that he'd judge her. They had the rest of their lives to deepen their trust and support one another as they each healed from their histories.

The establishment in Olread Cove had a wide alleyway behind the building where customers could arrive and leave discreetly through a red door. Cal jumped to the ground and lowered the steps of the carriage.

"Quiet and quick, ladies. Shove him my way, and I'll take it from here."

"You aren't handling this alone," Phee said.

His Phee would never expect him to do the dirty work to rescue her. Future countess or not, she would always be a scrapper at heart.

"Apologies, milady. I was thinking to protect your gown."

"You'll buy me another," she said cheekily and he laughed.

They looked at Emma, who shook her head. "I'll hold the horses."

Together, they shifted Milton off the seat. Cal slung the man's arm over his shoulder and maneuvered them through the alley to a window. On the other side of the glass, the working ladies entertained their customers in a public parlor.

"Is this place what I think it is?" Phee hissed, her eyes wide in the dim light.

"Depends. Do you think it's a brothel?"

"How did you know this was here?" A trace of suspicion colored the question.

Cal shot her an exasperated look. "It's a port. Every port has a brothel. I couldn't find it at first, so we circled around and I asked a man on the street." Cal raised his right hand— the one not wrapped around her dead uncle. "I solemnly swear to never visit another brothel for as long as I live. Not that I've frequented them in years, anyway. You're stuck with every last one of my lusty intentions." He winked at her over his shoulder. "I hope you're well rested."

"I can't believe you can joke about sex while carrying a dead man."

"It's not as if he was a friend. Here. Let's check this window." They propped Milton against the wall, and Cal peeked over the sill. "This will do nicely." Leaving the couple inside to their privacy, he surveyed the area for a sizable rock.

"What are you looking for?"

"Something believable for him to crack his egg on."

Phee searched the ground down the alley, then returned with a decent-sized lump of limestone. "This will do the trick."

Working as quickly as possible, Cal rolled Milton, and she set the stone in place under his head. Together they stepped back and observed the scene.

"Perfect. Outside a brothel window is a nice touch. After all, we don't know that he *wasn't* a Peeping Tom. I wondered a few times as a child, so this is fitting."

Cal wanted to kill the man all over again at the casual reference to her hellish childhood.

"If he's going to look like the degenerate he was, it needs to be worse. If you want to go back to the carriage, now would be a good time."

Phee crossed her arms, her ring flashing in the meager light spilling from the window. "Partners, remember?"

"Even partners in crime?" he teased.

"It was an accident," she hissed.

"I know. But moving a body is certainly murky legal territory. You're staying?"

"I'm staying."

"Fine, don't say I didn't warn you." Grimacing, Cal unfastened Milton's trousers and set one cooling, dead hand in place. "Poor chap," he murmured at the sight of one of the most pathetic penises he'd ever laid eyes on. Cal rubbed his palms on his breeches, then stepped back from the body, motioning for Phee to follow.

Inside the brothel, someone lit a lamp, sending a pool of light over the tableau they'd made on the ground. Milton, may he rest in peace, got the ending he deserved.

Cal and Phee hurried back toward the carriage, where Emma held the horses.

"You seem surprisingly fine with how this evening progressed," Phee said.

Cal shrugged. "For better or worse doesn't begin on the wedding day."

The white of her teeth flashed in the flickering light. "Speaking of wedding days, I'd like to get a special license and have Vicar Arcott marry us. What do you think?"

His cheeks ached with the width of his smile. "I like that idea. Ethan and Lottie could meet us in Northumberland. They're the only ones besides Emma I'd want to have present anyway." A shout echoed into the night from the direction they'd come. They exchanged a look and quickened their pace.

"Granted, when I proposed a couple hours ago, fleeing the scene of a death wasn't how I'd envisioned spending the night. Not that I'm complaining exactly. But a relationship with you is full of surprises, my love." Cal opened the door and held out a hand.

"Well, I wouldn't want you to get bored." Phee winked and jumped into the carriage.

Epilogue

London, eight months later

Their arrival in Town had been strategic. The Whit-bournes' ball was one of the final social engagements of the Season, and the perfect time for Phee to make her first appearance in society as Countess Carlyle before retreating to Lakeview for the rest of the year.

Phee smiled a welcome as her husband returned with refreshments. The Earl of Carlyle's marriage to a nobody of modest means and no title had been a brief scandal. She and Cal had enjoyed weathering that particular gossip feast from a distance.

Emma's house in Olread Cove had been the perfect place to spend the winter. Winds had buffeted the paned windows, and cozy fireplaces had kept the small rooms comfortable. By Christmas, both Emma and Phee could make a decent pastry crust, and they'd even mastered bread and sweet buns under the patient tutelage of Mrs. Shephard.

Standing in this glittering ballroom, surrounded by the

elite of society and their curious stares, Phee thought wist-
fully of the cottage. The warm kitchen. Phee and Cal's big
bed upstairs by their fireplace. The bedroom window facing
the sea, and the piles of quilts they'd spent months making
love under. It had been an idyllic winter.

Emma had given birth to a healthy boy. Little Alton
immediately stole every heart in the room and didn't seem
inclined to give them back anytime soon. He was all chubby
rolls and giggles, and his head only recently had lost that
intoxicating baby smell. Lordy, she missed Alton and his
mama.

Taking a glass of champagne from Cal, she took a sip.

"You look good enough to eat, my love. How are you
holding up?" Cal asked.

"Everyone is talking about us."

He shrugged, having become more comfortable being the
center of gossip these days. "Let them talk. They're just
jealous because you are the most vibrant woman in the room
and I'm the happiest man alive. Except perhaps for this
fellow." Cal added the last sentence as an afterthought when
Viscount and Lady Amesbury joined them, accompanied by
Lottie's godmother, Lady Agatha Dalrymple.

Phee had always liked Lady Agatha, and Cal held a special
place in his heart for the older woman. Having the blessing
of a grande dame like Agatha would certainly ease Phee's
acceptance to the *ton*.

A black feather quivered in Lady Agatha's silver curls.
"That gown is one of Madame Bouvier's designs. I'd recognize her work anywhere. You wear it well, Lady Carlyle,
with distinctive style."

Smoothing a hand over the emerald silk, Phee smiled her thanks. Precise folds and swaths of silk across the bodice gave the illusion of a larger bust and a more dramatic dip at her waist. Phee loved it—even after having to don the gown twice. The first time, the dress had drifted to the floor around the same time Cal had tumbled her back onto the bed. It had been a delightful reason to arrive late to the Whitbournes' ball.

"How do you like your first evening in society?" Lottie asked.

Phee fought a grimace. "All the gawking makes me nervous. Then someone asked Cal where he'd met me, and he said I was under his nose all along, and I nearly choked him in front of God and everyone."

Lady Agatha laughed. "If I may offer a word of advice, child? Embrace your status as a misfit. Be *you*, as gloriously and shamelessly as possible. Their speculation will turn to envy. All these people are wondering where you came from, but that's a question you don't have to answer. The only thing that matters is who you are now."

Lottie reached over and squeezed Phee's hand. "And you, my dear, are a treasure—not to mention a countess. You have the second most handsome husband in London"—at that, Ethan and Cal laughed into their wineglasses and Phee grinned—"and you're surrounded by friends. All the gossips can only wish for a life as good as yours."

"Do you know, I've realized something. During the countless social events I've attended with you over the years, there's one thing we've never done." A wicked smile lit Cal's face, much like the one he'd worn earlier in the evening. She flushed at the memory of why they'd been late and how he'd put that remarkable mouth to use.

"Something you've never done…Gotten me drunk in public?" Phee downed the last of her champagne and placed the glass on a nearby tray.

The others laughed, but Cal set aside his glass and offered a hand to his wife. "Danced with you. Come along, Puppy. Let's really give them something to talk about."

Want more of the
Misfits of Mayfair?

Don't miss Emma's story in

ALL ROGUES LEAD TO LONDON

Coming in Summer 2022

About the Author

Bethany Bennett grew up in a small fishing village in Alaska where required life skills included cold-water survival, along with several other subjects that are utterly useless as a romance writer. Eventually settling in the Northwest with her real-life hero and two children, she enjoys taking in mountain views from the comfort of her sofa, wearing a tremendous amount of flannel, and drinking more coffee than her doctor deems wise.

You can learn more at:

> *BethanyBennettAuthor.com*
> *Twitter @BethanyRomance*
> *Instagram @BethanyWritesKissingBooks*

Looking for more historical romances?
Get swept away by handsome rogues and clever
ladies from Forever!

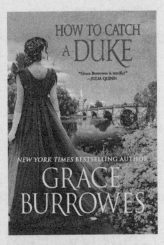

HOW TO CATCH A DUKE
by Grace Burrowes

Miss Abigail Abbott needs to disappear—permanently—and the only person she trusts to help is Lord Stephen Wentworth, heir to the Duke of Walden. Stephen is brilliant, charming, and absolutely ruthless. So ruthless that he proposes marriage to keep Abigail safe. But when she accepts his courtship of convenience, they discover intimate moments that they don't want to end. Can Stephen convince Abigail that their arrangement is more than a sham and that his love is real?

NOT THE KIND OF EARL YOU MARRY
by Kate Pembrooke

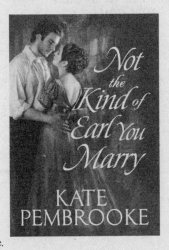

When William Atherton, Earl of Norwood, learns of his betrothal in the morning paper, he's furious that the shrewd marriage trap could affect his political campaign. Until he realizes that a fake engagement might help rather than harm...Miss Charlotte Hurst may be a wallflower, but she's no shrinking violet. She would never attempt such an underhanded scheme, especially not with a man as haughty or sought-after as Norwood. And yet...the longer they pretend, the more undeniably real their feelings become.

Follow @ReadForeverPub on Twitter and join the conversation using #ReadForever

A DUKE WORTH FIGHTING FOR
by Christina Britton

Margery Kitteridge has been mourning her husband for years, and while she's not ready to consider marriage again, she does miss intimacy with a partner. When Daniel asks for help navigating the Isle of Synne's social scene and they accidentally kiss, she realizes he's the perfect person with whom to have an affair. As they begin to confide in each other, Daniel discovers that he's unexpectedly connected to Margery's late husband, and she will have to decide if she can let her old love go for the promise of a new one.

SOMEDAY MY DUKE WILL COME
by **Christina Britton**

Quincy Nesbitt reluctantly accepted the dukedom after his brother's death, but he'll be damned if he accepts his brother's fiancée as well. The only polite way to decline is to become engaged to someone else—quickly. Lady Clara has the right connections and happens to need him as much as he needs her. But he soon discovers she's also witty and selfless—and if he's not careful, he just might lose his heart.

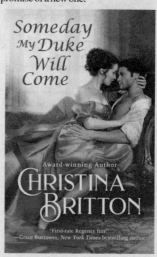

Discover bonus content and more on read-forever.com

Connect with us at
Facebook.com/ReadForeverPub

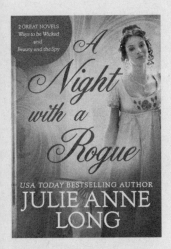

A NIGHT WITH A ROGUE
(2-in-1 edition)
by Julie Anne Long

Enjoy these two stunning, sensual historical romances! In *Beauty and the Spy*, when odd accidents endanger London darling Susannah Makepeace, who better than Viscount Kit Whitelaw, the best spy in His Majesty's secret service, to unravel the secrets threatening her? In *Ways to Be Wicked*, a chance to find her lost family sends Parisian ballerina Sylvie Lamoureux fleeing across the English Channel—and into the arms of the notorious Tom Shaughnessy. Can she trust this wicked man with her heart?

A ROGUE TO REMEMBER
by Emily Sullivan

After five Seasons turning down every marriage proposal, Lottie Carlisle's uncle has declared she must choose a husband, or he'll find one for her. Only Lottie has her own agenda—namely ruining herself and then posing as a widow in the countryside. But when Alec Gresham, the seasoned spy who broke Lottie's heart, appears at her doorstep to escort her home, it seems her best-laid plans appear to have been for naught...and it soon becomes clear that the feelings between them are far from buried.

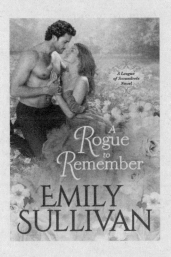

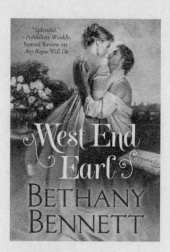

WEST END EARL
by Bethany Bennett

While most young ladies attend balls and hunt for husbands, Ophelia Hardwick has spent the past ten years masquerading as a man. As the land steward for the Earl of Carlyle, she's found safety from the uncle determined to kill her and the freedoms of which a lady could only dream. Ophelia's situation would be perfect—if she wasn't hopelessly attracted to her employer...

HOW TO SURVIVE A SCANDAL
by Samara Parish

Benedict Asterly never dreamed that saving Lady Amelia's life would lead to him being forced to wed the hoity society miss. He was taught to distrust the aristocracy at a young age, so when news of his marriage endangers a business deal, Benedict is wary of Amelia's offer to help. But his quick-witted, elegant bride defies all his expectations...and if he's not careful, she'll break down the walls around his guarded heart.

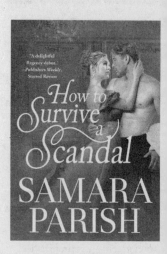